Beryl Kingston was born in 1931 in Tooting, where she spent the first four months of the Blitz. She was evacuated twice during WWII, the first time to Felpham and the second to Harpenden in Hertfordshire. She kept a diary from the time she was seven until she was nineteen, the content of which assisted the factual accuracy of this book.

PRAISE FOR BERYL KINGSTON:

'Beryl Kingston understands how to weave dialogue, character, theme and a thumping love affair into unity' – *The Sunday Times*

'A new novel by the warm and observant Beryl Kingston is not to be missed. Each one is special.'
– Elizabeth Buchan, bestselling author of *The New Mrs Clifton*

CITIZEN ARMIES

BERYL KINGSTON

LUME BOOKS

LUME BOOKS

First published in 2019 by Lume Books
85-87 Borough High Street,
London, SE1 1NH

ISBN 978-1-83901-157-3

www.lumebooks.co.uk

*For Charlotte Howard, my granddaughter and amanuensis,
without whom this book wouldn't have been possible.*

CHAPTER ONE

It was chilling to be sitting round the wireless in the middle of a sunny Sunday morning, waiting to be told they were at war again. The room was too ordinary for such a dreadful thing to be happening there. Too ordinary and too peaceful, just a well-used, comfortable, family room: the battered three-piece suite in a welcoming circle round the fireplace, the coal scuttle crouched ready for use, the brass fender dented, the fire irons lolling against each other, their special picture over the mantel-piece. Everything in it had a purpose: shelves in the chimney corners for their precious books and the wireless, a table in the window where the light was best and the girls did their homework, an ancient clock on the mantelpiece to keep the time like the guardian it was. And now this precious time was going to be disjointed – because war was coming and they all knew it.

Jim Jackson sat in his armchair with his hands on his knees, his face so quiet it was almost impassive. Looking at him, Rosie thought how old he looked, that thick mane of tawny hair greying at his temples and more lines on his face than she'd noticed before. My poor Jim, she thought, he's only forty-four and he looks old. He works too hard in that market stall of his, that's the trouble.

7

He'd been so quiet yesterday morning, when their Mary went off to school to be evacuated, and he hadn't really said much since. Of course, she'd had Gracie with her to keep her company until she got on the train and she *is* sixteen and very sensible… but even so, it's a hard thing to have to say goodbye to your child, especially when you don't know where she's going.

Gracie Jackson sat on the sofa with an arm round her mother's shoulders because she could see how anxious she was. She didn't know which of her parents she felt most sorry for. Dad, because he was being so stoical, or Mum because she looked so upset. None of them said anything, for really, now that the war was so close and children were being evacuated, what could they possibly say?

The music on the wireless was coming to an end. The clock clunked round to mark a quarter past eleven, the announcer called them to attention for the prime minister. Jim turned up the volume, they listened attentively.

Chamberlain's voice was reed-thin and very sad. 'This morning,' he said, 'the British ambassador in Berlin handed the German government a final note stating that, unless we heard from them by 11 o'clock that they were prepared at once to withdraw their troops from Poland, a state of war would exist between us. I have to tell you now that no such undertaking has been received, and that consequently this country is at war with Germany.'

His tired, sombre voice made Rosie's heart lurch with foreboding. Anguished memories jostled into her mind: finding her poor Jim gaunt and haggard and stinking of dysentery in that hospital bed, and watching him weep with anguish on their wedding night because he was so torn with pity for all the men who'd died. Opening Mrs Taylor's terrible letter and reading the hammer-blow words that told her Tommy had been killed – her lovely brother Tommy, taken so young. Seeing dear old Mr

Feigenbaum's face crumpling into grief when he told her his son had been killed, too. Nursing her poor mother as she struggled with the Spanish flu and calling that pompous doctor, who took his half a guinea before he'd go upstairs and examine her and then told them there was nothing he could do. Dear God, dear God, are we to have this all again?

'What are we going to do now?' she said.

'Now,' Jim told her, practical as always, 'I'm going to put the kettle on an' make us a cup-a'-tea.' Which he did.

What a dear man he is, Rosie thought, watching him and admiring his calm. If they do start bombing us the way people say they will, he'll be a splendid air raid warden.

So the tea was made and they all sat round the kitchen table, ready to enjoy it, but they'd barely drunk half a cup before the aid-raid siren sounded. The noise of its long upward howl was so loud and sudden, it made Rosie jump. She was used to hearing the horrid thing because it had been sounded quite frequently in the last few months so that people knew what it was, but that was a rehearsal —and now they were at war, and this was the real thing.

'Good God alive,' Jim said, putting his cup in the sink. 'They're not bombing us already, surely to God?' He went out into the hall at once, donned his warden's white tin hat, picked up his haversack of first-aid kit and slung it over his shoulder. 'Go to the shelter,' he said, and was gone.

'I shall finish my tea first,' Rosie said, determined not to be put out by a siren.

But Gracie had other ideas and stood up, cup in hand. 'Better do what he says,' she advised. 'We can take it with us. We don't want to get stuck in the house if they're going to drop bombs on us.'

The shelter was a source of constant irritation to Rosie. It annoyed her every time she looked at it. Four years ago, when they moved from their old flat to Coney Street and had a house and a garden all of their own, which was a rare thing in the Borough, she'd set to at once to nurture the soil. It had been horribly unpromising when they moved in; grey and lifeless and littered with broken flower pots, spent matches and crumpled cigarette packets, and it had needed a great deal of care and nourishment. But she'd cleared it and dug it over, and she and Jim had built a sturdy compost heap which she'd turned and aerated at regular intervals. And when the compost was finally ready to use, dark brown and moist and full of nutrients, she'd dug it into the ground she'd set aside for a vegetable patch and fruit bushes, feeling quite the countrywoman again. The moment when she'd planted her first seeds and potatoes and dug in her first soft fruits was such a red-letter day she'd marked it in the calendar, singing with the sheer joy of it.

And then that wretched ARP had announced that they were going to deliver air raid shelters to all the houses that needed them and had room for them and, although she tried to tell Jim that they really wouldn't need one, he'd overruled her and the dratted thing had been dug in. Now it bulged in the garden where her vegetables should have been planted, with the good rich earth that Jim had packed down over its reinforced steel roof growing grass as thick as a lawn, and the deck chairs they'd put inside ready for them to sit on spotted with black mould and beginning to split. She didn't want to sit out there in the dratted thing at all.

But Gracie was adamant. 'Come on,' she said. 'Dad's right. If they're going to start dropping bombs, we'll be safer out there than in the house.'

So although she scowled and grumbled, Rosie took her tea and went out to sit in the shelter and a horrible, dank, uncomfortable place it was. But they'd only been there about half an hour when the all clear sounded.

'Well, that was quick,' she said, feeling a bit surprised. 'How peculiar.'

'Tell you what,' Gracie said, 'if we wet the pot we can have another cup of tea.'

But as they walked through the kitchen door, the phone began to ring and her mother forgot about tea and ran into the hall to answer it.

It was Mary and she sounded quite perky. 'You'll never guess where we are,' she said.

Rosie was too disgruntled by the shelter to have the patience for guessing games. 'Well tell me then,' she said.

'We're in Hastings. By the seaside. What d'you think of that? It's no distance at all, is it? And me an' Margaret have got a billet with a lovely old couple, they're called Mr and Mrs Patterson, he calls her Maud but I don't know what his name is because she always calls him Father, which is a bit odd. Anyway, we'll be all right here. You'll love them. Mr Patterson's a bit like Grandpa –he's got the same sort of white beard and he used to work on a farm, imagine that –only now he's a baker and works all night and Maud says she's a fair old cook, which she is, and to tell you she'll look after us and put roses in our cheeks in no time.'

What a sauce! Rosie thought, miffed by the suggestion that her Mary looked peaky. But she didn't say anything. She just passed on the news, without embellishments, to Gracie who was standing beside her, and Gracie blew a kiss at the phone.

'Gracie sends her love,' Rosie said and changed the subject. 'How was the journey?'

'Not too bad,' Mary said. 'They were good kids, considering. One or two of them were a bit weepy. We jollied them along. But listen. They gave us all a postcard when we got here so's we could write and tell you where we are. You should get it tomorrow. I've put my address on it.'

She sounded so hopeful that Rosie understood at once what she was hinting at. 'We'll come down and see you as soon as we can,' she promised. 'Let me know what you want us to bring.'

'Could you bring my sandals for a start?' Mary said. 'My school shoes are so hot. And some of my ordinary clothes. I can't wear uniform all the time or I shall wear it out. I'll send you a list. Oh! There's the pips. I'll have to go.' And the phone cut out.

'Well at least that'll be something good to tell your Dad when he gets in,' Rosie said, walking back into the kitchen. She grimaced at the teapot. 'That tea'll be stewed. Let's make a fresh pot and then I must get the joint in or it'll never cook.'

The air raid had been a nuisance, nothing more. They were back to normal now. The sun was shining. Mary was all right.

*

Jim came home half an hour later. 'Dunno what all that was about,' he said as he hung up his tin hat. 'Fellers in the wardens' post reckon they was testing us to see if we was ready.'

'Listen, Jim,' Rosie said, and told him her news.

'There you are,' Jim said, grinning at her for the first time that day. 'She's a good kid. You needn't've worried. '

'*I* needn't have worried!' Rosie mocked him. 'Well I like that! You were the one fretting. You've had a face as long as a wet week ever since she walked out that door. Daft ha'porth.'

'We was both worried,' Jim said easily. 'Stands to reason. But she's all right now. She's fell on her feet. When'll you go an' see her?'

'Sunday, I expect,' Rosie said, putting the potatoes on the table. 'Or Saturday. Gracie'll be at the hospital all week, won't you Gracie?'

'All week and then some,' Gracie said, making a grimace. 'They warned us things would hot up once war was declared. I told you. Don't you remember?'

'You did,' Rosie said, remembering as she spoke. That damned shelter had put everything out of her head. 'And I might be at work too. It wouldn't surprise me. Mr Korda's bound to press on with *The Lion Has Wings* for a start. He's got it all planned, so Hamish was telling me the last time I was in, when we did that commercial. D'you remember? He only needs the money for it, that's all, an' Hamish reckons he'll get that come hell or high water.'

Jim wasn't interested in the film or its finances. 'Did you go in the shelter like I said?' he asked, unlacing his boots.

'Yes,' Gracie said, handing him his slippers 'Course.'

'Was it all right?'

Rosie was busy peeling the potatoes. 'It was filthy dirty and stank to high heaven,' she said. 'I shall have to give it a scrub round if we're going to have any more raids. Will you be coming to Hastings with us?'

'If I can,' Jim said, sighing as he eased off his left boot. 'I'll probably be on duty. Depends if we have any more raids. We'll have to see.'

*

There weren't any more raids for the rest of the week, and rumours began to circulate that the first one had been caused by a stray plane flying in across the Channel from France. But Jim was detailed to be on duty over the weekend even so, with orders to check every house in the street to make quite sure that everyone had black-out curtains to cover their windows. Gracie cycled off to Guy's Hospital on Monday morning, promising to phone when she knew what time she'd be back for the weekend, Mary sent a letter with a long list of all the things she needed, and the next morning, Rosie had a letter from Denham Studios telling her to report for work at the start of the following week, just as she'd predicted. They might be at war but their lives had a pattern nevertheless.

She was in the middle of answering the letter when the phone rang. That'll be Mary, she thought, with a lot more things she wants me to bring. She went to answer it.

But it was Gracie, to say she was learning so many things about injuries that her head was spinning, and to report that she'd be home late on Saturday afternoon.

'OK,' Rosie said. 'In that case, we'll go down and see our Mary on Sunday. Your Dad's on duty all weekend so it'll just be you an' me. We can take a bag each, can't we? I'll start packing them now, I've got plenty of time because I shan't be at work for the rest of this week.'

But in fact she didn't have plenty of time, because that afternoon her sister Tess phoned from Chichester, her voice bubbling with excitement.

'Listen,' she said. 'I've got a bit of news for you. Our Johnnie's got himself engaged, at last! What d'you think of that? Ent it a hoot!'

Rosie laughed out loud. 'Tell him it's about time,' she said. Her baby brother had turned thirty in July and although he and Connie Taylor had been walking out for five years, they'd all given up hope that he'd ever get around to getting married. It was a family joke.

''pparently they been planning this since Easter, only they never said nothing to no one –daft things –and now with the war started and everything, they thought they'd better get on with it. We was thinking of having a nice dinner to celebrate, nice bit of roast pork perhaps, apple sauce an' everything. Sorta family get-together. We was thinking tomorrow perhaps. Could you get down, do you think?'

'It'd only be me,' Rosie said. 'The others are all at work or evacuated, but I'll come. Wouldn't miss it for words.'

'See you tomorrow then,' Tess said. 'What fun, eh? Oops, there's the pips. Dratted things. They don't give you no time to talk at all.' And the phone cut out.

*

Early the next morning, Rosie packed a bag with fruit for the feast and took a train to Chichester, then another to the familiar halt at Lavant, where she stood on the empty platform and looked across the unchanging fields to the squat, square tower of St Mary's church where she and Jim had got married all those years ago. And for a few seconds she could almost imagine she'd gone back in time and there were no wars and no air raid sirens and everything was all right.

The feeling continued as she walked through the same fields. The Downs stretched their green flanks in the distance in their usual expansive way, the birds were singing the same songs, the little hamlet of Binderton hadn't changed by so much as a brick. It still smelt of the same reassuring things: the sharp scent of green leaves, warm earth, cows in the byre. She had to remind herself that the guns were going to be fired again, and men were going to be killed the way poor Tommy had been killed, or injured like her poor Jim, and bombs were going to be dropped on London and people were even going to be killed in their homes this time round. It was all wrong.

As she turned off the footpath and onto the trampled earth track that led to Binderton, she passed Binderton House, half hidden behind its screen of trees and hedges, and the cottage where she'd been house-keeper for Anthony Eden and his brother all those years ago. What memories that brought back. But then she saw Pa's cottage set beside the road, with Tess, and Jim's sister, Kitty, waiting for her at the gate, and quickened her pace.

'The dinner's all cooking,' Tess called, grinning. 'Come on in, quick.'

'I brought you some fruit,' Rosie said, waving her shopping bag. But Tess and Kitty were already in the cottage and beckoning to her to follow.

The room was full of people. Tess' daughter Anna and Connie's mother were setting the table, and Johnnie and Tess' husband Sydney were arranging borrowed chairs and putting up the bench for the kids to sit in, the way they always did at family parties. Kitty's twins were opening beer bottles and looking very pleased with themselves, and Tess' boy Dickie was passing the bottles across to them. The twins had grown taller since she last saw them and were wearing moleskin trousers and stout boots in the same style as Johnnie's. A bit of hero worship going on there, Rosie thought. I wonder whether they'll go farming too. They've turned twelve now, so they'll be leaving school in a couple of years' time.

And there was her dear old Pa, sitting at the head of the table, smiling across the room at her. He looked so frail it tugged at her heart to see him. He's so thin nowadays, she thought, and that hair's like thistledown. He looks as if a puff of wind could blow him over. She eased through the crowded room to kiss him.

'What a lark,' he said. 'Our Johnnie getting hisself married at last! He's a-blushing all the time these days. Ent yer Johnnie?'

Rosie blew her brother a kiss. 'Better late than never Johnnie, you daft ha'porth!' she said.

Johnnie pulled Connie towards him, blushing scarlet. But then he didn't know what to say and had to examine his boots for a considerable time.

Rosie looked at Connie's squat figure, her round face, her discoloured teeth and her funny little snub nose, and watched as she smiled at Johnnie and patted his arm. She might not be a beauty, Rosie thought, but she's very fond of our Johnnie and always has been. They'll make a good match.

'I think it's lovely you're going to marry our Johnnie,' she said. 'And you must take good care of *her*, Johnnie.' At which he grinned but blushed all over again.

He was rescued by Tess, who'd gone into the kitchen and now emerged carrying the roast pork on its familiar dish, and set it down on the table in front of Pa, ready to be carved. Rosie was touched to see how tenderly Johnnie took over the carving when he could sense their Pa was tiring. Poor old Pa, she thought, watching him.

When all their plates had been piled high, the conversation turned at last to what the newly-engaged pair would like as a wedding present and when the wedding was likely to be.

'November,' Johnnie told them, 'when the harvest's in. That's about the soonest we can do it, ent it Con?'

'We don't think he's likely to be called up,' Connie said, 'at least not yet awhile, on account of he works on the land, and they're supposed to be reserved or whatever it is, but you never can tell these days, can you? They ent said nothin' yet.'

Rosie agreed that they couldn't, but all this talk was making her remember those stupid Eden boys and how passionately they'd wanted to join the first war. They'd called it a 'good show' and said they didn't want to miss it, as if it was some sort of game. We should've learnt the hard way, she thought, given what we all went through. We certainly shouldn't be starting *another* war.

'I hope he *is* reserved,' she said to Connie. 'Don't let him go rushing into anything, that's my advice. We don't want him ending up like our Tommy.'

'And our Charlie,' Connie said sadly, looking at her mother. 'They was killed the same day.'

Wrong topic, Rosie thought, and pulled them back to considering their wedding.

'Will you get married in St Mary's?' she said.

'Course!' Connie said, cheering up. 'And I'm gonna have young Anna here as one of my bridesmaids. And afterwards we're coming back here to live, so's we can all look after Pa. We couldn't leave Pa on his own, could we Johnnie? And I can give Kitty a hand with things, can't I Kitty?'

Kitty looked across at Rosie and made a grimace, so it obviously wasn't going to be entirely to her liking. But Connie was waiting to be praised, so Rosie made an answering grimace at Kitty and then approved.

'Lovely,' she said.

'And you'll all come?' Connie said. 'Won't you?'

Rosie leant across the table and kissed her. 'We wouldn't miss it for all the tea in China,' she said. 'I promise.'

But she was thinking: no matter what happens.

CHAPTER TWO

Gracie and Rosie got up early that Sunday morning and cooked a good breakfast to set themselves up for the day. Then they kissed Jim goodbye, slung their gas masks obediently over their shoulders because he insisted on it, picked up the two bags they'd packed for Mary the night before, and set off for London Bridge and their trip to Hastings.

It turned out to be a rather uncomfortable journey, because they talked about the coming war all the way. Rosie would have preferred to chat about Johnnie's wedding, but Gracie was full of information about the injuries she was being trained to deal with and she wanted to tell her mother every ghastly detail. It was obvious to both of them that the authorities expected London to be bombed – like Prague and Guernica, and with the same terrible results.

'They've got thousands of cardboard coffins waiting in the warehouses, all made and ready,' Gracie said. 'Thousands. Isn't that gruesome? And a special train to take them out of London because there won't be room to bury them where they're killed. Imagine that.'

Rosie found it hard even to accept it, but there'd been millions of deaths in the Great War, so it was horribly possible.

'Yesterday they taught us how to protect people with crushed limbs and amputations from the weight of the bed clothes,' Gracie said, her young face serious beneath her mop of dark hair. 'We've got special cradles for it. And on Monday we're going to learn how to deal with shock, because Sister says that's the most important thing with casualties, and we've got a lecture on how to cope with injured children. *And* we're not going to get home much now the war's started. They warned us about that, too.'

Rosie gazed out at the peaceful fields smoothing past their window and listened with anguished pity. It seemed appalling to be talking about casualties and injuries and to be travelling to an evacuation zone on such a lovely, sunny day. And, when they got off the train and smelled the sea and heard seagulls screaming over their heads as if life was completely normal, she felt so confused that she just stood where she was, until she could gather her senses. Then she became aware that Mary was rushing towards them from the other side of the road, waving and calling as if they'd been apart for months instead of a week.

'Hello Mum,' she called. 'Hello Gracie. How's Guy's?' And when she'd reached them and was hugging them, 'Did you bring my sandals? My feet are killing me. I never knew school shoes could be so ghastly hot. Me and Maggie have been walking about barefoot. She said I was clomping about like an elephant.'

'Elephants don't clomp,' Gracie said, looking superior.

'That's all you know, clever clogs,' Mary said. 'They do too.'

Why must they do this? Rosie thought, watching them as they squared up to one another. It's so childish and they're grown women now, not kids. They should have grown out of it years ago.

'Elephants glide,' Gracie insisted, 'and roll from side to side. Like ships at sea.'

'I've never seen an elephant gliding anywhere,' Mary said, glaring. 'So there!'

'Well then you've forgotten the zoo,' Gracie said. 'I'd have thought—'

Rosie moved in on their tiff before it could get out of hand, as it too often did. 'Are we going to stand about on the pavement all day talking about elephants?' she said. 'I thought we'd come down to see your lodgings.'

Mary changed on the instant and was her smiling self again. 'And so you have,' she said, turning to hug her mother. 'Oh it *is* good to see you.' And she gave Gracie a grin, adding, 'Both of you.' And got an answering grin back – to her mother's relief. Then she took Rosie's bag and set off down Station Road at a very brisk pace. 'Come on,' she said. 'I've got such a lot to tell you.'

She talked all the way, the words bubbling from her in a never-ending flow. 'We're billeted in the high school,' she said, as she rushed them down Station Road. 'It's not as big as St Olave's but it's not bad, all in all. We share the building turn and turn about. We use it in the mornings and they have the afternoons for one week and then it's vice versa the next week. We've got the most complicated timetable you ever saw. The high school kids don't seem too keen on us, as far as I can see. I mean, the teachers are all right about it but some of the juniors give us looks. Anyway it suits us fine. It means we get half the day off to explore. Only trouble is it's not going to last very long, according to old Jonesey. She says not to bank on it. Apparently they're going to rent a hall or some such where we can have our dinner and classes and they're looking for a large empty house somewhere too, so she says, so we can have form rooms and classrooms there. That could be quite fun. One good thing, they don't make such a fuss about uniform down here. Although they might start putting the pressure on again when we've got all our clothes here.' They'd reached a small square where there was a large Woolworths – shut for Sunday of course – and several shops. 'Now this is where we meet up when we're not at school.'

It was an unnecessary explanation, because the square was full of girls in St Olave's uniform wandering about and chattering like a flock of starlings. Several of them had bicycles and stood leaning on the handle bars to talk to their friends. Many of them turned to wave at Mary as soon as she set foot in the place, so she had to stop and talk to them. And after a while, a few of the older girls came over to say hello to Gracie and ask how she was getting on at Guy's.

Rosie stood in the easy sunshine and watched them, feeling proud to think that her daughters were so popular and got on so well with their friends. But eventually Mary said she'd have to go or they'd be late for dinner and then they'd cop it, so they set off on their trek again and she resumed her commentary.

'That's West Hill over there,' she said, waving her hand at it. 'The old town is on the other side of it. I'll show you round when we've had our dinner. It's ever so old. You'll love it. Now we're going uphill. It's all hills round here. Old Mother Maudie says climbing'll keep us healthy.'

Old Mother Maudie's an idiot, Rosie thought, as they climbed through the narrow streets. 'I shall be glad to get there,' she said.

Mary grinned at her. 'We all said that the first day,' she said. 'But we're used to it now. Soon be there. This is Plynlimmon Road we're in now and Gladstone Terrace is just round the bend at the top.'

Which, after a brief halt to catch their breath, it was.

They stopped in front of a sturdy Victorian house in the middle of the terrace. It was two storeys high under a slate roof, like all the others, and had a short flight of well-scrubbed stone steps to the front door, bay windows on both floors, with lace half curtains – as Rosie was quick to notice – and a gleaming door knocker smelling of Brasso. In every respect a well-kept, proper house – at least from the outside.

Mary had taken a key from her blazer pocket and was fitting it into the lock. 'It made me think of London the minute I saw it,' she said, looking back at her mother. 'I mean, there're lots and lots of houses just like this in London.'

She wants me to agree with her, Rosie thought, reading her daughter's anxious expression. 'Yes,' she said. 'It *is* like a London house. I'll bet you feel quite at home here.' Actually, the old houses and hilly streets had been reminding her of Arundel, not London, but that was something she would keep to herself.

'I do,' Mary said, and she led them cheerfully into the house, calling, 'I'm back, Mrs M,' as she went.

It was dark in the hall after the dazzle of sunshine outside and it took a little while for Rosie's eyes to adjust. But all her other senses were fully alert, noting that this was indeed a clean, well-kept house, that it smelled of polish and soapsuds and cooking, fresh bread, pastry, a roast of some kind, something spicy – cloves, was it? Then the door to the kitchen opened and two people came out, one after the other. The first was a short, stout rosy woman in a flowery apron, who waddled towards them, smiling and holding out a hand in greeting. The second was a tall, skinny man who stooped behind her, looking anxious. He seemed to have been dunked in a flour bin. His hair was quite white with it, and so were his bushy eyebrows and his beard, and his shirt and trousers were as much grey powder as cloth.

'Hello,' the rosy woman said, shaking Rosie's hand. 'You must be Mrs Jackson. And you must be Gracie. I've heard so much about you I almost feel I know you – though p'rhaps that's a silly thing to say. P'rhaps

I shouldn't say it. You never know, do you? Anyway, your Mary's such a good girl and we talk about anything an' everything, and you learn a lot talking, don't you? Come through into the parlour and I'll show you where she and Margaret do their homework. Father'll keep an eye on the dinner, won't you Father?'

The lanky man gave them a shy smile and retreated to the kitchen, and Mrs Ferguson led the rest of them into her front room, talking all the way. 'Of course, this was the breakfast room when we ran the B and B. Me and Father eat in the kitchen, it being more convenient, like. I mean to say we always have. We thought it would be just the place for the girls to do their homework, not the kitchen I mean, no, course not, this nice front room. Nice and quiet, like, and lots of room for their books an' all.'

'Yes,' Rosie said, taking it all in, from the aspidistra in the window in its dark green Victorian pot, past the pairs of fading seaside prints on the walls, to the heavy oak dresser with an old fashioned condiment set at one end of its well-polished top and a bottle of Parker's ink standing, rather incongruously, on a neat tray at the other. There were school books piled on the table and open in front of two of the chairs, so she gave Mary a nod of approval, thinking what a good girl she was. She was obviously getting on with her work, despite all the disruption.

Mrs Ferguson was still chattering on. 'I mean to say, paying guests ent the same, are they? Not that I got nothing to say against 'em. I mean to say they was our bread an' butter for a good long time, paying guests was, an' most of 'em was very nice. It's just they're not the same. Don't you think so Mrs Jackson?'

Rosie had been paying so little attention to her, she didn't know what to say. But luckily she was saved by the arrival of Mary's friend

Margaret, who came rushing into the room bringing a waft of sea air with her and saying she hoped she wasn't late for dinner.

'No, no, dearie,' Mrs Ferguson reassured her, beaming. 'You're in plenty of time. I've just got to put the finishing touches to it an' then I shall start dishing up.' Then she turned to Mary. 'Why don't you show your mum your bedroom?' she said. 'You'll just about have time.'

'Good idea,' Mary said. 'Then I can get out of these ghastly shoes.'

They trooped up the stairs one behind the other, Mary and Gracie carrying the bags and Margaret bringing up the rear. 'She does run on,' Mary said, when they were on the landing and out of earshot of their host. 'Don't get me wrong, she's really kind and everything… but she will talk. Here you are! This is it.' And she walked into the room, opened the bag she'd been carrying and emptied it all over the nearest bed. 'Now, where're my plimsolls?' she said, rummaging in the pile. 'Oh God! I can't find them. Did you pack them?'

'We did, and they're in *my* bag,' Gracie told her severely. 'As you could've found out, if you'd asked instead of throwing everything all over the place.' And she started to unpack *her* bag, tantalisingly slowly and methodically.

Here we go again, Rosie thought, and stepped in quickly to find the plimsolls and hand them over to Miss Impatience before her two girls could get into another spat. Mary put them on at once and sighed with dramatic relief.

'Thank God for that,' she said. 'Another five minutes in those ghastly shoes and my feet would have burst into flames.'

'Where do you put your clothes?' Gracie asked.

Margaret was lying on her own bed as if she was exhausted, but she waved a languid hand at two tallboys. 'Hers is the one on the left,' she said.

'Come on,' Rosie said to Mary. 'We'll unpack together. Many hands

25

make light work and you'll be able to help us, won't you? Now your feet aren't on fire.'

Mary grimaced but set to work re-folding the clothes she'd tossed about and handing the now neat piles to Gracie, who put them away. The job was almost finished when they heard Mr Ferguson calling to them from the hall: 'Grub up, gels!' and Margaret sat up, then stood up and straightened her skirt and blouse.

'That's it,' she said. 'That's the call that has to be obeyed *instanta*. Capital sin to keep the food waiting. She likes to serve it piping hot.'

By now, what with the endless chatter and the insistence on being on time for meals, Rosie was having serious misgivings about her daughter's landlady. But she had to admit that the meal was very well cooked – the roast lamb done to a turn, the roast potatoes crisp outside and fluffy within, the mint sauce fresh and vinegary and a very tasty dish of cabbage, fried onions and diced bacon. She couldn't have done better herself, and said so.

'They learned us well up the big house,' Mrs Ferguson told her. 'That's one thing I *will* say for 'em. It's not much fun being in service, to tell you the truth, specially when you're just a young un, but they did learn us well.'

She was another one like me, Rosie thought. 'Very true,' she said. 'How old were you when you started work? If I may ask.'

Mrs Ferguson looked shamefaced. 'Day after me twelfth birthday,' she admitted. 'That was what they done to us in them days.'

They had found common ground. 'I know,' Rosie said, 'they did it to me too,' and beamed at her.

Mrs Ferguson was so surprised her mouth fell open. 'Was you sent to a big house an' all?' she asked.

'Very big,' Rosie told her. 'It was Arundel Castle. I was a nursemaid there.'

'Lawks a mercy, I don't envy you that, an' that's the truth,' Mrs

26

Ferguson said. 'Terrible job that is. I wouldn't ha' wanted to do it for all the tea in China. All them dirty nappies an' all. Not that they never asked us our opinion.'

Mary had been following the conversation with great interest. 'Well I never,' she said to her mother. 'I thought you only worked in the films.'

Rosie grinned. 'You don't know the half of what I got up to when I was young,' she said.

Her hosts were very impressed. Mr Ferguson's eyebrows had risen into his floury hair. 'My stars!' he said. 'We got a fillum star at our table, Maud. Imagine that!'

'Not quite, Mr Ferguson,' Rosie said. 'I was only a bit part player. And only from time to time.'

'Even so,' Mr Ferguson said, admiring her, 'to be in the fillums. I mean for to say, that's...' But then he couldn't find the words he needed and had to stop.

'Very hard work,' Rosie told him. 'Though it was nice to be on the set with the real film stars.' And she told them about Ralph Richardson and Merle Oberon and how unassuming they were, while Mr Ferguson listened with his mouth open and his wife was so enthralled she forgot to stack the dirty dishes.

'And that's not all,' Gracie told them, when her mother finally paused for breath. 'She was an artist's model too. Imagine that!'

Now the Fergusons were gobsmacked. 'Artist's model?' Mr Ferguson said. 'I mean for to say, I mean. My stars! Did you 'ave to pose...um... were you...?'

His confusion made Rosie laugh. 'Fully clothed, every time,' she reassured him. 'Sometimes I had to wear fancy dress of some kind, as a gypsy or a skater or some such.'

'I remember you as a skater,' Mary said. 'You had a lovely blue coat with a fur collar and cuffs and a pretty hat to match. And he painted *us* in that one too, skating alongside you. On the Serpentine.'

Now it was Rosie's turn to be impressed. 'You've got a good memory,' she said.

'Was he famous?' Mrs Ferguson said. 'I mean for to say, would we know his name?'

'His name's de Silva,' Rosie told her. 'He's a friend of Augustus John's.' But she could see that neither name meant anything to her hosts. 'He don't live here now so I ent modelled for quite a while. He's Jewish, you see, so he went to America a few years back, because he knew this war was coming and he wanted to get out the way of it. I can't say I blame him, knowing the way the Germans have been going on.'

'He gave us one of his paintings as a goodbye present,' Gracie said. 'It's me and Mum and Dad in the Borough Market. It's hanging on the wall above the fireplace. Margaret'll tell you. She's seen it.'

'Yes, I have,' Margaret said. 'But I never knew it was you and Gracie, Mrs Jackson. You never said. I'll have to take a closer look next time I'm there.'

Which won't be for a long time, Rosie thought, if I'm any judge, and she decided to change the subject. 'Would you like a hand with the washing up, Mrs Ferguson?' she asked.

'No, no, dearie,' Mrs Ferguson said. 'Thank you for the offer, but no. Me and Father do the washing up, always have, haven't we Father? And besides, we haven't had our apple crumble yet.' And she got up and waddled off to the cooker to get it.

So Rosie changed the subject again, and got the girls talking about the complicated timetables they had and how they walked around town when they weren't at school and what a lark it was to meet up in

Woolworths. So the meal ended peaceably. And after that, Mary told her hosts that she had to show her mum round the old town because she'd promised, and Mrs Ferguson said of course she must, it was only right and proper and a promise is a promise, so Gracie collected their empty bags from the bedroom and the three of them set off into the afternoon sunshine.

*

It was warm and peaceful out in the Sunday streets and, after a little while, Rosie began to feel the tension that had been coiling itself around her in Mrs Ferguson's loquacious kitchen, was gradually easing. 'It's so peaceful here,' she said to Mary. 'Just the three of us, out in the sunshine. In the quiet.'

'You don't want to take any notice of Old Mother Maudie,' Mary said, linking her arm in her mother's. 'She's just an old jaw-me-dead, that's all. Me and Margaret ignore her. She'd drive us bonkers otherwise. Come on. The old town's just ahead. Wait till you see *that*.'

The last wisp of Rosie's tension melted away in the delight of that splendidly scathing description. Yes, she thought, that's just what she is and here *we* are, all three of us and all together again and the sun's shining and we've got the rest of the afternoon to enjoy ourselves.

'Lead on!' she said.

They explored the old town from the top to the bottom, walking the length of All Saint's Street with its raised pavement and its handsome houses, and took detours to see the old pump house because Mary insisted on it. 'You must see that. It's half timbered.' And the High Street 'because the shops are lovely. You can get Butterkist in that one, when it's open.' And they finally arrived down by the sea, where the air was raucous with seagulls and there was a strong smell of fish, and lots of fishermen busy disentangling their nets, and more boats than they could count. They walked around the harbour and were duly impressed by the fishermen's huts, which were made of wood and as tall as a house and painted black.

'They've got the biggest fishing fleet on the south coast,' Mary told them. 'Just look at all those boats.'

Gracie was looking at their registration numbers. 'Why have they got RX and a number painted on them?' she wanted to know. 'That's a bit peculiar, isn't it?'

'It's because they were registered in Rye, according to one of the fishermen,' Mary said. 'I asked him when we first came down here. Come and have a look at the pier. That's very grand. It's got a pavilion and everything.'

'So has the one in Worthing,' Gracie said, looking superior. 'We're no strangers to piers, you know.'

'Actually, it's better than the one at Worthing,' Mary told her firmly. '*And* we've got a funicular railway to get us up to the top of the hill. If you're going to get snooty about the pier, come and see *that*.'

Even Gracie was impressed by the railway. 'Now *that* is a very good idea,' she said, gazing up at it. 'It can take us back to the station. How do you get on it?'

'You don't,' Mary said, with rather too obvious satisfaction. 'It's closed. They only open it in the season and that's over now because of the war and everything.'

'We'd better start getting back, with or without it,' Rosie said. 'It's getting on a bit and we've got a train to catch. Is there a short cut?'

'I'll take you the shortest way I know,' Mary said. 'But it's all uphill.'

'It would be,' Rosie sighed.

30

It was a long climb and, half way there, Rosie said she'd have to stop for a few minutes to catch her breath. 'This place would wear me out if I lived here,' she said. 'All this climbing. It's murder on the feet.'

'That reminds me,' Mary said. And then stopped and hesitated and gave Gracie an anxious look as if she wasn't sure whether to say any more.

'Spit it out,' Rosie said. 'You've started now so you might as well, otherwise we'll go home wondering.'

'Well…' Mary said, and when Rosie looked at her encouragingly, 'it's like this. It's not just that it wears you out walking up and down hills. I mean, it does but I'm not complaining. I mean, we're getting used to it. It's not that. It's the time it takes to get from one place to another. And if we're going to use the High School for half a day and then halls and things for the rest of the time, we've got to be able to get about a bit quicker. So…'

Rosie went on encouraging. 'So?' she said.

'So, the thing is,' May said, 'it would be a lot easier if I could have a bike. Lots of the girls are getting them. I wouldn't want a new one or anything. There're quite a lot of second hand ones on sale – I've been looking – and some of them are quite cheap.'

Rosie look at her anxious, hopeful face and grinned at her. 'Oh Mary-Lou,' she said, unconsciously using her old nickname 'How cheap is quite cheap?'

'I could get a good one for seven and six.'

Gracie was furious. 'Ridiculous!' she said. 'What's the matter with walking?'

'I told you,' Mary said. 'It's not the walking, it's the time it takes. You don't listen.'

'Oh, I listen,' Gracie said. 'And I know what you're doing. Don't think I don't. And you won't get away with it. In this family we get

31

a bike when we have to go to work, like me and Dad. When we're at school we walk. You walked to St Olave's in London, right? Then you can walk to St Olave's here.'

'It's different here,' Mary said, fighting her corner but trying to be reasonable. 'We're walking all over the place. I told you.'

Her sister was implacable. 'Rules are rules,' she said.

'Oh for heaven's sake, Gracie. You can't talk about rules. We're at war.'

'I can. I am.'

'Well you shouldn't.'

They were toe to toe and flushed with anger.

'In this family…' Gracie said.

I've got to stop them, Rosie thought. I can't let them go on like this.

'In this family,' she said, stepping towards them, 'the rules are made by the parents, not the children. And so are the decisions. How much did you say this bike was going to cost, Mary? Seven and six, wasn't it?'

'It doesn't matter,' Mary said, shrugging her shoulders. She looked tired and alone and so much like Jim, it made Rosie yearn with pity for her. I must put this right, she thought, and she took her purse out of her handbag and rummaged through it until she found two half-crowns, a florin and a sixpenny bit. I shall be earning again next week, she thought. I might be a bit short for a day or two but I can run to seven and six.

'There you are,' she said, handing it over to her daughter. 'And make sure you wrap up warm when you're riding the thing.'

Mary threw her arms round her mother's neck and kissed her. 'You're such a dear,' she said. 'It's going to make such a difference. You don't know how much.'

But Gracie was so cross she snorted and walked away from them, up the hill towards the station.

'Now we'll have to look sharp or we'll miss our train,' Rosie said. And followed the snorts.

*

It was another difficult journey and for a different reason this time. On the way down Gracie had talked non-stop; this time she stared out of the window for more than half an hour before she said a word. Rosie glanced at her from time to time, trying to gauge her mood and thinking what hard work it was trying to keep the peace between two young women who were as determined as her daughters. I don't know what I did wrong, she thought, but it must have been something, or they wouldn't pitch into one another the way they do. And yet they're fond of one another underneath all this nonsense.

As they were pulling out of Stonegate, Gracie turned her head away from the window and gave her mother a bleak smile. 'I'm not looking forward to tomorrow,' she said.

'No,' Rosie said, making the word carry as much sympathy as she could.

'I shan't mind learning about shock,' Gracie said, leaning forward towards her. 'At least that's a fairly normal sort of thing – if you know what I mean – but they're going to give us a talk in the afternoon about how to nurse injured children. I told you, didn't I? And that seems too awful even to be talking about. I'm not sure I can bear it. I mean, the thought of children being bombed is just…'

'But they will be,' Rosie said. 'If they bomb London, they'll bomb any children who are still there. Quite a lot of them weren't evacuated.'

'Madness,' Gracie said. 'And now they'll be hurt – killed, even – and we're going to have to deal with them. Why on earth did we declare

33

war? Someone must have known things like this would happen. Why didn't they stop it?'

'Mr Chamberlain tried,' Rosie said, 'to give him his due. He thought if he gave Hitler what he wanted, he could keep the peace. He didn't understand what sort of man he was dealing with.'

'And now we're going to be bombed.'

'Yes,' Rosie said sadly. 'But there are lots of people in London trained to deal with it. Your dad's one of them. And there are firemen and ambulance drivers and rescue teams. And we've got shelters of a sort, even if they *have* dug up the gardens to make room for them.'

'You and your garden,' Gracie said, and grinned at her.

They talked about what was ahead of them all the way to London Bridge, and walked companionably down the Borough High Street arm in arm. By the time Rosie slid her key into their familiar front door, she felt as if she'd been away for weeks.

Jim was waiting for them in the kitchen with the kettle on the boil and sausages and spuds on the kitchen table, ready to be turned into bangers and mash. 'Right,' he said, spooning the tea into the tea pot. 'Tell me all about it. How's she doing?'

They told him everything they could remember, while their supper was cooking. That she'd settled in well, that she was billeted with her friend Margaret, that her landlord was a baker and her landlady was a jaw-me-dead, that she had a comfortable bedroom, that she was being well fed, that she was working hard. And when they finally paused for breath, he said, 'Yes! Course she is. She's a sensible kid.' And asked if there was anything she needed.

So Rosie dished up the bangers and mash and told him about the bike.

His answer to that was immediate and easy. 'Sounds like a good idea,' he said. 'All depends how much it's gonna cost, a course.' And when she told him, he grinned and said, 'That's OK then. We can run to seven an' a kick'.

'Actually,' Rosie said, grinning back at him,' 'we've run to it already. I gave it to her out of my purse.'

'Well, there you are then,' he said.

Gracie was scowling but he was so busy eating his supper, he didn't seem to notice. Which Rosie thought was just as well.

But later that night when they were in bed and he was smoking his last cigarette of the day, he suddenly said, 'What was up with our Gracie? She seemed a bit miffed.'

So while he finished his smoke, she had to tell him. 'I don't know which of our girls I feel sorriest for,' she said when she'd explained what has happened. 'Mary's lonely down there and she misses us a lot. She didn't say so, naturally, but I could see it. Anyone could see it. And she *did* need that bike. An' our Gracie's worried sick about all the children who are going to be injured when the Germans start bombing. She doesn't know how she's going to cope with them. And I don't think I do either. It's horrible waiting to be bombed.'

'Always was,' he said, stubbing out his cigarette in the ashtray.

In her concern over her girls, she'd almost forgotten the dreadful things he'd seen in those disgusting trenches.

'I know,' she said, putting her head on his shoulder, partly as a sort of apology for reminding him and partly because she needed his comfort. When she'd given Mary the money she needed, she'd done it out of tenderness and because she wanted to stop their quarrel, even though she knew it would annoy poor Gracie. Now, having talked to Gracie all the way home, she wasn't so sure of herself or her decision. If only bringing up a family wasn't so damned difficult. 'I wish we weren't at war,' she said. 'There ought to be some way we could stop it.'

'Me an' all,' Jim said, stroking her hair. 'But there ain't a blamed thing any of us can do now. Except get ready for it. What's to come'll come.'

'Yes,' she sighed. 'I know.'

'Tell you one thing though,' he said, and his voice sounded as if he was teasing, so she sat up and looked at his face to read the signs. And there they were. 'I ain't had a kiss for nearly five minutes.'

'Oh diddums,' she teased back. And kissed him, thinking how much easier this was than worrying.

'That's more like it,' he said. 'Live for the moment. We don't none of us know what tomorrow'll bring.'

'I do,' she said. 'I'm starting work at Denham Studios.'

'Never mind Denham Studios,' he said, nuzzling into her neck. 'They'll wait.'

CHAPTER THREE

Denham Studios was waiting in its usual way that Monday morning, sitting importantly in the September sun, with the usual row of cars parked beside it and the familiar sign saying 'London Film Productions' across its long frontage. Now that bad times were coming, Rosie was comforted to see it again, because it was so ordinary and unchanged.

There were changes inside the building but she supposed she would have to accept that. For the first time in her experience, there was no one she knew on duty in reception, and when she walked down the corridor there were very few people there either. Butwhen she reached studio 4, the first person she saw was Hamish Gordon, and he was the same cheerful young man she'd known for years, with his shock of ginger hair and his ready smile and the same old clipboard in his hand.

'Hi there,' he said, ticking her name on his check list. 'Now we're all here except Mr Korda. You know the others, don't you?'

There were two other women and a dozen young men sitting on two rows of chairs, talking to one another, and she waved at them because she'd worked with them all at some time or another and knew them quite well.

'Who are the stars?' she asked.

'Ralph Richardson, Merle Oberon and June Duprez,' Hamish told her. 'You're playing a friend of Miss Duprez, called June.' Then he looked away because someone was coming in. 'Ah!' he said. 'There he is. Find a seat and you'll hear all about it.'

The great man was exactly the same as he'd always been, taking up his position in front of them and smiling and adjusting his spectacles before he began to speak, but what he had to say was quite unlike anything Rosie had ever heard him say before.

'Some months ago,' he told them, 'I had a meeting with Mr Churchill. It was a productive meeting and, by the end of it, we had reached an unwritten agreement that as soon as war was declared, I would set my team to work on a new project. That project is now planned and written, some of it by Mr Churchill himself. It is designed to show the British public what a warmonger Herr Hitler is and how brutally he has butchered anyone who disagrees with him, and therefore how necessary and inescapable this war has become. In addition to that, it will show people how well prepared we are, which will be good for morale. This is the task we are to embark upon this morning. It is hush-hush, for obvious reasons, so I trust you will not spread the news about it for the time being. I have called it, *The Lion has Wings* and work will start on it today. Work on *The Thief of Baghdad* stopped on Saturday, naturally. Now we must turn all our energies and skills to this new venture. We shall be filming in various locations, on various RAF bases and, at the same time, indoor scenes will be shot here. I have promised Mr Churchill to have it completed in five weeks or less and to distribute it at the start of November.'

There was a sharp intake of breath from his artists and one of them said, 'My God, sir. That's a rushed job.'

'It is,' Mr Korda agreed. 'But it is a highly important one. I am asking a great deal of you. I realise that. But I hope you will enter our endeavour with heart and mind and soul. This is extremely important work we shall be doing. I fear we are on a very tight budget, so I can only afford to pay you a flat rate of five pounds, but there will be bonuses if we can complete in time. Hamish will give you your scripts. Dressers and make-up are ready for you. Thank you for your attention. Good luck to us all!'

And that was that.

The grumbling began on the way to the dressing rooms. 'Five weeks!' they said to one another, as they mooched along the corridor.

'I never heard the like.'

'He'll run us ragged.'

'You can't shoot a film in five weeks!'

'It's unheard of!'

By the time they returned, made up and in costume, they were in a better mood, as if their change of appearance had changed their minds. 'Ah well!' they said, 'A job's a job. On his head be it, if it doesn't come off.'

But they were right in their prediction. They *were* worked extremely hard. Rosie was so tired by the time she clocked off that day that she fell asleep on the train.

It was quite a relief to be home with her dependable Jim. Especially as he'd peeled the potatoes, cut up the beans, laid the table and had everything ready for supper, bar cooking the chops.

'You look all in,' he said, as she set to work with the frying pan.

'I *feel* all in,' she admitted and told him all about it. 'He'll never get it made in five weeks,' she said. 'I mean, it's unheard of.'

'And what's he gonna pay you for all this graft?' Jim said, prodding the potatoes. 'These are done.'

He wasn't impressed by her answer. 'Five quid?' he said. 'Bloody slave labour.'

'There'll be bonuses,' she told him, mixing the gravy powder.

'There'd better be.'

'It's in a good cause,' she told him as they settled at the table and began their meal. 'So Mr Korda said. I mean, it's not just play-acting. He's gonna film on the airfields as well so people can see what a lot of fighter planes and bombers we've got and how well prepared we are.'

Jim cast up his eyes. 'What a load of old cobblers!' he said. 'We ain't got near enough planes. We all know that. This is propaganda.'

Time to change the subject, Rosie thought. 'I've half a mind to go up Petticoat Lane on Sunday,' she said. 'See if I can get a dress or a bit of cloth for our bride.'

He recognised the change of direction and went along with it, grinning at her. 'Good idea,' he said. 'I might come with you.'

'Could you?' she asked.

'Oh I reckon I could swing it,' he said. 'Just this once. Josh'll look after the stall. Make a nice day out.'

And it did. It made a very nice day out. It was so good to be strolling down that familiar street, dodging among the crowds between the familiar stalls with the sun on their shoulders and the smell of old clothes wafting over them from every doorway they passed. They found little Mr Levy in his long Jewish coat and his embroidered yarmulke, still in the same shop, beaming at them and asking 'Vhat I can do for you, my darlink?' and trying so hard to find what they wanted, and Mr Segal of the kindly eyes and the impossibly tangled beard, who emerged from behind a row of evening dresses in *his* shop, to ask 'Vat I can do to help you?' and went off immediately to find 'just the thing.'

'Will it be?' Jim asked, when he'd gone.

'You can never tell with Mr Segal,' Rosie said. 'He's got a good eye and he knows his cloth. He found my wedding dress for me.'

'Ah, well then,' Jim said.

The tangle of beard reappeared from behind the evening dresses a few seconds later, its owner carrying a roll of spotless cream brocade. 'Bought for a wedding vhat it vas called off. Vhat sadness! But for you maybe?' And he unrolled some of it and held it out for inspection.

It *was* just the thing. There wasn't any doubt about it. But Rosie remembered how Kitty always bargained in this place and pretended not to be sure about it. 'Well…' she said. 'Yes. It's a good piece of cloth. I'll grant you that. A very good piece of cloth. It'll depend how much you want for it.'

'Two pound ten,' Mr Segal said. 'Like you say. It good cloth. Vhat don't come round every day the veek.'

'How about two pounds?' Rosie said, hoping she sounded business-like.

'Two guineas maybe?' Mr Segal tried.

And two guineas it was and a bargain at the price. Rosie was so pleased with herself she was grinning all the way back to the tram.

'I *do* like the East End,' she said, as their cumbersome tin ship went swaying off along the rails. 'They're such a friendly lot and they never change. Specially my nice Mr Segal. That's twice he's sold me just the thing I wanted. I shall parcel this up this afternoon, when we've had our dinner, and send it off to Edie the first thing I can.'

'If that boss of yours is gonna work you into the ground, 'Jim said, 'you won't have time till Saturday. I'll take it for you tomorrow.'

'You're a sweetheart,' she said, cuddling his arm.

He laughed at that. 'An' I always thought I was a lion,' he said.

'Oh you're that an' all,' she told him, smiling into his eyes. He was such a good man, her Jim. She couldn't have married anyone better. If only they weren't at war, everything in her life would be perfect.

But actually, so little was happening that they hardly seemed to be at

41

war at all, despite being issued with ration books and identity cards, and despite having to put up with the blackout which was a real nuisance, especially on a cloudy night with only a little torch to light your way. The papers never had anything to report from France, and although they occasionally wrote about merchant ships being torpedoed by the German U-boats, after a while some of them were beginning to say it was 'a phoney war'. That idea suited Rosie very well. They didn't want to be bombed or to watch their soldiers being shot to ribbons like they were last time.

If it is phoney, she thought, let it keep on being phoney for a good long time.

*

But even if the war continued to be blessedly phoney, the work she had to do in the next five weeks was very real indeed and extremely hard. To her relief and Mr Korda's satisfaction, they hit their deadline and, on their last afternoon in the studios, the great man thanked them 'from the bottom of my heart' for all for the effort they'd made, and told them that their bonuses were secured and that the film would be released on November third, according to plan.

Rosie wasn't interested in the film now that her part in it was over. She wished it well but she was too busy organising her brother's wedding to waste any time thinking about it. There was a cake to cook and hats to be trimmed and all kinds of arrangements to be made. She and Tess sent postcards to one another every day and Kitty phoned her twice a week to keep her up to date on all the news, and it was all happily exciting and exactly as it should be. Gracie reported that she'd managed to get two days off for it and Mary rang to say that she was coming home for the wedding weekend, because all the kids were going home for weekends now, and could Rosie sort out her winter clothes so that she could take them back with her?

'I shall go down first thing Thursday morning,' Rosie said, when she and Jim sat down to their supper on the last Monday before the great day. 'Give them a hand with the cooking an' setting the tables an' the flowers an' whatnot. You can bring the girls down, can't you?'

'Yes sir, boss,' he said, saluting her. 'Anything to please you, boss.'

She blew him a kiss across the table. 'It's all very well you teasing,' she said. 'I want to make sure this is a lovely wedding. We're having it just in time before that damned Hitler starts up again an' I want it to be perfect.'

'It will be,' he promised, grinning at her. 'How can it be anything else with all you lot working on it?'

*

It was certainly one of the noisiest weddings either of them had attended, because the Taylors and the Goodisons were out in force. Rosie's sister Edie arrived early from Worthing with her husband Joey and their two kids: eleven-year-old Dorothy, looking grand in a new dress, and fourteen-year-old Frank, looking very uncomfortable in a starched collar which he tugged at every five minutes when he thought nobody was watching him. He'd reached the awkward stage in his life when he was long-legged and skinny and horribly embarrassed to be kissed by elderly relations, who all came swooping down upon him to do so as soon as he arrived at the church gate. Personally, he couldn't see the point of all this kissing, but as they were all shrieking and kissing one another when they reached the church and his mother was watching him sternly, he had to put up with it.

Kitty's twins grinned at him in sympathy but they didn't have a chance to come and commiserate because Kitty had dressed them up in identical grey suits and bright pink ties, and told them to stand just inside the church door and be ushers. They didn't have much luck with the job either, because the first group that arrived just roared with laughter at them when they asked 'Bride or groom?' and the group replied, 'Both.'

'Don't you go a-worritin' your little selves,' an elderly lady said to them. 'We know where our pews are. We've sat in 'em offen enough. Just make sure your Granpa's at the front.' And she gave them both a resounding kiss and led her chattering group into the aisle.

The twins stuck it out for the next four or five arrivals but then they gave up and went to mooch among the gravestones until Kitty arrived. She was none too pleased to find them in the wrong place.

'Now what did I tell you?' she said. 'Stand still while I tidy you up. You look a right pair a muckpots. What was you thinking of to get yourselves in such a state? An' today, of all days!'

She was still scolding as she marched them into the church and made them sit on either side of her, and by that time Johnnie had arrived with his best man and was standing at the altar rail, blushing and fidgeting with his tie. 'There you are, you see,' she hissed at them. 'All your silly carry-on an' you could've made us miss it.'

But when the bride arrived, all Kitty's irritability vanished, because their dear, dumpy Connie had been transformed. Now, she was elegant and almost graceful in Rosie's white brocade, and carried her enormous bouquet as if to the manner born, her face glowing with happiness.

Nobody in the church was a bit surprised when Johnnie came to give his responses, because he mumbled and shuffled and blushed until the tips of his ears were scarlet. But Connie spoke up clearly, as if she knew the words by heart and, when the vicar told the groom, 'You may kiss the bride,' she took Johnnie's blushing face between her hands and kissed him so soundly that the congregation broke into a cheer.

They went on cheering and singing as they followed the newly-weds back to Pa's cottage: 'Here comes the bride!' and 'For *they* are jolly good fellows,' while the fat clouds grew pink-cheeked above them in the autumn light and the humpbacked downs glowed in the distance like blue whales. The kids skipped and danced and waved their arms above their heads as if they were carrying garlands. And it suddenly reminded Rosie of a commercial she'd made, years ago, when the players were told to 'look joyful' and to sing and cheer and the children had to jump about. Only this time, it didn't stop when the director called 'Cut!' This time it went on right up to the gates of Pa's cottage.

And then what a crush there was, cramming so many people into such a small space and all of them laughing and buoyant and happy. Connie and Johnnie were led to the seats of honour, with their backs against the wall, and Pa and Mrs Taylor sat on either side of them and Rosie's wedding cake was set in all its beribboned splendour on the table in front of them, among plates and dishes stacked high with sandwiches and pies and buns and jam tarts. And the rest of the guests milled around the table gathering food and holding out their glasses for beer or lemonade or Tizer, which the twins were serving, and found places to sit or stand wherever they could, on the stairs, in the kitchen, out in the garden. It was noisy and happy and just what a wedding breakfast ought to be.

When half the plates on the table had been emptied and quietly removed by Tess and Kitty, and all the glasses had been topped up, Pa struggled to his feet and held up his hand for silence. Even though they'd been alerted by the topping up, it took several seconds for the party to shush itself sufficiently to listen to him, and several minutes of manic sardine packing before they were all more or less in the living room.

Watching her father's face, Rosie could see that for a fleeting second he was daunted by being expected to speak to so many people, but he took a sip of beer to sustain him and began.

'What I mean for to say, is to wish my son John an' my new daughter Connie a long, sunny life, what is no more'n they both deserves, so help me if it ent, being as they been walking out so long.' And he gave them a smile.

Johnnie was blushing again. 'I ent so sure about the sun Pa,' he said, trying a joke to make himself feel more comfortable. 'We had a thunderstorm Thursday, don't forget. They give me the goose pimples, them ol' thunder storms.'

That produced ribald laughter all around the room and some cheerful suggestions from his cousins as to the real reason for the goose pimples, which made him blush so deeply he had to hide his face in his hands.

'Be that as it may,' Pa said, starting his speech again, 'but what I means for to say, is that I hopes you have as good a marriage as me and my ol' gal. We was a good pair an' we come through thick an' thin, allus loving and kindly like. What I hopes will be the same for you. Now what else was there?' And he looked across at Tess, who raised her glass. 'Ah yes. Raise your glasses all of you an' drink the health of our bride and groom.'

Glasses were raised and sipped at, and Pa and Johnnie and Connie were cheered until the sound reverberated in the room like the thunder.

But Rosie was watching her father and aching because he looked so frail, remembering what a strong stocky man he'd been when she was little, when his cheeks were always red and his hands were brown and strong and capable. She had the clearest vision of them digging the garden, driving his heavy cart, mucking out the milking shed, lifting the heavy churns. He'd been such a hearty man and now he looked like a ghost, his dear old face so thin and lined and those white hands skeletal shadows of what they had been. Dear Pa, she thought, and shuddered with a sudden spasm of anguish. Dear, dear Pa.

Jim put his arm round her. 'All right?' he said.

'Course,' she said, shaking her spasm away with her memories. 'It's a lovely wedding.'

She and the girls talked about the wedding all the way back to the Borough, reliving every choice moment and laughing themselves silly, while Jim dropped off to sleep. When a sudden jolt woke him, he explained that he hadn't been asleep, to which his daughters chorused, as they always did, 'We know, Dad. You were just resting your eyes,' and shrieked with laughter all over again. Oh it *had* been a good day.

'We shall be like dead things in the morning,' Rosie said, when they finally yawned up to bed.

'It's half past one,' Gracie told her, 'so technically speaking it *is* morning. But it's Sunday morning, so we can have a nice lie in.'

Which they did. And, as they were up too late for breakfast, they set to and cooked their Sunday dinner while Jim strolled off to get the papers. It was a gentle meal because they were all still sleeping off the exertion of the previous day but, in the middle of it, Jim found something in the paper that made him grin.

'Take a look at that,' he said to Rosie, handing the paper across the table. 'Your film's been panned.'

She read it, with her fork half way to her mouth. 'Well it *was* cobbled together,' she said. 'I'll give him that. But calling it propaganda's a bit harsh.' And she went on reading as she ate. 'Well that doesn't surprise me at all,' she said when she handed the paper back. And when Jim looked a question at her, 'Mr Korda's going to America.'

'Will that mean no more film parts, then?' Gracie asked.

'Probably,' Rosie said. 'Never mind. I shall just have to find myself another job.'

'That was lovely,' Mary said, putting down her knife and fork. 'Now I'm ready for that apple pie.'

That made them all laugh again and the film and Mr Korda were forgotten. And remained forgotten until Rosie was walking home with two full shopping baskets after a trip to the Borough Market two days later and saw something that gave her an idea. It was a full sized poster of a woman in Air Raid Precautions uniform looking neat and purposeful, with a simple slogan alongside it, urging '*Join the ARP.*' Now that's a possibility, she thought. I'll see what Jim has to say about it.

'I been thinking,' she said to him, when she was dishing up their supper that evening.

He was taking off his boots but, alerted by the determination in her voice, he looked up to ask her, 'What about?'

'Well,' she said. 'There's not much work for me to do at the moment now Mr Korda's gone to America, an' I can get through the housework in no time at all now it's only you an' me. I think I'd like to join the ARP.'

He wasn't too keen on the idea of her being out in the streets during an air raid. It would be too risky, as he knew only too well, but he could see that she'd made up her mind to it. 'Well, I s'pose you could,' he said, trying to be diplomatic. 'Depends what you want to do. I mean, I wouldn't want you getting yourself hurt.'

'I reckon I could drive an ambulance,' she said. 'I know how to drive a car. I used to drive Mr de Silva's. And it can't be all that different.'

He wasn't over keen on that, either. Ambulances would be expected to drive through the thick of it. But at least she'd have some cover from the shrapnel and if she wore her tin hat all the time… 'I'll see what I can find out for you,' he promised.

*

Two days later she took a tram to the ambulance station at St Olave's hospital and demonstrated her skill behind the wheel.

Her instructor was a white haired man with a gentle manner and, as she quickly discovered, a steel resolve. 'First,' he said as they walked towards the ambulance shed, 'I must warn you that being an ambulance driver is not a glamorous job. It will be dangerous and dirty and exhausting.'

'Yes,' she said, 'I know. My husband told me. He's a chief warden.'

He looked at her curiously. 'What did you say your name was?

'Rosie Jackson.'

The instructor's expression changed. 'Course,' he said. 'Old Jim. He's a good man.'

'He is,' she agreed.

'Name of Kennedy,' he said, holding out a hand, which she shook. 'Now then, let's get down to brass tacks. You will be expected to look after your vehicle and keep it in full working order at all times, which means checking the tyres and the radiator and the battery every time you come in, and, when there's been a raid and you've picked up casualties, cleaning the interior thoroughly. Are you up for that?'

She was.

'And I'd better tell you they'll be hard to handle, being they're converted lorries. Can you double declutch?'

She was proud to say she could.

'Well, there they are,' he said, pointing to a long corrugated iron shelter. 'There's the key to the last one in the line. Let's see how well you can reverse out.'

By that time, Rosie was determined to put on the best show he'd ever seen and she climbed into the driver's seat at once, adjusted the rear view mirror, put the clutch into reverse, and inched out of the shelter, gritting her teeth and scowling.

He seemed satisfied, although he didn't say so, but climbed into the passenger seat and watched her as she turned the ambulance round and drove carefully through the gate between the two main buildings. Then she simply drove wherever he told her, growing more confident with every mile, even though she found driving over the tramlines more difficult than she expected.

'You know this area,' he said at one point.

'I've lived here a long time,' she told him.

'It shows,' he said. 'Right. You can drive back to base now. That's enough for one afternoon. Come back tomorrow evening and I'll see how you are in the blackout.'

As the tram rocked her homewards, Rosie gave this new venture careful thought. Now that she'd driven her first ambulance, she knew it was something she wanted to do and could do well, with a bit of practice. But she was a bit too aware that Jim didn't want her to do it – the expression on his face had told her that – and that was only natural because they both knew it would be dangerous. He was putting himself in danger being a warden, but then they were both going to be in this war when it stopped being phoney, whether they liked it or not, and everyone who lived in London would be in danger, one way or another. I shan't say anything to him until they've taken me on, she decided, just in case they don't. I might not be able to drive so well in the dark. Those headlights won't give much light and there's no moon to speak of at the moment. Still there's no point worrying about it. I'll face it tomorrow.

It was every bit as difficult as she'd feared it would be. For a start it took far too long for her eyes to adjust to the darkness and, when they did, she was confused by the sudden eerie gleam of the white bands that had been painted round tree trunks and pillar boxes. It wasn't until she started to use her wits and worked out the white bands that marked the edges of the kerbs were the ones that were useful to her now, that she began to feel confident and to obey Mr Kennedy's instructions more readily. But by the end of her drive she was driving well. Now, she thought, as she parked her vehicle, he'll have to tell me whether I've passed muster or not.

But he didn't.

'Same time tomorrow,' he said. 'I want to see how you can cope in an area you don't know.'

So, same time tomorrow it was. But this time she knew what to look out for and drove better in a strange part of the town than she'd done in her own.

'Yes,' Mr Kennedy said, as she scrambled down from the driver's seat. 'You'll do. Come and meet some of the rest of the team.' And he led her into the hospital.

The rest of the team were in a large room that had obviously been a ward. The windows were high and set in a long row. They were all shielded by heavy black-out curtains but their positioning revealed what they'd been, originally. There was a large table in the centre of the room, which seemed to be covered in telephones and cups of tea. More than a dozen people, all in uniform, were sitting or standing round it, all talking to one another. But they looked up when Mr Kennedy came in.

'Meet our new recruit,' he said, and introduced her. 'Rosie Jackson, wife of our Jim.'

They waved at her and one of them called out, 'Welcome aboard.' And she waved back and said 'thank you,' feeling suddenly and inordinately pleased with herself.

Then they gave her a cup of tea to drink while she signed on, and a splendidly friendly woman, called Mavis, explained her duties to her. 'We work three shifts every twenty-four hours,' she said. 'All eight hour, one on duty, one on standby and one off. Most of us arrange to work double shifts some days so that we can get a weekend off. Once the air raids start, that'll change, of course, but for the time being it's quite useful. Drink your tea and then I'll sort out your uniform and find you a tin hat.'

And oh! What a wonderful hat it was. Brand new and glossy black with a big white A painted on the front. Rosie carried it home like a crown and wore it as she walked into the kitchen, saying, 'Whatcher think a that?'

Jim looked up from his evening paper, grinned and answered her in the same words they'd used at the control station. 'Welcome aboard!' he said.

Now, she thought, whatever we've got ahead of us, we shall be in it together.

But although they couldn't know it at that moment, what they actually had ahead of them was the worst winter since 1895.

CHAPTER FOUR

It was the light that woke Rosie up that morning. She was alert to it even before she opened her eyes, a sense of whiteness and unfamiliar movement that wasn't usual at seven o'clock on a midwinter morning. Then she opened her eyes and saw the fat flakes tumbling past the window and clapped her hands with pleasure.

'It's snowing Jim,' she said, struggling into her dressing gown. 'We're going to have a white Christmas.' And she ran to the window and pulled the curtains right back to get a good look at it. 'Oh look! It must have been snowing all night. The roofs are covered with it an' all the pavements an' everything. It's really snowing.' The snowflakes drifted against the window as fat and fluffy as goose feathers. Even though the dawn had barely begun, she could see them quite clearly. 'We're going to have a white Christmas. Ent that lovely?'

Jim was still half asleep with the eiderdown heaped round his shoulders. 'Never mind Christmas,' he growled. 'You'll get chilblains, you stand at the window with nothing on your feet.'

So she skipped back to bed and slid her cold feet between his warm legs, the way she always did when she needed warming up. And they *were* cold. He was right.

He complained, as *he* always did. 'Gaw dearie me, Rosie! Do you have to do that?' But he put his arms round her to cuddle her warm, the way *he* always did. 'I'll go down presently and put the kettle on,' he said. 'An' you can dress up warm while I'm about it.'

'I'll wear me trousers an' a thick pair of socks,' she said, grinning at him. 'Will that suit you?' Her uniform trousers were the warmest garments she possessed.

He was pulling a jersey over his head. 'You'll wear 'em out,' he laughed at her.

'No I won't,' she said. 'They're sturdy. An' anyway, I like wearing 'em.'

'So I've noticed,' he laughed. 'You'll end up driving that amberlance a yours in your knickers. See if I'm not right.'

'I'll be a sight for sore eyes then,' she teased.

'You'll get chilblains on your bum,' he warned. And went off to make the tea.

But Rosie was too happy to be thinking of the time when she would have to drive the ambulance in earnest. That was in the future and she would deal with it when she had to. For the moment, all that mattered was that Christmas was a mere four days away and she and Jim and the girls were all going to be together again and Kitty was coming up with the twins to join them. The pudding was made, the cake iced, the goose ordered, there were chestnuts to roast round the fire and plenty of coal in the coal shed. She'd spent every penny of her bonus but so what? It was Christmas and it was going to be a good one.

And it was. Mary came home as soon as St Olave's broke up and set to at once to help with the cooking; Gracie swapped shifts so that she could be with them for the whole of Christmas Day; and, early on Christmas morning, Kitty arrived with her twins in tow, all of them red-nosed, booted and bundled up in mufflers and extra jerseys, and were sat by the fire to thaw out after their journey. The snow had melted by then and the road and pavements were clear, although it was still ominously cold. The sky was grey, so there was obviously more snow coming, but what did it matter? They were together again, cracking all the old jokes, tucking in to Rosie's excellent meal, ignoring the war and the weather, as if it was still peacetime and they hadn't a care in the world. And afterwards they turned on the wireless and sat round the fire and listened to ITMA.

'I wouldn't miss that for worlds,' Kitty said, wiping her eyes, when the programme was over. 'The speed they go at! Takes your breaf away.'

'It makes me feel as if we were in a sort of cocoon,' Rosie said. 'As if the war was a long way away an' nothing to do with us.'

'Me too,' Gracie said. 'That's what comes of laughing so much. It makes you feel better.'

'I wish we *were* in a cocoon,' Mary said, 'an' we could stay in it for ever till the war's over an' done with, an' I wouldn't have to go back to Hastings.'

'Make the most a the time you've got, kid,' Jim advised. 'You don't have to get back yet awhile, do you?'

Mary grinned at him. 'Not till after the New Year, anyway,' she said.

'Well there you are, then,' he said. 'You've got plenty a time. We could go to the pantomime. That's a laugh, too.'

Bobbie and George had been sitting at their mother's feet, listening with their mouths open. 'I wish we could come an' all,' Bobbie said. 'We ent never seen a pantomime, have we Georgie?'

His wistful expression gave Rosie a sudden, happy idea. 'Well, why not?' she said. 'Why don't you stay till the New Year? You'd have to go on sleeping in the camp beds, but if you can put up with *that*, why not?'

Two identical faces turned to Kitty, eagerly. Two identical voices spoke at once. 'Could we Ma? We could, couldn't we? Oh let's!'

'You'll have to put up wiv me an' Rosie an' our Gracie being on shifts now an' then,' Jim warned. 'But you're more than welcome.'

'We could keep the place warm for you, while you're out,' Bobbie said, 'an' keep our Mary company. That'd be good, wouldn't it?'

*

So it was decided, and their two-day cocoon became an eight-day holiday. They went up west to the pantomime on Boxing Day and out to the local pictures at the Elephant and Castle the day after, and spent a nostalgic evening at the music hall, where they saw Flanagan and Allen. They had fish and chips for supper one night and pie and mash the next and listened to the wireless every day. And, on the last day of the year and the end of their holiday, they all sat up to see the new year in, singing the old songs and eating shrimps and cockles and brown bread and butter and Rosie's cheese straws, and Jim and the twins drank a great deal of beer while their women sipped port and lemon, and they were warmly and ridiculously happy together.

'Best holiday we've ever 'ad,' Kitty said as they parted. 'Ain't it boys? Wrap that muffler round you good an' tight, Georgie, or you'll catch yer death.'

Jim was putting his coat on and winding his own muffler round his neck. 'Hang on a tick,' he said, 'an I'll walk you to the tram. I need to get me *Mirror*.'

So they walked off, arm in arm, Jim hobbling the way he usually did when it was cold, while Rosie and the girls waved to them from the doorstep. Poor old Jim, Rosie thought, that wound still troubles him and he never complains.

'Now what shall we do?' Gracie asked.

'Now,' Rosie said, 'we'll do the washing up an' stoke the fire an' put the boiler on for the washing an' get those camp beds folded up.'

'Slave labour,' Mary said, grinning at her. 'Come on then.'

They were hard at work in the scullery when Jim came in on a rush of icy air. He had the *Mirror* under his arm and a scowl on his face.

'Now what?' his daughters said, speaking together.

'Conscription,' he told them, and held up the paper for them to see the headline. *'Call up for two million men.'*

Rosie was lifting a sheet out of the boiling water with her copper stick. It hung in front of her eyes, heavy and steaming. 'Well it was bound to happen sooner or later,' she said, trying to be sensible about it.

Jim opened the paper and read it aloud. '*All men between the ages of 17 and 27, with the exception of those in reserved occupations, will be receiving their call-up papers today.* Poor sods. Didn't we have enough last time?'

There was such anguish in his voice that Rosie let the sheet fall back into the copper, put her stick down and strode across the scullery to hug him. 'Maybe it won't be so...' she began.

But he shook her off, his face set. 'Death's death,' he said, 'an' it's always bleedin' awful. Always.' And he turned away from her and left them, tossing the paper onto the kitchen table as he went.

They waited until he'd closed the front door. 'Should we go after him?' Mary asked, anxiously. He must have been really upset to walk out of the house like that. She'd never seen him do such a thing before. Ever. 'Poor Dad.'

'No,' Rosie said. 'Leave him be. He'll come round to it in his own time. Let's get these sheets rinsed.' And when Mary still looked stricken, 'Don't worry, chick. He'll handle it.'

Gracie put down the dish she was drying and flicked her tea towel over her shoulder so that she could put her arms round her sister and give her a hug. 'He'll be all right, kid,' she said.

But Mary began to cry. 'I've got to go back to that rotten Hastings tomorrow,' she wept. 'Miles away from all of you. An' I hate it there. I can't leave him when he's so upset.'

'I thought you liked it there,' Gracie said.

'Well I don't.'

'Come on,' Gracie said, putting the tea towel down and leading Mary towards the door. 'Don't cry. Let's you and me go upstairs and get you packed. The weather forecast is hideous – they're talking about blizzards – so you'll have to take all your warmest clothes and we only brought some of them down for you that time. You'll need your fair isle for a start, and some good thick socks. He'll be back. You'll see.'

'Oh Gracie, I *do* love you,' Mary said, and, to their mother's relief, she allowed her sister to lead her towards the hall. 'He *will* be all right, won't he?'

'Course,' Gracie said, turning her head slightly to nod at Rosie as she cuddled Mary out of the door.

But Rosie crossed her fingers, just to be on the safe side, before she got on with the wash. What he'd said was right. They'd had quite enough of war the last time and nobody in their right mind wanted this one. It made her sigh. The steam in the scullery was already running down the wall and her back was aching something chronic and she'd only done half the wash, and now they'd started conscription just to make things as bad as they could be. If human beings had any sense, she thought, as she hauled the sheet into the air again and lowered it into the bucket, they'd invent machines to do all this endless work instead of wasting their time firing guns at one another and dropping bombs.

She allowed her mind to slip into a familiar daydream. They could have a machine to scrub the doorsteps. That'ud be nice. And one to wash the floors and one to clean out the grate and set the fires and get them going of a morning. They might even invent a machine to keep their food fresh so's the milk wouldn't go off in the summer. There was already a machine that swept the floors. She knew that. It was called a Hoover and all you had to do was push it about. One of the drivers at the ambulance station had bought one for his wife and she reckoned it was the best thing they'd ever bought. I'd have one too, Rosie thought, if I ever earned enough. She pushed her damp hair out of her eyes and straightened her back to ease it. Then she put the next lot of sheets into the boiler and picked up the bucket to lug the first lot out into the garden and put it through the mangle.

By the time Jim finally came home, the day had become a normal washday. The first lot of sheets was hanging on the drier, and steaming up the kitchen, Mary's bags had been neatly packed, the potatoes were almost ready to mash and yesterday's joint was waiting on the table alongside the pickles.

To everyone's relief, he seemed to be quite himself again, smiling at them as he came in and with a copy of the *Evening Standard* under his arm.

'They've had a blizzard up in Scotland,' he said. 'It's gonna be a really bad winter, so they say.'

'Just as well we packed you all those warm clothes then,' Gracie said, grinning at Mary. 'I'll mash the potatoes, shall I Mum?'

*

The forecasts were right. As January progressed, it got steadily colder and, by the end of the month, the snow was falling again. This time it was very thick indeed and it went on falling, day after day, until the roofs were white and the roads and pavements were perpetually covered, no matter how often people came out with their shovels and tried to clear them. After the first few days, every gate had an ugly mound of frozen snow beside it, grey with dirt, embedded with fag ends, spent matches and empty cigarette packets and streaked smelly and yellow by the local dogs.

Out in the countryside, so the papers said, there were drifts twenty feet high, farm carts were stranded, sheep shivered in the fields and vegetables were frozen into the ground, so they were in very short supply in Covent Garden, which made Jim's life difficult, even though his customers took it philosophically. And to add insult to injury, bacon, butter and sugar were rationed. 'As if we didn't have enough to contend with,' people said.

At the beginning of February, the Thames froze for eight miles between Teddington and Sunbury and there were pictures in the paper of people skating on the frozen Serpentine, just the way Rosie and the girls had done, when Mr de Silva painted that picture of them. How long ago that seemed. Mary wrote to tell her mother and father that the hilly streets in Hastings were so icy she couldn't ride her bike anywhere and she was jolly glad of all the jumpers Gracie had packed for her, otherwise she'd freeze to death on the street. Even the sea froze, as Edie phoned to tell Rosie in some excitement, because it was unheard of.

'Great chunks of solid ice,' Edie said. 'Sort of clunking against one another on top of the water. They make the most peculiar sound. Really eerie.'

The one good thing to come out of such weather was the fact that it seemed to have brought any fighting to a complete halt. Occasionally the papers would print pictures of British soldiers in bulky white suits struggling among the snow drifts in Norway but apart from that, the news was all about snowstorms and blizzards.

'An' thank God for that,' Rosie said. 'At least weather's natural, even it *is* bad. I hope it goes on for a good long time.'

'It don't stop the buggers sinking our merchant ships, though,' Jim said sourly. 'We'll be nothing but skin an' grief by the time the spring comes.'

'I'd rather be skin an' grief than bombed,' Rosie told him. 'The spring can come as late as it likes as far as I'm concerned.'

But spring arrived on time, as soon as the last snows had melted away. The bright heads of the daffodils were dancing in the local gardens by the middle of March, just in time for Easter, and in the first week in April, Rosie saw the first tender buds on her lilac tree. The sight of them filled her with such a mixture of emotions it was quite painful. Pleasure to see them there, of course, because they'd always been her harbinger of spring, but anxiety too because this fine soft weather could only have one outcome. The Germans would start another campaign. The war would stop being phoney and begin in earnest. She didn't talk about it, for what could she say? What could any of them say? Or do?

And sure enough, on April the ninth the papers headlined the news that German troops had invaded Denmark and Norway. Denmark surrendered six hours later, which was a shock, but Norway seemed to be putting up a fight. As far as Rosie could make out, the Germans were invading Norway from the sea. She looked up all the places where they were landing troops in Gracie's atlas, Trondheim and Bergen, where one of their cruisers was sunk by the British Navy –which she thought was good riddance to bad rubbish –then on to a place called Stavanger and another one called Narvik, right up in the north. She couldn't understand what they were doing, and she didn't like to ask Jim in case it upset him. So she waited until she and Gracie were on their own one evening, when Jim was on duty and, after they'd finished supper and were enjoying a ciggie together, she asked *her*.

'They're ports,' Gracie said, blowing smoke out of her nostrils like a dragon. 'That's what he's after. He's going to need a lot of equipment for that army of his.'

It made sense. 'It makes me wonder what he'll do next,' Rosie admitted, 'now he's conquered Denmark.'

'He'll invade France,' Gracie told her, coolly. 'And then he'll have airfields within striking distance of London and he'll start bombing *us*.'

She was quite calm about it. But Rosie was gripped with fear and foreboding, thinking of all the dreadful newsreels she'd seen of German soldiers marching like robots in their hideous jackboots with their arms held rigidly in the air, and tanks rolling inexorably towards the troops they were going to kill and injure, and great black planes armed with bombs and machine guns, ready to kill anyone that lay beneath them, like they did at Guernica. You couldn't stop planes coming, that was the awful thing about them, and you couldn't defend yourself against them when they did, and they were flown by men who'd been trained to kill. Trained to kill! God help us all! And she had a sudden, shattering memory of the British fascists she'd seen marching off the pier at Worthing behind that horrible man Moseley, with their hands held in the same rigid salute and their faces full of hatred, baying 'England for the English! Moseley! Moseley!'

God help us all!

'You know what I think,' Gracie said.

Rosie dragged her mind back to the present and tried to concentrate. 'No,' she said. 'What do you think?'

'I think you ought to get a bike.'

'I don't need a bike,' Rosie told her. 'I can get anywhere I want on a tram.'

'Ah, but you might not be able to,' Gracie said, stubbing out her cigarette in the ashtray. 'Tramlines can be bombed as easily as shops and houses. And if the lines were out of action the trams'd be stuck. But if you had a bike, you could just wheel it over the wreckage until you could hop on again and Bob's your uncle. We were talking about it this morning, after the lecture.'

How mature she is, Rosie thought, admiring her daughter's brown eyes and that determined chin, and thinking how like Jim she was, despite her dark hair. She got that from me, she thought, but everything else is like her father. She looks a lot older than eighteen, especially when she's in uniform. 'I'll give it thought,' she said.

*

She didn't think for long because when she talked it over with Jim, he said it was a good idea too. So the bike was bought a week later. And not a minute too soon.

On May the tenth the news broke that they'd all been dreading and expecting. A huge German army had smashed through the great Ardennes forest, that the French politicians had been so sure was impenetrable, and had invaded Holland, Belgium, Luxembourg and Northern France. Gracie had been proved right. They had moved –and they had moved quickly.

Rosie was off duty that morning, so she kept the wireless on and listened to the bulletins so that she could follow the news as it came in. It was frightening. The German army seemed to be advancing like some hideous juggernaut, swallowing countries whole and trampling over everything and everyone in its way. And nobody seemed to be resisting. Where are our armies? she thought, thumping her mop on the kitchen floor in exasperation. Why isn't somebody doing something?

By six o'clock when Jim came home for his supper, the bulletins had changed direction. Now they were reporting that Mr Chamberlain had stepped down as prime minister and handed over to Winston Churchill and, in a later bulletin, that all Germans and Austrians who lived in Great Britain and were between the ages of 16 and 50 were going to be interned.

'Battening down the hatches,' Jim said, 'in case they're spies.'

'Would they be?' Rosie asked. 'I mean, some of them have lived here years.'

'Doubt it,' Jim said. 'The Jerries in the market are the same as us only they don't speak so good. You leaving the dishes in the sink or shall we wash 'em?'

Rosie checked the clock and turned on the geyser. 'We'll wash them,' she said. 'We've got time. I don't like leaving the place in a mess.' There were standards to maintain even if the war *had* begun in earnest.

But oh! She did so wish it hadn't. It seemed wrong to be cycling through the familiar streets, dodging trams and wobbling across tram-lines on such a gentle evening. Everything was so reassuringly, peace-fully familiar, the shops, shuttered and quiet, settling into evening, the pubs loud with laughter and exhaling their usual fragrance of beer and cigarette smoke on everyone who passed, the sky streaked with sunset colour, gorgeous above the darkening roofs. And all the time that dreadful juggernaut was rolling across Holland and Belgium, bringing death and destruction, unstoppably.

Three days after the invasion, Queen Wilhelmina arrived in England, bringing her family, her government and her country's gold reserves with her. And a mere two days after that, the Germans sent their bombers to blitz Rotterdam while their army occupied the Hague. And to everybody's horror but nobody's surprise, the Dutch army surrendered. Now France lay wide open to the invaders.

That evening, Churchill gave his first speech as prime minister. It was powerful and frank because it gave words to what most people were thinking and opened with a warning. 'I have nothing to offer you,' he said, 'but blood, toil, tears and sweat.'

That needed saying, Rosie thought, and she felt a rush of unexpected affection towards this plummy-voiced man. We need to know what's happening, if we're going to be asked to cope with it.

From then on, whenever she wasn't on duty, she kept Gracie's atlas open on the kitchen table and referred to it during every bulletin she listened to as she followed the German advance. She knew she ought to be getting on with the housework and baking a cake for Gracie's birthday, which was only a few days away. She'd got all the ingredients and bought her daughter a pretty blouse, and Gracie had swopped shifts so that she could be at home for it. But everything was happening so quickly it was impossible not to listen.

As she wrapped Gracie's present in clean brown paper and tied the string with a bow, the BBC announced that German tanks had crossed the Meuse at Sedan and, later that day, news came through that the French army, under a man called Colonel de Gaulle, had made a stand against the tanks and had halted their advance, but had then been driven back when they came under attack from Stuka dive bombers. The British army was fighting near Amiens. By Wednesday, when Rosie was finally mixing the cake, the announcer reported that Amiens had fallen to the Germans and that German tanks were heading for Abbeville. British divisions, according to the announcer, were 'taking up strategic positions'. She didn't know what he was talking about. But the direction the Germans were taking looked ominous.

That evening Jim came home with his usual copy of the *Evening Standard* under his arm and a grim expression on his face. He threw the paper on the table as if he were glad to see the back of it.

'It's bad, ent it?' Rosie said.

'About as bad as it can get,' he told her, sitting wearily at the kitchen table. 'They're driving our poor sods into the sea. Gawd help 'em.'

'Yes, they are, ent they,' she said sadly. 'That's exactly what they're doing. I been following the bulletins all day.'

'We all have,' he said, drinking the tea she'd set before him. 'One a the lads brought a wireless in.'

He was being so calm, it sparked Rosie's anger. 'What's the matter with the Germans?' she said. 'They're so brutal. I can't understand it. They just go on and on and on, in those God-awful tanks, knocking everybody out of the way, bombing and killing. It's not human. Why doesn't somebody do something to stop them?'

'Because they can't,' Jim told her. 'That's the long an' the short of it. The French tried an' they used Stukas on them. Poor sods. We ain't got enough tanks to fight that lot, nor enough men.'

'We've got an *army* out there,' Rosie argued, 'a whole army. An' nobody's doing *anything*. And they should be. The Germans are just pushing everybody around. I mean, what'll happen to our men if they get pushed into the sea?'

'No good asking me,' Jim said, and now he sounded irritable. 'I'm just one of the poor bloody infantry. Millions of us there was, first time round, an' they never asked us nothin'. They jest sent us off ter get killed. And that's what we done, God help us. Millions of us. It's the same now. Don't keep on about it.'

'It's no good saying "don't keep on",' she said, crossly. 'We can't just sit here an' do nothing. It's too awful for that.'

'War *is* awful,' he said. 'But once you're in it, you 'ave to get on with it. It's no good going on to me about it. I can't do nothing. Never could.'

She tried to explain, her face anguished. 'I keep listening to the wireless and it keeps saying "British divisions are taking up strategic positions" and they're not doing anything, are they? They're just getting pushed further and further back. I mean, it's getting worse all the time. It is, isn't it? I'm worried sick.'

'We're all worried sick,' he shouted at her, 'an' you're making it worse going on about it. There's sweet FA we can do about it. Can't you get that into your thick head?'

The shock of being shouted at took her breath away. 'Don't you dare speak to me like that,' she shouted back. 'I've got as much right to my opinion as anyone. Why shouldn't I speak?'

'Because it's fucking useless,' he said, on his feet and in a fury. 'I'm off up the pub.'

'Oh that's right,' she shouted. 'You go up the pub. I should! That'll solve everything.' But she was shouting at his back and even as the words were in her mouth, he was gone.

She stood in her empty kitchen with the echoes of their quarrel reverberating in the air around her, while her anger drained away, taking all her energy with it. She felt alone and utterly bleak. How *could* that have happened? She and Jim never had rows. Ever. It wasn't the way they went on. The odd spat now and then but never rows. And he didn't call her names either. That was horrid and it was still hurting her.

The kitchen clock gave one of its sudden clunks and she looked at it idly, wondering what time it was. The sight of its familiar face restored her to her senses and she remembered that there was a demonstration on the use of splints at St Olave's that evening, and that she was supposed to be attending it. She still felt muddled and confused, but she knew that if she didn't leave the house in five minutes, she'd be late for it or miss it altogether, and that would never do. After all, if London was going to be bombed, she was one of the people who were going to have to deal with the casualties. She found a piece of notepaper, wrote a short message to Jim and left it on the kitchen table. 'Just off to St Olave's for the lecture. Fish and chips for supper?' Then she wheeled her bike out of the hall and set off.

It was a difficult evening. For a start, her mind kept wandering away from the subject, returning to that horrid row, again and again, like a tongue to a sore tooth, even though she was trying really hard to concentrate. The lecturer didn't help much either, because he spoke too quickly and didn't give them time to digest what he was saying before he rushed on to the next thing. And on top of all that, she kept wondering what she was going to say to Jim when she got home. Not knowing how she was going to face him made her feel lost.

He was sitting at the kitchen table when she got in and looked up at her, almost as if there was nothing wrong. 'Right,' he said. 'I'll nip off now and get the fish an' chips. D'you want a pickled onion? Shan't be long.' And that was that.

They ate their meal in an uncomfortable silence. She toyed with the idea of switching on the wireless to fill the silence but there were bound to be bulletins and that would upset them all over again.

'Now then,' she said to him, when she'd eaten all she could and she was clearing the table. 'When Gracie comes, we won't say nothing about what's going on in France. I don't want her upset on her birthday.'

He answered her stiffly, his face set. 'D'you take me for a fool?'

'No,' she said, equally stiffly. 'I just don't want her to be upset. That's all. I'll wash these up and then I'm off to bed. You'll lock up, won't you?'

When Gracie arrived the following afternoon, it was soon obvious that she knew more about the situation than they did, and when she'd been given her presents and kissed them both and thanked them, she settled at the table for her birthday supper and told them about it at length.

'We've got two divisions out there,' she said, 'and they've been fighting all the way, so we're expecting a lot of casualties if the navy can get them home. There are six destroyers standing by, so Matron was telling us. We're all ready to receive them. We've got everything we need.'

How sensibly she's taking it, Rosie thought. But she knew it was going to be very difficult to bring two divisions home, even with six destroyers heading off to do it.

'Take care of yourself,' she said as she kissed Gracie goodbye. 'Phone us when you can.'

'Don't worry,' Gracie said, hugging her. 'I'll be all right. I shall be taking care of other people now. Whatever's coming, we're ready for it, and that's half the battle.'

'She'll cope,' Jim said, standing beside her as Gracie cycled away. 'She's a good kid.' And he put an arm round her shoulder and gave her a hug. It was the first time he'd touched her since their row.

'She is,' she agreed, looking up at him.

'Forgiven?' he asked.

'Course,' she said. She was waving to Gracie and spoke instinctively and without giving it much thought. But then she wondered and turned to face him so that she could look him in the eye. She was touched and surprised by what she saw. He looked anxious. There was no doubt about that. Apologetic and anxious. But he didn't push her to say anything more. He just waited.

'I never say nothing I don't mean,' she said, recognising the truth of it as she spoke.

He smiled at her, almost in his old way. 'Thank Gawd for that,' he said. 'I thought I'd had it.'

'You on duty tonight?' she asked.

''Fraid so. Or we could go to the flicks.'

''Nother time,' she said. There was always another time.

CHAPTER FIVE

That next week was a nightmare. Every day brought bad news, which Rosie followed like everyone else, feeling more and more anxious. On Monday and Tuesday the Germans continued their inexorable march towards the sea despite a valiant attempt by the British troops to hold them back. By Wednesday morning, it was obvious that the British army was being hemmed in at Boulogne and Calais and a place called Dunkirk, where thousands of men were waiting for rescue on a dangerously exposed beach.

Later that day, the news bulletins announced that six British destroyers had been sent to Boulogne, and although they'd come under very heavy fire from the Germans, they'd managed to rescue 4,400 French and British troops from the harbour there. But, as everyone knew by then, that was nothing compared to the huge numbers who were still waiting on the beaches, and there had been a heavy price to pay for it. As well as the men who had been killed or injured in the harbour, two French destroyers had been sunk with what the announcer called 'considerable loss of life'. It made grim listening and was the main topic of conversation wherever Rosie went next morning.

'Them poor sods on the beaches,' the women said to one another as they stood in little groups, passing on what news they'd gleaned. 'They'll never take all that lot prisoner. Stands to reason. I mean to say, there's thousands of 'em. They'll just mow 'em down. Poor devils.'

Their anxiety cast a pall over the entire market. It was so quiet the place seemed to be holding its breath and the air around them was smoky and peculiarly still. It was as if they'd been cut off from the rest of the world by a sea mist. The handful of children who were still in the Borough had caught their adults' anxiety and clung to their mothers' skirts, pale faced, owl-eyed and speechless. Even the stall-holders were subdued and not calling and chivvying the way they usually did. Now they stood waiting for trade instead of urging it, and they spoke quietly and gently. Some of them patted their customers' hands as they handed over their change, or packed their baskets for them, as if they were the ones who were wounded. The sudden noise of a train passing over their heads startled them all because it sounded so much louder than usual and so out of place.

'What'll become of all those poor men?' Rosie's next-door neighbour said, when they met at the fish stall.

'God alone knows, Sonia.' Rosie sighed, looking at the anguished expression on Sonia's face. 'You got someone out there?'

'My cousin, Phil,' Sonia told her. 'You remember him. Great big chap with curly hair. Always whistling. He used to come an' visit me when he was on leave. He's with the British Expeditionary Force, poor devil. I ain't heard from him for weeks. He could be anywhere. An' that's the truth of it.'

'I *am* sorry,' Rosie said, giving her a hug. It was just an impulsive gesture, but it made Sonia cry and that wasn't at all what she intended. 'Oh Sonia. We never expected this, did we?'

'No we never,' Sonia said, wiping her eyes. 'For the life a me, I can't see why we had to declare war in the first place. Now we got all them poor buggers out there on the beaches and we can't get 'em home.'

'The navy's doing its best,' Rosie said, trying to be comforting.

'It ain't big enough, duck,' Sonia told her sadly. 'Not for all those men. Thousands and thousands of 'em there are. It'd take months to get all that lot off the beach and they've only got a few days 'cause the Jerries are advancing at a rate a knots. It can't be done. I only wish it could.'

And although it was miserably depressing for Rosie to admit it, it looked as though she was right.

*

For the next three days, the BBC broadcast regular bulletins about the situation in Normandy. They were smoothly read and sounded comforting, but they actually told their waiting audience very little. The navy was still rescuing as many men as it could but it was a slow process and they were under heavy fire most of the time and losing ships.

Jim came back from his stint in the ARP post on Wednesday evening to say that one of his mates had bought a wireless in and they'd all been listening to it. 'God awful business,' he said. 'I can't see 'em getting many more men off the beaches, the rate they're going.'

Rosie made a grimace because she didn't trust herself to say anything in case it upset him.

But he was being sensible. 'We'll just have to listen to the news an' see,' he said. 'There ain't much to do at the post at the moment, so we might as well. I mean, we got everything good an' ready. We ain't neglecting our duties or nothing. An' we ought to know what's going on.'

That was the opinion in the ambulance station too. One of the drivers had brought his wireless in on that first Monday and they had it on all through the day shifts and kept it going at night until the last bulletin was over, desperately trying to find some hope in what they were being told, but growing steadily more and more despondent.

And then on Saturday evening, the bulletins told them the news that they all dreaded and certainly didn't want to hear. Boulogne and Calais had surrendered.

Jim and Rosie heard it as they were sitting in the front room after their supper. There wasn't anything either of them could say, although they were both thinking hard and unhappily. Eventually they lit up and smoked cigarettes together which was at least companionable, even if it didn't solve anything. And just as Rosie was stubbing hers in the ashtray and wondering whether she'd light another, the phone rang.

She rushed to answer it, eager to know who it was and what they would say – and was surprised to hear Mary's voice on the other end of the line. She was a good daughter, her Mary, and sent a postcard home at least twice every week, but for her to phone was so rare that Rosie started to worry as soon as she heard her voice.

'Are you all right?' she asked.

'Yes, yes,' Mary said, dismissively. 'I'm fine. Listen. Something really odd's happened. All the fishing boats have gone.'

That didn't make sense. 'What?'

'They've all left the beach,' Mary said, 'every single one –and they're not out fishing. They've been gone too long for that. It looks really peculiar without them. And the lifeboat's gone too. It wasn't called out. We do know that. But it's gone. *And…* this is odd too…Old Mother Maudie says they've gone to Dover. What d'you make of that?'

Rosie didn't know what to make of it. She stood in the hall with the receiver to her ear, feeling very frightened. Were they expecting the invasion to start? Was that it? Or preparing to be bombed? She couldn't ask because she didn't want Mary to be frightened too. In the end she temporised by saying, 'Is everything all right at school?'

'Lots of work,' Mary said. 'It'll be the exams in a coupla weeks so it's all revision and last minute notes and stuff. Bit boring really. I'll let you know if there's any news on the boats. Everyone OK your end?'

They spent the last part of the call on family news – such as it was. And Rosie went back to the front room to tell Jim and find out what *he* thought about it.

'Well, something's up,' he said in his stolid way. 'That's for sure. I shouldn't think they're expecting an invasion though. I mean to say, they'd've evacuated all the schools if that'd been the case. Anyway, the Jerries'll want to take France first, if I'm any judge. But there's certainly something going on. It'll be interesting to see what it is. Don't worry. They'll get the kids out of it PDQ if it's anything dangerous.' And when she still looked worried… 'Like a cuppa tea?'

The tea was produced within minutes, but it was no comfort to Rosie at all. Whatever this was, she knew it was serious. It could hardly be anything else, after all this time hearing bad news pretty well non-stop. She washed the dishes and dried them up and tried not to worry, but the harder she tried, the more concerned she became. Oh please, she thought, don't let them be invaded. Not with all those children there.

It was a long sleepless night and, when she finally got up to start her day, she felt as if she hadn't slept for weeks. 'Turn on the wireless,' she said to Jim when he came yawning into the kitchen. 'There might be some news.'

There was –and it wasn't what either of them expected.

'Early this morning,' the newsreader said, in his calm, cultured voice, 'an armada of more than four hundred ships set sail across the English Channel heading for Dunkirk, where they will assist at the evacuation of the British army. The operation is under the overall command of the Royal Navy and the armada consists of a variety of boats gathered from all over the south and east coasts: life boats, dock yard launches, river tugs, yachts, cockle boats, fire boats, pleasure craft, French and Belgian fishing boats, oyster dredgers, even Thames barges.'

'Good God!' Jim said. 'They're never gonna take the poor buggers off the beach in yachts. I mean to say! They'll be shot to ribbons!'

'It might work,' Rosie said. The news had given her hope. 'I mean, they wouldn't send them if they didn't think it'd work.' But it was hard to imagine all those thousands of men being taken off a beach in seaside boats. It'd take hours to shift a few hundred. 'We'll have to wait an' see.'

Which they did, tuning in to the wireless whenever they had a free moment, breathless with hope and fear.

By the end of that first anxious day, the newsreaders were telling them that a total of 7,669 men had been rescued. It didn't seem many when they considered how many thousands were waiting, but it was better than nothing and, from then on, the numbers rose, taking their hopes with them. On Monday it was nearly eighteen thousand, the next day it was over forty seven thousand and Gracie rang them that evening to tell them the first of the casualties had arrived in Guy's.

'Some of them are in quite a bad way,' she said to Rosie, 'but they're so cheerful you wouldn't believe it. It's really impressive. There's one here called Sam. Ever so young. He can't be much older than me. And so brave. He had shrapnel wounds to his legs and we had to clean them with alcohol and dress them and it must have been excruciatingly painful... but he was making jokes all the time. We made him a medal of honour out of an old picture postcard and pinned it to his pyjamas.'

On Thursday the total was just under fourteen thousand, which was lower, but impressive even so. The newsreader reported that the fleet had been under very heavy fire and that several ships had been lost, including three destroyers, which Jim said didn't surprise him at all. But the next day's total was sixty eight thousand and that was so good that he and Rosie felt like cheering. They sat in their quiet front room drinking a last cup of tea before they went on duty and grinned at one another.

'That's more like it,' Jim said.

'Do you think they'll do it?' Rosie asked, putting on her shoes.

'There's no way a knowing,' Jim told her. 'Depends on the weather an' how many ships are sunk an' how long the rear-guard can hold the Germans off. All sortsa things.'

Rosie crossed her fingers. 'Well, let's hope everything goes their way for once,' she said. 'It ought to, after all they've been through.' Sitting there in their quiet, peaceful room, hope *did* seem possible.

She went on hoping and hoping all through the next day, as if hoping for good news would make it happen. But when the BBC newsreader finally announced the total that had been rescued, it was so good it made her cry. One hundred and thirty-two thousand men were home and safe. 'In nine days,' the newsreader said, 'a total of 192,226 British troops and 139,000 French have been rescued by seven hundred small ships and 220 warships.' He followed that up with a postscript to tell his listeners that four thousand BEF troops were still in the perimeter, along with a hundred thousand men of the French army.

'What'll happen to *them?*' Rosie said. 'Will they be brought home too?'

'No,' Jim told her. 'They'll be took prisoner, poor sods. They're the men who've been holdin' the Jerries back. The ones what've made this rescue possible. All honour to 'em.'

It upset her to think they weren't going to be rescued too. It didn't seem fair.

Jim watched her, thinking how hideous war was and wishing he could give her what she wanted. But he could do the next best thing. 'Take a gander at that,' he said, holding out his copy of the *Evening Standard*. 'That bit there.'

She took it, read it – and grinned at him. Oswald Mosely had been sent to Brixton Prison. 'Good,' she said. 'I hope they kick his rotten teeth in. He's had it coming to him for a long time.'

He laughed out loud at her. 'That's what I like about you, kid,' he said.

'Not so much a the kid,' she said. 'I'm nearly as old as you.'

'You ain't caught up yet though,' he said. 'I'm still the eldest.' And he gave her a hug, looking up at the ceiling with a question.

'What, now?' she asked, laughing.

'Why not?' he said, happily. 'No time like the present.'

'What about the washing up?' she teased.

'Washing up can wait.'

'And you can't?'

'No,' he said, and he took her arm and walked her to the stairs.

How easy love is, Rosie thought, leaning against his warmth, even now with a war going on all round us.

*

It was such a good evening and it was followed by such a warmly gentle morning that they were late getting up. So they were still sitting around in their kitchen finishing their breakfast when Sonia came knocking at the door. She had a postcard in her hand and was waving it excitedly.

'It's jest come,' she said. 'I had to show you. He's all right. My Phil. He's home. Come back yesterday.' Then she noticed they were at breakfast and looked embarrassed. 'I've interrupted you,' she said.

'Sorry about that. It was just I was so…'

'We've finished, ent we Jim?' Rosie said. 'Would you like a cuppa, Sonia? There's one in the pot.'

'I shall 'ave to go to work,' Jim said, standing up. 'Young Josh is good at holding the fort but it ain't right to leave him on his own long. He's only a kid. Glad you got good news, Sonia. Come in tonight an' have a beer.'

Rosie was pouring the tea. 'Now,' she said when Jim had gone, 'tell me all about it.'

The card was displayed and passed to and fro across the table, all four pages of the daily newspaper were read and devoured, the rescue was declared a miracle, over and over again. They were still enjoying the amazement of it as they walked down to the market together. And the market was transformed. During the last nine days it had been anxiously subdued; now it was bubbling with excitement and triumph, faces beaming, neighbours hugging one another and the word 'miracle' singing from stall to stall, clear as a bird.

But as Rosie walked home through the summer sunshine, with her laden shopping basket over her arm, she was wondering what would happen next.

That evening, Mary rang to say that she would be coming home the next weekend. 'The exams are going ahead as planned,' she said, 'but we're breaking up early. I'll tell you all the gossip when I see you. There's a lot of it.'

'I'll cook you a nice meal and we can sit round the table and you can tell us all about everything,' Rosie said. 'Gracie should be here too. At least I hope so. They usually give her time off over the weekend.'

But that weekend Gracie phoned her on Saturday morning, a mere hour or two before she expected Mary to arrive, to say that she couldn't come home this time because she was going to St Albans, wherever that was, to meet 'Sam's mother', whoever that was. 'She wants to thank me for looking after him,' she explained. 'I'll see you next week.'

'Mary'll be taking her exams next week,' Rosie said crossly, scowling at the wallpaper. 'I thought you'd like to see her today. Don't you want to wish her luck?'

'She doesn't need luck,' Gracie said lightly. 'She'll sail through. Give her my love. Must go. There's a queue.'

And that was that. It upset her mother terribly. 'I don't know what she's thinking of,' she said angrily, when she'd reported the phone call to Jim. 'Rushing off all over the county to see some stupid old lady she doesn't even know, when her sister's coming home before her exams. It's made me so cross. And I'd got the joint and the vegetables and everything. And I did so want us all to be together.'

He laughed at her. Out loud! Actually threw back his head and laughed. What was the matter with the man? 'It's all very well you laughing,' she said. 'It ent funny. Not one little bit. She ought to be here, supporting her sister, not rushing about all over the country.'

'Our Mary'll pass her exams with flying colours,' Jim said easily. 'It don't matter how many people are sitting round our table. You'll see. Don't worry.'

The careless assumption that she could cope with anything broke what little was left of Rosie's control. 'Don't worry?' she shouted at him. 'Don't worry? I'm worried sick. Don't you understand? We none of us know what's ahead of us. None of us. We could be bombed or invaded or anything. We should all be here together. Not charging about all over the country visiting people we don't know.'

Now, and a bit late, Jim realised that she was frightened, and in exactly the same way they'd been in the trenches when they were waiting to go over the top. He stubbed out his cigarette in his saucer, got up and strode across the kitchen to put his arms round her and hold her tight, stroking her hair. 'It's all right, old thing,' he said. 'We're all scared. That's how it is in a war. Shit scared but we get on with it, on account of there ain't a thing we can do *except* get on with it. Not a single damn thing. But we'll manage! You'll see.'

'We could be bombed any time, now,' she said, weeping. 'Or invaded, which'd be worse. Or anything. We're just sitting here like rats in a trap.'

Somebody was scrabbling a key into the front door and the little grating sound made them both turn. Rosie glanced at the clock, in a panic. 'Oh dear God,' she said. 'It's Mary. And here's me…' She was struggling to pull her handkerchief from the pocket of her apron.

But Mary was calling to them and already moving towards them. 'Coo-ee, Aged Ps! I'm home.' She crashed into the kitchen, put her bag down in its usual corner, grinned at her father in her usual way. But then she looked at her mother and was alarmed. 'What's up?' she said.

'Onions,' Jim said. 'You know what they do to her.'

'Oh Mum,' Mary said. 'You should have left them to me. I'd've done them for you.' Then she sniffed the air. 'Is it roast lamb?'

'Well, it will be when it's cooked,' Rosie said.

'Can't wait,' her daughter told her, happily. 'I'll set the table, shall I?'

So the table was set, the meal served, praised and enjoyed and then, over a cup of tea, they got down to pumping Mary for her promised news. It wasn't good.

'The school's going to be re-evacuated,' she told them. 'We've all been busy packing.'

Rosie could feel her heart sinking. 'Where to?' she asked.

'Wales,' Mary said. 'We're supposed to be going as soon as the exams are finished. Don't worry. I shan't go. I've talked to the Head about it

81

and she doesn't mind. If I'm home here, they might let me start my training as a nurse a bit early. Gracie thinks it likely. She knows who I ought to ask.'

'Good,' Jim said. 'Very sensible.'

'They're going to evacuate the Hastings schools, too. They're going to Hertfordshire. Couple of weeks after us.'

'So they think the Germans are going to invade,' Rosie said. She was feeling quite calm by that time, now that she was facing what was going to happen. But then hadn't they known that all along?'

'Looks like it,' Mary said. 'It's been muddle and upheaval in Hastings ever since Dunkirk. They've closed all the beaches, and taken down all the road signs and sign posts and anything with the name Hastings printed on it and there are ack-ack guns on the prom. And they're not allowed to ring the church bells anymore. They're to be kept to warn us if paratroopers start landing. Which is a bit daft, if you think about it. We reckon we'd probably see them drifting down towards us long before anyone started ringing bells. And there are road blocks all over the place too with soldiers guarding them. No one's allowed in unless they're residents. We have to show our identity cards.'

'Ye gods!' Rosie said.

'Actually,' Mary said, grinning at her, 'I think all this fuss about taking down road signs is just nonsense. If the Germans invade us, they'll bring all the maps they need. They're bound to, when you think about it. There's no shortage of maps. They're all over the place. Anyway, me and Maggie don't think they're anywhere near invading. They'll have to beat the RAF first. And conquer France.'

How shrewd she is, Rosie thought.

'You got the right of it there, kid,' Jim said, taking out his cigarettes. 'Want a ciggie?'

Mary said 'Ta,' and Rosie held out her hand too, so it took a few seconds for them to light up and take their first lungful. Then Jim said, 'All things considered, I don't think they'll invade us yet awhile. An' I'll tell you for why. Hitler's got it in for France on account a they beat the Germans first time round. Now he's gonna get his own back. I don't think we need to worry about him invading us. Not yet awhile anyway. He's thrown us out an' he's taken Dunkirk an' now he'll head for Paris. You see if I'm not right.'

Rosie was enjoying her ciggie and thinking hard. They might not be planning to invade us yet, she thought, he's probably right about that, but they can bomb us whenever they want to, now they've got airfields in France. She didn't say anything because she could see that Mary was taking comfort from what her father was telling her and it was *so* important for her to do well in these exams. But she couldn't push her own thoughts away although she *did* try. Her mind kept returning to them all evening, over and over again, that familiar tongue to that familiar rotten tooth. They'll attack us one way or the other. They'rebound to. And it won't be long before they do. Well then, she told herself, as Jim and Mary listened to the wireless, all the more reason to make this visit as happy as I can.

Which she did, cooking the best meals she could contrive and even making a sponge cake for their final tea, which was rare now that the ingredients were so hard to come by. To her delight and relief, Gracie came to join them for tea and to walk her sister to the station afterwards, and nothing was said about her trip to St Albans, although it took painful self-control on Rosie's part to avoid it, so the weekend went well. But she was too down to listen to the news, self-control being more exhausting that she expected, so she went to bed early and tried to ignore it. If bad things were happening she would hear about them in the morning.

Which they were and which, miserably and inevitably, she did.

The papers had quite a lot of news that day, all of it from France and some of it trying to convince their readers that the French were putting up a valiant opposition to the German advance but, when she'd read both the morning and the evening papers, it was obvious to Rosie that the German panzers were powering south and well on their way to Paris. We're all in limbo, she thought, stumbling through the day, waiting for something terrible to happen and powerless to stop it.

The next day the papers reported that Mussolini had declared war on Britain and France.

'Jumping on the band-wagon,' Jim said, tossing the paper aside. 'Nasty little squirt.'

Rosie didn't answer him because the phone was ringing and she was pretty sure it would be Mary reporting on the latest exam, which was Human Biology and probably the most important one she had to take.

'How did you get on?' she asked eagerly when they'd said 'Hello'.

'Quite a good paper, really,' Mary said. 'More or less what we expected, pretty straightforward. We all said so afterwards. Now it's just two more to go and I can come home. I've started packing.'

'Good luck with the last ones,' Rosie said, and nodded to Jim who was standing in the kitchen door sending eye signals. 'Dad sends his love.'

'Give him a kiss from me,' Mary said. And the pips went.

In those dark, tormentingly sunny days, phone calls from Mary and Gracie were the only normal moments in Rosie's life. The news from France grew inexorably worse and worse as the Germans thundered towards Paris. The French government left the city on June thirteenth and the next day it was captured by the German troops, who were pictured jack-booting past the Arc de Triomphe.

For the next few days, the news was all about the French surrender.

Hitler had arranged for them to sign the articles in the same railway carriage that had been used when the Germans had to sign *their* surrender to the Allies in 1918.

'It's a neat revenge,' Jim said. 'You got to give him that. Nasty little growth.'

He was looking at a picture of the 'nasty little growth' dancing with delight just after the surrender had been signed. 'Makes you wanna spit.'

But Rosie was wondering what was going to happen next.

CHAPTER SIX

Rosie was in her garden, picking roses. It was a lovely summer's day, the sun warm on her shoulders, a blackbird singing loud and clear in the may tree, the luscious scent of the roses rising towards her with every movement she made. She had her back to that dratted air raid shelter so she couldn't see it and Mary was coming home on the four o'clock train. What could be better?

Mary had sent them a postcard that morning saying she hoped someone would be able to meet her at the station because she'd got piles and piles of luggage. Now the tea was prepared, the table laid and it only needed their old blue vase full of roses set in the middle for the finishing touch. It was good to be alive, war or no war.

Rosie was admiring the vase full of roses through the window when the phone rang. She walked dreamily into the hall, hoping it would be Gracie and that she was going to tell her that she was coming to welcome Mary home too. And it was.

'She sent me a postcard this morning,' Gracie said. 'Lot of luggage she said, and would I come and help her with it all? I was planning to come home anyway, so I said yes, naturally.'

'Good,' Rosie said, 'now there'll be three of us.'

'Well four, actually,' Gracie said. 'That was the other reason I'm phoning. Sam would like to meet you and I said I'd ask if it was OK for him to come this afternoon. He might limp a bit, but he's strong.'

Rosie was disgruntled. She didn't want a stranger joining their welcome home supper, even if he was strong. 'Sam?' she said.

'You remember Sam,' Gracie urged. 'Sam Marsh. The soldier with the shrapnel in his leg. The one who was so brave. I told you. We made him a medal.'

'You went to visit his mother,' Rosie said, now very definitely disgruntled. 'St Albans or somewhere.'

'That's right,' Gracie said. 'I did. So that's all right then. I'll tell him he can come, shall I?'

'Well…' Rosie said, trying to think of a way to say 'no'. But the pips were sounding and the call was nearly over.

'We'll see you at twenty to four,' Gracie said. And the phone cut out.

Oh for heaven's sake! Rosie thought, glaring at the phone. Now I shall have to rustle up more food and set another place at the table and that'll mean bringing down a chair from the bedroom. Damned boy, she thought, as she stomped up the stairs. Pushing in. And after me picking all those roses and making a meat pie and everything. By the time she reached the landing she was determined not to like him. But in the event everything happened in such a rush she didn't have time to work out whether she liked him or not.

Gracie arrived late, on her own and at great speed on her bike, which she skidded to a halt by the alley-way. She looked so full of life it was a joy to see her, dark hair tousled, cheeks pink and excitedly out of breath.

'Sorry I'm late,' she said. 'Come on. We'll have to look sharp or the train'll be in before we can get there and that won't do.'

There was no sign of the Sam person. Perhaps he's not coming, Rosie thought, as she followed her whirlwind daughter down the road, but she was being rushed along at such a rate she didn't have time to ask. And, as they reached the entrance to the Borough tube station, Gracie suddenly began to wave her arms about and a tall skinny soldier who was standing alongside the entrance, leaning against the wall, stood up and waved back.

'This is Sam,' Gracie said, as they charged up alongside him. 'Sam, this is my mum.' But she didn't abate her rush in the least, so she barely gave them a chance to say 'hello', never mind shake hands or talk to one another, before she'd swept them both up in her stride and rushed them along towards London Bridge.

'Late,' she puffed over her shoulder to the soldier. 'Sorry about that. Can you keep up with us?'

He grinned. 'Do I have a choice?' he asked. He was wearing his cap on his shoulder, so now that they were side by side, Rosie could see how fair his hair was, and how badly he was limping, and what very blue eyes he had.

'She doesn't give anyone a choice, my Gracie,' she told him. 'Never has.'

'I'm gettin' used to it,' he said, and gave her a shy smile.

'Come *on*!' Gracie called to them over her shoulder. 'No time to talk or we shan't be there before the train.'

And sure enough, they arrived on the platform just as the train was steaming in and, within seconds, there was Mary throwing her winter coat and an armful of carrier bags and parcels onto the platform and struggling out of the carriage carrying two bulging suitcases. She put the cases down among the pile of bags and waved to them. 'Just off to get my bike,' she called. 'Shan't be a tick.' And she left them standing while she pushed through the oncoming crowds towards the guard's van.

'Look at the mess she's made,' Gracie said in her disapproving voice. 'She never thinks. Come on you two. We'd better get it sorted out before someone goes a purler.'

She worked so neatly and quickly that the suitcases were set on one side and the mound had been reduced to four neat piles of carrier bags and parcels by the time her untidy sister wheeled her bike back to them through the crowds.

'You can wear your coat,' she said to Mary. 'Don't make that face. It won't kill you. And you can take those two lots in your basket and me an' mum'll carry the suitcases – OK Mum? Sam'll take the rest, won't you Sam?'

It was a surprise to Rosie and Mary when Sam gave their Gracie a loving smile and said 'No.'

Gracie scowled. 'What d'you mean, no?' she said.

'Simple word,' he grinned. 'I'll take one of the cases and your mum can take all this other clobber. That's fair.'

'And what about your leg? Gracie said. 'You know you shouldn't be–'

'It's good,' he said. 'It'll stand up.' And he picked up the case and walked off with it.

She stomped after him with the second case, grumbling, and Mary and Rosie let her go.

'Well, well, well,' Rosie said. 'What d'you make of *that*?'

'I think it's lovely,' Mary said. 'He's nice. He's a gentleman. He's standing up to our Gracie –I mean, imagine *that* –and it's because he wants to look after you.'

'Well he's got some spunk,' Rosie admitted. 'I'll give him that. I never thought I'd see *anyone* stand up to our Gracie. Though it wouldn't have been any problem for me to carry the case. I've carried worse.'

She was watching Sam and Gracie as she spoke, impressed by the fact that she'd accepted his decision and touched by the easy way they were walking along together, each carrying a heavy case but arm in arm. He's got a good way with him, she thought. I wonder what Jim'll think of him.

She didn't have to wait long to find out because it was obvious that the two men were taking to one another the moment Jim arrived home from work and walked into the kitchen. 'Name of Jim,' he said, holding out his hand. 'Gracie's dad, for my sins. I gather you're Sam.'

'Pleased to meet you sir,' Sam said, shaking his hand.

Jim laughed. 'Don't call me sir, he said. 'I left the army a lifetime ago. I'm just going down the off licence to get a few drinks. What's your tipple?'

'Could I come with you maybe?' Sam asked.

'Course,' Jim said and he called into the scullery, 'What d'you fancy, gels?'

They decided on lager and Gracie produced a basket for them to carry everything home in and off they went.

'Well?' Gracie asked, when the door had closed behind them. 'What d'you think of him?'

'He'll do,' Rosie said briefly. 'Let's get this pie out the oven and then it'll be all ready to serve when they get back.'

*

It was a happy meal, despite Rosie's initial misgivings about her unwanted guest, the food much appreciated and all of it washed down by Jim's plentiful supply of lager: Jenner's brown ale and Barclay's stout. And, once he'd discovered that Sam drove a tank, the conversation was lively.

'Fancy you being a tankie,' he said. 'Gaw dearie me! They was our saviours, tankies was, when we was in no man's land. Give us the first cover we ever had. We used to get behind 'em an' stay there. Great big lumbering things. You should ha' seen 'em crashing across the German trenches. Tanks an' yanks, we always said. That's what won the war for us.'

'They've come on a bit since then,' Sam told him with some pride. 'They're quite manoeuvrable now. I drove a Cruiser MK1 in France, but the new ones are even better. They say we'll be able to drive them through fields and along roads, even across rivers sometimes. They call them amphibians.'

Jim was impressed. 'Fancy!' he said.

'We had to leave our Cruisers behind when we retreated,' Sam said. 'Wicked waste but that's how it was.'

'What'll happen now?' Mary asked. 'Will they give you some of the new ones?'

'I expect so,' Sam said. 'I shall find out when they sign me off and I get back to camp.'

'Where's that?' Mary asked him.

'Salisbury Plain,' he said, 'whenever I get there.' And he looked a question at Gracie.

'You'll know on Wednesday, if I'm any judge,' she told him. 'But only if you behave yourself.'

He grinned at that and blew her a kiss. And watching them, Rosie thought again how easy they were with one another and how happy they looked. He could be the one, she thought, and even as the idea entered her head, she realised that it pleased her, which was extraordinary when she considered that earlier in the day – before she'd met him – she'd decided not to like him at all. Who'd have thought *that* could've happened?

'Well now,' she said. 'Who's for apple pie?'

After their meal, Gracie helped to stack the dishes and then told them that she and Sam would have to be getting back to Guy's or they'd

91

be drummed out the Brownies. Then she kissed them all goodbye and took hold of Sam's arm and steered him off to the alleyway to collect her bike. The kitchen seemed very quiet without them.

'Nice kid,' Jim said, carrying the dirty plates into the scullery. 'His parents did a good job with him.'

'Parent,' Mary corrected, following him with a tray full of glasses. And when Rosie looked surprised, 'His dad died before he was born. He was gassed at Ypres and never really recovered, so Gracie said.'

Rosie was at the sink and up to her wrists in soap suds. 'How horrible,' she said and looked up at Jim, remembering when he'd been wounded and all those awful weeks when she and Kitty hadn't known whether he was alive or dead. 'His poor mother.'

'Gracie says he looks after her ever so well,' Mary told them, picking up a tea towel. 'He goes to visit her whenever he can.'

'That's another thing we got in common then,' Jim said, with obvious satisfaction. 'I looked after my ol' gel too when *my* dad died. Told you he was a good kid.'

We're accepting him into the family, Rosie thought, and we've only just met him. It seemed extraordinary but, in an odd way, almost natural. I wonder when he'll come and see us again. We should've asked him. But then I don't suppose he knows. If he's got to go back to Salisbury Plain, like he says, they won't give him leave for quite a while.

There was a large, floppy soap bubble clinging to her little finger, shining with iridescent colour. She admired it idly as she digested the fact that this young man and her Gracie were going to be apart from one another, once he was sent back to camp, in exactly the same way as she and Jim had been apart when he got called up. Beautiful things hardly last any time at all, she thought, lifting her hand, bubble and all, to put a clean dish in the rack. It's a lovely hot June and Mary's home and the garden's full of roses so everything's perfect —except that we don't know when that hideous Luftwaffe's going to attack us and everything's put on hold while we wait. And that's not how life should be for any of us.

*

But it went on being like that for three more weeks. The lovely summer weather continued; Sam was signed off and sent to Salisbury Plain; tea and cooking fat were put on ration, which didn't please Rosie at all; the local papers reported that a disused tunnel on the Borough line of the Underground was going to be opened up as a public air raid shelter, which Rosie thought was rather ominous but Jim said was a damned good job. Mary cycled to Guy's Hospital and saw the sister in charge of student nurses, and was enrolled to start her training on the third week in July, and came home rather full of herself, because the regulations had been changed and she would be a fully trained nurse in two years rather than three. And Jim and Rosie did their regular eight-hour shifts and doubled-up so that they could have a weekend together with their girls.

And then, on the second Wednesday in July, the Luftwaffe suddenly moved into the attack, bombing Falmouth and Swansea, a factory in South Wales and an RAF airfield in Suffolk called Martlesham, which Rosie had never heard of. There'd been no sign of them in the sky over London but everybody knew that the threatened and dreaded attack had now begun. And, sure enough, from then on, ports and cities all over Great Britain were bombed one after another and airfields in the south were attacked every day.

Soon the newspapers were scoring the German losses every morning and evening – *"42 German aircraft shot down and 13 British fighter planes."*

'They make it sound as if they're reporting a cricket score,' Jim said, angrily. 'These are young men being sent up to fight in the air an' getting killed. Very young, some of 'em.'

But even he was impressed by the headlines on August fifteenth when the *Daily Mirror* claimed that the Germans had lost 144 planes to the British 50. By that time the battle in the skies was being called the Battle of Britain, and there was no doubt what a terrible struggle it was and what a toll it was taking. That afternoon, the Luftwaffe attacked Croydon airport and several houses in the vicinity were bombed and, according to what the tram conductors said, more than sixty people had been killed. The sirens were sounded all across south London when the raid was over. As Jim and Rosie were both on-standby, they cycled to their posts and saw the bombers in the sky to the south of them, all heading south-east.

'I'm afraid we're for it now,' Mr Kennedy said, smoothing his white hair, when his crews had gathered about him. He gazed around at them and paused before he offered them some advice. 'If I were you,' he said, 'I'd get as much rest as you can whenever you're off duty, because if I'm any judge, we're going to be under considerable pressure once the bombers start coming here.'

None of them had any doubt about that at all. But for the next few days the attacks on the airfields continued and the Luftwaffe went on taking heavy casualties. In the five days between August thirteenth and seventeenth, they lost 225 planes. But they still kept coming.

*

Down in Binderton, Tess and Kitty were following events very closely indeed, because they were right in the thick of the attacks on their local airfields and had been watching the dog fights from their vantage point in Pa's kitchen garden. One or other of them wrote a postcard to Rosie every day. They were full of admiration for the pilots in Tangmere and Hunston.

'*They're barely on the ground for more than five minutes before they're refuelled and up in the air again,*' Kitty wrote. '*I don't know how they do it. You should see the way they manoover. Stops your heart. It's so clever. The Germans give poor old Tangmere another pasting this morning and yet our boys still come back fighting. We seen a bomber brought down in flames yesterday and serve him right. People round here say they think that horrible Goering is trying to destroy the RAF. But he's not making a very good job of it, that's all I can say. Hope you and Jim are all right. The others say to ask you. We wouldn't like to think of you having bombs dropped on you.*'

That postcard arrived at breakfast time, after Jim had gone off to work and while Rosie was enjoying her second cup of tea and, once she'd read it, she found pen and paper and sat down to answer it straight away. It was important to tell them that she would keep them informed about what was going on, but she knew she had to admit that everyone in London knew that the Germans would bomb them sooner or later.

'*We're all well prepared for it,*' she wrote. '*We know what we've got to do and we know how to do it, and we've got lots of people in the ARP, wardens like Jim and firemen and rescue teams and ambulance drivers, and the London hospitals have evacuated most of their patients to safer places and now have wards standing ready. And I promise that when it starts I will send you postcards as often as I can and keep you up to date on how we all are. Try not to worry.*' Then she signed it '*Love to you all*' and put it in the post-box when she went to market.

And the waiting went on. And on and on.

At the end of August the weather changed and it was wet and cold. So wet, in fact, that the Luftwaffe seemed to have been grounded because there were no raids reported anywhere for five days. During the lull, Winston Churchill made a speech in the House of Commons, honouring the young pilots of the Spitfires and Hurricanes who'd been opposing the Luftwaffe so valiantly. It was widely reported and much approved of, because it was so powerfully and movingly expressed. '*Never in the field of human conflict*,' he'd said, '*has so much been owed by so many to so few.*' And neighbours meeting one another in the streets repeated his words and said how very true they were.

But the wait in London continued and, when the weather cleared, the Germans went back to bombing the airfields. Before long it was September, and the skies were summer-time blue and the sunshine as warm as it had been in August. Rosie did a big wash on the first September Saturday and hung it all out in the garden, and was pleased to find that it was dry by mid-afternoon. It had been such an easy, pleasant day. She'd spent it in happy domesticity, baking a cake with her now precious margarine, darning Jim's socks out in the sunshine, even taking time to sit in the garden and start reading *David Copperfield* again. Reading a novel was something she hadn't done in a long time. She was so absorbed in it that when the sirens started their long growl upwards they made her jump. Then she was afraid. Is this it? she thought. Are they coming to bomb us now?

She looked up at the sky, but there was no sign of any planes although she could hear their engines somewhere. And the sound of someone opening a sash-cord. And there was Sonia Cohen, leaning out of her bedroom window and peering up at the sky.

'Should we go down to the shelters, Rosie?' she called. 'What d'you think?'

The question brought Rosie to her sense of duty. If the bombers were coming there was work to be done. 'I'm on stand-by,' she said, 'so I shall have to go to the ambulance station, but you ought to go down.'

Sonia looked down at her, doubtfully. 'D'you really think so?'

'Yes,' Rosie said firmly. 'I do. I've got a nasty feeling about this, Sonia. And I'd make haste, if I was you.'

'Okey doke,' Sonia said, and closed the window.

The sound of the approaching planes was growing louder and more ominous by the second. I'd better look sharp too, Rosie thought, and she took the stairs two at a time and changed into her uniform as quickly as she could, checked that she had an extra hankie in her pocket, put on her tin hat and ran to the alleyway for her bike.

By the time she reached Long Lane, the noise of the planes was too loud to be ignored and she could see the barrage balloons going up from Southwark Park, huge and cumbersome and comforting, with their great ears flapping as they rose, so there was no doubt that a raid was coming. She knew she ought to get under cover but she was still quite a way from Lower Road and the ambulance station, so she kept going.

And then, as she pelted down Jamaica Road, her lungs straining, the blue sky over her head was suddenly and terrifyingly full of planes, hundreds and hundreds of them, flying in a huge formation towards the city with Spitfires tailing them. Dear God! she thought. What'll become of us?

Seconds later she heard the first bombs exploding and, glancing to her left, she could see a line of black bombs slanting out of the sky and flames leaping up along the north bank of the river… one, two, and then more and more, bright and terrifying. She could feel the heat of their burning, and her nose was full of strange and terrible smells, and she knew the docks were being bombed and she was horribly afraid.

Quick, quick, she urged herself. Get to the station. You must get to the station.

And then she was indoors among her friends and colleagues, drenched in sweat and panting but under cover, and Mr Kennedy was standing at the table, deploying his troops as the calls came in, and it was all exactly as they'd practiced – only this time it was for real.

'Ah, there you are,' he said. 'Splendid. You've got Joan working with you.' He paused so that she and Joan could smile at one another and then gave her the first order of the afternoon. 'You will be one of the next three on call,' he said. 'Get your breath back, have a cup of tea and then go and drive your vehicle up to the line.'

It was routine, it was normal, she could cope with it. Even when she and Joan were driving off on their first call, she was calm. They were prepared, they had all the equipment they needed, they were driving down familiar streets. The sky ahead of them was roaring with flames that towered higher than they could see, and the air was acrid with billowing smoke and full of the smell of burning wood. They could hear the steady *fer-dum*, *fer-dum*, *fer-dum* of the ack-ack, and from time to time a series of shattering explosions and the sound of falling masonry rather too close by. But what was important was getting to the address they'd been given, picking up their casualties and driving them safely to hospital.

Their first call was to one of the side streets turning out of Jamaica Road and they found it easily and quickly. But they hadn't driven into it for more than a hundred yards before their way was blocked by mounds of debris and obscured by such thick clouds of dust that they had to stop. For a few seconds Rosie sat perfectly still behind the wheel, while she tried to make sense of what she was seeing: her mind blocked it and refused to accept it. Nothing was real. She could hear the bombers overhead but she couldn't see them, and she could see the unearthly glow from the fires on the other side of the river and hear explosions, but that great pile of bricks with all those broken beams sticking out of it, and those three men in dark uniforms and tin hats scrambling over it towards the ugly gap where the house had been, felt more like a film set than reality. If Mr Korda had suddenly appeared and called '*Cut!*' she wouldn't have been the least surprised.

'There's our casualty,' Joan said above the noise, and Rosie turned her head to follow her colleague's glance and saw a warden sitting on the kerb, supporting a woman wrapped in his jacket, her facechalk white.

'OK,' she said, returning to normal, knowing what had to be done. 'I'll take the stretcher, you bring a blanket.'

They moved quietly and calmly, the way they'd been taught, diagnosed the woman's injuries as far as they could – shock, possible concussion, cuts needing suture – wrapped her in their blanket and secured her on the stretcher.

'There's a kiddie too,' the warden told them, putting his coat on. 'Boy aged seven, name of Alan. They're getting him out.' He checked his notebook. 'The lady's Mrs Godfrey.'

'We'll get her comfortable in the ambulance,' Rosie told him, 'and then we'll wait for the boy.'

It seemed to take a long time, and quite a bit of the dust had settled before one of the rescue team climbed out of the wreckage of the house with the child in his arms, unconscious, covered in dust and grime and smeared with blood.

'This one's serious,' Joan said. 'How fast can you drive?'

Rosie was reporting back to base. 'Right!' she said into the phone. 'We're on our way.'

'Guy's,' she said to Joan, and put the van in gear.

She drove fast and smoothly, determined to get her patients to hospital as quickly as she could, while Mrs Godfrey wept and the little boy was sick. Now I know what war's like, she thought, and hated it with a passion.

It was a relief to all of them that they were greeted at the hospital by a very competent nurse, who took the child at once, reassured his mother that he'd be all right, laid him gently on a bed in one of the cubicles and then stood aside while a doctor examined him. Mrs Godfrey was still weeping and clinging to Joan's hand but at least she'd stopped shaking.

'I'll go and take a mop to that sick,' Rosie said to Joan. 'I'm only in the way here. Follow me when you can.'

She worked quickly and surprisingly efficiently, given the state the ambulance was in and the fact that she only had a small bucket of water. While she was working and retching, Joan came back to write up her report and the next call came in. A shop in the Jamaica Road. Two ambulances called.

'We're on our way,' Rosie said.

This time they expected the piles of debris, the casualties covered in white dust and smeared with dirt and blood, looking stunned and shaken, the rescue squad digging in the wreckage. They took three casualties: a man with injuries to both his legs who kept apologising for being a nuisance and two women struggling to breathe and badly shocked. This time, the practised words of reassurance came more easily. 'You're all right. Don't worry. We've got you. We're taking you to hospital.'

It wasn't until they were on their way back to base that they realised they couldn't hear the bombers and minutes later, as they turned in at the gate, the all clear sounded.

'Thank God for that,' Joan said.

'They'll be back,' Rosie told her, grimly, looking up at the sky. The fires on the other side of the Thames were still blazing and the sky above them was orange. 'This is like a torch. They'll follow it in.'

That was Mr Kennedy's opinion, too. 'Well done all of you,' he said to his team when they'd gathered in the control room. 'You've been impressive. Now, I'd advise you to get a bit of rest and have something to eat while you can. The canteen's open and ready for you. Clean your vehicles first, because we don't know when they'll be back. But they *will* be back. You can be sure of *that*.'

He's got some sense, Rosie thought, as she trudged wearily to the compound to start her chores. Like my Jim. I wonder what he's been doing. And my girls. They'll have been busy too. And she felt very proud of them. Whatever happens now, she thought, we shall cope with it.

CHAPTER SEVEN

Jim had had an exhausting afternoon and was feeling jaded, although he was doing his best not to show it; he knew how demoralising it would be for the others in his team if they felt they were carrying a passenger. He and his fellow wardens had attended five incidents on their patch during the raid and they'd been hard at work the entire time, so he knew they would all be as tired as he was.

His present call was to a rather cantankerous neighbour called Mrs Baker, who, if she'd taken his advice, ought to be sheltering in her Anderson in the garden. When he arrived, he found that the bomb had blown the back off the house, roof, chimney and all, so that it was sliced open like a piece of pie and stood exposed to anyone who looked up at it, the kitchen table still covered in dirty cups and messy saucepans, a grubby tea towel hanging on a hook by the door, two down-at-heel shoes on a chair, while in the room above it, an unmade bed balanced precariously on three legs while the fourth hung in the air over the gap, luridly lit by the glare from the fires raging on the banks of the river. He felt like a peeping Tom glancing up at it, as though he was poking his nose into other people's private lives. But there wasn't time to think about it. There was work to be done and it was his business to get on and do it.

The chimney was still in one piece, leaning drunkenly against what remained of the fence, but the shelter was smothered by the rest of the debris, piles of broken bricks, torn curtains, smashed beams, vicious shards of glass, and the air was full of dust, the way it always was after a bomb. While he'd been in the street he'd noticed a strong smell of gas, so he knew there was a gas main broken somewhere, and, now that he was in the garden, he could see at once that the shelter would have to be dug out. He sent a message to the ARP post, reporting back and asking for assistance, and then climbed over the debris to where the door to the shelter should be to see if he could make contact with Mrs Baker.

It took him a little while to lift away as much of the debris as he thought safe, so that he could call to her through the gap at the top of the door, but to his relief she answered him at once.

'Bleedin' Hitler,' she said, crossly. 'I knew this bleedin' shelter was a rotten idea.'

'Are you OK?' he called back.

'Don't ask me, mate,' she said. 'How should I know? I can't bleedin' move.'

Not short of breath though, Jim thought, noting how firm her voice was. It was a hopeful sign but not a dependable one. 'We're gonna have to dig you out,' he explained. 'The rescue team is on its way. Is Gladys with you?'

'No she ain't,' the cross voice came back. 'Don't talk to me about Gladys. I've 'ad jest about enough of her for one day.'

'D'you know where she is?'

'Street raking wiv her mates I shouldn't wonder. She's always off out somewhere or other. I'm sick a telling her.'

Jim's fatigue tipped him into momentary irritation. Poor kid, he thought. She can't be more than seven or eight an' she's been out in these streets with all this going on. She must be scared stiff. Why couldn't the stupid fool woman go an' look for her? I can just imagine my Rosie letting one of ours play out in an air raid…

'Mr Jackson,' Mrs Baker called.

He remembered his duties with a palpable effort and adjusted the chin strap on his helmet. 'Still here,' he called back.

Her voice was plaintive. 'Put a jerk on will you? I can't breave in 'ere.'

'They're coming,' he told her. 'We can't hurry 'em. They was probably digging someone else out when I called 'em. We got to take our turn, same as everyone. There's been a lot of people hurt this afternoon.'

She grunted but didn't answer. He took out his notebook, licked the end of his pencil and got on with the next part of his job. If he'd got a missing kid on his hands, he'd better find out what she was wearing.

'Don't ask me,' Mrs Baker growled. But then added, rather surprisingly, 'Her red jersey. Now I *do* remember that. Made me so cross. I bought it for best, not for her to go traipsing round the streets in.'

'What colour skirt?' Jim tried patiently.

'She's only got the one,' Mrs Baker said.

He tried again. 'What colour is it?'

'Sorta like porridge. I dunno.'

Jim could hear voices in next door's garden, and turned to see the rescue team removing what was left of the battered fence to make way for their equipment. He was relieved to see that the leader of the team was a friend of his, called Fergie.

'What we got here then?' Fergie asked, looking at the wreckage of the shelter. But before Jim could tell him, the all clear began its slow growl upward. Both of them were surprised because the noise of the raid was still going on all round them, and they looked up into the sky at once to check. And comfortingly, although there was still a great deal of smoke and the flames from the fires were still worryingly high, there was no sign of any bombers.

'Well, thank the Lord for that,' Fergie said. 'Now let's get that shelter cleared. How many you got in it?'

'One woman,' Jim said.

'Conscious?'

'And talking.'

'Right,' Fergie said. 'Let's get her out. There's an ambulance waiting. They said they'd give us twenty minutes. Saucy buggers!'

It took them a great deal longer than twenty minutes, but eventually the corrugated iron roof was shifted sufficiently for Mrs Baker to be eased out. She was covered in dust, plainly weary and had a sizeable lump on her forehead.

'We got an ambulance in the street waiting for you,' Jim told her. 'Can you walk there?'

'You callin' me an invalid?' she said tetchily. 'Course I can walk.' But he noticed she hung on to his offered arm and walked unsteadily. Fortunately the ambulance was still waiting.

'You nearly missed us,' the ambulance driver said to Jim. ''Nother minute and we'd ha' been off. We got another call come in. Hop aboard missis.'

'Hop!' Mrs Baker said, as she heaved herself into the ambulance. 'Never mind hop. I can barely put one foot in front a the other.' Then she turned to Jim. 'When you find that kid a mine,' she said, 'give her a clip round the ear an' tell her it's from me.'

If I find that kid a yours, Jim thought, as the ambulance drove away. Poor little blighter. If she's been street-raking in all this, anything could've happened to her. She could have been injured in the blast or cut to bits by flying glass or hit by shrapnel or anything. I shall have to report her missing and then ask around.

But first he had to wait for the men from the gas board to arrive and, after that, he had to check the neighbouring houses in the terrace and make a note of what state they were in.

This time it was easy enough because they were his neighbours and he'd known them a long time. The house to the left of Mrs Baker's was empty because Mrs Lewin and her kids had been evacuated and Mr Lewin had been called up and gone to join the navy, but Jim opened it with his key and went in to check it, noting that one of the ceilings had come down but that otherwise it was intact and seemed sound. Then he moved on to the house to the right.

This one was occupied by one of his old biddies and one he was particularly fond of. Her name was Winnie Totteridge, which she thought was a great joke now she was old, because she was often very tottery, although, as she was quick to point out, 'I ain't fell down yet, mate.' He found her in the kitchen, trying to pick up the broken plates that had been blown from her dresser onto the tiles.

'Hello our Jim,' she said, as he walked in. 'What a carry-on, eh! I never heard such a racket in all me life. I thought the whole street'd be blowed up when I come out the shelter. It's made a right ol' mess a me plates.'

He got down on his knees to help her pick up the pieces. 'You got an old newspaper, have you?' he asked. 'If you can just put it on the table, I'll wrap this lot up for you an' we can put it in the dustbin. I'll hand the bits up to you.'

'Best place for it,' she said, taking an old newspaper out of the dresser drawer and spreading it out on the table. 'What a carry on! Good job Mrs Lewin an' them kiddies was gone. Is she all right next door? I seen the ambulance go off.'

'Bit of a lump on her head,' Jim said, and took a breath to tell her about the damage, but before he could get a word out there was a thunderous knocking at her door and someone calling, 'Mrs T! Mrs T!'

'Hang on a tick,' he said and went to answer it. It was Gladys, in a dirty red jersey, looking extremely grubby and wildly distraught.

'Where's my mum?' she shrieked at him. 'What you done wiv 'er? I can't get in the 'ouse. My key don't work. I tried an' tried. Why can't I get in the 'ouse, Mister Jackson? What you done to it?' And then she burst into tears and stamped her feet in a hysterical combination of temper and fear.

Old Mrs Totteridge was in the hall behind them, leaning on her stick and calling to her. 'Gladys, come on in an' stop crying an' then we can tell you. You'll make yourself sick you cry like that. Come on. Lean on my arm.' And she led her grubby little neighbour into the kitchen. 'Now, you sit there and I'll just take a little cloth to your face an' clean you up a bit.' Which she did, while Gladys sobbed to a halt. 'Now,' she said. 'I'll just find you a little hankie, so's you can blow your little nose and then we'll have a nice cuppa tea, how would that be?'

But handkerchiefs and tea were the last things on Gladys' mind. '*Where's my mum?*' she wailed.

'Well now,' Mrs Totteridge said, handing her the handkerchief, 'as to that, your mum's had to go to the orspital for a little while on account a she 'ad a bump on the 'ead. You're gonna stay with me till she comes back. If you're a good gel, we can have some fish an' chips later, if the chippy's open. We'll nip down the road presently an' see.'

And that, at last, brought a smile. 'Wiv a pickled onion?' Gladys asked.

'Pickled onion, top brick orf the chimbley, anythink you fancy,' Mrs Totteridge said, 'providing you're a good kid. An' no wandering off.'

So the matter seemed to be settled, to Jim's relief. Now he could get back to the ARP post and find out what his next set of instructions

107

were going to be. It had been a long afternoon. He got on his bike and pedalled off slowly, aware that he felt tired and that his leg was painful, as it often was when he'd been standing or walking for too long. The fires were still blazing, down on the river side, smoke and flames rising to a terrifying height above the rooftops, and the air was hot and heavy with the smell of burning. He recognised wood and burnt sugar and there were other smells too, strong and potent and pervasive, that he couldn't place. Leather, maybe? It was hard to tell. On an impulse he turned right up Battlebridge Lane and cycled towards the river. Whatever was going on down there, he felt he needed to be a witness to it.

What he saw was so overpowering, it stopped him in his tracks. He sat on his bike, with one foot on the ground to steady himself, and stared in horror and disbelief.

There were so many warehouses on fire he couldn't count them and they were burning like torches. The sky was full of thick brown smoke and the flames that towered through it were in a variety of terrifying colours, through every lurid shade of red, orange and yellow to occasional alarming spurts of emerald green and electric blue. Below them, the firemen were playing their hoses on the blackened hulk of the buildings, working together to keep the flow steady.

There were fireboats on the river pumping out the water and all around them the peaceful Thames was blood red, as if the City was bleeding. It made him think of a picture he'd seen of the fires of hell in some mission hall somewhere when he was a kid. He'd stood in front of it for ages, horrible thing, and it had scared him stiff. But this was worse than anything he'd ever seen, even in the trenches. This is hell on earth, he thought, staring at it. That's what this is. Total, absolute bloody hell on earth. We thought we was in hell in the trenches, but this is worse. Least when we was there we stopped firing at one another while we was having our grub. This lot are deliberately burning our food an' bombing people in their homes, old women an' little kids, an' we can't stop 'em. We're in the middle of it with nothing to protect us 'cept a tin hat. An' they'll be back again tonight with a fire like this to guide 'em, sure as God made little green apples. God help us all.

He was filled with a sudden impossible yearning to go home. He wanted to sit in his comfortable chair in his comfortable room, right out of the way of all this horror, and have a beer and talk to Rosie, and put his arms round her and cuddle her until he felt better. But he knew there was no point even thinking about it, because she'd be as busy as he was and the house would be empty. Then he was ashamed to think he was being so childish. He had a job to get on with and people to be responsible for. But even so, he couldn't help wondering how Rosie'd been coping and how the girls were getting on in that hospital, and he ached because he couldn't see them and talk to them and find out. Bleedin' war, he thought, as he cycled wearily back the way he'd come. Bleedin' Hitler. He should ha' been strangled at bleedin' birth.

*

Gracie and Mary were eating their supper in the canteen. They'd been hard at work since the first casualties started coming in and they were almost too tired to talk. But the ward sister had told them they were to eat a good meal and get as much rest as they could, because the bombers would be back as soon as it was dark and then, like as not, they would be on duty all night. Gracie tried to cheer them up when she saw that the cooks were serving cottage pie, but Mary was too down to do more than nod to show she'd seen it too.

'I've never seen so much blood in all my life,' she said, as she struggled with the first mouthful. It seemed wrong to be sitting here in this warm canteen, trying to eat a meal when so many people were lying in the ward they'd just left with dreadful injuries, and so many of them in pain.

'That's nursing for you,' Gracie said in her brisk way. *She*'d been upset by the sights she'd seen too but she wasn't going to admit it. Sister Luke warned them that they'd never get used to it, but she wasn't going to admit that either. 'And nursing in wartime is worse. Bound to be.'

'Will they really come back tonight?' Mary asked. All the senior staff had been sure of it. She'd heard them talking about it when they were in the sluice and they thought she wasn't listening.

'Sister Luke says they will,' Gracie told her. 'She said it's the way the Germans go on. They call it a blitzkrieg. We could be in for a long night. I'm going back to my room when we've had supper to see if I can get a bit of a nap. You can come with me if you like.'

'Yes,' Mary said, struggling with her meal and smiling bleakly at her sister. 'I would like.'

Gracie smiled back. 'That's settled then,' she said. 'And you never know. Sister might be wrong and it might not happen.'

*

But the sirens wailed their alarm as soon as it was dark. And all over London people who'd been working all day and had endured that afternoon's raid, gathered the things they needed – or thought they might need – and headed for the cellar or the shelter in the garden or under the stairs or went down the Underground wherever it was open for them. And the rescuers and defenders like Jim and Rosie and their daughters, straightened their uniforms, checked their vehicles, their phones and their tin hats, and made sure everything they needed was to hand and in good order. The ack-ack gunners stood ready, guns loaded, the barrage balloons were already rising into the air in their cumbersome way, the crews of the Spitfires and Hurricanes were waiting for the order to fly, the tea urns were on the boil. They were, as they told one another, as ready as they would ever be.

CHAPTER EIGHT

In Binderton, all the local members of Rosie's family were gathered round the supper table, screaming with laughter at her brother Johnnie, who was wriggling in his seat and blushing to the roots of his hair. The harvest had begun that morning so most of them had spent a long day in the fields, either reaping, or stacking the sheaves or gleaning, and the room was heady with the smell of ripe corn and summer sweat. But just as the meal had been served and they were all ready for their first well-earned mouthful, Connie stopped them with their forks on the way to their mouths by making an announcement.

'Ma says I ought for to tell you,' she said, speaking boldly but looking oddly ill at ease, 'on account of you ought to be the first to know.' Then she stopped and put her hand over her mouth.

'Well, go on Connie,' Tess said. 'You can't stop there. Tell us what, for pity's sake? We're all on tenterhooks now.'

And when she still seemed to be dithering, the others joined in. 'Come on, Con!' 'Tell us!' 'Spill the beans! Come on!'

'Well,' Connie said, 'it's like this. What I means for to say is... the thing is... I mean...' Then she took a deep breath, swallowed and confessed. 'Me an' Johnnie's expecting.'

The room exploded into shrieks of delight and a flurry of happy movement, as Tess and Kitty rushed round the table to hug her and Anna gazed at her in admiration and Pa struck the table and said, 'Well dang my eyes! I never thought our Johnnie had it in him.' At which Johnnie's face burst into flames.

'Oh there's plenty a life left in us old dogs, eh Johnnie?' Sydney said, winking at Johnnie and then beaming at Tess and Anna. 'Ent there, Tess?'

'Do give over,' Johnnie protested. 'I ent *that* old.' Which provoked mocking cheers and made him blush so much he had to study the tablecloth for a good five minutes.

'When's it due?' Tess asked, trying to rescue him.

'January,' Connie told her, 'according to Ma.'

'And she should know,' Tess said. 'I'll have to write to Rosie and Edie now you've told us. We can't leave them out. I'll send 'em a postcard, soon as we've done eating. What a lark, eh!'

But when they'd done eating and the dishes had been scoured and put away, Pa suddenly decided that they should all go off to the pub and have a quick pint to celebrate. He was so happy about this coming baby and so determined to celebrate it that, although Tess and Kitty were worried that he'd never be able to make the walk there and back because it was a fair old way, off to the pub they went, ambling through the shaven fields together arm in arm, Pa using his stick and leaning on Johnnie's proffered arm.

It was a peaceful summer's evening and pleasantly warm after the heat of the day. The setting sun left a trail of gently coloured ribbons across the darkening horizon. They grew slowly and tentatively, pale rose pink and duck-egg blue, while the sky high above them was still cobalt blue and cloudless. The birds sang their evening chorus; the convolvulus gleamed in the hedges; the air smelled of ripe corn and warm earth;

there was no sight or sound of Spitfires and German bombers: all was well with the world.

They stayed in the pub till the landlord chivvied them out at closing time and strolled home telling one another it had been the best day ever. The moon was a disc of pearl in a dark blue sky and peacefully benevolent.

*

In the Borough, the moon was totally obscured by the smoke and flames from the warehouses, where the fires still weren't under control despite the most exhausting efforts of the fire brigade. Rosie and Jim and their daughters were waiting at their posts, ready for the sirens to sound and the night's action to begin. The City was holding its breath.

Rosie surprised herself by how calm she was feeling. Her ambulance was clean and stocked with everything she and Joan could need. She'd had a good supper and even managed a catnap. She was so well prepared that when the sirens sounded she didn't even jump.

'Well that's it,' she said to Joan, who'd been asleep in her chair and woke with a start.

'I wonder how long this one'll go on,' Joan said, rubbing the sleep out of her eyes.

'It can go on as long as it likes,' Rosie said. 'Providing people take shelter or go down the tube, which they ought to after this afternoon. We're ready for it.'

Twenty minutes later they could hear the bombers droning overhead and the ack-ack firing and, looking up, they saw the long white beams of the searchlights scanning the dark sky and the flames still rising, bold as beacons, from the burning warehouses. The explosions sounded twice as loud in the darkness as they'd done that afternoon, and they were coming one after the other in sequences that could have been frightening if they hadn't been prepared for them. As it was, Rosie counted one of them down, recognising that there really were six bombs in a stick, and thinking that there must be a very large number of bombers in the air above them because there were so many explosions. She wondered how long it would be before the wardens reached the bomb sites and asked for ambulances. And she looked at the clock on the wall and began to time them.

It was half an hour, while they waited and wondered and tried not to think too much, but then the first calls came in so quickly that she and Joan had only just moved their ambulance up to replace the ones that had left when they were called out themselves.

Their first casualty was an elderly man who'd been out in the street when the bomb fell and had been blown right across the road into the doorway of a tobacconist's shop opposite.

'Another six inches an' he'd ha' been blown through the winder,' the warden said. 'He's been in an' outta consciousness ever since, poor ol' feller. We can't get much sense out of him.'

Joan knelt on the pavement and examined him as well as she could by the light from the warehouse fires. 'Internal, as far as I can see,' she said. 'We need to get him in fairly sharpish.'

It was easy enough to lift him, although he was a dead weight, and that made him quite heavy to carry on their cast iron stretcher. But they got him into the ambulance as quickly as they could and, after checking that there weren't any other casualties, they took him to hospital.

Their second call-out was more disturbing. This time they arrived to find two dead bodies laid out on the pavement, a man and a woman, both very bloody and covered in brick dust, and some distance away, sitting in the rubble of her bombed house, a confused old lady, who was coughing her lungs up. She was covered in white dust from the plaster and trailing an obviously broken arm.

'My gel's… in there,' she managed to say, clutching Rosie's hand and peering up at her in the light from the fires. One side of her face was outlined in an unearthly red, like something in a nightmare. 'Tell 'im to get 'er out, miss.'

A dark shape in a warden's white tin hat was walking towards them, outlined in the same lurid colour. As he got close enough for Rosie to see his eyes, he shook his head in warning and glanced over at the corpses.

Rosie knelt down in the rubble so that she and the old lady were face to face. 'We're going to take you to hospital,' she said, shouting because the raid was making so much noise and she wanted to be sure the poor old thing could hear her. 'Can you stand up, do you think?'

'What about my gel?' the old lady insisted. 'She's in there wiv 'er ol' man.'

'We're takin' care of 'em,' the warden assured her. 'D'you want a hand standing up?'

'No,' she said, 'I'm all right. I can manage.'

But in that eerie half-light, they could see she couldn't do it –although she was struggling for all she was worth, screwing up her poor old face and trying to wriggle her bum on the rubble so that she could rock forwards, leaning on her good arm.

'Tell you what,' Rosie said, stooping so that they were face to face again. 'Why don't you let me an' Joan here lift you onto our stretcher?'

'If I could just get my stupid back to give a little, I'd be all right,' the old lady said, struggling on. 'I wouldn't want to be a trouble to you.' But Joan and Rosie gave one another a quick unspoken message and moved to lift her.

'Ups a daisy!' Rosie said, as they scooped her from the rubble. 'There you are, you see. You're as light as a feather. No trouble at all. Now we'll have you comfy in no time.'

Which they tried to do, as soon as they'd settled her in the ambulance. Joan put a splint on her broken arm and, noticing how often she was groaning, asked if she had pain anywhere else.

'My back's givin' me a bit a gyp,' the old lady admitted. 'It'll go orf. You won't forget about my gel, will you?'

'No course not,' Joan said. 'That's all took care of. Don't worry. I'm going to give you a little injection to take away that pain.'

Rosie climbed into the driver's seat, ready to reverse out of the street, but having got there, she didn't start to drive because she could see two limping figures being helped over the debris, towards her, by a man from the rescue team.

'You got room for a couple a walking wounded?' he said when he reached her window. And when she told him she had, he turned to his patients and began to walk them round to the back of the ambulance so that he could help them aboard. 'There you are, gels,' he said, as he handed them in. 'Just need a bit a stitching here an' there, an' you'll be as right as rain.'

He was giving them a smile when there was an enormous explosion which sounded much too close. The blast rocked the ambulance and knocked him off his feet and, within seconds, the air was full of dust and falling debris. 'Blimey!' he said as he picked himself up. 'That was close. Get off quick, gels, before there's any more a the buggers.'

Rosie already had the ambulance in gear and was reversing out of the street as the second bomb fell, a little bit further away as far as she could judge, but she didn't stop to ask or check, she simply drove as quickly as she could, given the darkness and the swirling dust.

It was a great relief to all of them to arrive at Guy's, which felt like a haven of peace and order, despite the fact that reception was full of casualties and their attendants. With the help of morphine and reassurance, Joan had managed to get all three of her patients to give her their names and addresses during the ride, so she was the one who booked them all in, while Rosie sat on a bench and caught her breath, feeling suddenly exhausted.

'What's the time?' she asked wearily when Joan finally returned to her.

Joan lifted the watch from her bosom, and looked at it. 'Going on quarter to twelve,' she said. ''Nother quarter of an hour an' I'm off duty. Thank God! What about you?'

'I've got four more hours,' Rosie said, and she could feel her heart sinking as she did so. The night had already gone on quite long enough and the thought of working another four hours without Joan's comfortable presence was upsetting. I'm being childish, she thought. We all know we work shifts. We've just got to get on with it. And she stood up, straightened her jacket and stuck her chin in the air, as much to accept the position she was in as to show she was going to deal with it.

There were no calls waiting for them when they got back to the ambulance, so they drove back to base, taking the journey slowly because the roads were full of debris and, even with the great fires to guide them, the light was poor. They seemed to be having a lull. There was less noise than there'd been when the raid began, there seemed to be fewer bombers overhead and the sound of the explosions was further away. But lull or not, it was good to be back, almost like coming home, with Mr Kennedy to welcome them and the kettle boiling for tea, and their mates arriving two by two and sprawling in the chairs to rest while they could.

Joan's replacement was Sister Maloney, who was brusque, skinny and fresh from what she called 'a nice long sleep,' although how she'd managed to sleep through the racket of the raid, Rosie couldn't imagine. But the lull only went on for another twenty minutes and then they were called out again, so there wasn't time for conversation.

Their first casualty on that sortie was a fireman from one of the warehouses, who was gasping for breath and covered in a horrible black slime: face, hands, uniform, boots and all. Sister Maloney dealt with him efficiently, giving him oxygen and examining his face and hands for burns while Rosie drove to Guy's as quickly as she could. When they arrived and she and Sister Maloney were wheeling their patient into reception, she wondered whether she might see one or other of her daughters there. But there was no sign of either of them and, as soon as they got back to their ambulance, another call came in for assistance at a block of flats.

'Holy Mary, Mother a God,' Sister Maloney said. 'That'll be a major incident, then. I never did hold with flats. Nasty, dangerous t'ings, so they are. Give me a farm any day of the week.'

It irritated Rosie to have to listen to such silly talk when they were in the middle of an air raid. 'We don't have farms in the middle of London,' she said, sternly.

Sister Maloney seemed impervious to rebuke. 'More's the pity,' she said. 'We'd all be a deal better off if we did.'

But she was right about it being a major incident. Theirs was the third ambulance to arrive on site and more came soon after they did, and, even in the darkness, Rosie could see that a quarter of the block had been blown away and that the debris had fallen into a huge mound almost as high as the flats. The heavy lifting team were already at work along with more wardens and helpers than Rosie had ever seen together in one place, and there were electricians there too, setting up spotlights, and gas men standing beside their vans. *A major incident.* As she watched, the first casualty was eased gently out of the wreckage and carried off at once to the nearest ambulance. It was going to be a long job.

'I shall be more use out there than sitting in here, so I shall,' Sister Maloney said, and she wrapped her cloak warmly round her and was gone.

More helpers were arriving by the minute and, watching them, Rosie was full of admiration for them. They were all so calm and careful, doing what had to be done, but standing quite still and perfectly silent whenever the team leader held up his hand for quiet. There was no panic, no excitability, no fuss, just a group of hard working people doing what they could to rescue the injured. We're a sturdy lot we British, she thought. Hitler can rant and roar all he likes, but he needn't think he can beat us. The thought sustained her through the rest of the night, even though it was full of suffering and revealed more grief than she cared to see. We do what we can, she told herself, as she carried the injured into her ambulance; we do what we can, as she cleaned and serviced her vehicle when the all clear finally sounded.

*

She and Jim didn't get home until after half past five that morning and by then they were both totally exhausted. Jim arrived five minutes after she did and brought a copy of yesterday's evening paper with him.

'They had it hot off the press last night,' he said. 'After all that. You gotta hand it to 'em.'

The headline was huge as befitted the news. '*Three hundred and fifty bombers in daylight raid in London,*' it said, and went on to give the details. '*It is estimated that three hundred tonnes of bombs were dropped on the docks and the streets of the East End of London. There was considerable damage and many casualties. The RAF shot down ninety-nine planes and lost twenty-two of their own.*'

'I wonder what they'll say about the night raid,' Rosie said grimly, when she'd glanced at it. 'I'm sure we had a lot more than three hundred and fifty bombers over our heads last night.'

'Bad?' Jim asked.

She answered him truthfully and wearily. 'Grisly.'

He set the paper aside on the table so that he could put his arms around her. 'That's war,' he said. 'It was bad everywhere.'

She laid her head on his familiar chest as if it was a pillow. She felt so tired she could have slept where she stood. 'Mr Kennedy reckons they'll come again tonight,' she said. 'D'you think they will?'

He wanted to comfort her and say no, but he didn't. Now that this blitz had begun, they both knew it would go on until one side or the other admitted defeat. That was the nature of it. He'd learnt that in the trenches, if he'd learn nothing else. 'Let's have a bit a breakfast and get to bed,' he said. 'We'll have to sleep when we can, now.'

'I promised to send a postcard to Tess if the bombing started, to let her know we're all right, sorta thing,' she remembered. 'I better had, hadn't I? I'll get breakfast when I've done it.'

'No,' he said, kissing the top of her head. 'You write your postcard an' I'll get the breakfast. What we having?'

'A large amount a not very much,' she told him, ruefully. 'I didn't get to the shops yesterday what with one thing an' another. We'll have to make do with tea an' toast.'

He grinned at her. 'Leave it to me,' he said.

So she wrote her postcard to Tess and another identical one to Edie. *'Just to let you know, we had two air raids yesterday. You'll probably see it in the papers. We are all OK.'*

'Put 'em on the sideboard,' he said. 'I'll take 'em down the postbox presently. Now eat your toast while it's hot, an' then you can get up to bed.'

He's taken over, she thought, and although it wasn't the sort of thing that had ever happened before, she was glad of it, and went meekly to bed when she'd finished her breakfast.

When she woke, it was past midday according to the clock on the mantelpiece, and the room was rich with Sunday sunshine. For a few minutes she lay on her back in the blissful warmth and gazed at her lovely, familiar, peaceful room. It was as if she was seeing it for the first time, although every detail in it was as familiar as her face in the mirror. The pink rosebuds and blue forget-me-nots in the wallpaper, sharp-edged in the sunshine; the white curtains blowing in the breeze from the top of the window; the rag rug, prettily patterned, on her polished lino; the glint of light reflected from the mirror over the fireplace; the china shepherdesses on either side of the clock, holding their crocks and facing one another, the way they'd done ever since she'd first set them there; her clothes hanging over the back of the chair where she'd flung them that morning. Everything in its place and cared for and as it should be.

Then, she became aware that she could smell a joint cooking and put on her dressing gown and went downstairs to see how that could possibly be.

Jim was in the kitchen, stooped over the oven, basting half a leg of lamb and looking very pleased with himself.

She smiled at him. 'How did you manage that?' she asked.

'Guile,' he said, happily. 'I been down the market to see what's what an' Johnnie Macham was there so I done a swap, my fruit an' veg for his half a leg. No coupons or nothing. Good, eh? I picked the mint for the sauce an' there's a marrow an' some spuds on the table.'

It was a sumptuous meal and they followed it by going back to bed for the next two hours, making love, slowly and luxuriously, as if they had all the time in the world.

'What a way to go on,' Rosie said happily, when they were finally sitting up among the pillows, relaxed and satisfied, smoking their usual cigarettes.

'You have to take *what* you can, *when* you can, when you got a war on,' Jim said, smiling at her.

She turned her head to look at him. 'In other words, you think we're gonna have another raid tonight.'

'I don't think there's any doubt about it,' he said. 'When the Nazis start a blitzkrieg, they go on an' on until their victims give in. They've done it every time an' now they're gonna try an' do it to us.'

'Well, it won't work,' she said, flicking the ash from her cigarette, 'because we won't give in.'

'No,' he agreed. 'We won't.'

She drew on her cigarette, thinking. 'If that's the case,' she said, practical as ever, 'we'd better have a good filling supper and get everything cleared up before they sound the sirens.'

'That's my gel,' he said, and kissed her.

*

The ambulance teams turned up for work late that afternoon in a state of grim determination.

'Looks as though they'll be coming again tonight,' they said. And one or two of them said they didn't think much of that for an idea. 'They might have let us off on a Sunday.'

'We're going to have to face the fact that we're in for a long haul,' Mr Kennedy warned them. 'Check you've got all the supplies you need for the night'

'Same as yesterday then,' Joan said wryly.

'I would like to hope not, but it's best to be prepared,' Mr Kennedy told her.

So they checked supplies and petrol while they waited for the sirens to sound, and sat about the table drinking tea and knitting and not saying much because they were trying not to think about the horrors ahead of them. And, just as Mr Kennedy had predicted, the sirens started their long upward wail as soon as the sun had set, and the new pattern to their night began.

'At least all the fires are out tonight,' Rosie said. 'That's one good thing.'

'They'll soon light some more,' Joan said sourly. 'Don't you worry.'

Which they did, although this time they seemed to be aiming at the City and the fires were smaller. The first calls came twenty-five minutes later and Rosie and Joan were the second team to be sent to respond.

Even though they'd only lived through two raids, there was a hideous predictability about the bomb sites they visited that night. But, however terrible it was, at least they knew what to expect this time and how to respond, remembering to keep calm no matter what injuries they saw, and using the same comforting phrases over and over again to reassure their patients. 'You're all right. We're here. We've got you. We're just going to give you something to take away the pain and then we're going to take you to hospital.'

At midnight, to Rosie's relief, the next shift arrived, so as soon as she and Joan had cleaned their ambulance and put everything to rights, she was able to cycle home slowly and carefully through the ever-present dust and the new piles of debris. She knew it was risky to be out on the streets when the bombers were overhead and bombs were falling, but it was such a relief to be heading for her own comfortable, normal house that she almost managed to ignore it.

And there it was, still peacefully, comfortingly the same, with the windows in their frames just as they ought to be, and the curtains hanging neatly, the way curtains ought to hang, and the kettle on the hob ready to make tea. I'd better go in that dratted shelter, she thought, or Jim'll have something to say. I'll make myself a thermos, and take the spare eiderdown because it's bound to be cold.

And suitably provided, that's what she did. The deck chair was very uncomfortable but she was so tired she managed to sleep in it, and only woke from time to time when an explosion was a bit too near and a lot too loud. It wasn't until the all clear sounded that she really woke up, and by then Jim was sprawled in the other deck chair, rubbing the sleep from his eyes.

'Hello,' she said. 'What time did you get in?'

''Bout threeish,' he said. 'You was snoring.'

She aimed a cuff at his ear. 'Shall we have breakfast, then? The sun'll be up in a minute.'

'Not till I been down the market,' he said, smiling at her. 'I don't know about you, but I need something a bit more sustaining than bread an' marg this morning.'

So they walked down to the market together, skirting the debris as though that was a normal thing to be doing. It was so quiet and peaceful, they could hear the birds singing to the new day. All hell was breaking loose here last night, Rosie thought, and now here we are listening to the birds as it if we were in the country. And she thought of Binderton and wondered how they were there and if they knew what had been going on in London. I'll write two nice long letters to Tess and Edie when we've had breakfast, she thought.

Which she did, even though trying to decide what she should tell them and what she should leave out was a great deal more difficult than she expected. She wanted them to know how bad it was for the people who were being bombed but on the other hand she didn't want to worry them. In the end she found a sort of compromise for her final paragraph.

'*Jim and I and the girls are safe and well,*' she wrote. '*There has been a lot of bombing, like I told you, but the fire brigades and rescue teams are doing great work. You would be proud of them. We are living a rather topsy-turvy life now, working all night and sleeping during the day. I will write again soon. Love from Rosie.*'

That night it was no surprise to her when the sirens sounded. She was on duty at midnight but she cycled to the depot earlier when there was a lull so as to be there in plenty of time and avoid the worst of the raid. Getting the ambulance ready was routine now and so were the first two calls.

Her companion was Sister Maloney, but she didn't seem anywhere near as irritating as she'd been the previous night, and she certainly knew how to deal with a serious injury. At one point they saw a German bomber caught in the searchlights and hit by ack-ack fire, which pleased them both. When the all clear sounded they parted company like old friends, saying 'See you again soon.'

Three days later, Mr Kennedy gave them all new shifts, explaining that as the night raids were obviously going to go on for some time, it had been agreed that two new shifts should now be run to cover the night, with a change over at around midnight. 'That will give you time to rest during the day,' he said, as he handed them the details of their new shifts. 'And please make sure you do. Remember you are valuable.'

'Quite right,' Jim said. 'We're going to adjust ours, too. An' while we're talking about it, I think we ought to bring the camp beds down to the shelter, so if either of us needs a bit of a kip an' there's a raid on, at least we can sleep in comfort. Them deck chairs are giving me gyp.'

'How long d'you think this is going to go on?' Rosie said.

'Weeks, certainly,' he told her. 'Maybe even months.' And then, because she looked tired and upset, he changed the subject and told her he'd been round to see old Mrs Totteridge on his way home to check on Mrs Baker and Gladys, and he'd discovered they'd taken themselves off to live with a relative in Wales.

'Lucky relative!' Rosie grimaced. 'And how's old Winnie?'

'Soldiering on, so she says.'

'Like the rest of us,' Rosie said, with feeling.

From then on the raids became so regular they were almost ordinary. September dragged into October and the nights grew colder and still the sirens sounded. By that time, news of the worst incidents was being passed along the tram routes the next day by the drivers and conductors. They called it the tram telegraph and were quite pleased by their ability to get the news out quickly. On 9 October they reported that St Paul's Cathedral had been bombed. 'The bomb went right through the dome,' they said. 'The high altar's in ruins.' On the fourteenth they brought the news that a 'massive great bomb' had been dropped on Balham tube station, which was full of people taking shelter. 'Ever so many killed an' the crater was so big a bus fell right into it. Bleedin' Hitler!'

People got so used to walking past the rubble of bombed buildings that they barely noticed them. And it wasn't very long before weeds began to grow in the debris, and among the nettles and ivy was a tall, bright pink, flowering plant that was too eye-catching to miss. They certainly noticed *that*. Its official name was rosebay willowherb, but Londoners who worked on the railways, and knew it because it grew on the embankments, had always called it London Pride, and felt that its appearance after all those raids was right and proper and encouraging.

127

'It's a sign we ain't beat,' people said, and they welcomed every new patch of it with a nod and a grin. 'Life goes on, you see.'

*

On one of their rare afternoons off together, Jim and Rosie actually took time off and went to the pictures at the Troc at the Elephant and Castle. The film they chose was *Old Mother Riley in Society*, and they surprised themselves by enjoying it very much and laughing immoderately and, as they travelled home, they both said how much it had cheered them up. They knew the sirens would sound again that evening but their lives had returned to something approaching normal for the afternoon.

'Thank Gawd for the flicks,' Jim said.

And then it was the night of the fourteenth and fifteenth of November and, to everybody's amazement, they didn't have a raid. 'Good God,' people said as the hours passed and the bombers still didn't come, 'have they stopped?' But it was a night off, that was all, and the next day they discovered from the papers that the bombers had gone to Coventry instead and flattened the cathedral and killed thousands of people.

'Poor sods!' people in the Borough said to one another when they went to market that afternoon. 'I wouldn't wish that on my worst enemy. I bet the buggers are back here this evening.'

And sure enough, that night the London blitz began again with a vengeance, and Londoners all over the city wearily picked up the pieces just as they'd been doing before. Although they didn't know it then, they were to be bombed nearly every night for the next six months.

CHAPTER NINE

Kitty and Connie built up a nice big fire in the cottage the next morning, and that afternoon they went off into the kitchen to cook a big meat pie. It was getting cold now that they were into November, and they were determined that everyone would be warm and well fed that evening, because Tess and Edie were coming over to sort out baby clothes and do some sewing. They had the kitchen to themselves because Pa was upstairs having his afternoon nap with the cat sleeping on his chest, as it always did, and the twins had gone to school, although very reluctantly. They'd tried hard to get out of it that morning, complaining they 'never learnt nothing'.

'You just go over an' over the same old stuff,' Bobbie said, as Kitty buttoned him into his coat. 'It's ever so boring.'

'That's as may be,' Kitty said, pushing up her new glasses, which were forever slipping down her nose. She'd bought them in Woolworths and, like so many things in her life these days, they were a necessary evil, but she hadn't quite got the hang of them. 'You can't keep 'opping the wag or they'll smell a rat an' you'll have the school board down on you.'

'You let us off last week,' Georgie pointed out.

'That was to help your uncle in the cowshed,' Kitty told him.

'Couldn't we say we had to help you in the kitchen?' Georgie hoped.

'No, you could not,' Kitty said, firmly. 'Cowshed's one thing, kitchen's quite another. Don't make that face. You've only got a few more months to put up with it an' then you can leave it all behind you an' get to work.'

'It ent a few more months,' Bobbie protested. 'It's *eight*. We'll be bored out of our wits by then.'

Georgie joined forces with his brother as he usually did. 'Eight months is a lifetime, Ma.'

Kitty wound his muffler round his neck and kissed him firmly. 'Now then,' she said. 'You're all wrapped up nice an' warm, an' you know where the door is, dontcher?' And she gave Bobbie an equally firm kiss and pushed them both out.

'Saucy beggars,' she said to Connie when they'd gone scowling off along the path, but her voice was full of affection. 'They'll try anything on if you let 'em. Right. Now we'll get cleared an' swept round an' then we can get cracking an' start preparing that pie an' the vegetables an' all.'

'I never thought much to school myself,' Connie confessed, waddling out to the kitchen to fetch the broom. 'Not if I'm honest. It was all sums an' such an' I couldn't be doing with sums.'

'Didn'tcher want to be a midwife then, like your Ma?' Kitty said.

'No,' Connie said. 'Not really. Never thought I'd be a wife, did I? Never mind a midwife.'

Kitty grinned at her. 'Well you was wrong, wasn't you?'

'I'm good at clearing up though,' Connie said. 'An' peeling tatties an' carrots an' such.'

'We make a good pair,' Kitty told her. And although it surprised her even to think such a thing, it was no less than the truth. They had nothing in common. Connie was short and stout, even when she wasn't expecting, and cheerfully slow-witted, even though she was always loving and meant well. But she had no interest in what was going on in the world, didn't read the papers and didn't see any point in voting, while Kitty was still essentially a Londoner, despite her years in Binderton, skinny, sharp-witted, quick tongued, a one-time suffragette and passionately interested in politics. Even so, almost from the first day Connie moved into the cottage, they'd cooked all the meals together and, as the weeks passed, had gradually started to do most of the other chores together too, discovering that they were glad of one another's company, especially when Johnnie was at work and the boys were at school and Pa was upstairs having a nap, as he so often was these days. It was oddly like having a sister. She would have preferred to live with Rosie and Jim, naturally, because they were her own kind and understood her, but Connie was the next best thing.

The meat pie was well cooked, piping hot and ready to dish up when Edie and Tess arrived that evening, both of them red-nosed and swathed in shawls and carrying bags full of baby clothes. Pa was already up at the table, holding his knife and fork at the ready and declaring that his mouth was 'fair watering', the gas lights were lit, and Johnnie and the twins were fetching in more logs, filling the coal scuttle and stoking the fire.

'Eat hearty!' Pa commanded, not that any of them needed any bidding.

When the meal was over, Johnnie and the twins went off for a quick one, that being their habit nowadays, Pa dozed in his easy chair, with his hands contentedly folded across his belly, and Maggie's old work-box was brought out of its corner and opened for action to an accompaniment of long-stored family memories.

'I don't think I can ever remember a day when our Ma wasn't working,' Edie said, taking out her mother's ancient pin-cushion and setting it on the table. 'She was always at something or other, cooking or sweeping up, or darning or letting out seams or putting on a patch.'

'Or churning butter,' Tess said. 'She was always doing that. Round an' round an' round. It's a wonder her poor old arms never fell off.' Then she turned to her sister-in-law. 'Now then Connie,' she said, 'we got two skirts what are nearly the same colour. See? We're gonna cut 'em into panels an' turn 'em into a nice new wrap-around what you can let out as you go along. An' this ol' smock, what we're gonna make over for you. You won't know yourself when it's done. Just slip it on and we'll see what's got to be done to it.'

'Over me jumper?' Connie said.

'Course,' Tess told her. 'You'll need room for lots a jumpers when it's really cold.'

It was a very tight fit, so the two sisters set to at once to unpick the arms and the side seams. 'We got a nice bit a sheeting,' Edie explained as they worked. 'Almost the same colour. It'll look a treat when we've done with it. You won't know yourself.'

'I don't feel much of a treat at the moment, an' that's a fact,' Connie said, rubbing her belly. 'This baby's kicking me sore, all on an' on an' on. I shall be glad when it's born an' it can kick the cot. An' I shan't want another one in a hurry, I tell you that.'

'You don't 'ave to 'ave babies if you don't want 'em,' Kitty said, holding out her hand for a sleeve and its inset, so that she could start pinning them together.

'I don't see how,' Connie said. 'I mean for to say, if he... if you... I mean for to say...' But then she couldn't find anything at all to say that was even half-way decent, and had to cover her face with her hands to hide her blushes.

'I never 'ad no more after the twins,' Kitty told her. 'They was quite enough for me. Our Rosie told me what I had to do, an' I done it, an' that was that.'

132

Connie stared at her, round eyed. 'Heavens!' she said.

'I done it an' all,' Edie said. 'We're in the twentieth century now, Connie. There's things you can do.'

'Heavens!' Connie said again, staring from Kitty to Connie and back again.

Tess was laughing at her. 'We've all done it,' she said. 'Two was enough for me an' all. Our Rosie told us what we needed to know an' where we had to go an' everything an' that's what we done. It was easy. If you really don't want any more babies, Connie, you just ask our Rosie. She knows all about it. She'll tell you.'

'I wonder how she is,' Kitty said, biting off her tacking thread and handing the sleeve back to Edie. 'They'll be in the middle of an air raid in London now.' And she sighed. 'I think of her an' Jim an' the girls every night an' wonder how they are, an' wish I could be with 'em. I know she writes to us every day but that don't stop you wondering during the night.'

'They'll be right as rain, you'll see,' Connie said, leaning across the table to pat her arm.

Kitty looked at Connie's silly, empty face and was suddenly flooded with anger.

'What a bloody silly thing to say,' she said, jerking her arm way from Connie's patting hand. '"*Right as rain!*"' she mocked. 'For crying out loud. You don't know the half of what's going on in London. They're being killed in their hundreds, every single bleeding night. Killed. Don't you understand? You can't be "right as rain" when you're being bombed. You just get blown to bits. Don't you understand? Blown to bleedin' bits.'

The fear she'd kept under control for so long was out and blazing. 'My ol' Jim an' my Rosie ain't hid away in a shelter. They're out in the streets every single bleedin' night, pulling people out the wreckage an' taking 'em off to the orspital. Out in the open wiv nothing but a tin hat to protect 'em, an' a fat lot of use a tin hat is against a bleedin' bomb. They could be blowed up an' killed any time at all. Any time at all. Don't you understand?'

Connie was blushing and looking confused, covering her mouth with her hand as if she was trying to squash her offending words back inside it, and the others were all eyes, looking from one to the other. Pa had woken with a start and was looking round at them, plainly baffled.

Edie tried to placate Kitty. 'She didn't mean no harm,' she said. 'Did you, Con?'

'You get a bleedin' newspaper delivered here every single bleedin' day a the week,' Kitty raged, 'an' she never reads a bleedin' word of it. Not one single bleedin' word. "Right as rain".' She was shaking with fury and very close to tears.

Tess put down her sewing and, leaving Edie to comfort Connie, crossed the room and put her arms round her poor Kitty. 'It's all right,' she said, hugging her. 'We're all worried silly, being stuck down here not knowing what's happening to them two. If we could make it easier for anyone we would. It's the knowing there's nothing we can do, issen it?'

And Kitty began to cry and at that Connie cried too.

'Come on, Connie,' Edie said. 'Let's you an' me put the kettle on. We need a cup of tea.'

'What's going on?' Pa asked, looking from one to the other, his old face wrinkled with concern.

'Jest a bit of a spat, Pa,' Edie said. 'All over now.' And she patted his shoulder as she led Connie towards the kitchen.

'She will be all right, won't she?' Connie whispered. 'Our Rosie.'

'We must hope so,' Edie said. 'Let's make the tea, eh.'

*

But at that moment Rosie was very far from all right. She was sitting in the ambulance, pale faced and aching with fear and anxiety, because Mr Kennedy had just been on the phone to tell her that Guy's Hospital had been bombed and to let her know that she couldn't take her casualties there. She could still hear his voice giving her instructions but it sounded a long way away, as if he was in a tunnel, and nothing he said was making sense.

'I've been in touch with St Thomas',' he was saying. 'They'll be expecting you.'

She said 'Yes,' automatically, but her mind was spinning in a most unpleasant way, hurling terrible thoughts at her and giving her no time to make sense of them. What if they're injured? Oh dear God, please don't let them be injured. Or dead! What if they're dead? No, no. no, they mustn't be dead. They mustn't. I've got to find out what's happened to them. Now. This minute. I must. But how can I do that if I'm stuck here? I can't just drive off an' leave everyone. Oh God they might be injured. Anything could've happened to them. Please, please God.

She became aware that someone was standing behind her and had put a hand on her shoulder, and that a voice was saying 'Are you all right?' She turned her head and saw Sister Maloney.

'They've bombed Guy's Hospital,' she said. 'My girls work there. Nurses.'

'Ah!' Sister Maloney said, 'then it's tea you'll be needing.' She peered through the windscreen at the bomb site. 'They're not calling for us yet. Stay there. I shan't be a tick.' And she wrapped herself up in her cloak, straightened her cap and was gone.

Rosie was too stunned to move and too anxious to think. She simply sat where she was as if she'd been glued to her seat, staring through the windscreen at the nightmare scene in front of her. Until that moment she hadn't really looked at the bomb sites she'd attended. She'd been too busy coping with the wounded to notice anything else. Now it was as if she was seeing what was happening for the first time.

There was a fire burning in the wreckage, shooting out very bright flames like jagged tongues, and she could see the dark outline of a fireman, the AFS on his helmet stained red by the firelight, expertly aiming his hose at the blaze. She thought, inconsequently, what a hard job he had to keep the weight of it on target. The light of the fire revealed the rubble from the house which had fallen into the street and filled the pavements. The pile was half the size of the house, full of broken bricks, roof tiles, wooden beams, blackened bed linen, a battered teddy bear, a single broken shoe and a chipped jerry lying on its side, and down in the crater, she could see a tangle of wires – more wires than she could count or understand – and more broken beams, where the rescue team was hard at work. There were two gas men waiting to one side, their yellow helmets very noticeable. So much destruction from one bomb, she thought, and they're falling on us six at a time. She could hear the bombers labouring overhead but they were a malign presence, and there was no sign of them in the dark sky above the dust clouds and the smoke; only a small, apologetic moon and the long white beams of the searchlights, tirelessly moving.

As she watched, the rescue team lifted a woman out of the wreckage. She was covered in white dust from the plaster and even at this distance, Rosie could see that she was shaking. The first thing they did was to wrap her in a blanket. The second was to ease her towards the first ambulance, supporting her one on either side, and as she watched, Rosie saw another stick of bombs falling out of the sky, one after the other, no distance away, and held herself ready for the explosions that she knew would come. This is hell on earth, she thought. Nobody should have to endure this sort of thing. Nobody, ever.

There was a waft of the usual stinking mix of gas and soot and brick dust and shit, as the ambulance door was opened and Sister Maloney climbed aboard, carrying two steaming mugs of tea.

'Drink it down nice an' quick, while it's hot,' she said, handing one to Rosie. 'It's brass monkey weather out there tonight, so it is, an' you'll need to be on top a things when we start picking up patients. Which we'll be doing any minute now, be the looks of it, d'you see. Now then, do you have such a thing as a scarf about you? You've had a bit of a shock, so you have, an' you need to wrap up warm.'

Rosie took the tea and drank it automatically, aware that it was hot and sweet and that she was thirsty for it. But talk about a scarf was trivial beyond her comprehension. She sat where she was without moving, watching the horror beyond her windscreen, as three more people were lifted out of the wreckage. Somewhere, a long way behind her back, Sister Maloney was chuntering on, 'Not to worry, me dear. You can have mine. I'll go and get it for you now, so I will. It wouldn't do for you to take a chill on top of everything else, now would it?'

There was a warden beckoning to her to reverse so that the first ambulance could drive out. She obeyed him without thinking, backing neatly into a side street, waiting for the ambulance to leave and then driving out to take its place. There was a job to be done and she was there to do it. She had no idea what had happened to her daughters and there was no way she could find out. The ache of fear and anxiety was still gripping her stomach, but she'd seen that there were two people lying in the wreckage who would have to be lifted onto stretchers and she was aware that the ack-ack were putting up another barrage, and knew that the bombers were overhead again. Sister Maloney was still fussing round her, tying a scarf round her neck, but she let her do it because she didn't have the energy to argue about it. And then they were out in the darkness, carrying a stretcher towards their first patient and their work took over and pushed everything else to one side.

It wasn't until they'd delivered their casualties at St Thomas' that Sister Maloney looked at her watch and announced that it was past midnight and that their shift was over.

'Back to base,' Rosie said with relief.

'No,' Sister Maloney said. 'Not just yet. I'll tell you what we're going to do first.'

Rosie was too weary to do more than look a question at her.

'First,' Sister said firmly, 'we're going to drive over to Guy's and find out how your girls are. It won't take a minute. Come along!'

Yes, Rosie thought. Of course. They'd always been told to drive straight back to base when their shift was completed and until that night they'd always obeyed, but that *was* the thing to do. She drove carefully because so many roads were blocked by new heaps of debris and waiting ambulances and busy rescue teams, but she made as much speed as she could, given that her panic was increasing with every second, because the sooner she got there, the sooner she would know.

It was a disappointment to find that reception was virtually empty except for one very old man snoring noisily in a chair and a quiet sister on duty. She walked to them at once when she saw their uniforms and started to explain that the hospital couldn't take any casualties at the moment, but Sister Maloney forestalled her.

'We know,' she said, gently. 'We were told. We're not here with casualties. We've come to ask after this lady's daughters, so we have. They're nurses here. Name of Jackson.'

'I don't have a casualty list, I'm afraid,' the sister said. 'We're still dealing with it. But, if you'll hold the fort, I'll go and see what I can find out.'

Rosie found her tongue at last and managed to thank her. And then with a swish of her starched apron and the softest sound from her rubber shod feet, she was gone. Sister Maloney took over her position behind the desk, Rosie sank onto the nearest chair, and they waited. It felt like a very long wait and every minute of it was painfully full of frantic thoughts. But at last the sister came brisking back along the corridor and, to Rosie's anguished relief, she was smiling.

'They're both well and hard at work,' she reported. 'Gracie says she'll ring you in the morning, when she comes off duty.'

The relief was so overwhelming that Rosie began to cry. She simply couldn't help it although she *did* try. Soon the tears were rolling down her nose and into her mouth, making her gulp. 'Thank you so much,' she said, thickly.

'A pleasure,' the sister said. And meant it.

It took several minutes before Rosie had recovered enough to drive back to base and then she drove with exemplary care and patience. It took rather longer than usual to clean and service the ambulance because she and Sister Maloney were very tired, but they did it diligently and handed it over to the next pair feeling proud of themselves. And then at long, long last she could cycle home.

The raid was still going on all round her although the bombers weren't directly overhead, which was a mercy. From time to time, as she wobbled through the debris, she glanced to her right and could see that they were bombing the City and the docks again. There was a huge fire on the other side of the river, burning fiercely, and air was heavy with the smell of burning rubber. The flames rose as high as a block of flats and above them the sky was full of billowing pink smoke. As she looked at the black silhouettes of the firemen struggling with their powerful hoses, she became aware that there was a flock of white birds, soaring and wheeling in the smoke above them. Doves? she thought. Surely not. We don't have doves in the City. And, even though she knew it was a stupid thing to do in the middle of an air raid, she stopped peddling for a minute or two and rested on her handlebars to look up at them. If they fly any closer to that fire, she thought, they'll get roasted alive. But they were wheeling away from the heat, turning in the smoke and, as they flew upwards, she saw that they weren't doves after all, but pigeons, ordinary common or garden pigeons from Trafalgar Square. That's the second time tonight I've got hold of the wrong end of the stick, she thought, as she cycled on. It's a bit too easy to make mistakes in the middle of a raid. All these bombs addle your brain. And she felt suddenly weary and longed to lie down and sleep.

It was very cold in the shelter and Jim wasn't back to keep her company. She wrapped herself up in her eiderdown, switched off her torch and tucked it under the pillow and settled as well as she could, convinced that she would never be able to sleep out there in the middle of the raid. She woke to the sound of the all clear.

Jim had been back and slept in the other bed, as she could see from the crumpled eiderdown he'd left there. It was still dark but, when she yawned out of the shelter and headed for the kitchen, the first light of dawn was easing the sky with green.

Jim was standing by the cooker waiting for the kettle to boil. 'Tea?' he said.

She sank into the nearest chair. 'Please.'

'The girls are all right,' he told her, spooning the tea into the pot. 'I called in on my way home.'

'So did I,' she said, managing a smile.

'I expect one of 'em'll ring us when they come off duty,' he said, stirring the tea.

He was right. The phone rang just as they were finishing their breakfast.

It was Mary reporting that they'd had 'quite a night' but that everything was sorted out now. 'It was a bit of a to-do when it fell,' she reported laconically, 'but we coped. Now then, will you be at home next Sunday? We're going to try and get the afternoon off together.'

'That would be lovely,' Rosie said, feeling how wonderfully normal it sounded. I'll have to see if I can run to a little joint, she thought. I ought to have enough for that. And we'll have to rearrange our shifts.

But she had more to cope with then the rearranging of shifts, because that night the raid was centred on the Borough and the John Bull Arch in Southwark Park Road was bombed and destroyed. It was a major incident because the great arch carried several railway lines in and out of London Bridge, and one of the huge steel girders had come down on top of the row of houses underneath. All the ambulances in the area were called out to it and Jim attended it too, because they needed more wardens to check the number of casualties. Over one hundred people were killed and many more injured, so he and Rosie were hard at work coping with it all night, along with all the others who'd been called out. They saw more dead bodies laid under tarpaulins than they could count, and Rosie took back one ambulance load of badly injured after another, driving through the smoke and dust with as much care as she could so as not to jar them too much. She and Jim returned home early the next morning, aching with pity and completely exhausted.

It took them both several days to recover, and the raids went on every night there and elsewhere. Nevertheless, Rosie went shopping on

141

Saturday as if life were normal and bought a half leg of mutton ready for Sunday. She cooked it very slowly and carefully to make it as tender as she could, and Jim provided the vegetables and laid the table, and between them they made quite an event of it. And oh! it was *so* good to see the girls after all the dreadful things that had been happening to them that week. She sat on the opposite side of the table to them while Jim carved the joint and was warmed simply by the sight of them. They weren't in uniform, naturally, but anyone could tell they were nurses because they looked so competent. Tired – there was no denying that – but the sort of women you could trust and depend on.

None of them said anything about Sunday night's terrible raid, which didn't surprise Rosie at all. There were some things that were better put behind them. In any case, Gracie was full of information about the war in Africa and started to talk about that as soon as they were all settled round the table.

'It's hotting up in Africa,' she said, gathering her first fork load.

Rosie wasn't sure whether she was talking about the weather or the war, so she just looked interested and didn't say anything. But Jim seemed to know what she was on about. 'That's bloody Mussolini for you,' he said. 'What's he up to now?'

'Sam reckons he's shot his bolt,' Gracie said. 'His troops are surrendering in thousands but I expect you know that. It was in all the papers. Wavell captured an Italian camp last week near Sidi Barrani. Did you read about that? Over a thousand of them surrendered there, so the papers said. And that's only one place.'

Rosie had a vague recollection of a picture in the paper showing a long crocodile of Italian troops marching along with their hands in the air. 'Good,' she said.

But what Gracie said next was alarming.

'Sam reckons they'll be sending the Eighth Army Tank Corps out there soon. They're getting prepared for it, they've got new tanks coming and the latest equipment and everything. In fact, he's gone to see his mum this weekend to tell her.'

'But they won't do it before Christmas, will they?' Rosie said. And was ruffled when the others laughed at her.

'Oh Mum!' Mary said. 'You are funny. This is war. I don't think the generals pay any attention to Christmas – or anything else, come to that.'

'No,' Rosie said, sadly, 'I suppose not.' But it was miserable to have to face the fact they would have to endure the raids even at Christmas time. They deserved a night off now and then, for crying out loud. Just one. If there was a God, and she had to admit she was very dubious about it, He ought to freeze the bombers to the ground so that they couldn't take off and then keep them pinned down there for weeks and give us all a chance to catch our breath. But no. The damned things just kept coming, night after night. And if they weren't bombing London they were bombing somewhere else. There was no end to it. And all we can do is say *God help us!* she thought. And it's a fat lot of good saying that.

'Anyone for any more? Jim asked, picking up the carving knife.

'*Is* there any more?' Gracie asked, grinning at him.

'Not much,' he admitted. 'I'll share out what there is, shall I?'

'Sounds good to me,' Gracie said and held up her plate.

'Me too,' Mary said and followed her example.

'Rosie?' he asked.

Rosie was admiring her daughters' good sense. We must enjoy what we can when we can, she thought, and raised her plate too.

CHAPTER TEN

When Rosie walked into Borough market that December morning, Jim was balanced on his rickety step ladder, hanging up his usual Christmas decorations of newly-cut holly and battered baubles above the stall, and young Josh was holding the ladder firm and watching him.

He's such a good lad, Rosie thought. My Jim made the right choice when he took him on. Even though he very nearly didn't. What an extraordinary day that was! She remembered every minute of it as if it had been yesterday, and the memories were so vivid and powerful they glued her feet to the ground. It was three and a half years ago – how well she remembered *that* – in the middle of the summer holidays, not long after the King had been crowned and when they were still at peace. Jim had been grumbling over breakfast about what a waste of money a coronation was and how it would have been much better spent finding jobs for the unemployed, and the girls scolded him and told him not to be such an old kill-joy, which made him grin because they'd got a great treat planned. They were going on a day trip to Worthing on a charabanc, and Tess and the twins and Edie and Kitty and their kids were all going to meet them there. They'd planned it down to the last little detail. Fish and chips on the beach and ice cream sundaes afterwards. And the weather had been just right for it. It was early in the morning but the sun was already so hot she could smell her roses in the kitchen. They'd packed their towels and their swimming costumes and they were on their way to the front door when somebody rang the doorbell. She and Jim made a face at one another, she remembered. But he'd shrugged his shoulders and opened the door. And there stood the most peculiar old woman dressed in black from head to toe, with a young lad hiding behind her, looking sheepish.

'I do hope I'm not disturbing you coming so early, Mr Jackson,' she'd said, ducking her head and looking apologetic. 'Only I come in answer to your advertisement for a boy, d'you see, and I vanted to make sure I catch you.'

'You'll have to be quick,' Jim warned her. 'We're just on our way out.'

'Yes, yes,' the old lady said. 'I vill.' And she pushed the boy forward. 'This is my nephew, Josh, Mr Jackson sir, vhat is my brother's son. A good boy. He been in an office the past year but between you an' me, Mr Jackson sir, it don't suit on account of he's got trade in his blood, so to speak. So vhen I see your advertisement I know I must come and see you at once, on account of I know you vill understand.'

Jim didn't understand at all and his face showed it. 'Could you come to the stall tomorrow?' he said. 'We're in a rush.'

'So I tell you vhat I got to tell you quick,' the old lady said, doggedly. 'Vhat I got to tell you is his great uncle vas old Mr Feigenbaum. Vhat I know you'll remember him.'

The atmosphere changed at once. She and Jim looked at one another in surprise and then they both looked at the boy and remembered.

'He was a good man,' Jim said to the old lady. 'He took me on when I was at me wits' end an' trained me up like a father. A very good man. I owe him a great deal.'

'So take his boy,' the old lady urged. 'He von't disappoint you, Mr Jackson sir. You have my vord.'

It was agreed, of course, there and then.

And he never has, Rosie thought, watching him. He's so like Mr Feigenbaum. They don't look the same but he's got the same patience and the same gentleness and the same trick of knowing what you need before you know it yourself. A good lad.

She was brought back to the present by a cackle of laughter. A small crowd of customers had gathered round the stall to watch the work in progress, and were happily cheering.

'Go it Jim!' they called.

'You missed a bit a holly back there, duck.'

'Whatcher gonna have as a centre piece?'

'Farver Christmas, aincher Jim?'

'No, he ain't. He's gonna have a pig's head wiv a lemon in its mouf, aincher Jim?'

'Quite right,' he called back to them. 'Wouldn't be Christmas wivout a pig's head wiv a lemon in its mouf.'

'Here's yer missis come,' old Mrs Totteridge said. 'Watcher think a this then, Rosie?'

'Very Christmassy,' Rosie said. 'You got any fresh sprouts, Jim?'

'Got 'em this morning,' Jim called down to her. 'I'll be finished presently.'

''E's a one, your Jim,' Mrs Totteridge said, admiring him. 'He always does us proud come Christmas time. War or no bleedin' war.' And it was true, Rosie thought; we clear away the debris from the bombs, we repair the old bridge and tidy up the market, and bring things back to normal as quick as ever we can. And now we're going to have the most normal Christmas we can and sod the bloody Jerries.

'He'll do,' she approved, happily admiring him, and at that he looked down from his perch and blew her a kiss. 'But he'd better look sharp. I'm on duty at four.'

'Plenty a time,' Jim said, grinning at her.

But that wasn't Rosie's opinion. Duties dominated her life as the months grew colder and the weather got worse, and it grew more and more difficult to stay cheerful when she was out in the dark streets with her ambulance. Rain made it hard to see the way in the blackout, frost underfoot struck cold even through her boots and a thick pair of socks, and snow was the worst of the lot. If it wasn't for the Women's Voluntary Service with their tea wagons, it would be really bleak out there some nights. She and Joan or Sister Maloney would make a bee-line for the nearest one whenever the raid gave them a minute to do it. It was almost worth waiting in line at a major incident for the chance to nip off quick for one of their steaming mugs.

As they did that night. Their first call was at a little after midnight to an office block near the Elephant. It had taken a direct hit and there were reports that there'd been at least four fire watchers on duty inside. The rescue teams were having a very hard job clearing the rubble and finding their casualties, and Rosie knew that she and Joan were in for a long wait. So when Joan said 'Cuppa?' she agreed at once and off they went.

The stall was set well back from the action as usual, where it wasn't in the way but was easy to see and near enough to be handy. There were two firemen standing beside it, one drinking tea and the other wiping the sweat from his forehead.

'Two nice big mugs a tea for my mate Rosie an' our Joan,' he said, standing back from the counter to make way for them, and the woman who was serving them smiled through the hatch and said 'Two teas coming up.'

But when she handed the mugs to them she gave Rosie a long, searching look. 'You're Rosie Goodison,' she said. 'You *are* aren't you?'

147

'I was once,' Rosie admitted, squinting at her in the darkness. There was something familiar about the face under the WVS hat, something about the set of the mouth, the tilt of the head. She couldn't quite place it, but...

'We worked together when we was girls,' the woman said, as two more firemen arrived. 'In Arundel Castle. I'm Maisie.'

Memories pushed the chaos of the raid aside and crowded into Rosie's brain; she could see them walking the babies in the grounds, cleaning their nappies and feeding them those horrid bottles, strolling up and down the High Street in Arundel on their afternoon off, feeling like swells in their Sunday best.

'D'you remember our tea shop an' the sticky buns?' Maisie asked, and turned to her next customer to ask, 'What can I do for you sir?'

But she didn't get an answer to either of her questions, because at that moment there was a blinding flash of light and a deafening roar, and Rosie and the three firemen were punched off their feet by a force that felt like a blast from a furnace. It was so powerful it pushed the air out of their lungs and left them gasping for breath. Rosie landed painfully and stayed where she was, huddled on the ground with her face away from the blast, stunned and still, while the debris fell all around her. It had happened too quickly for her to feel afraid and, as far as she could tell, she was still in one piece, but she was too numb to know whether she was hurt or not. When there was no more debris falling, and the air had settled a little, and her breathing had righted itself, she tried to sit up and found she couldn't do so. But she managed to raise her head and saw that the mobile canteen was lying on its side and was badly damaged, that the tea urn had been blown right out of the canteen and was lying yards away, crushed under a pile of bricks and leaking tea, that her ambulance had vanished, and that there were five dark shapes lying higgledy-piggledy on the ground a few feet away from her, half hidden by the dust cloud.

Then she heard a voice calling to her. 'We're on our way, Rosie. Stay where you are!' And she tried to answer it but couldn't. A face loomed into her line of vision and she recognised it, but couldn't remember who it was.

'You're all right,' it said. 'We're here. Don't try to move.'

'I can't,' she said, and was annoyed to hear how croaky her voice was. It was a struggle to focus her eyes too, but she knew her rescuer was one of her fellow ambulance drivers, even though she couldn't see him properly. 'John?' she said.

'That's me,' he agreed. 'I'm just going to check you over. OK? Have you got any pain anywhere?'

She was struggling to say no when the pain suddenly began, almost as if he'd given her permission to feel it by asking. It was so overwhelming it made her pant. 'Right arm,' she managed to say, and then there was blackness.

When she came to, she was travelling in the ambulance and a nurse she knew from the station was standing beside her, smiling. 'Soon be there,' she said.

'Where?' Rosie said in her croaky voice.

'Guy's,' the nurse told her. 'You're going to see your girls.'

It was too much. Bad enough that she couldn't talk properly or see without squinting, bad enough that she was finding it hard to breathe and had pains in her arm and all down her side and felt as if she'd been beaten up, but the thought that Gracie and Mary would see her like this was too much to bear. Tears swelled in her nose and rolled out of her eyes, and she let them run because she couldn't move a hand to wipe them away, and she couldn't stop them. Soon she was sobbing and groaning, shameful though it was, and the nurse was patting her hand. Oh please God, she thought, make it stop.

She cried until the ambulance came to a halt and John opened the doors. Then she made an enormous effort by concentrating on the lights in the ceiling that were jumping in and out of focus in a most peculiar and irritating way, and managed to get herself under control before they carried her into reception. She was still outwardly calm when John removed her tin hat and they eased her onto a bed in one of their cubicles. The familiar smells of the place filled her nose – carbolic and disinfectant, the starched aprons of the nurses as they walked from bed to bed, a strong smell of blood and shit and dirty clothes.

Now I know what it's like to be a casualty, she thought, and I'd rather not, because it's bloody uncomfortable. I wish I could see properly. It's horrible not being able to focus. She thought there was a nurse coming towards her, but she wasn't sure about it. She could see one side of her white apron and one shoe quite clearly, but the figure had a fault line running diagonally through it, and that made it impossible to judge the direction in which the figure was moving. But while she was still struggling to get her eyes to work, a hand held hers and a face swam into focus and it was Gracie, her dear, dear Gracie, smiling at her and bending down to kiss her, and she knew how very, very glad she was to see her. 'Oh Gracie!' she said.

'I've come to cut your clothes off, so doctor can examine you,' Gracie grinned, and when Rosie looked startled, she explained, 'It's OK. I'm a dab hand at it. I shan't cut *you*, only your clothes.'

'You can't do that,' Rosie protested. 'I'd never hear the end of it. It's my uniform.' It was unheard of for anyone to cut up their uniform.

'They'll give you another one,' Gracie said, easily. 'This is filthy dirty and ripped to shreds. Now then, I'm going to take off this splint so that I can get at you. Keep quite still. Right. Now I'm going to take the sleeve out.'

Rosie kept as still as she could on her hard bed and closed her eyes. There wasn't much point in keeping them open and she would rather not watch what her determined Gracie was going to do. It was bad enough to have to feel it and hear those scissors scratching and snapping. There were so many sounds in this place. She could hear every footfall, every voice, recognising an ambulance driver from the calm way he was giving his report: 'Fractured femur, lacerations, shock,' as if he was writing a shopping list. There was a child weeping piteously somewhere, calling for its mother, 'Mummy! Mummy! Mummy!' and a nurse trying to soothe it, 'You'll see her soon, sweetheart.'

'That's the sleeve got rid of,' Gracie said. 'Now I'm going to cut off the rest of the jacket. Could you roll over onto your good side a little bit, d'you think?'

'I'll try,' Rosie croaked, and opened her eyes so that she could see what Gracie was doing. The sleeve from her jacket had been tossed into a bucket alongside the bed and, despite the fractured state of her sight, Rosie could see it horribly clearly. It gave her a shock because it wasn't just torn and dirty, which she expected, it was bloodstained. For a second she gazed at it, wondering where all that blood had come from. Then she glanced down at her denuded arm and saw the state it was in. The break was obvious from the peculiar angle at which it was lying, and her hand was streaked with long, dirty cuts, oozing blood. 'What a mess,' she said.

Gracie was easing the remains of her battered jacket from underneath her. 'It always looks worse than it is,' she said, and when Rosie winced, 'Have you got pains anywhere else?'

'Chest,' Rosie said. 'Hard to breathe.'

'Let's get you comfy,' Gracie said, 'and then I'm going to cut off your jumper and wrap you in a blanket.'

But Rosie was staring at a tin hat which was lying on a chair just within her limited focus. 'Is that mine?' she said.

'It was,' Gracie grinned. 'And you're not going to say you want us to keep *that* for you.'

Rosie shook her head, gazing at the terrible dents in her helmet and thinking, if that hadn't been on my head, I'd have been killed. She was completely dispassionate about it. The time for fear was over. Not that she'd felt afraid, even when she was lying on the ground waiting for the debris to stop falling. Stunned, yes. But no more than that. And now she was injured and in hospital like so many other people before her, and really that's all there was to it. But it made her remember all the bodies she'd seen lying on the ground and that made her think about the others: Maisie and the firemen and the other woman who was pouring the tea, and she wondered how they were and who she could ask about them. If she could get to a phone she could give Mr Kennedy a call and ask him. As it was…

There was a movement at the foot of her bed and she turned her head towards it, recognising one of the doctors who was talking to Gracie. He's checking the nurses' report, she thought, and watched his face to see how he was reacting to it, noticing how blood-stained his white coat was and how tired he looked. It wasn't until he walked round to the head of the bed that she realised she could see properly again.

'Mrs Jackson,' he said. 'I hear you're Nurse Jackson's mother. Sorry about this dirty coat. We've had a night of it.'

'Yes,' she said. 'I can see that.'

He smiled wearily. 'I'm going to send you down to x-ray. And then we're going to get you into theatre to have that arm set. When did you last have something to eat?'

'Six o'clock,' she remembered. 'Supper.'

He looked at his watch. 'Which was seven hours,' he said. 'Good. Did you eat anything else later?'

'I got a mug of tea from the WVS, around midnight,' she remembered, 'but the Luftwaffe blew it out my hand before I could drink it.'

That made him grin. 'All set then,' he said.

And all set it seemed to be; 'set' being the operative word. She waited patiently until an orderly arrived to wheel her to x-ray, where she endured being lifted from her trolley to the x-ray table, which was painful. She lay 'perfectly still' as she was instructed, was lifted again and wheeled somewhere else, and after a very long time, she found herself on an operating table with lights above her that hurt her eyes and, on being told to count to ten slowly, counted to three and was gone. Finally she woke to a quiet ward, where she found she couldn't focus her eyes properly, and was told by a wonderfully gentle nurse that her bone had been set and her arm had been put in plaster of Paris, that she had two cracked ribs so they'd bound her chest to protect them, and that both her hands had been stitched. She also said that everything had gone according to plan and, feeling relieved, Rosie fell into a deep sleep, waking to find that she was in yet another ward and that Jim was sitting beside her, watching her, anxiously.

'What time is it?' she said, reaching for him with her left hand.

He held it and stroked her fingers, which were the only part of it that hadn't been stitched and bandaged. 'Quarter to three. You been asleep a long time.'

'You look as if you ent slept at all.'

'I ain't.'

'Nor shaved,' she teased.

'I been worried about you.'

He looked so woebegone she was torn with pity for him. 'Daft ha'porth,' she said lovingly. 'I'm all right.'

'I couldn't bear to lose you, Rosie,' he said.

'Well I've not gone,' she said. She was brisk with him because he looked as though he was going to cry, and she couldn't have that. 'I've got a broken arm an' a few stitches here and there an' the odd cracked rib but that's all.'

'You was lucky to survive,' he said, dourly. 'Except for you and one a the firemen, all the others was killed. Mr Kennedy told me when he rang me. He said it was a very bad incident. Your ambulance took the force of it. Blow'd to smithereens, it was. They found bits of it three hundred yards away.'

She could feel her heart sinking. She'd been thinking about herself all this time; what was happening to her, and she'd hardly spared a single thought for the others who were there. 'Oh dear God!' she said. 'That's awful. What happened to the women in the WVS van?'

'They was killed an' all, so Mr Kennedy said.'

'Oh my dear good God!' she said. 'One of them was a friend of mine. We worked together in Arundel Castle. We'd just found each other again when…' And then she began to cry, because it was all too awful.

He sat on the bed and put his arms round her as well as he could for the plaster and the bandages, and stroked her hair and did what he could to comfort her.

'I hate this bleedin' war,' she sobbed. 'Hate it, hate it, hate it!'

'I know,' he said. It sounded trite but what else could he say?

When he finally left her, right at the end of visiting time, he went to find the ward sister to ask when she would be allowed home. 'We'll look after her,' he said. 'She'll be all right wiv us.'

'I know your daughters, Mr Jackson,' she smiled, 'so I'm sure she will. But we shall have to see what sort of a night she has first. A lot depends on that. Then we'll decide. I can't promise anything but, all being well, she should be home by mid-morning.'

*

And she was. She arrived in one of Mr Kennedy's ambulances in the middle of the morning, wearing Gracie's cloak over her vest, carrying the rest of her bloodstained underwear in a carrier bag and feeling very self-conscious. Luckily, she was driven by one of the drivers she'd met at the station and he was quiet and kindly and blessedly tactful. Neither of them said anything about Joan either, which was right and proper, although it made her think about her poor friend all the way home.

But once she was indoors, she had such a surprise she cheered up at once. The kitchen seemed to be full of people: not just Jim as she expected, but old Mrs Totteridge and Sonia Cohen too, and all of them busy. The table was set with teacups, there was a plate full of homemade scones and the kettle was on the boil, and Sonia had brought an old cardigan for her to wear.

'It'll do a turn now you can't wear your usual clothes,' she said. 'We can't have you getting cold. You can leave the arm sorta flopping an' just do up the buttons.'

Rosie put it on at once and was very graceful for it, thinking what a lovely welcoming committee they were.

'Now then, duck,' Mrs Totteridge said, when the tea had been made and they were all settled round the table. 'We don't want to push in or nothing, but if you need a bit a help now your poor arm's broke, you only 'ave to give us a call an' we'll be right round. We can unpick a few sleeves for you, for a start.'

'What with Christmas coming an all,' Sonia said, 'there's gonna be a lot to do, as well we know, don't we Mrs T? I know you got Jim an' the gels but many hands make light work, an' you've only to say.'

'I call that really kind,' Rosie said, thinking how good they were. 'Thank you.'

'We could pop in of a morning just to see how you are, sorta thing,' Mrs Totteridge said. 'Find out if there's anything you need, sorta thing.'

So it was agreed, and as the days passed and Rosie got used to the fact that there were a great many things she simply couldn't do one-handed, she was very glad of their help. They went shopping together every morning and Mrs Totteridge and Sonia carried the baskets between them, and on Monday they turned up to help her with the wash.

By that time she'd learnt how to make the beds, tidy up, sweep the floor, fill the kettle and the coal scuttle one-handed, and could even make a passable job of lighting the fire. But she enjoyed their company, especially after a bad night in that horrible shelter. It was so cold out there and the raids seemed right overhead.

'D'you reckon they'll give us a break over Christmas?' Sonia asked, as they were unpacking the shopping after one particularly noisy night.

'I can't see that bleedin' Hitler giving nobody a break over nothing,' Mrs Totteridge said, sourly. 'Rotten little bugger. He just keeps all on an' on. There's never any end to him.'

The others agreed with her. But they were proved wrong.

*

Christmas Day was a better occasion than Rosie had dared to hope. Mary and Gracie made long strings of paper chains and came home for an hour on Christmas Eve to hang them up, which they did so quickly that Rosie said they took her breath away, Jim treated them to a goose from Leadenhall Market, and between the four of them, with occasional help from Mrs Totteridge and Sonia, they prepared a surprisingly good meal which they all shared.

After the meal they left the dishes to soak in a sink full of soapy water and took themselves off to the front room, where Jim had a splendid fire ready for them and two bags full of chestnuts to roast round it. So they ate roast chestnuts and drank port wine and listened to the wireless, and it was almost as if there was no such thing as war.

'My eye!' Mrs Totteridge said, happily, 'we'll all go orf bang after all this grub. You done us proud you two.'

'Here's to Mum an' Dad,' Gracie said, raising her glass.

And there's still the presents to come, Rosie thought. She'd bought a pair of fur-backed gloves for both her daughters and couldn't wait to hand them over. What a Christmas this is turning out to be.

By the time their presents had been exchanged it was beginning to grow dark, but they sat on in the firelight enjoying the peace and normality of the day. Jim made a pot of tea and carried in Mary's first Christmas cake, which was much admired and enjoyed, although she explained that she really didn't have all that much to do with it. 'Mum told me what to do and I just did it.'

'They'll be sounding the sirens soon,' Mrs Totteridge sighed, looking at the clock. 'We'll give you a hand wiv the dishes, Jim, an' then we'll have to start thinking about going home.'

Gracie looked at the clock too. 'Me an' Mary'll have to be off in twenty minutes,' she said. 'We're on duty at six.'

It was sad to think that their happy Christmas was coming to an end, but the inevitability of the night's raid was hurrying them on. The girls left for the hospital, the dirty dishes were washed and put away, Sonia and Mrs T said goodbye and Jim set about putting the house to rights and damping down the fire.

'Everything's ready,' he said, as he kissed Rosie goodbye. 'You've got your boots and your greatcoat. Your torch an' your whistle are in the pockets. See you around midnight.'

Then it was simply a matter of waiting for the siren's upward howl. But it didn't come. Ten o'clock passed. Half past ten. And still there was no sound. I've half a mind to go to bed, Rosie thought. I haven't slept in my own bed for ages. It'd make a nice change. I'll put my coat and boots ready on the chair, just in case, and I'll have a bit of comfort while I can. I'll just put the milk bottles out, and then I'll go to bed.

It took her quite a while to carry her coat and boots upstairs one handed, and to ferry the empty milk bottles to the door, one at a time. And when she opened the door to put the bottles on the step, it was so dark and cold it made her shiver. Get back in the warm quick, she told herself, and turned to do it.

But as she turned, she became aware of an odd movement just beyond the doorstep and, on an impulse, turned back to see what it was. There was a small bedraggled animal crouched beside the step and, even in the poor light, she could see that it was soaking wet and covered in dust and dirt and shivering violently. Then it opened its eyes and made a plaintive mewing sound, and she knew that it was a kitten and that it needed help, and she bent down and picked it up very gently and took it indoors into the warm.

Now that they were in the light, she could see what a terrible state the poor little thing was in. Its coat was matted with dirt and dust, and it was pitifully thin. First things first, she thought. I'll get it cleaned up and wrap it up warm, and then I'll find some scraps for it to eat and warm up some milk for it. Which she did. It took a very long time because she was aware of how fragile it was and didn't want to break any of its bones. But she cleaned it thoroughly, discovered it was a female, and that it had been neutered, and even found an old baby's hair brush and brushed its clean fur until it lay flat again. Then she fed it. It was pathetically grateful, purring at her and narrowing its eyes and, when it had eaten everything she put in front of it, she lifted it onto her lap and stroked it and talked to it. Now that it was clean, she could see that it was a green-eyed tabby and very prettily marked, with a decided M on its forehead and soft white paws.

'I shall call you Moggie,' she told it, 'because that's what you are.'

Then it occurred to her that the sirens still hadn't sounded and she began to wonder whether they were going to be spared a raid, after all. 'Let's go to bed,' she said to the little cat. 'We can keep one another company.'

Which they did, and very pleasant it was, cuddled up together under the eiderdown. It was a fitting end to an excellent day. And the sirens still hadn't sounded.

*

Jim came back from the wardens' post just after midnight. He'd left old Harry taking care of the place and told all the others to go home and get some rest while they could. 'We can sleep in our own beds fer once,' he'd said. He'd been looking forward to it all the way home. And there it was, when he'd climbed the stairs: his familiar, comfortable bed, lit by moonlight, with Rosie lying on her back in the middle of it, her mop of tousled hair dark against the pillow and her plastered arm lying rather awkwardly on the eiderdown, as if it didn't belong to her. He was full of admiration and affection for her. She's a good old girl, he thought. She'd made so little fuss and things couldn't have been easy for her. Now he couldn't wait to get into bed and give her a cuddle.

Rosie opened her eyes as he took off his clothes and smiled at him sleepily. 'No raid,' she said.

'No,' he said, and turned back the covers to make room for him to get into his nice warm bed. His mood changed in the instant. 'What the hell is *that*?' he said.

'She's a casualty of the blitz,' Rosie said, stroking the cat, which had put back its ears at the sound of Jim's voice. 'I've taken her in.'

'Well you can just take her out again,' he said.

'She needs looking after,' Rosie told him. 'You should have seen the state she was in when she got here. I thought she'd crack her bones, she was shivering so. An' it took me hours to clean her, poor little thing.'

He tried to persist. 'We don't have cats in the bed.'

'We do now,' she said, and her face was determined.

'What if there's a raid?' he persisted. 'What'll you do then?'

'I shall take her in the shelter with me,' Rosie said. 'She'll be company. Oh get into bed, do. You'll catch your death standing out there in the cold.'

So he got into bed, feeling disgruntled, and she cuddled him until he was warm and good humoured again. And the cat slept beside them and didn't move.

CHAPTER ELEVEN

Jim and Rosie didn't wake until nearly ten o'clock the next morning, and then they did so slowly and luxuriously. There was no need for them to get up. There was plenty of food in the house, Jim wasn't on duty until the evening and neither of them had to go to work – not that Rosie *could*, now that her arm was in plaster and her hands were stitched. They had a whole day to do whatever they liked and they were going to make the most of it, partly because it was such a rarity, but mostly because they were both sure there'd be an air raid that night. The Jerries would hardly let them off two nights in a row.

But for the moment, they were warm and comfortable and faintly amorous. Jim ran his fingers through Rosie's tangled hair, enjoying the strength and wildness of it. 'If I was to hug you,' he said, hopefully, 'would I hurt you?'

'No idea,' she said, smiling at him lazily. 'Let's try it an' see.' If he wanted to do more than hug and it didn't hurt her, she could nip out to the bathroom and get ready later.

He rolled towards her as gently as he could, breathing in the easy, familiar smell of their musky bed, thinking what an unusual thing it was to have slept a whole night there together and feeling ridiculously happy. It was a bit awkward to try to hug her lying on his side, but he gathered her towards him, as gently as he could, and managed to nuzzle into her neck, enjoying the lovely musky smell of her sweat and the lingering smell of ciggies in her hair, faint traces of that scented soap of hers whenever she moved, the skin on her body so soft and the skin on her hands so rough, even the harsh stink of that horrible plaster that she was enduring so patiently. 'My lovely Rosie,' he said, kissing the hollow in her throat, 'sweet, sweetheart...'

But then his love-making was brought to a sudden and unexpected halt. The cat sprang out of the bedclothes, shrieking like a banshee, and leapt straight up into the air. Jim jerked his head towards the noise and, for a fraction of a second, he saw the animal suspended just above his back, its eyes wild and its fur standing on end, and then it landed on him, claws first. He sat up at once, swearing and trying to shake it off. 'Bleedin' hell, Rosie! Get this damned thing off a me!'

Rosie laughed. She simply couldn't help it. It was all too ridiculous. And that made him worse.

'It ain't nothing to laugh at,' he said, his face red. 'I'm scratched to bits. Look at me! Bleedin' cat. I ought to fling it out the winder.'

'She ent a bleedin' cat,' Rosie told him. 'She's young an' upset. That's all. Poor little thing. Where's she gone?' And she hung her head over the edge of the bed and peered into the darkness there.

'*She's* upset!' he roared. 'What about *me* then? I'm ripped to pieces.'

'You'll live,' Rosie said. 'Ah, there she is. Right up against the wall. Moggie! Moggie-Moggie-Moggie! Come here! Don't be scared.'

'If you're going on like that, I'm off downstairs,' Jim said. But he was talking to the back of her head and she wasn't even looking up at him. Bleedin' cat!

It took Rosie a long time to coax her frightened animal from underneath the bed and, by the time she'd managed it, they were both so cold they went back under the covers to warm up. She could hear Jim riddling out the grate in the kitchen and shaking coal from the scuttle, so she knew she would come downstairs to a warm room and softened towards him with every sound. He'd looked after her so well since she got hurt. Dear Jim. But it was well past eleven before she finally bestirred herself and put on her slippers, wrapped herself in her dressing gown and yawned downstairs with the cat under her arm.

The kettle was on the boil, there was a good fire burning in the grate and Jim was sitting at the kitchen table writing one of his familiar notices for the stall. She watched him for a second or two, feeling immensely fond of him. Then she went and stood behind him so that she could see which of his goods he was going to be pushing the next day. And got a shock.

'*HAVE YOU LOST A CAT?*' the notice said in unnecessarily large capitals. '*Small tabby female. If you have, she is here. Collect her at your conveeniense or see me at the Market. Jim Jackson fruit & veg.*'

'Oh!' Rosie said, glaring at him. 'How can you be so heartless? I never thought I'd live to see the day when my Jim was heartless.'

'It ain't heartless, Rosie,' he told her calmly. 'Somebody could be looking for her. You ain't thoughta that, have you?'

'If I'm any judge, from the state she was in when she turned up here, she's been in a bombed house, for one reason or another,' Rosie said quite crossly, 'an' probably for quite a time. Or the house where she lived was bombed, and she stayed in it because she was too scared to do anything else. And if *her* house had been bombed, everyone in it would be gone, one way or another. She could be all on her own. Have you thought of that?'

'She could've just took fright when the bombs was falling, an' run off,' he said, arguing back. 'Have you thoughta *that*?'

She had, but only briefly. All sorts of thoughts had crowded into her mind in those first confused seconds. But what was important to her then, and was even more important to her now, was the fact that the cat was small, terrified and needed care. For four long months, she'd seen one terrible injury after another and been torn by pity for the suffering of her casualties, and all she'd been able to do was to soothe them and patch them up and pass them on to the hospitals. It had never been enough and she knew it clearly now. This shivering, skeletal kitten had focussed her compassion in the most powerful way. She couldn't give her up now, not without putting up a fight.

'She needs looking after,' she said stubbornly.

'An' so she will be,' Jim said. 'One way or another.'

She sensed an advantage and pressed it home. 'So if nobody comes to claim her, we'll keep her. Right?'

'OK,' he said, but he said it grudgingly.

'And how long will you give them before you take the notice down?'

'Fortnight? Week?'

She compromised. 'Say ten days.'

So Rosie's unwanted visitors were given until the fifth of January to put in an appearance, and they could turn to more mundane and pleasant matters. 'Shall we have a late breakfast or an early dinner?'

'Dinner,' Jim said decidedly. 'Then *we* can have the rest a the Christmas pud, an' the cat can have the giblets.'

Their compromise eased them effortlessly into the rest of the day. They made a good meal and they both fed the cat until her belly was as tight as a drum. Then, while the little animal was sleeping off her excesses by the fire, they gentled upstairs and made awkward but increasingly tender love for the rest of the afternoon.

'If only we weren't going to have a raid tonight, this would have been

164

a perfect day,' Rosie said, as she made a pot of tea afterwards. She'd forgotten how close they'd been to having a row. 'What time have you got to be on duty?

He left her at a quarter to eight. And twenty minutes later the sirens set up their horrid growl. Rosie put on her boots, her thick cardigan and her winter coat, working automatically as she always did, and took Moggie and her torch, her eiderdown, an extra blanket and a hot water bottle down to the shelter with her. It took two trips and such a long time that the bombers were overhead before they were settled, the sound of their laboured engines loud and unmistakable. It was no surprise to Rosie when the little cat crawled into the bed with her and hid under the eiderdown, its heart beating like a hammer against her chest. From time to time she put a hand under the covers to stroke the poor thing. 'It's going to be a long night,' she said.

She was right. It *was* a very long night and so was the next night. But the night of the twenty-ninth was the worst she'd ever experienced. The bombs were falling far too near them. 'They're after the City again,' she said to Moggie when they'd settled in the shelter. And as if to prove her right, it wasn't long before the first fires began to cast their glare through the gap at the top of the door. She'd have liked to have gone out so that she could see what was going on for herself. It felt more alarming, hidden away. But she stayed where she was until the first lull, and then she tucked the cat into her coat and held her close and eased out into the garden to see what had happened.

The sky was lit by a lurid crimson and yellow glare. Incendiaries, she thought, and they're in the City, if I'm any judge. Not warehouses this time. It doesn't smell like warehouses and the colours are different, but there are a helluva lot of fires.

For a few seconds she was tempted to go indoors and take a look out of the window of the back bedroom, but she thought better of it because she'd never hear the end of it if the house was bombed while she was in it. Jim'd have a fit. Even so, she stayed in the garden watching the glare until the bombers were back overhead, and she saw the bright white flash of six exploding bombs and ran back into the shelter as quickly as she could.

It was half past six before the all clear sounded and the sky was still full of yellow and crimson clouds. 'That was a bad one,' she said to Moggie, and carried her indoors to comfort her with a saucer of warm milk. 'I wonder what Jim will say when he gets home.'

He was full of information. 'They was after St Paul's,' he said. 'Crafty buggers came when the tide was low, an' the poor devil firemen used so much water the level dropped even further, an' they couldn't get no more an' they had to stand by an' watch while everything burnt. Terrible, it was. They say there's nothing left a the City round St Pauls' an' *that* only came through because there was twice the number a fire watchers there an' they managed to put the incendiaries out. There was twenty nine a them all told, in just that one building. But they had to climb through the rafters to get at them. It's been a bad old night.'

Just how dramatically bad the night had been was revealed in a picture published on the front page of the *Daily Mail* on Tuesday morning. It showed St Paul's standing huge and untouched in the thick smoke and flames that were destroying the City, under the caption '*War's Greatest Picture.*' And it was bought in large numbers and passed from hand to hand all through the day.

'I'd like to go and see it for myself,' Rosie said, gazing at the picture. 'I've half a mind…'

'Wait till Sunday an' I'll go with you,' Jim said. 'We'll have to be very careful. There could be UXBs an' all sorts in that lot.'

And as he looked so anxious, she promised she would wait. That'll make two things I'm waiting for, she thought, and there's safety in numbers. Nobody's come to claim my cat and Sunday will be the last day they can.

Mary turned up for a couple of hours on New Year's Day, eager to see 'your new pet' and with a letter to tell her mother that she was to attend the outpatients at Guy's on Friday morning to have her stitches out. She was very taken with the cat and spent the whole time sitting by the fire, cuddling it. They'd been inundated with casualties on the twenty-ninth, so she said. 'Mostly burns. Poor devils. They say it was a firestorm. Have you seen the picture in the *Mail*?'

'We have,' Rosie said. 'And we're going to go and see it for ourselves on Sunday. Ent we Jim?'

'Wear warm clothes,' Mary advised. 'It's bitter out, and it'll feel worse with no houses around to keep the heat in. What will you do with Moggie while you're out?'

'I shall leave her by the fire,' Rosie said, and she looked at Jim. 'She's very good, ent she Jim? Ever so clean. She meows at the door to be let out in the garden to do her business, regular as clockwork every morning. No trouble at all. She's quite safe to leave, ent she Jim?'

Her second appeal, being more pointed, drew a wry grin and a grudging admission that she was a good little cat. It felt like a victory.

'Well *I* shan't want to leave her, when I have to go, I can tell you that,' Mary said, tickling the cat behind her ears. 'She's a sweetie.'

'She is,' Rosie agreed, but she was thinking, *Please don't let anyone come and claim her*. Ten days was proving to be a painfully long time. Still, at least she was going to have her stitches out in a couple of days and, once they were out, she might be able to get back to work. You have to take things one step at a time in the middle of a war, she thought, and for someone who'd always rushed at life, that wasn't easy to accept.

*

Friday was a very wintry day. The sky was the colour of pewter, there was a sharp frost in the garden and the air smelled of brick dust from Thursday night's raid. Rosie wrapped herself up in her warmest clothes: her uniform trousers, the jumper she'd borrowed from Sonia, her winter coat with her left arm in the sleeve and her right sleeve dangling and as many buttons done up as she could manage, and added a thick scarf and gloves and an old woolly hat that looked a bit disreputable but at least kept her head warm. Then she set off to walk to the hospital. She went at such a pace she was ten minutes early, but that was all to the good because it gave her a chance to take off her hat, scarf and gloves, and unbutton her coat and make herself look a bit more presentable before she was seen.

She felt at home in outpatients. It smelled like a hospital should; of clean floors and starched aprons and carbolic soap. And the sister who attended her knew who she was.

'Ah!' she said, smiling as she walked into the cubicle. 'Our ambulance driver.'

'You recognise the trousers,' Rosie said.

'I recognise *you*,' the sister said. 'You've brought in a lot of casualties over the last four months. We get to know our regulars. And now you're the casualty. How have you been getting on?'

'Not too bad.'

'Does your arm still pain you?

'The odd twinge now an' then.'

'That's normal. So let's have a look at those stitches.'

The bandages were removed and both hands examined carefully. Then the stitches were taken out, very gently and with approval.

'You've healed very nicely,' the sister said.

'Now all I want is to get this plaster off,' Rosie said. 'Then I can get back to work.'

'You've got a few more weeks to go before we can do that for you,' the sister told her.

It was probably quite the wrong thing to ask, but Rosie asked anyway. 'You wouldn't happen to know when, would you?'

The sister consulted her folder. 'February tenth,' she said. 'Nine thirty.'

Rosie thanked her and took herself off to the waiting room where she'd left her coat and her gloves and things. She was thinking hard. If she had to sit around at home doing nothing till February, she'd go crazy. There was nothing for it but to go to Tooley Street and take a tram to Lower Road and see if Mr Kennedy could find another sort of job for her. Which she did.

There were five people in the station that morning: Mr Kennedy and two crews, and they made her a cup of tea at once and sat her down, to hear her news.

'It *is* good to see you again,' she said, when she showed them her hands and told them how much longer she'd got to wait to have her plaster off. 'I can't wait to get back to work. I feel such a fraud sitting at home doing nothing. I can't drive an ambulance until I can get this cast off, but if there's anything else I could do, I'd do it like a shot. I ent got a uniform no more. They had to cut it off of me, but…'

'Don't worry about the uniform,' Mr Kennedy reassured her. 'We'll get you a new one. You wouldn't like to man the phone of a night time, would you? We've lost two drivers now, so we're a bit hard pressed.'

Rosie didn't answer at once because she was thinking hard, planning it all out in her head. I shall have to get someone to look after Moggie – Sonia can't, because she goes down the tube of a night, but I'll bet old Mrs Totteridge would. I could buy a cat basket for the little thing to sleep in while she's there. I could get here on the tram of an evening and go back on the first one out in the morning and pick her up on my way home.

'Yes,' she said. 'I think I could. It wouldn't be till Monday because I shall have to get things organised, but I could start then.'

So it was agreed.

I won't tell Jim till we've been to the City and seen the bomb sites, Rosie decided as the tram swayed her home. She had a nasty feeling that he wouldn't like it and would try to put her off, so she'd have to choose her moment. He might be in a better mood to accept that they all had to do whatever they could when they'd seen the full extent of the damage for themselves. In the meantime she'd go down and see old Mrs Totteridge and make arrangements for Moggie.

But she didn't have to go down the road because Mrs Totteridge came up, eager to find out how she'd got on with having her stitches out. So naturally Rosie made her a cup of tea and sat her by the fire and displayed her hands, which were approved of.

'You've healed up lovely, ain't she cat?' the old lady said, as she settled her feet on the fender, and the cat jumped into her lap, ready to be stroked and petted.

So it was easy for Rosie to admit that she'd found herself another job at the ambulance station and to add, 'providing I can find someone who'll look after Moggie during the night.'

Mrs Totteridge beamed at her. 'I'll have her if you like,' she said. 'She's a good little cat. She can come in the shelter with me. Bit a company, like. She won't be no trouble, will you, Moggie? You could bring her an old box or a basket or sommink for her to sleep in, couldn'tcher?'

'I'll go down the market, this afternoon, an' see what I can find,' Rosie told her. And did.

What she found was a second-hand cat basket. It was very dirty but it scrubbed up well and, when she'd found an old blanket to arrange in it, it looked quite the thing. She took it down to Mrs T's when it was ready and they installed it in 'just the right place' in her shelter. Now it was simply a matter of finding 'just the right moment' to tell Jim what she'd decided to do. And that, as she knew rather too well, was going to be a long way from simple.

That evening the two of them listened to the six o'clock news as they usually did and were impressed to hear that Winston Churchill had informed the House that afternoon, that he had a message to give 'to the Hun' about the recent bombing of the City. It was short and to the point and, although Rosie didn't know it at the time, it was going to prove very useful to her. 'You do your worst,' he'd said, 'and we shall do our best.'

'You gotta hand it to him,' Jim said, as he laced up his boots. 'He always finds the right words. That's as good as "blood, sweat, toil and tears".' He was still grinning about it as he went off to collect his bike and cycle to the post.

Rosie sat on by the wireless, nursing the cat. She was darning her stockings and wanted to finish them before she had to go down to the shelter. And besides, it was Noel Coward after the news and he was one of her favourite singers despite his upper-class voice. She'd been listening to him ever since he wrote the song called *London*

Pride. She'd heard it so often by then that she knew the words by heart and sang along with him as soon as he began it. '*London Pride has been handed down to us. London Pride is a flower that's free. London Pride means our own dear town to us. And our pride it forever will be.*' It was perfect. It said everything that needed to be said. They *were* proud of their city. And that bold weed was the perfect symbol of how they felt.

That night the sirens sounded when he was in the middle of the song, but she stayed where she was and sang it with him until it was over, feeling daring. The bombers were overhead as she carried Moggie to the shelter, but she didn't care. She felt she was giving them the V sign like Churchill. Damned bombers. This is our city, she thought, and you can't destroy it.

It was a long raid and a very cold night. When she and Moggie came out of the shelter in the morning she could hear the frost crunching under her feet as she walked up the path, and the first thing she did when they reached the kitchen was light the fire. It took a long time to take, and she was shivering by the time she saw the first comforting flames. How odd fire is, she thought, as she sat on her heels and watched it grow. It's such a comfort in the house and such a horror in a raid.

'Now for a cup a' tea,' she said to Moggie. 'An' then I'll find you something to eat.'

The day followed its usual pattern: a trip to the market, meals to cook, dishes to wash, the kitchen floor to scrub one handed, but she was full of edgy impatience, waiting for Sunday and the moment when she would have to tell Jim what she was going to do. From time to time she tried out various conversation openers in her head, but none of them sounded possible or even likely. And when Sunday afternoon arrived and they'd eaten their dinner, washed up and tidied round in their usual way and were ready for their walk to St Paul's, she was no nearer to knowing what she would say than she'd been when she first decided to say it.

It was bitingly cold on London Bridge and icy underfoot, and the Thames was choppy, sullen and grey as putty. Above them, the sun was just a pale disc that gave out very little light and no heat at all, and the sky was the dirty grey of unwashed underwear. The seagulls that wheeled and shrieked over their heads looked snow white by comparison. Rosie shivered and hung on to Jim's arm, but neither of them said anything. They just trudged on towards the bomb site, both of them wondering whether it would really be as bad as it had seemed to be in the photographs.

It was worse. There was virtually nothing left of the buildings that used to crowd the grubby alleys around the great cathedral. The heavy rescue squads had cleared the streets and carted away most of the debris, so that in some places there was nothing left at all except dusty earth and piles of broken bricks. Here and there the wreckage of a wall was still standing, but it was usually blackened by fire and looked crooked, as if it was about to lose its balance and topple over. The cathedral was desolate and dirty. There was hardly anybody about, no traffic in the road and only a handful of locals, wrapped and withdrawn in their winter coats, who walked as if they were in a daze. The place was an eerie wilderness, like something out of a nightmare.

'Dear God!' Rosie said, looking up at Jim. 'I never thought I'd live to see anything like this. They've flattened the place. There's nothing left.'

He put his arm round her and held her as close as he could for the plaster. 'They flattened everything in France,' he said. 'Just the same. There was nothing left there neither, come the finish, no buildings, no trees, no grass. Nothing. There was only dead horses an' corpses an' the stink of that God-awful mud. At least we ain't got *that* here. This smells clean enough. They done a good job cleaning it up.'

'I don't understand it, Jim,' Rosie said. 'I mean, what do they hope to gain by all this? The more they try to destroy us, the more we're going to fight them. Stands to reason. We're not gonna give in.'

'The Dutch gave in,' Jim pointed out, 'an' the Belgians, an' the French. Didn't take 'em no time at all. I s'pose they think we're the same.'

She stuck her chin in the air, in the old familiar gesture. 'Then they'll have to learn to tell the difference,' she said.

'You do your worst an' we shall do our best,' he said, quoting Churchill.

'This is our town,' Rosie said, 'an' we're not gonna run away from it.' And the words of Noel Coward's song came powerfully into her head; she sang them, loud and clear, standing among the wreckage with her chin in the air. '*Every Blitz, your resistance toughening, from the Ritz to the Anchor and Crown. Nothing ever could override the pride of London town.*' And two passers-by stopped in their tracks and listened to her and burst into applause.

'Quite right,' Jim said, caught up in the drama of the moment. 'If they think they can override us, they got another think coming.'

It was too good an opportunity to miss and Rosie took it at once. 'So you won't say no if I tell you I've got a job?' she said.

Caution returned. 'Depends what sorta job.'

'Manning the phone at the ambulance station,' she told him.

He answered her grudgingly. 'Just so long as it ain't driving that amberlance.'

She took his arm and began to walk home. There was no need to talk about driving the ambulance yet. 'Starting tomorrow night,' she said. 'Mrs Totteridge is going to look after Moggie. All right?'

He grinned at her. 'Can't very well say no, can I?'

'No,' she agreed happily. 'You can't.'

CHAPTER TWELVE

Mr Kennedy was very impressed by the way Rosie Jackson handled his incoming calls and told her so at the end of her first week. 'You are commendably calm,' he said.

'There's no point being anything else,' Rosie said, warmed by his praise. 'If there's an incident, the sooner we deal with it, the better.'

'Quite,' he said, smiling at her.

It had been a hard week. There'd been a raid every night and the ambulances had been on call from the first cluster of fallen bombs to the aching relief of the all clear. There was a routine to life in a blitzed city and it was often exhausting. Rosie worked all night and caught the first tram home, as she'd planned, and, since nobody had ever come to claim her cat, she picked her up from Mrs Totteridge on the way back and fed her as soon as they got home. Then Rosie and the cat went upstairs and slept until midday. Jim came wearily up to join them when *he* got home, but they were too sound asleep to notice him.

They swapped such news as they had over their dinner but most of it was predictable and could hardly be called 'news'. That came via the wireless, courtesy of Alvar Lidell, Bruce Belfrage and Stuart Hibberd, and it was usually bad, no matter how skilfully they wrapped it up in their velvety voices.

For a start, because so many merchant ships had been torpedoed, there were going to be serious restrictions on the import of food. There would be no more bananas and only a small quantity of oranges, less wheat and a great deal less sugar. It was a depressing list and it would have a serious effect on Jim's trade. Well over half the nation's food was already home grown, and the Ministry of Food was hoping the percentage would grow even higher. Farmers were urged to grow sugar-beet and a new 'dig for victory' poster, urging gardeners to dig allotments, appeared on the hoardings and at the pictures. It showed a merchant ship divided down the middle with the slogan, '*Use spades, not ships*' on either side of the divide. And to punch the message home, magazines ran columns on cookery, explaining how housewives could make do with less.

Mrs Totteridge wasn't impressed. 'Make do with less,' she scoffed. 'I never heard such tosh. We're skinny enough al-a-ready. We'll be skin an' grief if this goes on, like we was the last time. I hope they don't go putting our beer on the ration.'

'Beer an' skittles,' Jim teased her. 'They're the next thing they got planned.'

It was late on Sunday morning and the old lady had nipped in for a few minutes to see how they were, as she did now that she'd been looking after the cat for nearly three weeks, and especially when there'd been a heavy raid the previous night. In an odd sort of way she'd become a member of the family and was quite at home in their kitchen. Now she was sitting by the fire, enjoying a cup of tea, with her feet on the fender and Moggie on her lap, while Rosie prepared the Sunday dinner, peeling potatoes left-handed, and Jim read the papers.

'Bleedin' Hitler,' Mrs Totteridge said inconsequentially. 'He don't care what he does to no one, just as long as he gets his own bleedin' way. Someone oughter give him a good seeing-to.'

'I'd sort him out mesself,' Jim laughed, 'if it wasn't for the stall.'

'I know you would,' she said. 'You're a good lad. Your gels coming over today, are they?'

'They can't come till Thursday,' Rosie told her, putting the last of the potatoes in the saucepan. 'They're on duty all day today but they'll be here at teatime Thursday. I'm going to make a cake, and then we can have tea and cake while we listen to ITMA.'

It was hard to find a day when they could all be together now that they were all on duty or on stand-by and at so many various times. Rosie had got into the habit of making a timetable week by week, pinning it on her cork board by the dresser so that she could keep tabs on them all.

'That'll be nice,' Mrs Totteridge said. 'That's a good programme that ITMA. I been listening to it ever since this bombing nonsense started up. Wouldn't miss it for worlds.'

'You can come an' join us if you like,' Rosie offered.

'I would an' all, thankee kindly,' the old lady said. 'It'd be lovely. But Sonia comes round of a Thursday. She gets lonely, you know, poor gel. She likes the company.'

You're a good soul, Rosie thought, smiling at her. And it occurred to her, not for the first time, that one of the few good things to come out of this horrible war was that neighbours talked to one another, and offered each other help when it was needed. She knew more about Sonia and Mrs T now than she'd known in all the years they'd lived in the same street, and she was sure it was because they'd only passed the time of day back then and now they were telling her all sorts of things, not just about the latest horrors of the Blitz, but about their lives and how difficult they had been.

Or perhaps it was because she'd got a cat. There was something wonderfully soothing about stroking a purring cat, something about the softness of fur under your fingers and that contented rhythmical sound in your ears. They made confidences possible. Sonia had been stroking the cat when she told her how terribly her husband had suffered when he was dying.

'Consumption's a terrible disease,' she'd said, her face creased with remembered anguish. 'There's so much blood. You'd never believe how much. An' they cough up great chunks a their lungs, come the finish. My poor Charlie. An' only thirty-one.' Her tears dropped on Moggie's head, but the little cat went on purring.

Mrs T had been cuddling Moggie too when she told Rosie how her husband had been killed at Ypres. 'Never stood a chance, poor beggar. Well, none of 'em did, did they? An' that was the end a that. They sent his cap home to me. Fat lot a' good *that* was. An' then, as if that wasn't enough, my little lad took the diphtheria. Only six he was, an' the bleedin' doctor wouldn't so much as look at him until I'd give him his bleedin' half guinea. That was all the money I 'ad. Should ha' lasted me for weeks. Fat lot 'e cared. An' then 'e took one look at the poor little mite an' he says "Diphtheria," he says. "Nothing can be done." An' buggers off. Heartless lot they was them doctors.'

Rosie had made them mugs of sweet tea and hugged them until they'd recovered and told them how well she understood.

'They was bad times,' Mrs Totteridge said. 'An' now here we are again. Gawd 'elp us!'

But they'd remembered the good times too; the larks they used to get up to in the shops and stores and big houses where they'd worked. 'They never knew what we was doing behind the scenes,' Sonia said, laughing.

There were some days when they gossiped so much that Rosie thought it was more like living in Binderton than the Borough, except, of course, that they'd never cuddled the farm cats. She wrote to Kitty or her sisters every morning to tell them they'd got through another raid and were all in one piece, and one or other of them sent her a postcard every day to keep her up with the gossip.

The most recent was lying on the kitchen table at that moment, among the sprouts and potatoes. It was from Tess and it had made Rosie laugh. Now as she set the potatoes on to cook and turned her attention to baking the cake, she read it again.

'We are all well. Connie is as big as a house. You should see her. It's a wonder she don't burst. She says she is heartily sick a being pregnant, what I don't wonder given the size of her. Roll on the end a January an then we will get a bit a piece from her grumbling.'

Jim folded his newspaper and put it on the dresser. 'I'm off to check things over down the post,' he said. 'Shan't be long.'

At which Mrs Totteridge decided she ought to be going too and put the cat on the floor. 'Give my love to the gels,' she said. 'Enjoy your tea Thursday.'

'Oh we shall,' Rosie said.

And they did. It was always so good to be together again, and especially now, when the weather was miserably cold, and the raids went on and on, and the nights were full of injuries and deaths. They sat round the fire and ate Rosie's cake and dreamed of the time when the war would be over, and they could build a better world out of the ruins.

'We've got a long way to go until we get there though,' Gracie warned, looking stern. 'The news from north Africa is dreadful. We keep losing places and re-capturing them and losing them again. I expect you've heard it on the news. They've told the tank corps it's going to be a long campaign.'

The stern expression alerted Rosie. She's worried that her Sam will be sent out there, she thought.

Jim wasn't so tactful. 'Is your feller likely to go there?' he asked. 'Have they told 'em that?'

Gracie answered him calmly. 'Not yet,' she said. 'But it's likely. They're waiting for their new tanks. He's coming down to tell you about it as soon as he can. He said to warn you he wants to see you and talk to you.'

Ah, then he wants to marry her before he goes, Rosie thought. But she didn't say anything in case she'd jumped to the wrong conclusion. They'd know soon enough. And in any case, Mary was changing the subject.

'How's your pregnant sister-in-law?' she asked, grinning at her mother.

'Big as a house and fed up with it, so Tess says,' Rosie told her. 'I got a card this morning. I'll show you presently.'

'When's it due?' Mary said, poking the fire, which was rapidly becoming more ash than flame and needed attention.

'End of January,' Rosie told her, as Jim took the hint and put on more coal. 'Could be any time now.'

Gracie joined in, grinning at them. 'Or it could keep her waiting till the middle of February,' she said. 'You know what babies are like. They come when they're ready.'

'Don't they just,' Mary said. 'D'you remember the one that came in the middle of that awful raid?'

Rosie let her mind wander, drowsed by the warmth of the fire and the ease of being together with Jim and the girls in this comfortable, familiar room. There might be a war on, but here everything was exactly the same as it had always been. The old clock still kept good time, there was still a dent in the fender where it had been battered during the move, Gerry de Silva's picture still held sway over the mantelpiece, the same books were still arranged on the shelves. It was peaceful and soothing. And soporific. After so many months of incessant bombing, she tired easily and slept at any opportunity, lying in the bath, or sitting in an armchair with the cat on her lap as she was then, or even with her elbows propped on the table as she struggled to prepare a meal with her left hand.

She woke to the sound of the opening chorus of ITMA. '*It's that man again. It's that man again. It's that Tommy Handley is here.*' And opened her eyes to see all three members of her family grinning at her.

She defended herself at once. 'I wasn't asleep.'

'No, course you weren't,' Gracie chortled. 'You were resting your eyes.'

So the programme began with a laugh even before the first joke had been cracked. Oh, it *was* good to be together.

*

January limped by on chilblained feet. The raids continued, although, to everyone's relief, not every night. The weather was dismal, far too many people had coughs and colds, there was less food in the shops, Rosie grew more and more fatigued, and the news from north Africa was depressing.

'We need some good news to cheer us up,' Rosie said, when Jim folded up his newspaper and sighed.

But when the good news came, it didn't lift her out of her fatigue at all.

It was the last day of January and half way through the morning, and she was yawning down the stairs, sleeping off her night shift and still feeling much too tired, when the phone rang.

'Yes?' she said as she picked up the receiver.

'It's a girl,' an excited voice said. 'Eight pounder. Born in the middle of the night. Wouldn't you know it? Half past one. You should've heard the row she made, screaming an' hollering an' carrying on. They could hear her the other side a the village. Mr Tennant gave me a lift into Chichester. That was nice of him. He's a good neighbour, even if she *did* keep him awake all night. He said they could hear her right over there. Imagine! They're going to call her Maggie after Mum. Ent that lovely?'

Rosie stood in the hall with the receiver in her hand, feeling chilly and confused. It was such a rigmarole, and she was so tired she couldn't make any sense of it. 'Tess?' she said.

'Course,' Tess' voice said. 'Who else would it be, you daft ha'porth? Ent it good news? Whatcher think a the name? Another Maggie, eh?'

'Yes,' Rosie said. 'Very nice.' But she didn't have the energy to enthuse about it. All she wanted was to get into the kitchen, light the fire and make herself a cup of tea and sit as close to the warmth as she could get while she drank it.

Tess was still talking. 'Pa says when can you get down to see her?'

'I'll have to look at my timetable,' Rosie said. 'I'll let you know.'

She could hear Tess drawing in breath for her next question and struggled to think of something positive to say, but fortunately she was saved by the pips. And thank God for that, she thought, as she headed for the kitchen and the warmth she needed. The cat was waiting patiently by her bowl. The fire was laid. The teapot was standing ready. If only she wasn't quite so tired.

She sat by the fire with the cat purring on her lap for a very long time, drinking tea and waiting for the fire to warm up – and thinking. It wasn't like her to feel so tired that she couldn't take in what Tess was saying. But since she'd been blown across the road by that horrible bomb, she'd been constantly aware of the danger they were all in and the knowledge exhausted her. She'd known it in a vague sort of way ever since the Blitz began – how could anyone be off knowing it? – but now she knew it in her bones, aware every time she left her house in the evening, that it might be blown to pieces when she came back in the morning, waiting hour by hour during the night for news of one incident after another, knowing there would be people there who would be killed or dying or horribly badly injured.

Eventually, she had to bestir herself to build up the fire and, since she was on her feet, she went to look at her timetable and find out when she could go down to Binderton. She discovered that the first day that was possible wasn't until Monday. So, feeling dutiful, she put on her coat and went into the cold front room where she wrote a postcard to Tess, left-handed, which was the only way she could write those days and which was still awkward and ugly no matter how much effort she put into it. But she managed to tell her which day she'd be coming. Then she shivered down to the postbox to post it. They were such small tasks to do but, when she got home again, she felt as tired as if she'd done a full day's work.

As she inched the key into the lock, the phone began to ring, but by then she was so tired she lugged a chair out of the living room and sat down before she answered it.

'This'll have to be quick,' Gracie's voice said. 'Is it OK for me an' Sam to come an' see you an' Dad at teatime on Friday?'

'Hang on a minute an' I'll look at my timetable,' Rosie said, and did, discovering that she and Jim were both off duty that day. 'Yes,' she said, picking up the phone again. 'That's OK. I'll see if I can make a cake.' Then she thought she ought to pass on the family news. 'Your aunt's had her baby. Little girl. I'm going down to see her on Monday.'

'Good,' Gracie said in her brisk way. 'You can tell me all about it on Friday, and we've got lots to tell you. Got to go. I'm on duty.'

They're going to tell us they want to get married, Rosie thought as she hung up the receiver. It's bound to be. Especially if he's going to be sent to north Africa. And she felt warm with affection for both of them, knowing what was ahead of them.

*

That Monday morning was bitterly cold. There was a vicious north wind, which pushed Rosie sideways as she walked home and bit at her cheeks until they were sore. I shall be glad to get indoors and light a fire, she thought as she struggled against it with Moggie yowling in her basket.

'Soon be there,' she said, and it was as much to comfort herself as the cat. It was going to be a cold journey to Binderton.

It was a great relief to open the kitchen door and find that Jim was already home and had got the fire lit and the kettle boiling.

'Rough night?' he asked as she let the cat out of the basket. It was only just a question.

'So-so,' she said vaguely, looking in the larder for the scraps she'd left for the cat. 'I could go a cup a' tea.'

It was on the table before she sat down.

'You look all in, kid,' Jim said, watching her as she drank.

'I am.'

'Whatcher want for breakfast?' he asked. 'Don't worry. I'm the cook. Bacon an' egg be alright? Then I'll get you wrapped up warm for your journey. Got to look after you.'

Which he did, escorting her to the tube and buying her a ticket to Victoria and kissing her goodbye very gently, as if she was fragile and likely to break.

'Take care a yourself,' he said, and watched until she'd disappeared down the escalator.

It was warm in the tube, which made her feel sleepy, and warm among the crowds in Victoria station. But once she was on board the train to Chichester, she wasn't just warm. She was so tired she knew she'd be rocked to sleep as soon as it moved, and thought she'd better check whether there was any one in her compartment who was going to Chichester and could wake her up when she reached the stop.

A quiet woman sitting opposite her volunteered that she would do it, adding, 'You look all in.'

'I've been on duty all night,' Rosie told her.

'Ah well, that accounts,' the woman said, smiling at her. 'Don't worry. I'll look after you.'

How kind people are, Rosie thought, but she didn't have time to say so because sleep was already drifting her away.

She slept until the train was pulling into Chichester, and she dozed on the train to Lavant, and consequently she arrived at Pa's cottage feeling more like herself. And once there, she was rushed upstairs to see the new baby before she'd had a chance to take off her coat and gloves and unwind her scarves.

It worried her that she felt absolutely nothing for the baby at all, even though her sisters were cooing over it. She thought it was fat and rather ugly and decidedly smelly, that was all, with small piggy eyes. She agreed with Tess when she said 'Ent she lovely?' because it wouldn't have done to upset her, but she felt nothing. A piglet would have been much prettier. It wasn't until they led her downstairs and skinned off her coat and scarves and sat her down at the table that she realised her lack of feeling was because she was too tired to feel anything. Now that she was sitting down waiting for Tess and Kitty to serve the meal, she knew that all she wanted to do was go to sleep. She didn't even have the energy to talk to Pa, who was sitting in his usual chair at the head of the table, looking frail and pale and smiling at her.

'How's your arm?' Kitty said, coming in with the joint.

'Heavy,' Rosie told her.

'You'll be glad to get that horrible thing took off,' Pa said.

'Yes,' Rosie said, thinking what a dear he was and how much she loved him.

'You look wore out,' Kitty said.

'I been on night duty.'

'Ah. That accounts. D'you want to go up an' have a lie down?'

Rosie shook her head. 'No,' she lied. 'I'm all right. Just a bit tired.'

Tess and Edie were carrying in the vegetables. 'Get some a this inside you,' Edie advised. 'Good stuff, is this. That'll put some colour in your cheeks.'

Rosie ate as much of the meal as she could so as to please them and remembered to ask after their children. She was told that the twins couldn't wait to get to work on the farm with their uncle Johnnie, Edie's Frank had settled in well as a footplate man on the railways and that Tess' daughter Anna was working as a milkmaid on a farm in Lavant, 'although,' as Tess said rather sourly, 'why she couldn't work on one of our farms I really don't know.' There was so much information that it made Rosie's head spin, and although she made more or less appropriate answers, she forgot most of it as soon as it was spoken. It was no surprise to her later that day, when she was on her way back home, that she slept right through the second stage of her journey and only woke when the train was pulling into Victoria.

If only we could have a night without an air raid, she thought as she yawned down the escalator. But Hitler had other plans.

That night the sirens sounded ten minutes after Jim had cycled off to the wardens' post and, as she was off duty, there was nothing for it but to put on her boots, her greatcoat and her balaclava helmet, gather all the things she needed and put them in the basket, checking them off as she did it – thermos flask of tea, torch, hot water bottle – tuck her rolled up bedding under her arm, pick up the cat and head off to the shelter.

It was dank and very cold out there and smelt of mud and damp.

'I hate war,' she said to Moggie as they settled into their uncomfortable bed, but the cat just purred and snuggled deeper into the eiderdown. 'If they'd only stop all this awful bombing, it wouldn't be so bad –but they don't, do they? They just keep on and on. We're into our seventh month of it now an' I'm worn out with it.' It was possible to confess things to the cat that she would've kept to herself if there'd been anyone else around. 'I don't know how much longer I can keep going, to tell the truth,' she said. 'It's like having a ton weight on your back all the time, pressing you down an' down an' down. An' I'll bet the buggers come back tomorrow. Bound to. I'm on duty. Hark at 'em now. They're right overhead. Bleedin' Germans! They should never have been born. Roll on Friday. That's what I say. I could do with some good news.'

The news for the rest of that week was generally depressing, although out in Africa, the Italian troops were surrendering in droves. There were pictures of them walking along in dismal lines with their hands in the air and two grinning Australians guarding them, which everyone in the market that morning thought was a very good thing. But the German reaction to it wasn't good at all. They were sending one of their crack panzer units to Africa, under a newly-promoted lieutenant general called Rommel. The news was all across the front page when Sam and Gracie came to tea.

'Whatcher reckon to all this then?' Jim asked, pointing to the paper when they were settled round the fire.

'Not good,' Sam said, taking his cup of tea from Rosie. 'Rommel's got a powerful reputation. An' our generals are just a load of old fuddy-duddies. He'll make mincemeat of 'em.'

'They was fuddy-duddies last time,' Jim said, grimacing. 'Didn't have the first nor last idea how to run a war.'

'We need a good strong general to oppose this new one,' Sam said, 'an' that's a fact. I hope to God we get one before we get sent out.'

'Any idea when that'll be?' Rosie asked, glancing at her daughter's serious face.

'Not yet,' Sam told her. 'The first lot'll go in March, so they say. We've got to wait for our new tanks.'

And I hope you wait a good long time, Rosie thought, but she didn't say so because Gracie was giving Sam a meaningful look. And he was grinning at her.

'Well, go on,' Gracie said. 'Tell them.'

'OK Bossy-Boots,' he said. 'Have a bit a patience.' And he turned to look at Jim and Rosie. 'She thinks we ought to tell you something,' he explained. And then stopped.

'Well go on then,' Gracie urged.

Sam took a visibly deep breath. 'The thing is,' he said, 'we want to get married.'

Rosie could feel her smile spreading all over her face. 'That's wonderful,' she said. 'When?'

'Well, pretty soon really,' Sam told her, smiling back. 'April or May perhaps? As soon as we can. Before I get sent out, anyway. I've put in for some leave.'

'We'll start organising it tomorrow,' Rosie promised him. 'Won't we, Jim?'

'No,' Jim said sternly, 'we won't. Sorry kids, but we ain't doing a thing till she's got that great lump a concrete off her arm. It's wearing her out.'

'Quite right,' Gracie said, laughing. 'We can't have you worn out. When's your appointment?'

'Monday,' Rosie told her. 'And we'll go shopping up Petticoat Lane the first chance we get afterwards. I promise. You can still get some splendid outfits up there.'

Sam was looking baffled so Jim enlightened him. 'It's a family tradition,' he said. 'All the brides in this family have to get their dresses from Petticoat Lane. Every single one a them. It's the first rule a the wedding.'

'Oh well,' Sam said, grinning at him, 'if that's the case, who am I to argue?'

Gracie turned towards him on the sofa and kissed him full on the lips. 'Wise man,' she said. 'Never argue with Mum when she's in one of her organising moods.'

He was a bit abashed to be kissed so openly in front of his future in-laws but they were all beaming at him so happily, he soon recovered and grinned back at them.

'Now then,' Rosie said. 'First things first. Where do you want to have this wedding? Church or registry office?'

They answered at the same time but with different words; he saying 'registry office,' she saying 'church.' Which made them all laugh. And one of the burning coals hissed at them as if it was disapproving. Which made them laugh again.

'I s'pose you could have both if you wanted,' Rosie said, grinning at them. 'It would take longer but…'

It was a problem that needed disentangling but they were all in such a happy mood it was easily done. 'Is it important to you to be married in a church?' Sam asked, blue eyes earnest.

'I think it would be more serious,' Gracie told him. 'As if we really meant it.'

'Wouldn't you really mean it in a registry office?' he teased.

'Yes, idiot,' Gracie said. 'You know I would. But it would be more serious in a church. I like the vows. I think we'd mean them.'

He was suddenly serious. 'Yes,' he said. 'We would.' And hugged her.

'Sold to the lady in the nurse's cap,' Jim said, bringing his fist down on the table so hard that the milk jug jumped in the air.

At which they all laughed and grinned at each other. Problem solved. Easily and with affection. And Rosie thought what a good pair they were going to make, and was lifted into a flowing happiness she hadn't felt since the Blitz began.

*

It was still flooding her senses as she walked to Guy's that Monday morning. It was cold out there in the streets, so she kept up a brisk pace to keep warm. The place smelt of last night's air raid, and she noticed that there were several new bombsites, some still smoking, but there was still good in the world and the possibility of happiness despite everything, and they were going to have a wedding. And in a few minutes time, she'd have this 'great chunk a concrete' taken off her arm, and she could get on with her life properly again.

It was quite a disappointment to discover that her arm felt weak when it was released from the plaster and that it was horribly shrunk and wrinkled.

'I look like a lizard,' she said.

'That's normal,' the nurse told her, smiling. 'It's actually healed very nicely. Have a warm bath, and put plenty of hand cream on it, and you won't know yourself. I'll give you some exercises to do to strengthen it. They'll be a bit painful to start with but persevere with them. The more regularly you do them, the quicker you'll get your strength back.'

'The quicker the better,' Rosie said. 'I've got an ambulance to drive.'

'Take your time,' the nurse advised.

But Rosie had no intention of doing any such thing, and that afternoon she stuck her chin in the air, mounted her bike and rode off to the ambulance station, feeling that even if her arm did hurt a bit, her life had returned to normal at last.

Three nights later she took her new ambulance out for the first time. Sister Maloney was with her, which was reassuring but, even so, she felt unexpectedly nervous, aware that she was out in the open, without any shelter, and knowing how painful it was to be injured. It took her several nights to relax into confidence again, and that made her feel ashamed of herself for being so weak for so long.

But she kept her feelings to herself because there was work to be done, and she was there to do it.

CHAPTER THIRTEEN

'Come on, kid,' Jim said, standing at the kitchen door. 'Aintcher ready? I got work to do an' I can't leave young Josh on his own much longer.'

'I feel so sorry for those poor daffodils,' Rosie said, gazing at them. Yesterday afternoon, when she'd opened the door to let the cat in, they'd been nothing more than a row of tight green buds, but now they were in full bloom, and the one remaining border in her garden was bright with them, fluttering and dancing on their long stalks, yellow as butter.

Jim didn't have time for flowers. 'Are you coming or aintcher?' he said.

'They're so young,' Rosie mourned, 'an' so pretty.' She was full of anguished emotion, struggling to find the words she wanted. 'Innocent. Vulnerable. Standing here in the garden, not doing any harm to anybody. And now they're going to be bombed and blown to bits, or burnt black in one of those awful fires, and covered with filth and debris. It's not fair. What did they ever do to deserve that?'

Her mind was choked with terrible images, the unearthly brightness of exploding bombs, the size of those huge fires, dead bodies laid out on the pavements; filthy dirty and torn to pieces, wounded children crying and groaning.

'What did any of us do?' Jim said bitterly. 'That's bleedin war for you.'

She turned to look at him and, with a spasm of sudden pity, he saw that her face was fraught and her eyes were full of tears. 'Oh Jim,' she said. 'When are they going to stop? How much more have we got to put up with? They can't go on forever.'

He was across the garden in two strides and had his arms around her, holding her against his chest, kissing her forehead and her tangled hair. 'Oh my dear gel,' he said. 'You've got battle fatigue.'

'What?' she said, looking up at him.

He tried to explain. 'Battle fatigue,' he told her. 'We had it in the trenches. A lot of us did. We was stuck out there in that bleedin' mud, with bits a bodies an' dead horses everywhere an' lice crawling all over us all the time, an' great fat rats running about everywhere you looked, an' it stank to high heaven, an' we thought it would go on an' on until there weren't a soul left alive. It feels as if you're sort a sinking in it. Ain't that right? As if it's just gonna go on an' on, an' there'll never be any end to it.'

'Yes,' she said. That was exactly what she was feeling. As if there was no hope for any of them. As if they were all stuck in a trap and nobody cared, and the bombers would go on and on until there was no one left.

'But we was wrong,' he said, stroking her face. 'There *was* an end. It was just a bloody long time coming, that was all. We got there come the finish.'

A blackbird perched at the top of the may tree and began to sing, but every note was a needle reminding Rosie how close to death they all were. 'An' millions was killed,' she said.

'Yes,' he agreed. 'They was, poor sods. But they couldn't kill all of us. *We're* still here, you an' me an' the gels. Still here, keeping up the good work.'

It was comfort of a sort and she recognised it even if she couldn't share it. 'You'd better get to the market,' she said. 'Poor ol' Josh'll wonder what's become of you. I'll get my hat on.'

They walked up the Borough High Street, comfortingly arm in arm, past the tube station and the bakers and that stupid war memorial that he hated so much, and into the noise and bustle of the market, where Josh had a queue of customers, first among them being old Mrs Totteridge and Sonia Cohen.

'Oh there you are, mate,' Mrs Totteridge called out to Jim. 'We thought you'd left the country. Didn't we Sonia?'

'We was just gonna send out a search party,' Sonia said, grinning at him.

'All right, all right,' Jim said, grinning back at them. 'Put a sock in it. Now then, what can I do for you?'

It was all so familiar and warm and friendly that Rosie knew it should have lifted her spirits just listening to it, but it didn't. Nevertheless, she stuck her chin in the air and squared her shoulders and set off to do her shopping, determined not to give in, even if that was what she really wanted to do. Battle fatigue, she thought, as she headed for the butcher's, ration book in her hand. It's about right, because this *is* a battle, no matter which way you look at it. Please God don't let *this* one go on for four years.

The day staggered on, dragging its feet. Even the cat was lethargic, and all Rosie wanted to do was lie down and sleep for weeks. It was a great relief to her when the sirens didn't sound that night.

'We've got another night off,' Mr Kennedy said, when she rang him, 'so we shan't need you till tomorrow. Make the most of it. They'll be back again tomorrow night, you can bet your bottom dollar.'

It was luxury to sleep in her own bed with Moggie at her feet and Jim beside her, warm and comfortable and comforting. She could almost imagine there was no war going on at all, and she surprised herself by sleeping well. And then, as if she were being rewarded for good behaviour, she found a postcard from Tess on the door mat when she got up, with the news that the baby was going to be christened on Sunday week, after the service. '*We hope you can come*,' she wrote. '*It seems a long time since we last seen you.*'

'You'll go, won't you?' Jim said. He looked so hopeful and encouraging, and there was such a lot of grey hair at his temples now, and she'd loved him so much and for so long that she assured him she would. But she knew he was hoping it would cheer her up and, given how deeply down into hideous thoughts she'd fallen, she couldn't be at all sure of *that*. My poor Jim, she thought. This is every bit as bad for him as it is for me and he don't make any fuss about it at all, and here I am, groaning and moping about and complaining. I must make more of an effort. And she stuck up her chin once again and smiled at him, and was rewarded with a kiss.

But in the middle of an air raid, vowing to make more of an effort and actually making it were two very different things, as she discovered that night.

It was a very heavy raid and she and Sister Maloney were called out as soon as they'd driven their ambulance into the holding bay.

'Block of flats,' Mr Kennedy said when he'd given them the address. 'Direct hit.'

'Holy Mary, Mother of God!' Sister Maloney said as they drove onto the site. 'I should just think it *was* a direct hit. That was a mine, if I'm any judge. Will you look at the size of that crater!'

The site was full of rescue teams digging by floodlight, their white helmets glinting in the artificial light. Half the block was still standing, but a huge chunk had been blown out of the other half, and the debris from it had fallen into a pile that covered twice as much ground as it had taken when it was standing, filling the pavements and the roadway to almost as far as the flats on the other side of the road. As there was nothing they could do for the moment, they sat in the ambulance and watched until two men from the nearest rescue team lifted a limp body from the pile and laid it on the nearest stretch of clear ground.

'That's the first of them,' Sister Maloney said in her brisk way. 'Come on.'

Rosie didn't need telling. She was already out of the ambulance and striding along the road to her casualty. This was a major incident, and the sooner they started dealing with the injured, the better. But she hadn't gone more than six paces before she realised that this wasn't a casualty, but a dead body. Even from where she stood she could see that it was a young woman, that her left arm had been torn off and there was a gash in her side so deep that her intestines were exposed. The two men straightened their backs and looked across the debris at Rosie and Sister Maloney.

'Two for the morgue here,' the nearest man said, as they approached.

'Two?' Rosie asked.

'She had a kiddie,' the man said, looking down at the body.

Rosie looked too. Lying in the crook of the girl's remaining arm was a very small, very pretty baby. It couldn't have been more than a few weeks old and, although it wasn't torn to pieces, it was filthy dirty just like the girl, smeared with soot and brick-dust and grime, and obviously dead, its little round face pearl white, its eyes tightly closed and plainly not breathing. So young and so pretty, Rosie thought, and killed like this. She was overwhelmed with pity for them both. It was what she'd felt for her daffodils, only a hundred times worse. War is a wicked, cruel business, she thought. What have these two poor young things ever done to deserve a death like this? That girl's barely out of her teens, and her baby's been killed before it had a chance to know it was alive. She was yearning with useless pity for them, aching with it.

And then her belly began to shake, and she knew she was going to be sick and had to turn away from them to vomit.

'We're needed over there, so we are,' Sister Maloney said, gently. 'Are you up to it?'

Rosie made a tremendous effort to recover, breathing deeply to get herself under control. There was work to be done, and she was there to do it. 'Course,' she said, wiping her mouth on her handkerchief. 'Come on.'

For the rest of the night she worked automatically, saying the comforting things to her casualties, '*We've got you. You're all right*', carrying stretchers, cleaning the ambulance, driving through streets littered with debris, doing whatever she could to keep the nightmare away.

It returned to reduce her to anguished tears when the all clear had finally sounded and she was back home and asleep in her own bed. She woke with a start, her heart juddering, and cried in Jim's arms for a very long time, as he gentled her damp hair out of her eyes and tried to comfort her. 'Don't cry, my little one. I've got you. You're all right.'

'It'll never be all right,' she wept. 'Never. Not till this God-awful Blitz is over.'

'No,' he said sadly, 'you're right. It won't. It was a bad night.'

'It was bloody awful,' she said, and told him about it as he held her and kissed her hair. He was torn by the state she was in, because he understood exactly how she felt and couldn't think what to do to help her. But eventually she fell asleep again and slept fairly peacefully, as far as he could tell. He lay awake beside her, struggling to find something he could do or say to help her. And failing. The only hope he had was that the christening would cheer her. And maybe the girls would have some ideas.

The next morning he got up relatively early, leaving her asleep, and crept downstairs as quietly as he could so as not to wake her. Then he made himself tea and toast, fed the cat, and got ready for work. And, just before he left the house, he tiptoed into the front room and found two postcards and the stamps to match, and put them in his pocket.

It was a busy morning, and for the first two hours he was too hard at work serving his customers to think of anything else, but when there was a lull, he took his postcards out of his pocket, found the stub of a pencil in the till and sat down to write to his daughters.

They were short notes, because he found writing anything rather difficult, but they were to the point, and the point was affectionate.

'Your Mum is a bit upset. The air raids are getting on top of her. I hope the chrissening will cheer her but it mite not. Could you come over Sunday to be there when she gets home?'

They answered him by return of post and wrote their postcard together.

'We have arranged our shifts and will be there at teatime. Don't worry. We will think of something between us. We can't have her upset.'

They're such good girls, he thought, as he hid the postcard in his pocket. And looking at their bold, elegant writing, he felt hopeful for the first time in days.

*

That Sunday was a bright spring day and, now that the weather had improved, the trains were running on time, so the journey to Binderton was easy. Rosie arrived at St Mary's as the congregation was gathering for the service, so she was able to greet some of her neighbours as they walked in together through the slender archway and under the lantern, which cheered her. It seemed right and proper to be in the church again, sitting in the usual pew among her chattering family, waiting for Father Selwyn to make his important entrance and looking round at the curved choir stalls and the golden pipes of the organ, and the stained glass windows shining sky blue above the altar. She'd seen it all from this same pew, on every Sunday of her childhood until she went away to Arundel, and although it didn't lift her spirits, she felt she fitted there.

But when the service was over, and the family had gathered around the font for the christening, and the three godparents were holding their candles and promising to renounce the devil and all his ways, and the little, fat baby, who looked more like a piglet than ever, was looking puzzled, having just had water sprinkled across her forehead, she was suddenly and unexpectedly seized by that terrible memory. The dead baby lay on the ground before her, pearl white and perfect and inexorably dead, tucked into the crook of the filthy arm of its poor mangled mother. And within a second she was completely overwhelmed and finding it hard to breathe, just as she'd been at the incident, and the need to weep was so overpowering that she had to cover her face with her hands as if she was praying, so that none of them would notice the state she was in. It was a useless ploy because Kitty saw through it at once.

'Not like you to be praying,' she observed as they walked back to the cottage arm in arm. 'I thought you was an atheist like our Jim.'

'I don't know what I am, to be truthful,' Rosie said. 'I can't believe in a "God of Love" when I see all the dreadful things that are going on in London.'

'Bad?' Kitty asked, her face wrinkled with concern.

'Dreadful,' Rosie admitted. 'Don't let's talk about it.'

So Kitty changed the subject and they walked on, still arm in arm and talking about how well the christening had gone. And then there was the breakfast to be eaten and family news to catch up with, and she sat next to Pa and served him whatever he fancied and talked to him nearly all the time. She was worried by how frail he looked, but he was quite himself and so pleased to see her it warmed her to be with him.

And when the meal was over, and they were clearing the table, and she was passing his cup and plate to Kitty, he caught hold of her arm and said something so unexpected and loving that it took her by surprise.

'You're a good gel, my Rosie. You allus was, helping with your Ma an' all, an' looking after the little'uns, an' a-going off to work without a bit of fuss, when you wassen much more than a little'un yourself. Dear little soul you was. An' now you're driving that great amberlance about in all the bombs. I take my hat off to ee, so I do. You make me proud as Punch an' that's a fact.' And he gave her hand a squeeze and raised it to his lips and kissed it.

'Oh Pa!' she said. 'What a lovely thing to say.'

'Meant every word,' he said, smiling at her. 'You're a dear, good gel.'

It buoyed her up to be so lovingly praised, especially as she wasn't expecting it. She carried the dirty dishes out to the kitchen feeling there were good things in the world after all, and when she left her family to walk across the fields and catch her train, she kissed them all and promised she would come back and see them again as soon as she could. But once she was on the train going home, the terrible images broke into her mind again; needle-sharp and unavoidable, and she wept because she couldn't do anything else and there was no family to see her and be upset by her. Her fellow travellers smiled at her sadly, but none of them said anything. Grief was too commonplace to provoke comment in those bomb-shattered days.

By the time she reached Victoria Station she had recovered herself and went down the escalator like any ordinary traveller; blank-faced and patient. She would soon be home and that was what mattered. Home with her dear, understanding Jim. She opened the door, feeling limp with relief, and there was her dear Gracie walking out to greet her, and two paces behind her, her dear, serious Mary.

'Oh,' she said, 'if I'd known you were coming, I'd've got a special tea for you.'

'Don't worry,' Gracie said laughing. 'We're going to have special fish an' chips. We've got it all planned.'

It was a splendid understatement. She and Mary and their father had planned this evening over tea in the front room and arranged it all down to the last word that was to be spoken. 'We must sweep her along,' Gracie had said. 'Keep her focussed on the pleasant things. And there *are* pleasant things. It'll just be a matter of getting her to see them.'

She moved into action as she'd helped her mother out of her coat and hung it on the coat stand. 'We've come here to talk about the wedding,' she said. 'I've got a list of the people Sam wants to invite. There aren't many because he hasn't got any relations at all, except for his mother and an aunt.' She was leading them all into the front room as she spoke. 'We can have our fish and chips while we plan things, can't we?' Now she grinned at her father and gave him his instructions. 'Off you go, Dad.'

He saluted her mockingly. 'Yes sir, boss.' And went.

'Now then,' Gracie said, 'let's start.' She took a list out of her pocket and put it on the kitchen table in front of her mother. 'It's a bit short, as you can see.'

There were nine names on it, neatly written, one below the other.

'Is this all?' Rosie said, feeling quite sorry to think that this was all the family Sam had. There must be more of them, surely.

'Apparently,' Gracie said, sitting down beside her mother and looking at the list. 'It's a bit sad, really. That's his mother, and next one's his aunt Maud, who lives in the same house – she and Ruth brought him up so they're very close – and the others are his mates from the tank corps.

Cuthbert O'Connor's his best man. They were together at Dunkirk. I haven't met him yet, but he's always talking about him. He calls him Bertie.'

'So who are we going to invite from our side of the family?' Mary said.

'Everybody,' Gracie said cheerfully. 'Why not?'

'We don't want to overwhelm his people,' Rosie said.

That made Gracie laugh. 'They're tankies,' she said. 'You can't overwhelm tankies! They're the toughest things in shoe leather.'

So Gracie's list was written – Kitty and the twins, Pa, Johnnie and Connie and the baby, Edie and Joey and Frank and Dorothy, Tess and Sydney and Anna and Dickie. And after a little thought, they added Mrs Taylor, because as Gracie said, 'she's as near family as dammit.'

'Right,' Gracie said. 'So that's done.' And she moved on to the next part of their plan. 'Now we've got to decide where we're going have the reception and when we're going to get our dresses. Don't you think so, Dad?'

Jim had just come in with two plates full of fish and chips but he said, 'It could be here,' following their plan. 'Whatcher think, Rosie? If we was to shift the furniture about a bit.'

Rosie was taking an interest almost despite herself. 'Be a bit of a squash,' she said.

'When have we ever minded a squash?' Mary said, laughing, as her father went off to collect the rest of their supper. 'Think how squashed we've always been in Binderton. It's part of the fun.'

'Trestle tables and benches,' Gracie said, decidedly.

'Well…' Rosie said, trying to get her thoughts in order.

'You get extra rations for a wedding,' Jim said. 'I'll go down the food office an' see to it. Nice ham maybe. I'll bet ol' Mrs T an' your Sonia would give us a hand. You'll have to eat this on your lap.'

The girls said 'OK,' but Rosie took her plate and went on with her thoughts about the wedding breakfast. 'If they do, we ought to give them an invite,' she said. 'That'd only be fair.'

'Good idea,' Gracie approved, shaking vinegar on her chips. 'Why not? They've been good neighbours to us.'

Rosie felt as if she'd just eaten an enormous meal and was still trying to digest it all. 'Well…' she said again.

'So now,' Gracie said, 'it's just the dresses. You were saying something about a trip to Petticoat Lane. How about next Sunday?'

Rosie blinked at the speed they were moving. 'Can you get the time off?' she said.

'Leave it to us,' Gracie told her.

*

She phoned two days later to say that everything was arranged. 'Look out your best bib and tucker,' she said to Rosie. 'We'll be with you at eight o'clock, sharp.'

'The speed of these girls,' Rosie said to Jim, as she hung up the receiver. She was beginning to feel swept off her feet. 'I hope there isn't a long raid Saturday night, or we'll all be like bits a' chewed string by eight o'clock in the morning.'

'No, you won't,' Jim said, pleased that their plans were working so well. 'It'll be a lark.'

And it was, even though it started with a set-back because the first tram that came along stopped running at the Borough.

'Road's blocked,' the conductor explained as his passengers got off.

'Not to worry,' Mary said, taking her mother's arm, 'we'll take the tube to Liverpool Street instead.'

So they all went giggling off to the tube. The air that wafted into the trains every time the doors opened was as ripe as ever, but they were used to the smell of sweat and piddle now and didn't comment on it. They changed at Bank, still chatting and giggling, and were jostled along the tiled corridors to the Central Line, where they took another train to Liverpool Street, and then they were out in the London air again, and *that* smelt of brick dust and smoke with traces of gas as it usually did after a raid, which made them feel quite at home. And then they were walking down Middlesex Street arm in arm and breathing in the pungent smell of old clothes.

'London's a smelly old place,' Rosie said affectionately.

It was a disappointment to her when they reached Mr Levy's shop and found it was being run by someone else, but Mr Segal was still there, his beard as long and tangled as ever, and full of his usual kindness.

'A vedding, my darlinks,' he said, clapping his hands with delight, when Rosie explained what they were looking for. 'Such a joy! Vait there. I see vhat I find for you.' And he disappeared into the darkness of his shop, leaving Rosie and her girls on the pavement, where they were engulfed in the passing crowds and watched as people picked over the clothes on his stall. He returned about ten minutes later with his hands full of bulging carrier bags and two rather grand dresses over one arm; one pale pink and the other pale blue.

'These vas a pair,' he said. 'Tailor made for two pretty sisters, but they sold them to me you understand, bride and bridesmaid. This vas the bride's,' holding up the pink dress, 'and this the bridesmaid's,' showing them the blue one. 'Crepe you see, vhat is the softest material you can find. Feel it.' And he held out the bride's dress, and Gracie felt it between finger and thumb and smiled at him

'It's like silk,' she said to Rosie. 'Feel it, Mary. Could we try them on?'

They could. Oh indeed they could. 'My vife, she vill help you,' Mr

Segal said. 'Plenty dressing room ve have. But just vait a second. I have shoes to match, d'you see, and liddle hats, vhat is the latest style. Vhat you think?' He produced them from the carrier bags with a flourish and laid them on the nearest chair.

Gracie made up her mind in an instant. 'Come on,' she said to Mary. 'Let's see if they fit. I'll take mine and you take yours.' And they disappeared with the hats, shoes and dresses into the shadows at the back of the shop.

It seemed to Rosie that they were gone a very long time, but she waited as patiently as she could while Mr Segal attended to the customers crowding round his stall and, when he wasn't busy, she asked what had happened to Mr Levy and was told he'd been bombed out and gone away.

'So many bombs ve have had,' Mr Segal sighed. 'Whole streets gone. Not a single brick left standing. Flattened.' He spread his hands in despair at the waste of it all.

Rosie couldn't answer him because the terrible visions were back again, bruising her brain. How could the Germans be so cruel? she thought. They must know what they're doing. Nobody can plead ignorance. Not now. We've seen enough pictures of bombed cities, God knows.

But then, just as she was slipping toward tears, she was rescued by a very different picture. Gracie and Mary were walking out of the shop doorway, looking so glamorous in their wedding dresses that the sight of them made her heart leap. The dresses had looked elegant when they were draped over Mr Segal's arm, but worn by her two darlings, they were superb. They hung so well for a start, almost as if they'd been made for them, and they looked so soft, and were wonderfully stylish with their high, round necklines and their hip-length bodices and those splendid skirts. Mary's was neatly pleated, which suited her quieter character to perfection. And those dear little hats set them off perfectly, the wide brims framing their faces. We could put flowers in those brims, she thought, to match their bouquets. I shall have to take in the seams here and there to get a perfect fit. But really she couldn't have asked for anything better, and from the look on her daughter's faces, neither could they. She stood for several seconds, just drinking in the sight of them, from the pretty hats to the elegant shoes. Court shoes, no less, and a perfect match for the dresses. And Mr Segal stood to one side, beaming at them all.

She bought both outfits, naturally, after the usual gentle bargaining, and then the girls went off to change and Mr Segal wrapped the dresses in tissue paper and laid them neatly in long cardboard boxes, and the hats and shoes were put back in their carrier bags, and the three of them set off to take the tube back home, feeling triumphant. It had been the best day out in years.

The joy of it kept Rosie going through the next week, even though there were two bad raids, which left her exhausted, and it rained incessantly. And to make matters worse, their stocks of coal were running low and, although they'd ordered more, they were still waiting for it to be delivered, so they'd had to economise and not light the fire so early or so often. But Gracie and Mary each came over for half an hour so that she could alter the dresses, so that was done, and she and Gracie had talked about the flowers, and she'd sent out the invitations and, all in all, she felt they were all doing rather well. And Jim and the girls were secretly purring because their plans had worked even better than they'd hoped.

And then Rosie had a phone call.

They'd had a short raid that night and had got home not long after one o'clock. When the phone rang they were clearing their breakfast things.

'You take it, Rosie,' Jim said. 'It's bound to be for you, this time a day. I'll finish clearing up.'

So she walked into the hall and picked up the receiver. The voice on the other end of the wire was Kitty's, but it didn't sound right.

'Ah,' she said. 'Look. I'm ever so sorry to ring this time a day, an' I wouldn't have, ony we thought you ought to know. Mr Tennant give me a lift to Chichester in 'is milk cart so's I could ring you. 'He's been ever so good.'

Something's wrong, Rosie thought, instantly alarmed. Someone's hurt or ill. 'What's up?' she said. 'Is it Pa?'

'I'm ever so sorry,' Kitty said. 'Ony, I went in to take him his cuppa tea, this morning, like I always do, an' he was dead. We reckon he must ha' died in his sleep. He hadn't suffered or nothing. You could see. He looked ever so peaceful. Ony, we thought you ought to know.'

'Yes,' Rosie said. 'Thank you. Was Johnnie there?'

'He'd gone to work,' Kitty said. 'We had to send the twins out to get him.'

'Do you want me to come down?'

'Well,' Kitty dithered. 'We wouldn't want to make it difficult for you. I mean, what with the raids an' everything.'

'I'll be on the next train,' Rosie said. 'Buy a leg of mutton for supper. There are bound to be lots of us there.' And, after telling Jim what had happened and phoning Mr Kennedy to warn him that she wouldn't be able to get in for a couple of days, she was.

*

The cottage was full of people, most of them in shock and all four women weeping. Edie and Tess and Kitty were huddled together on the sofa, their faces blotchy with grief, and Connie was in Pa's chair, wailing and rocking to and fro, with her poor fat baby on her lap, screaming at the top of its voice. Anna and Dickie were clinging to their father's hand and crying hopelessly.

'Oh Rosie!' Tess said, piteously. 'He can't be dead. He just can't. Not our Pa. What are we going to do?'

Rosie squared her shoulders and took command. She was the head of the family now, and it was her job to do it. 'First,' she said, 'Kitty's going to put the kettle on and make us all a cup of tea. Then we'll write a list of all the jobs we'll have to do. Has anyone sent for the doctor?'

'What's the point of that?' Connie wailed. 'Doctor can't help him now.'

'No,' Rosie said patiently. 'But we'll need a doctor to sign the death certificate.'

Kitty was already on her way to the kitchen, followed by her boys. Rosie's arrival had given her the push she needed. 'We'll need to tell the undertaker too,' she said.

'We will,' Rosie said, 'and we'll need to see Father Selwyn to arrange the funeral, and we'll have to tell the neighbours.' She turned to her brother. 'Nip upstairs an' pull the curtains, Johnnie,' she said. 'That'll give 'em warning.' Then, as the twins carried in the cups and saucers and the milk jug and set them on the table, she turned her attention to her howling sister-in-law. 'If I were you,' she said quietly, 'I'd take that poor little mite upstairs, somewhere quiet, and feed her. She needs a bit of comfort as much as the rest of us. Johnnie'll bring you up some tea.'

She was restoring order, making things possible for her family, even if they weren't tolerable. By the end of the afternoon, when Joey and Frank appeared straight from work and still in their overalls, Mrs Taylor had come to lay Pa's body out, the doctor had visited and his death had been certified, their nearest neighbours had called and been told the news – although some of them confessed they'd known it since early morning because Mr Tennant had told them – and the leg of mutton was in the stew pot, surrounded by vegetables, and cooking gently. By seven o'clock Rosie was busy dishing up the supper, 'because we all need a bit a sustenance or we'll collapse.' It was past ten o'clock before she was able to slip away into Pa's quiet room and say goodbye to him. He seemed so cold and far away it made her ache to look at him, but he was peaceful. There was no doubt about that. And that comforted her.

That night she wept and slept in her old double bed with Kitty. And in the morning, she was awake at daybreak with her head full of all the things that would have to be attended to that day; a visit to Father Selwyn to arrange the funeral being the most important. Grieving would have to wait until everything was organised.

CHAPTER FOURTEEN

It shouldn't be spring on a day like this, Rosie thought. Not when we're burying our Pa. It should be raining and cold and miserable. But no, the sun was as warm as a blessing on their heads as they followed the coffin up the path towards the church, the sky was a tender blue and full of innocent cotton-wool clouds, the Downs were benign, the fields were fresh with new green grass. There was even a thrush singing in the may tree.

'He's saying goodbye to Pa,' Tess said, squeezing Rosie's arm.

Rosie thought that the bird was simply singing, the way it always did when the sun was shining, but she didn't argue because the idea was comforting her sister. In any case, she had other more troubling things on her mind. It wasn't just the unsuitable weather that was fretting her. She was worried about whether the speech she'd written for this funeral would do. She wanted to say something that would make her neighbours see what a dear, loving man her father had been, but the right words wouldn't come, and what she'd written had seemed stiff and formal and absolutely useless when she'd read it through the previous evening. But it was too late to change it now. She glanced over her shoulder at the crowd of people who were waiting to follow the family into the church and shrank to think what a big event this was going to be.

But big or small, it was going to start at any minute. The coffin had reached the church door, was being carried into the church, she and her siblings were getting ready to follow it. She straightened her spine, squared her shoulders and lifted her chin. She would have to do the best she could.

It was warm in the church and the air was full of the reverberating sounds of the organ. Rosie could feel the crowd building up behind her, shuffling and coughing as they took their places in their accustomed pews. And then Father Selwyn was climbing into the pulpit to welcome them, smiling gently round at them all, and when the words of welcome had been said, he announced their first hymn.

'The family asked for this hymn to be sung,' he told them, 'and it is particularly appropriate. It is '*He who would valiant be,*' and who more valiant than our John Goodison?'

They sang lustily, which made Rosie feel far more comfortable. And it *was* an appropriate hymn.

He who would valiant be 'gainst all disaster,
Let him in constancy follow the Master.
There's no discouragement shall make him once relent
His first avowed intent to be a pilgrim.
Who so beset him round with dismal stories
Do but themselves confound —his strength the more is.
No foes shall stay his might; though he with giants fight,
He will make good his right to be a pilgrim.
Since, Lord, Thou dost defend us with Thy Spirit,
We know we at the end, shall life inherit.
Then fancies flee away! I'll fear not what men say,
I'll labour night and day to be a pilgrim.

Yes, Rosie thought. That's true. No foe ever did stay his might. And if there *were* dismal stories, he simply didn't listen to them. But then it was time for Father Selwyn to address them, so she settled herself to listen to *him.*

He spoke gently and with obvious affection. 'John Goodison was a good, upright man,' he said, 'a family man. He lived a long, valuable life in our community. He was well known to all of us as a dependable and helpful neighbour, as a loving and much loved husband and father and as a member of this congregation.

'He started work in the fields when he was nine years old, and worked without complaint and always as well as he could, for nearly seventy years. He and Maggie married in this church and brought their babies here to be christened. Now we have come here to say goodbye to him and to remember him and to salute him as a man who never wavered in his faith and never changed, even though he lived through some of the most turbulent times we have ever known. It is a great credit to him that…'

Rosie's mind was drifting, shifting, leaping, changing gear. Now she knew what she wanted to say. It was all there in her head.

'…his daughter Rosie has something to say to us,' Father Selwyn was saying, smiling at her.

She got up, carrying her new idea carefully, and stood before the congregation, warmed by their expectant, friendly faces, proud of the sight of her two girls in their nurses' caps and capes and her Jim in his warden's uniform.

'Let me tell you a story,' she said. 'It's quite right that Pa started work when he was nine. That was the way it was in those days, and thank God it isn't like that now. You don't get much of a childhood if you have to start work when you're nine. By the time I had to go to work,

I was twelve and that was bad enough, because I had to go to Arundel and live away from home. Anyway, the point of the story is this. Pa took me there that first day, as you'd expect, in his old milk cart with his grey mare pulling us. Old Snowy. Do you remember her?'

Oh they did, and nodded and smiled at her. 'Well,' she said, 'it was a quiet ride, as you can imagine, and very peaceful out there among the fields. And then, all of a sudden, without any warning, there was an absolute racket behind us. I'm not kidding you. An absolute racket. And naturally I turned my head to see what it was, and it was a bright red motorcar, fairly racketing down the track towards us. There were two people in it. I remember them clearly. One was a grand lady in a fine blue coat and a huge great hat tied in place by a long scarf that was flapping out behind her, and the other was a gentlemen in a tweed suit and a deerstalker hat. The sight of it took my breath away because it was the first car I'd ever seen in my life, and I was just going to tell Pa how marvellous I thought it was, when it swooshed past us and spooked poor Snowy and she bolted. It took Pa an age to pull her to a stop, and then she was shivering and sweating and showing the whites of her eyes, and it took him another age to calm her down. He was *not* pleased, as you can imagine. He said it was a "dratted contraption" and should never have been allowed on the road.'

That provoked laughter, and she waited until it had died down. 'Now the point of the story,' she said, 'is that by the time he was old and frail, he had changed his mind about cars and changed it entirely. His character was unchanging – Father Selwyn's right about that – but he could change his mind. His opinion of motorcars is an example. I came to visit him a few weeks before he died, and he said something so lovely to me I can remember it word for word.'

She paused for a second to get her breath and steady herself, because she suddenly felt dangerously close to tears, and her audience waited with their faces full of sympathy and concern until she could go on.

'I was helping him to eat his tea,' she said, 'and he caught hold of my hand and held it and said, "You're a good gel, my Rosie. You always was, helping with your Ma an' all, an' looking after the little'uns, an' going off to work without a bit of fuss, when you wasn't much more than a little'un yourself. An' now you're driving that great ambulance about in all the bombs. I take my hat off to you, so I do. You make me proud as Punch." And then he kissed my hand, I remember. He kissed my hand.'

It was too much. The tears were rolling down her cheeks. She couldn't stop them. But Father Selwyn was beside her, easing her back to her pew and to Jim's comforting arm and the ordeal – for it *had* been an ordeal – was over.

Later, when they were all back in the cottage, eating sandwiches and milling in and out and telling one another all sorts of things they remembered about Pa, some of them came across to her to tell her what a lovely speech they thought it was. And she felt proud of herself to have done it so well. 'He was a good man,' she said, over and over again. 'And he had a gentle death, which is a rarity now.'

And they smiled and patted her shoulder, or hugged her and gave her a kiss, and some said 'True.'

*

By the time the Jacksons were walking along the footpath to catch their train, darkness was edging across the fields, the Downs were smoke blue and the sky was stained flamingo pink and orange with sunset. It was so beautiful and so peaceful and such a long way away from the endless stink and grime and death and destruction in London, that Rosie wanted to turn round and go back to the cottage and stay where she was. There was bound to be a raid that night, because they'd had two nights off, and she wasn't at all sure she could face it.

'You OK, kid?' Jim said, alerted by her expression.

'Yes,' she said. 'I was just wishing there wasn't gonna be a raid tonight.'

'Ah!' he said, understanding, and gave her a hug.

Gracie and Mary had been walking on ahead. Now Gracie turned and grinned at them. 'Come on, you two,' she called. 'Put a jerk on or we'll miss our train.'

'Yes, sir boss,' Jim said, which made them all laugh, and he and Rosie picked up speed obediently. But there was still a raid ahead of them and they both knew it.

*

That night they set off to their various duties feeling decidedly down. Rosie cycled slowly, loath to get to the ambulance station, dreading what lay ahead of her. The sirens sounded as she parked her bike in the quad, and even though she was the last to arrive, she and Sister Maloney were one of the first three crews to be told to bring up their ambulances and stand ready. Wouldn't you know it?

'When are they going to stop this malarkey?' Sister Maloney complained in her forthright way. 'They can't go on much longer, surely to goodness. They should be running out of planes be now, the number we've shot down.'

'I don't think they're likely to do that,' Mr Kennedy said, smoothing his white hair. 'They've got a massive armaments industry. Always have had. But on the other hand, I do think we might have reason to begin to look on the bright side.'

'There's a bright side?' Mavis teased. And the other crews laughed.

Mr Kennedy laughed with them but then he said, 'I've been keeping tabs for the last few weeks and there's a better pattern emerging. Four raids one week, three the next.'

'Yeh, yeh!' Mavis said. 'An' six the week after.'

The first call was coming in, so the teasing had to stop. But as she inched her ambulance out into Southwark Park Road, Rosie was offering up a silent prayer for her boss' predicted pattern to be proved true. We've had enough of it now, she thought. It's been going on for seven months, and they can't go on forever, surely?

It was a difficult raid but mercifully short, so she managed to pick up the cat and get some sleep at the end of it. But next morning, the newspapers brought her back to the rough earth again. The new German general, Rommel, had according to the paper, been sent to North Africa to 'stiffen the resolve' of the German panzer units and was making rather too good a job of it. The Germans were advancing and pushing the British army back.

'*We* need a new general an' all,' Jim grumbled, glaring at the paper. 'The ones we got now are bleedin' useless. Upper class twits, that's what they are, every man jack of 'em, just like the stupid block'eads we 'ad in the trenches all them years, poncing about in their staff cars an' their fancy uniforms, saying "One more push! That'll do it boys!" An' then, a course, we had one more bleedin' push an' thousands got killed an' it didn't make the slightest difference. We was still stuck in the same stinking trenches in the same stinking mud. We hadn't moved as much as an inch. Bleedin' ridiculous. If you ask me, ol' Churchill should sling all this stupid lot out, lock, stock an' barrel, an' put someone in with a bit more sense.'

'He'll have a job,' Rosie said, pouring herself a second cup of tea. 'Far as I can see, most of his MPs are the same toffee-nosed gits as the generals, bred in the same way, in the same schools, an' I'll bet all the generals are too. I keep thinking of that Anthony Eden an' his brother. They was the same age as me an' you couldn't've found a pair more arrogant an' cocksure if you tried. They thought the last war was going to be 'a good show'– if you ever heard of such a thing – like something at the theatre or a game. According to them, it wasn't going to last more than six months an' they didn't want to miss it. They were really peeved when their mother wouldn't let them join up. Sulking an' complaining an' throwing newspapers about an' all sorts.' She was scowling as she remembered it. 'An' they were bloody rude about our Keir Hardie.'

'Course they was,' Jim said. 'He stood up for the suffragettes. They couldn't have that.'

'He was a good man,' Rosie said, sipping her tea. 'We need a lot more like him, 'specially in the House a Commons. The Tories an' the Liberals have had it their own way for far too long.'

'That'd take a revolution,' Jim said, 'an' we don't seem to run to revolutions.'

'More's the pity,' Rosie said.

*

But although neither of them knew it then, away in Whitehall a quiet civil servant was chairing a committee that had been set up by Ernie Bevin, the Minister of Health, and was currently gathering information about the state of the nation so that he could write a report on it for the government. And that report, when it was eventually written and published, would advocate just the sort of revolution they wanted.

He was a serious and dedicated man, respected by his committee, and with the right credentials for the job, as he'd been trained as an economist when he was young and had been the director of the London School of Economics until just before the war. His name was William Beveridge.

*

In the meantime, Londoners went about their day to day business in their usual stolid away, coping with the Luftwaffe's spring offensive, enduring more and heavier rationing, wincing when income tax was raised to 50% and accepting bad news from Africa with stoical resignation. On April the third, the news came through that British troops had been evacuated from Benghazi as Rommel's advance continued and, by the end of the month, they heard that three columns of troops from his overpowering Africa Korps had crossed over from Libya into Egypt.

'Just as well the wedding's only days away,' Rosie said, when she'd read the latest news. 'They'll send Sam's lot out there now. Bound to.'

'Yes,' Jim said. 'They will. All the more reason to give him the best send-off we can.'

'It will be, don't you worry,' Rosie told him, chin in the air. 'I've got it all planned down to the last little detail.'

But she'd reckoned without the hiccups.

*

She and Jim got up early on the morning of the wedding day, and she made them tea and toast to keep them going until the wedding breakfast, fed the cat, checked that plates and glasses were all standing ready on the trestle tables and that the food was covered with white cloths. Then while Jim was off collecting the ham, she cooked egg and bacon for her two girls, made them a fresh pot of tea, arranged everything prettily on a tray with a lace cloth and a single newly-picked rose in her little blue vase and carried it up to their room.

They were awake and talking. She could hear them through the door. 'Breakfast time, girls,' she called, and she opened the door one handed and carried the tray into the room.

The bride was sitting up in bed, gasping and struggling for breath, with Mary behind her rubbing her back, her face serious and worried. Rosie was instantly alarmed. 'What's up?' she said, putting the tray down on the dressing table.

'Hiccups,' Mary explained. 'She's had them for hours. Ever since she woke up.' And as if to prove her right, Gracie gave an enormous hiccup and winced. 'We've tried everything, haven't we Gracie? Slow breathing, sipping water. I even hit her in the middle of her back. Nothing works. She just goes on an' on, and she can't have hiccups at her wedding.'

Someone was calling from downstairs. 'Coo-ee Mrs J. Anything you wants doing?' It was Mrs Totteridge, her face rosy. 'Need a hand?' she called hopefully.

'Gracie's got the hiccups,' Rosie called down to her. 'Could you bring us up a glass of water?'

'Oh nasty,' Mrs Totteridge said. 'She had it long?'

'Couple of hours.'

'Glass a water an' a bath towel,' Mrs Totteridge said. 'That's what we need. Won't be a tick.'

These were provided, and Gracie was shrouded in the towel and the glass of water put in her hands. 'Now all you got to do, dearie,' Mrs

Totteridge said, 'is to drink that water out the wrong side a' the glass. Take a good mouthful, mind. There you go. Swallow it down. That's it. Now another one. We'll soon have you to rights. You'll see. I've never know'd it fail yet.'

But it failed that time. As soon as Gracie had handed over the dripping towel to her mother, she started hiccupping again and even more frequently and painfully than she'd been doing before.

'Well I never did,' Mrs Totteridge said, much disappointed. 'Have another try.'

Gracie shook her head and sighed wearily. 'I don't… think I'm… supposed… to get married… today,' she said between hiccups.

They rushed to reassure her, all speaking at once, but before they could even finish what they were saying, the door was thrown open and Jim stood before them, looking rather splendid in his uniform, his eyes blazing and his shock of hair at its most leonine. 'Stop everything!' he yelled, waving his arms dramatically. 'The ceiling's fell in.'

'Oh for crying out loud,' Rosie said. 'That's all I need. Which one?'

'Kitchen,' Jim told her. 'You never saw such a mess in all your life. It's all over the food an' the floor an' everything. Come an' have a look-see.' And he turned and headed for the stairs, leaving them to rush after him, Rosie grim-faced, the two girls struggling into their dressing gowns, Mrs T looking anxious.

The kitchen door was shut. He flung it open and stood aside so that they could all rush in.

The kitchen was exactly the same as it had always been. There was nothing the matter with the ceiling at all.

Rosie was furious. 'For God's sake Jim!' she shouted. 'This ent the time to play silly buggers. Today of all days! What's the matter with you?' And she scowled at him as if she was going to hit him.

He caught her hands and held them against his chest. 'I done it for a reason,' he said, grinning at her. 'It ain't what's the matter with *me*, you see, it's what's the matter with our Gracie.'

They all turned to look at Gracie, who was standing by the door with her hand to her mouth.

'Well?' Jim asked her. 'How's the hiccups?'

She stood still thinking, for five seconds, ten seconds, twenty. And she didn't hiccup. 'Well thank Gawd for that!' Mrs T said, which of course made them all laugh. Partly with relief and partly with surprise.

'Where'd you learn to pull a trick like that?' Rosie said.

'Saw it done up the market once, never forgot it,' Jim said, and turned to Gracie. 'OK now kid?'

She rushed at him to kiss him to show how OK it was.

So after all that, and to Rosie's considerable relief, the wedding went according to her careful plan. She went upstairs and dressed in her best red cotton and put on her best white shoes and her red straw hat, and even had time to admire herself in the mirror. Then she and Mrs Totteridge covered the ham with another white cloth and, while they were doing it, Gracie came down for her bath, and Sonia arrived in her best hat, followed not long after by Kitty and the twins. The flowers were delivered and laid ready on the kitchen table. The button holes were distributed, Mary came down for *her* bath, and when they were all nearly ready except for Gracie and Mary, the first of their two cars arrived and she and her guests were driven smoothly off to St George's.

From then on, everything was a bit of a blur. Although it was a huge building, the church seemed to be full of people. She waved to the Binderton mob, as she passed, and they waved back, she gave the groom and his best man their buttonholes and pinned them to their tunics as they seemed to need a helping hand, she smiled at Sam's mother, who was sitting beside him and looked so like him it was obvious who she was, and gave her *her* buttonhole, and she nodded at all the soldiers who were sitting behind her. There seemed to be ever so many of them, all wearing their black berets on their shoulders and grinning at Sam whenever he turned his head. She assumed that the older lady in the mauve hat who was sitting next to Sam's mum was Aunt Maud, so she smiled at her and gave her a buttonhole too. Then she took her seat in the front pew with Kitty and the twins, being careful to leave a space by the aisle for Jim, and waited impatiently as the organ played and the congregation rustled and murmured.

It seemed to be a very long time before the organist changed his tune to the wedding march, but there they were at last, walking slowly down the aisle, her pretty Gracie holding her father's arm and her pretty Mary following behind them, smiling happily at her relations. And she felt so proud of all three of them and knew that this was going to be the best wedding ever. She didn't even worry about how she would fit all the guests into the house, which had been a major concern until that moment. Now, she knew she would manage it. If you'd grown up in Binderton you were capable of squeezing a very large quart into a very small pint pot.

The largest member of the quart pot brigade squashed herself into a corner of the living room with baby Maggie on her knee and her mother beside her. The bridal party sat at their allotted places at one side of the trestle table and Mrs Totteridge settled in the kitchen with Aunt Maud and some of the kids. Kitty and Sonia sat on the stairs and were soon immersed in memories of what the Borough had been like when they were kids themselves, and the twins managed to squeeze into the middle of one of the long plank benches between Johnnie and five of the soldiers, where they were glowingly happy.

Johnnie took over the ham and carved it expertly. Edie and Tess handed round the plates, and Joey and Sydney were in charge of the drinks. What with eating and drinking and talking, it didn't seem any time at all before people were squashing into the room from the stairs and the kitchen and the garden, and Jim was on his feet ready to make the first of the speeches.

He excelled himself. First he thanked them all for coming and making the wedding such a success. Then he told them he was going to tell them a horror story. That provoked disbelieving laughter, and Sonia called out 'No you ain't, Jim.' But he laughed back at them and said 'Oh yes I am. Wait till you hear this. First thing this morning I frightened the life outta the bride. Tell 'em Gracie. I did, didden I?'

And when Gracie had endorsed him, he told them the tale. They loved it and when it was done, they blew kisses to Gracie and applauded happily.

'He's a one, our Jim,' Mrs Totteridge said, beaming at him. 'You should ha' seen him.'

'I wish I had,' Sonia said.

Then it was the turn of the bridegroom, who looked very nervous but said all the right things, thanking them for coming and thanking 'my new father and mother-in-law' for providing such a sumptuous feast for them, and his own mother for 'being mother and father to me,' and finally thanking Gracie for marrying him. 'It probably sounds a bit trite,' he said, 'because all bridegrooms say things like that, but I mean it.' Then he turned and spoke directly to Gracie. 'I meant every word of the service too, Mrs Marsh, as long as we both shall live.'

She put her arms round his neck and kissed him lovingly, as their guests cheered. Then they stood with their arms round each other until Bertie rose to his feet and interrupted them, saying, 'Come on, Mooch. Cut it short. I got a speech to make.'

He was such an affable-looking bloke, with his chubby face, his broken nose, his wide-spaced brown eyes and mop of untidy brown hair, that the room hushed for him and waited.

'I asked my mum what I was supposed to say at this wedding,' he began, 'and she said, "Tell 'em a story. Everyone likes a story. Only make it a good un." So that's what I'm gonna do… or try to do. It can't be a story about what Sam here was like as a boy on account of I didn't know him then. We met in the army. So it'll have to be a war story.' And when Sam winced, 'Don't make that face. Truth will out, you know. Well then, it goes like this. We was on a beach in France, not sunning ourselves an' whatnot, but being strafed by Stukas; shelled an' bombed an' I don' know what else. Thousands of us there was an' we'd been waiting to be took off for so many days we'd lost count. And me an' Sam an' a bloke called Les, kept each other company an' swapped ciggies when they was running low and huddled up together at night when it was bleedin' cold. Pardon my French. An' finally, it was our turn to wade into the sea and be picked up by one a the little boats. And then wouldn't you know it, just as we was standing in line ready for the off, the Stukas came over, an' we was machine gunned.

'Les took a hit, poor sod. We could see the blood spurting out of his leg. So he says, "You two go on," he says. "They won't take me, not like this." And Sam says "Bugger that for a lark. You're coming with us. Just hop on your good leg an' lean on my arm. Don't worry. I'll take your weight."

'And that's what he did. Must ha' been nearly half a mile, struggling forward with the water getting deeper with every step. But we got there, and we was hauled aboard a fishing boat. And it wasn't till then that we saw Sam had been wounded as well. Hadn't said a word to either of us, an' his leg was bloody as Les'.' Then he turned to look at Gracie and spoke directly to her. 'You married a hero, Gracie,' he said.

His audience clapped and cheered and Sam blushed. So naturally Gracie had to put her arms round his neck and kiss him again. Which led to more cheering. And when the noise had abated a bit she made a short speech of her own.

'I know it's not the done thing for a bride to say anything at her wedding,' she said, grinning round at them, 'but there's a war on now and times are changing. So I'll tell you something. Bertie's right. My Sam *is* a hero. We knew that when we were nursing him at Guy's. He never made any fuss although we were hurting him terribly. In fact, we made a medal for him, didn't we Sam?' And when he nodded, 'It was very grand. Made out of cardboard with '*For Valour*' written on it in wax crayon. We pinned it to his pyjamas.'

'Correction,' Sam said. 'They pinned it to my chest. Now that *was* painful.'

That made them all laugh, and while they were laughing, Sonia carried in the wedding cake and placed it before the bride and groom. It was a very small fruit cake – how could it be anything else with rationing so tight? – but it had a layer of white icing to top it off and was duly cut and distributed, and every last crumb of it was eaten.

'And now,' Jim said, 'I'd like you all out in the garden so's I can take pictures of you.'

Rosie was very surprised. 'What with?' she asked.

'You'll see,' he said grinning at her. 'I been keeping it for a surprise. It's in the cupboard an' I can't get at it, can I, till you all go out?'

So they all went obediently out into the sunshine and, as there were going to be pictures, Rosie went into the kitchen and collected the bouquets which had been standing in water in the sink. And, having made sure they were dry and wouldn't drip on the clothes, she took them out to Gracie and Mary.

Jim was standing with his back to the shelter holding a Brownie camera in his hands and looking very proud of himself. 'Bride and groom, for starters,' he said.

For the next forty minutes, he arranged his groups and took pictures and joked about what he was doing, until they were all silly with laughter. Half way through, he had to stop and change the film, and they called out to him 'Are we allowed to move now?' and walked around the garden and in and out of house until he called them all back. And Bertie took advantage of the break to walk over to Mary, who was sitting on the grass, her bouquet in her lap.

'Hi,' he said, smiling at her. 'It's my job to look after you now.'

She squinted up at him through the sunlight. 'Do I need looking after?' she said.

'Probably not,' he admitted. 'But my mum said that's what I was supposed to do, so I'm doing it.'

She grinned at him. 'An' I suppose you always do as you're told?' she teased.

'Only when it's pleasurable.'

'Well, at least you're honest.'

'What you going to do when all this is over?' he asked. 'I suppose you've got to go back to the hospital.'

'Not till tomorrow morning.'

He grinned at that. 'Well in that case, how's about coming to the flicks?'

She considered it. It wasn't at all how she'd intended to end this day. 'Depends what's on.'

'We could go up west an' see. Whatcher think?'

'You're on,' she said.

'We're taking Sam an' Gracie to the station in our lorry,' he said. 'I'll come straight back after. Honour bright.'

Well, Mary thought, that was some conversation.

There were conversations going on all over the house and the garden that afternoon. Rosie and Ruth discovered that they were almost the same age and swopped notes on what it had been like when they were young; the twins told Aunt Maud how they were going to leave school in ten weeks to start work on the farm, and she told them how sensible she thought they were; the tankies talked war to Jim; Sonia and Mrs Totteridge told one another what a good wedding it had been as they were washing the dishes, and by the end of the afternoon, when Sam and Gracie had been given a riotous send-off and driven away in style in the army lorry, and Kitty and Rosie and Jim were putting the living room back to rights, Kitty made a confession that was to change her life.

'I don't half miss the old Borough,' she said as she folded the trestle table. 'I been in Binderton for years now, so I ought to be used to it. But the truth is I'm still a Londoner an' I don't 'alf miss the place. Going to the flicks an' the market, an' fish an' chips an' all.'

'Tell you what,' Rosie said impulsively. 'Why don't you stay here for a few days? We've got an empty room now an' no one to put in it.'

Kitty's face was creased with delight at the thought of it. 'Could I?'

'Why not, kid?' Jim said. 'Your twins are old enough to look after themselves now.'

So it was arranged, and when the guests had gone their separate ways, and the Binderton gang set off to catch their train, she was left behind.

'What a day it's been,' Jim said, as they waved goodbye.

'And quite right too,' Rosie said.

'What's for supper?' Jim said, grinning at Kitty. 'Need I ask?'

'Where's Mary?' Rosie said. 'We ought to ask her too.'

'Gone to the pictures with Bertie,' Jim told her. 'So it's just us.'

'Good heavens!' Rosie said. 'He's a quick worker.'

'He's a good bloke,' Jim said. 'He'll look after her. Now then you two, whatcher want? Cod an' sixpenn'orth?'

CHAPTER FIFTEEN

'Welcome to the Red Lion, Salisbury, Mrs Marsh,' Sam said, doffing his beret to bow before her like an actor in a play. His fair hair was spotlit by sunshine and he looked so handsome and loving, standing there in front of that extraordinary building with their heavy bag on the pavement beside him, and his beret in his hands, that it made Gracie's heart leap just to look at him.

'We're never going to stay *here*!' she said, staring at it in some awe. It was an impressive place: all oak beams arranged in patterns and old-fashioned leaded windows gleaming in the white walls.

'That's the plan,' Sam told her, happily. 'I knew it was the place for us the minute I saw it. Come on. I'm itching to show you round. Wait till you see the courtyard.' And he picked up the bag and limped off towards the entrance.

He shouldn't be carrying that great bag, Gracie thought, wearing her nurse's hat. But he won't be told and, even though she knew best, she had to admire his determination. It was one of the reasons she'd married him. Dear Sam. But even so…

He was waiting for her at the entrance so that they could walk in together, so she headed off to join him. But, as she drew near, he began to sing 'Here comes the bride! Here comes the bride!' in such a loud voice she was quite alarmed.

'Hush!' she said, putting her index finger to her lips. 'We don't want everyone to know.'

He grinned at that. '*I* do,' he said. But then he stopped singing because he could see it was worrying her, which was odd considering how tough she was, and simply picked up their bag and led her into the hotel.

They signed the register as easily as if they'd been doing it for years, and then a bell boy, who looked about fifteen, took their bag and escorted them to their room, and Sam gave him a tip as if he'd been doing that for years too.

And then they were on their own together.

'So what shall we do now?' she said, knowing very well.

'I don't know about you,' he said, smiling into her eyes, 'but I'm going to take your clothes off.'

Even thinking about it made her shiver with pleasure. 'Only on one condition,' she teased.

'Which is?' he asked.

'That I undress you at the same time.'

He turned her gently in his arms and began to undo the buttons on her dress, kissing her naked back as each button surrendered.

*

They were naturally very late down to their evening meal, but the waitress smiled at them as she took their order and didn't seem to mind that they were the last to arrive. And the food she served was manna. It surprised them both to discover what healthy appetites they had. Oh it was good to be married!

231

They were late down to breakfast the next morning, and by then they had discovered that this new life of theirs had acquired a delectable and satisfying pattern, and that all they had to do was follow it. So it wasn't until their fourth morning that they found they had enough energy to take a post-breakfast stroll around the town. And naturally, they were entranced by it.

'It's so peaceful,' Gracie said, as they wandered into the cathedral close. 'You'd never think there was a war going on. Who lives in those great houses?'

'Bishops and archbishops. Those sort of people,' Sam said. And as if to prove him right, a man in a long purple gown and an odd-looking hat walked out of one of the doors and ambled towards the cathedral, smiling at them briefly as he passed. 'D'you want to look at the cathedral?'

'Not particularly,' Gracie said. 'Do you?'

'Not much,' he told her happily. 'I'd rather look at you.'

So they admired the great building from the humble grass of the close and then they set off to find the centre of the town, where there was a market full of stalls and shoppers and felt 'much more like it,' as Sam was happy to say.

That night they finally took a look round the dining room and noticed what a lot of oak beams there were, and Gracie asked their waitress how old the place was. They were very surprised by her answer.

'Seven hundred years,' she said. 'Started off as a barn, so they say, somewhere around 1220. The workers who were building the cathedral put it up to give themselves somewhere to live. You can still see the rafters of the original barn in the lounge.'

'I like the idea of this place being built by men who built the cathedral,' Gracie said when they were eating their meal. 'The cathedral's too grand for me, if I'm honest, but this place is just right. Don't you think so?'

232

'I knew it was the right place,' Sam told her, 'the minute I saw it.'

That made Gracie think. 'Do you come in here a lot, then?' she asked.

'Whenever we can get a pass,' he told her. 'We usually go to the flicks or a pub. Anywhere to break the monotony of army life.' And when he saw how pensive she was, he said, 'We could go to the flicks tonight, if you'd like to.'

So that evening they walked down Milford Street into a road called New Canal and bought two tickets at the Gaumont. They got two seats in the back row so they didn't see much of the film, but it was a warm, familiar place and they enjoyed being there. And anyway, kissing was better than gawping at a screen.

The next day they wandered further afield and found the Harnham water meadows, where they lay side by side in the long grass and watched the swans swimming elegantly and effortlessly through the peaceful green waters of the river – when they weren't kissing one another. And the day after that, they made a discovery.

They'd drifted westwards and rather aimlessly that afternoon. The sun was warm on their shoulders, the houses they passed were quiet, old fashioned and peaceful, they had their arms round each other and they'd tempered their strides until they were walking in harmony, which was a new and delightful trick to have learnt. When they reached the end of the road they saw that they'd come to a bridge over the river so they stopped for a while, with their arms still round each other, and looked to see if there were any swans about.

'I'd like this honeymoon to go on for ever and ever,' Gracie said dreamily.

'Me too,' Sam agreed.

'We ought to have a month at least.'

'Or two.'

'Or three,' Gracie said, following the game. But then her face clouded.

It was all very well making jokes, but that little digit had reminded her that they'd only got three days left now, and then God knows when they would see one another again. 'It ought to go on for a lifetime,' she said, 'and it would too, if it wasn't for this foul war.'

He kissed her hair. 'D'you want to go back to the hotel?' he asked, trying not to sound too hopeful.

'No,' she sighed, missing the cue he was sending her, 'Not unless you do. I think I'd rather walk a bit further.' If she walked somewhere new it might cheer her up. You never knew what you might find round the corner.

So they ambled on again, past a grey clock tower with four clock faces and spires at each corner, that reminded them of Big Ben, so they stopped to admire it for a little while, but it didn't lift her spirits. So they went on along the street, heading northwest. And Gracie saw a building that stopped her in her stride.

It was four storeys high, built in solid red brick with an impressive roof, and was plainly an important place.

'Now *that*,' she said, 'is a hospital. Or I'm a Dutchman.' An idea was forming in her head, filling her with energy. 'Come on!' she said and strode off towards the entrance, which she could see a few yards ahead of them. And there, sure enough, was a tall notice board that said '*Salisbury Infirmary*' loud and clear. Hadn't she known it?

'Hang on!' Sam called. And when he'd caught up with her, 'What you going in there for?'

'A job,' she said.

'You've got one.'

'I want one here,' she told him. 'Then we can be together whenever you have a pass. Otherwise we shall hardly see each other when this honeymoon's over.'

'You can't just barge in off the street and ask a strange hospital for a job,' he protested, following her. 'I mean, that's not…'

But Gracie wasn't her mother's daughter for nothing. She was already walking through the entrance into the reception area.

They found themselves in a small admissions office, with a wooden desk at one side and a row of chairs at the other, very different from the huge bustling hall at Guy's. The receptionist was an elderly woman with a tight grey perm and horn-rimmed spectacles, who smiled at them vaguely and gave them the customary greeting. 'Good afternoon, sir. Good afternoon, madam. How can I help you?'

Gracie got down to business at once, giving her new name as effortlessly as if she'd had it for years instead of days, and telling the receptionist that she was a fully trained SRN, who was currently working at Guy's and was looking for a job in the Infirmary. And Sam watched her, caught between grudging admiration of her daring and irritation that she was wasting their honeymoon job hunting. She won't get a job here, he thought. Not like this.

But he was being proved wrong even as he watched. The receptionist was smiling at her and saying they were often on the hunt for new nurses.

'Staff come and go,' she said, rather sadly. 'It's the war.'

'Of course,' Gracie said. 'That's what's brought me here.'

The receptionist was writing on a small card. 'This is Matron's address,' she said. 'I suggest you write to her and tell her everything you've just told me. She has overall control of everything that goes on in this hospital. She'd be able to answer your question.' She handed the card to Gracie and smiled at her. 'Good luck,' she said.

'Right,' Gracie said, as she and Sam walked out of the building and headed off for the Red Lion. 'Now all I've got to do is write my letter.

I shall use a sheet of their fancy notepaper, I think, because that'll look good, and I'm sure someone'll lend me a pen and ink. Don't make that face. It won't take me long.'

'I've never heard of anyone going off job hunting on their honeymoon,' Sam said, crossly. 'Never, ever.'

He was looking at her as he walked, scowling so fiercely it upset her to look back at him. But this was something that had to be done. Surely he could see that? 'Things are different now,' she said. 'War changes things. Anyway, I'm doing this as much for you as I am for me. I mean, it's for both of us. So that we can be together when you have a pass. Think about it. If I can get this job or something like it, I can move down here and find a bedsit or a bed and breakfast somewhere nearby, and then we can be together whenever you can get out of the camp. Instead of being miles away from one another. I mean, you wouldn't be able to get to London for an evening, now would you? Whereas this way...'

He was still scowling. 'I thought we were going to the flicks tonight.'

'There's nothing to stop us.'

'If you're going to spend the evening writing letters,' he said stiffly, 'we shan't have time.'

'Oh how ridiculous you are,' she said, exasperated by the way he was going on. 'Five minutes a letter'll take. That's all. Five minutes.'

His face was stubborn. 'I don't see why you can't leave it till after the honeymoon,' he said. 'We've only got three days left. It can wait three days, surely to God?'

She was equally stubborn now. 'No, it can't,' she said. 'Because in that time someone else could have taken the job.'

They were nearly back at the hotel but instead of walking in together, Sam stopped at the entrance.

She hesitated, looking back at him. 'Aren't you coming in?' she asked.

'No,' he said shortly. 'You write your letter, if you must. I'm going for a walk.'

'You're being childish,' she told him.

But he didn't answer. He just walked off towards Catherine Street and didn't look back.

She was more upset than she wanted to admit, but she was determined not to show it so she took a few seconds to compose herself and put on a smile, the way she'd done so often for her injured patients, and then went to the desk to ask for her key and to see if she could borrow a pen and ink. There was work to be done, and she was determined to do it, no matter how silly he was being.

It took her quite a long time and two sheets of notepaper to compose the letter she felt she needed. But it was done, and she was writing the envelope when someone knocked at the door. And it was Sam, looking crestfallen.

This time she didn't stop to think and she didn't say anything. She simply put her arms round his neck and kissed him.

'I'm so sorry Gracie,' he said. 'I mean, I didn't want to upset you, it was just… Oh I don't know… I can't make sense of it.'

She stopped him with another kiss. 'It's all right,' she said. 'We've had our first row, that's all. It's perfectly normal. All married couples have rows. Believe me. You should see the way Mum and Dad go on sometimes.'

That surprised him. 'Seriously?' he said.

'No,' she said, laughing at his surprise. 'It's never serious. It just clears the air.' Then she remembered that he'd been brought up by a mother on her own, so he'd never seen a married row and didn't know how usual it was. And she smiled at him again, this time lovingly. 'Are we going to bed first, or down to supper?'

It wasn't really a question because the answer was on his face as clearly as if it had been written there.

The next morning, as it was a warm summer's day, they took another walk down to the water meadows and the swans, posting her letter on the way.

'There's an old mill down here,' Sam said. 'Do you want to go and have a look at it?'

'No,' she told him happily. 'I'd rather look at you.'

'It's so peaceful here,' Sam said, gazing at the swans, 'You'd never think there was a war going on at all.'

*

But although there wasn't a hint of war in Salisbury, it was certainly going on in plenty of other places. That night, London endured one of the worst raids they'd had in a long time, and Jim and Rosie and Mary were hard at work until the all clear. There were so many bombers overhead that the laboured droning of their engines was incessant and terrifying, and although the rescue services worked hard all night, there were more casualties than any of them could stop to count. The next morning, the tram telegraph reported that the House of Commons had been reduced to rubble and that the square tower of Westminster Abbey had fallen in.

'Bad night,' people in the Borough said to one another as they went to market. 'An' jest when we was thinking they might be stopping.'

'Don't count your chickens,' Mrs Totteridge said soberly. 'Them bleeders'll go on forever.'

But there was no raid the next night and no raid the night after, when Gracie reported for duty and Mary told her what a dreadful time they'd had of it on the eleventh. And there was no raid the next night, nor the one after that, which made four unbombed nights in a row. And that was something that hadn't been heard of in all the nine long months the Blitz had been going on. And the nights became weeks, and the city was so peaceful that the glaziers began to tell one another that maybe the glass they were replacing would be allowed to stay in place for a bit longer than it usually did and, if the Blitz really had stopped like people were saying, it might even be its final repair.

And hope began to grow.

*

Something else was growing in those hopeful weeks of summer, but that was private and personal, and for the time being at least, it was being kept secret. Ever since the wedding, Bertie O'Connor had been writing to Mary. At first his letters had been fairly short, but he wrote every other day and had gradually grown more confident about what he was saying. On the day after Gracie came back to the hospital, he wrote to tell Mary that he would be coming to London the next Saturday and to ask if she would like to go to the pictures with him. She wrote back at once to say 'Of course,' and to the pictures they went, feeling extremely happy in one another's company. He was so easy to talk to and such fun to be with, that when he left her to drive back to Salisbury Plain with his mates, she promised to go out with him whenever he could get a pass long enough to get to London to see her.

'Are we walking out then?' he asked her.

'I suppose we are,' she laughed. 'Not that we've done very much walking.'

'Then I s'pose it would be in order to kiss you?'

She supposed it might. And very pleasant it turned out to be.

After he'd left her, she wondered whether she ought to say something about it to her parents, or to Gracie. But Gracie was fully occupied. She'd had a letter from Salisbury Infirmary offering her a job – not as a nurse but as a *'temporary receptionist until such time as a nurse's job becomes vacant.'* She'd written back at once to accept the offer and was now working her notice and had gone to Salisbury that very weekend to find herself some lodgings.

Our lives are getting complicated, Mary thought, as she reported to the ward for duty later that night and took up her post at the nurse's station. I wonder what it'll be like when she's gone, and I'm on my own without her. She'd come to depend on her big sister for support in the hospital, and she knew she would miss her very much when she moved. But I daresay she'll come back when they send the tank corps to North Africa, she thought. I do hope she does. But that thought brought another that was far less pleasant. If they sent the tank corps to Africa, Bertie would go too, and she didn't want that. Not one little bit. Oh, she thought, why does life have to be so difficult? Then there was a patient ringing for attention so she had to stop thinking about herself and go and attend to him. But the questions remained and couldn't be answered.

*

Gracie came back from Salisbury bursting to tell her sister how well she'd got on.

'I found a very nice room, just round the corner from the hospital,' she said. 'Only bed and breakfast, but that'll do for me, I can get a main meal in the hospital canteen. I've sent Sam a postcard with my new address on it, so he'll know where to find me. Now it's just a matter of working out my notice.' She was so happy that Mary couldn't tell her how much she was going to miss her. Two weeks later, she packed up all the clothes she needed and her books and her ration card, and set off for her new life in Salisbury. Mary and her mother went down to the station to watch her go, Rosie determinedly cheerful, Mary feeling quite bleak to be losing her.

'I'll send you both a postcard as soon as I'm settled in,' Gracie promised.

But Mary knew that a postcard wouldn't the same thing at all as her company. And the lovely June days passed slowly without her. If it hadn't been for Bertie's arrival every other week and a happy trip to the flicks with him and considerable kissing afterwards, her life might well have been quite dull.

*

In their kitchen in Coney Street, Rosie and Jim were reading the morning paper, as they ate their bacon and tomatoes. It was 23 June, and the front-page news had given them the answer to the question they'd both been asking since 11 May. Germany had invaded Russia. Apparently, the Germans had issued a statement from Berlin claiming that their armies were *already deep into Russian territory.'* And, as the paper reported, *'there was evidence that German troops, supported by the Luftwaffe, had invaded along a front that was 1,500 miles long, from Finland towards Leningrad, from East Prussia towards Moscow and from Rumania towards the Ukraine. It is thought,'* the reporter said, *'that the Russians are taking up defensive positions along the Dneister river, where Russian artillery and air squadrons are reported to be massing. Reinforcements are arriving hourly. Here will probably be fought the battle for the Ukraine and its wheat and the oil of the Caucasus.'*

'So that's where they've gone,' Rosie said. 'The Blitz really *is* over.' It was wonderful news even though the Russians would have to pay the price for it. 'Poor Russkies!'

'They're a tough ol' lot,' Jim told her. 'An' there's millions of 'em. They'll sort Hitler out if anyone can.'

But Rosie didn't really care whether the Russians sorted Hitler out or not. She felt a vague fellow feeling towards them because they were under attack, but the great thing was that after ten terrible months, the Blitz of London was over.

There was another item of news that hadn't been in the papers and that Jim knew about although Rosie didn't. And for the time being, he was keeping it to himself. Now that the Blitz was over, the Ministry of Defence had issued the casualty figures for the ten month period, and as a chief warden, he'd seen them. They made grim reading. Over twenty thousand civilians had been killed and twenty-five thousand badly injured. And on top of that, there'd been heavy casualties among the rescue services. The firemen had suffered the highest losses with over five hundred of their men killed, but there were wardens and ambulance drivers and members of the rescue teams who'd been killed too. It had been a very high price to pay for not surrendering.

CHAPTER SIXTEEN

It was a late Sunday afternoon on one of the warmest days of the summer, and Jim and Rosie were in the garden. They ought to have been sitting in their dilapidated deckchairs enjoying a bit of well-earned sunshine but they weren't. They were in the middle of a row.

'Bloody ridiculous!' Rosie shouted, glaring at the shelter. 'I don't see why we can't dig the damned thing out and have our garden back.'

'So you keep saying,' Jim said. 'I'm brassed off listening to you.'

'The Blitz is over,' Rosie said, glaring worse than ever. 'Everybody says so. Well they do, don't they? You got to admit. Even the BBC. And I wouldn't've been laid off as an ambulance driver if they'd thought it was going to start again. So right. The Blitz is over so I don't see why we can't do what we like.'

'How many more times have I got to tell you?' Jim said, trying to be patient. She was annoying him so much, he was very close to shouting back at her. 'We can't because there's regulations. You can't just do whatever you want. Not in the middle of a war.'

'Well, I don't see why not,' Rosie said truculently. 'It's *our* shelter when all's said an' done, an' we don't need the damned thing. We could've had a crop of nice fresh runner beans by now if you'd listened to me instead of keeping on about regulations. And radishes. I'd've dug it out if you didn't want to.'

'It ain't I don't want to,' Jim said angrily. 'You know that as well as I do. I ain't *allowed* to. It's the regulations an' it's my job to see they're obeyed.'

'Bloody ridiculous,' Rosie said again, glaring at him this time. She was just drawing breath to give him another broadside, when she heard the phone ringing. So she stomped off into the house to answer it. It might be Gracie. She rang at all sorts of odd times these days.

'Saved by the bell,' Jim said to the cat.

But it wasn't Gracie, it was Kitty and she was breathless with excitement.

'You'll never guess what,' she said.

Rosie was still steaming and in no mood for guessing games. 'What then?' she said.

'My boys are starting work in two weeks' time,' Kitty told her happily. 'Whatcher think a that?'

Rosie's bad temper melted under the impact of the news. 'How did you swing *that*?' she asked.

'Ol' Mister Oddy's buying ten new cows, 'pparently,' Kitty said. 'He reckons there's such a demand for milk he can run to it, providing he can take my boys on for the extra work. Anyway, me an' Johnnie went up the school yesterday an' told the ol' headmaster an' he said they could leave early on account of it's for the war effort. Whatcher think a that? They're as happy as Larry.'

'I'll bet,' Rosie said.

'An' if they settle in OK, I can come home. Whatcher think a *that*?'

Jim was walking into the hall with a question on his face, so Rosie put her hand over the mouthpiece and answered it at once. 'It's Kitty,' she said. 'Coming home in a week or two. Tell you about it presently.'

The pips were sounding, and Kitty only just had time to say she'd send them a postcard, but it *was* good news, and it had knocked the row on the head, which was just as well.

'Time to make a salad I think,' Rosie said. She didn't point out how nice it would have been if she could have used home-grown tomatoes and radishes and lettuces, which she could've done if he hadn't been so pig-headed over that damned shelter. It was extremely forbearing of her, and she felt very smug about it.

Now, she thought, as she set the table, I'll write to Gracie and tell her what's happening and ask her if it's all right for Kitty to use her old bedroom and, if she's agreeable to it, which I'm sure she will be, I'll set to and get it ready. Those curtains could do with a wash for a start.

She'd felt very unsettled since she'd been laid off –not because she wasn't needed to drive that ambulance, she was only too glad to see the back of it and all the terrible suffering that came with it – but because she missed the company and the steady wage. She was a worker, that was the truth of it, always had been, and she wasn't used to being idle. Preparing this room for Kitty would give her something to do.

Gracie's postcard arrived by return of post. Of course Auntie Kitty could have her old room, she said. 'I've left home now and I've got my bedsit, which will do until we can find something else. It's high time Kitty left Binderton. She hasn't really been happy there for quite some time. I know Dad will be happy to have her home again. He worries about her a lot. Let me know how the move goes and give her my love.'

So Rosie set to and got the room ready, moving all Gracie's winter clothes into her own cupboards, washing the curtains, the bedspread, the windows, the floor, the picture rails, the skirting boards and every-thing else that looked even faintly grubby, until the room smelt fresh and new. She'd had very little time to read the papers or listen to the news bulletins, but that was just as well because the news was so bad it upset her to hear it.

The Germans were powering into Russia with their horrible panzers and their foul Luftwaffe in exactly the same way that they'd pushed into Belgium and Holland and France. The last thing she heard, they were heading for Moscow and Leningrad and the poor old Russians couldn't stop them, huge nation though they were. And things were just as bad in Africa. The British army seemed to be changing Generals every five minutes. The latest was a man called Wavell who'd taken over from another one called Auchinleck, and a fat lot of use that had been because neither of them knew what to do about Rommel, who was pushing the British army around whenever he felt like it.

'Bleedin' twits, the pair of 'em,' Jim said, scathingly. 'Same as last time. They ain't got a happorth a brain between the lot of 'em. Ol' Churchill should sack 'em all an' put someone in who knows what's what.'

But old Churchill didn't seem to be able to find a general who knew what was what, and the North African campaign stumbled on from small victories to small defeats without achieving anything. And it was nearly August. In another month they'd be into the third year of the war.

Kitty came back to the Borough on the first Saturday in August, in a sudden shower of summer rain and a battered old van driven by Mr Tennant. She was so happy she couldn't stop giggling.

'Gaw dearie me,' she said to Rosie, hanging out of her window and breathing in the smell of the city. 'It ain't 'alf grand to be back in the ol' smoke again. Breave that air! I couldn't be doing with all them cows.'

Rosie put the last of her cardboard boxes down on the bed and laughed at her. 'You are a caution Kitty,' she said. 'I rather like the smell of cows.'

'Well you would, wouldn'tcher?' Kitty said happily. 'You grew up with it. I'd rather smell a fish an' chip shop any day a the week, or a pub, or the ol' La-Di-Da. Is that still running?'

She was a bit disappointed to hear that it was closed. But she cheered up when she heard Jim calling to her as he ran upstairs, and bounded off at once to throw her arms round his neck and hug him and be hugged in return. And then Mr Tennant came toiling up the stairs with a pair of ancient wellington boots, a bookcase and a bedside lamp, which was the last of her luggage, and Jim said it was time for fish and chips all round, and what did they fancy, and he and Kitty went happily off to the chippy.

It was a riotous meal. The cat walked from chair to chair mumping for titbits and Mr Tennant was impressed by fish an' chips. 'I never tasted nothing as good as this,' he told Jim, shyly. 'Thankee kindly.'

'We couldn't have you driving all that way back on an empty stomach,' Jim said, beaming at him.

After their improvised banquet, Jim went back to the market saying he couldn't leave young Josh holding the fort forever, much though he wanted to, and Mr Tennant set off for his drive home, and the two women washed the dirty plates and went upstairs to unpack Kitty's cardboard boxes and put her bedroom to rights. It took them the whole afternoon, because they kept stopping to remember things, or so that Kitty could hang out of the window 'ter breave in some good ol' London air', so they were still hard at it when Sonia and Mrs Totteridge arrived with a welcome home cake for their tea.

That night Jim took his two women off to the Troc to see *In the Navy* with Abbott and Costello and they sat on either side of him like the old times, as if Kitty had never been away.

'What a day!' Kitty said, as they walked home arm in arm. 'I ain't 'ad one as good as this in years.'

'Whatcher want to do tomorrow?' Jim asked.

'Stay in bed till midday for a start,' Kitty told him, happily. 'I ain't had a lie-in since I don't know when. The boys are up at the crack a dawn, silly beggars.'

So it was a luxurious Sunday: a long lie in, late breakfast, Sunday roast in the middle of the afternoon and an evening spent happily listening to the wireless.

'You look like the Cheshire Cat,' Jim said, as they waited for the next programme to begin. 'You ain't stopped grinning since you got here. Has she, Rosie?'

'I'll have to keep a straight face tomorrow,' Kitty told him.

'Why's that then?'

'I shall be off job-hunting.'

'There's no rush,' Jim said. ''Ave a few days off.'

'Oh come on, our Jim,' Kitty said. 'You know me better'n that. I can't sit around all day. I'd go bonkers.'

'I've half a mind to come with you,' Rosie told her. 'It ent in my nature to be idle, neither.'

'Oh well,' Jim said. 'If you must, you must. Try the post office. They're looking for more posties, 'cording to Mr Moffat, an' you know the area.'

It was ridiculously easy. They strolled down to the post office after breakfast, applied, were taken on, given a uniform and told to report for duty the next morning.

'Blimey! That was quick,' Kitty said, as they powered back home. 'But there you are, that's London for you.'

'I think the war's got a lot to do with it too,' Rosie said, speaking her thoughts to try and make sense of them. 'I mean, time's sort of relative in a war. Sometimes everything hangs fire and we're all stuck, waiting for bad things to happen, and then they happen so quickly you can't take them all in.'

'Is that what it was like in the Blitz?' Kitty asked, her face concerned.

Rosie considered it. 'Yes, I suppose it was,' she said. 'Trouble is, being bombed addles your brain. But when you get the call out, you remember what you've got to do and how to do it. It's very odd.' They had reached the great bulk of St George's church, set well back from the road, sunlit and massive and imperturbable. 'On the other hand,' Rosie said, looking at it, 'when I was planning our Gracie's wedding, there were never enough hours in the day.'

'It was a lovely wedding,' Kitty said, remembering. 'How're they getting on?'

'Good, as far as I know,' Rosie said. 'She's still working in the office, an' I think that annoys her a bit because she wants to get back to nursing. She don't complain about it though, an' they seem happy together. He gets to see her whenever he can. Salisbury's no distance from his camp, you see, an' they give them passes.' And she thought of Mary and Bertie having to wait until he could get a long pass before they could see one another and felt quite sorry for them, because she had a feeling that their friendship was developing into a love affair, too. Not that she said anything. They would tell her in their own good time. War pushes people apart, she thought sadly. It don't give them nowhere near enough time together and that's not natural.

'We going up the pub tonight?' Kitty asked happily.

'I 'spect so,' Rosie grinned. 'After all, we got something to celebrate, ent we?'

It was a perfect summer's evening; soft, warm and easy. They went to the Royal Oak, where they met up with Mrs Totteridge and Sonia and had a good old sing-song and drank lots of beer, which Jim urged on them to whet their whistles. And afterwards they walked back to

Coney Street, arm in arm and still singing. The sky was a rich sapphire blue, pinpointed with snow-white stars, and there was enough moon for them to see their way without torches.

'What a day it's been,' Kitty said, and she began to sing again. '*By the light of the silvery moon, I want to spoon. To my honey I'll croon love's tune.*'

*

Mary and Bertie were strolling in the moonlight that evening too. They'd been in the Windmill on Clapham Common that evening, sitting as close together as they could get and enjoying a pie and a pint, feeling comfortably at home among the cheerful London voices, the clink of glasses, the constant buzz and bustle and the enveloping clouds of blue cigarette smoke. Now they were ambling between the chestnut trees in the peace of the common, where the trams were just a distant whir and the trees above their heads seemed to be whispering, stopping for kisses whenever the spirit took them, which it did with stronger and more passionate feelings every time.

'We oughter get married,' said Bertie, lifting his head after a particularly long kiss.

Mary was so drowsed with kisses that she heard the words in a vague, rather distant way and didn't pay any attention to them. 'Um,' she said, dreamily. Then she became aware that he was grinning at her.

'What?' she asked.

'I've just asked you to marry me,' he said.

That was a bit of a surprise although it shouldn't have been. 'Really?' she said and then felt guilty as she watched his face change. 'I mean, could we?'

The moon was shrouded in a dark cloud. 'If we both wanted to,' he said, doggedly. 'That's why I asked you.'

'Then we will,' she said. She hadn't been sure that this was what she wanted until she spoke the words, but now and suddenly the matter was settled.

He put his arms round her and held her tight. 'Oh my dear, darling Mary-Pary,' he said and kissed her most lovingly. 'Only the thing is,' he said, when the kiss was over, 'they've delivered our MK11s an' we're going to start training with 'em tomorrow an' then I don't know how long it'll be till we're sent out to the desert. But it won't be long, I can tell you that, an' I thought we ought to have a taste of married life 'fore I go, even if it's just a short one.'

'Right,' she said, instantly becoming clear-headed and practical. 'Then we'd better start planning it straight away. When can you come an' see Mum and Dad?'

'Good question,' he told her, grimacing. 'I might not get the chance for weeks. I'll write to them tonight, if that's all right.'

'OK,' she said. 'I'll get over an' see them as soon as I can swing it.' The moon had shaken off its shroud and was shining brightly. She could see his dear, loving brown eyes so clearly, she put her arms round his neck to kiss him.

But he was looking at his watch. 'We got ten minutes,' he said, 'and then I'd better take you back to Guy's and go and catch my train.'

Ten minutes sounded like no time at all to Mary. 'Then we'd better not waste a minute,' she said.

*

Bertie's letter turned up in the afternoon post that Rosie was delivering and, even though it was addressed to Mr and Mrs Jackson, she opened it and read it where she stood. Ah, she thought, so that's why Mary was so keen to come and see us tonight. And she couldn't wait to see what Jim would think of it.

He was late home that afternoon, so he only had half an hour to read Bertie's letter, but he took over as soon as he'd digested it.

'It'll take a bit a doing,' he said, 'but we'll manage between us. Least we know the ropes this time. They'll have to get a special licence, for one thing. He don't say where they wants to get married.'

'No,' Kitty said. 'I noticed that.'

'Mary'll know,' Rosie told them, filling the kettle. 'Sit down an' I'll make you a cup of tea. She'll be here in a minute.'

She arrived like a whirlwind, blowing facts and figures and information at them so quickly they could hardly take them in. Bertie had sent her a letter in the same post, and she'd brought it with her so that she could show them what he'd said – or *almost* all he'd said. Since their amazing conversation on the common, she'd lain awake for most of the night giving the matter a lot of thought and, by the time the sun came up, she'd decided that however her marriage might turn out, there was one thing she was sure about. Her wedding wouldn't be like Gracie's and Sam's. It was going to be *her* wedding and quite different.

'Now then,' she said, taking her cup of tea from Rosie, 'we haven't got a lot of time, so this is going to be a bit of a rush. He reckons they'll be sent to North Africa by the end of September, maybe even sooner, so we've only got six or seven weeks. I've written to tell him you'll need the names and addresses of all the people he wants to invite, and I've sent a postcard to Maggie asking her to be my bridesmaid.'

Rosie's eyebrows rose with surprise. 'What about Gracie?' she asked.

'I rang her this morning,' Mary said. 'She's finally got her job as a nurse. Took long enough, heaven knows, but she's got it now, and she doesn't want to ask for time off till she's settled in, which is under-standable. She'll come to the wedding, naturally, and so will Sam if he can get a pass. She said she thought Maggie would make an excellent bridesmaid. So that's all settled.'

Actually it hadn't been as easy as she made it sound. Gracie had been very miffed not to be asked, and they'd come uncomfortably close to having words over it, but Mary had managed to smooth it over, and they *had* agreed, come the finish.

'It'll have to be by special licence,' she went on, 'because we won't have enough time to call banns an' all that sorta thing. Bertie'll take care of that, but I shall need to get down to the registry office an' fix a date an' a time for us.'

Rosie and Kitty were staring at her, unmoving, as if they'd been transfixed, but Jim had recovered his breath. 'Right,' he said. 'I'll have to come with you, mind, to sign the consent form. Can you get time off We'nesday afternoon?'

Mary had forgotten that she'd need her parents' consent to get married, but she took it in her stride and tried not to show she was surprised. 'I'll ring you an' tell you,' she said and smiled at him. It was the first smile she'd given anybody since she breezed into the kitchen and, seeing it, Rosie and Kitty relaxed at little.

'It's in the town hall, opposite the ambulance station,' Rosie told her. 'You could catch the tram and meet him there. Corner of Neptune Street and Lower Road. An' there's a hall not far away, by the Wells tene-ments. We'll never get everyone in here this time. Not if your Bertie's got family, which I'll bet he has.'

'Hordes of them,' Mary said, grinning at her. 'Mum an' Dad an' two sisters, aunts an' uncles an' cousins, *and* a grandma he's very fond of.'

'Well there you are then,' Rosie said, feeling relieved to think that she would be involved in all this. While Mary had been pummelling them with information, she'd wondered whether her newly fierce daughter was going to do everything herself. 'We'll book the hall as soon as you've got a date.'

Now that she'd told them her plans, Mary felt smitten to see how much she'd surprised them all. 'I'm sorry it's such a rush,' she said to her mother. 'Only with him going away…'

'Don't worry, my darling,' Rosie said. 'We'll manage. Once we've got a date, we can get cracking on the food. There's plenty of us. I'll make a little cake tomorrow an' then it'll be all nice an' ready. It'll have to be a small one, but there'll be enough for a slice each. It'll all work out, you'll see.'

'Just so long as you don't get hiccups,' Jim warned, assuming a stern face. 'I had quite enough a that with your sister.'

That made them all laugh and remember.

'Are you staying to supper?' Rosie asked.

'Can't, I'm afraid,' Mary told her, making a rueful grimace. 'They let me have an hour off but that was all. I'm on night duty, you see.'

But she kissed them all most lovingly when she left them and promised to phone whenever she could. 'See you soon,' she called, as she cycled away.

'Well blow me down with a feather,' Kitty said as they all walked back into the kitchen. 'I never thought I'd live to see the day when your quiet little Mary'd come over all bossy-boots.'

'That's all you know kid,' Jim said, laughing at her. 'She can be a right little tartar when she likes. You should ha' seen her squaring up to Gracie when they was young. They was at it hammer an' tongs.'

'I think it's a bit more than sparring this time,' Rosie said. 'I think she's anxious.'

Jim was surprised. 'Why?' he said. 'She ain't on her own. She's got all of us rooting for her.'

'I don't know exactly,' Rosie said, 'but I know she's anxious. Bertie going to the desert, maybe. That's enough to make anyone anxious.'

'Right,' Jim said agreeing with her. 'What's for supper?'

'Fish an' chips?' Kitty hoped.

*

During the next few busy weeks none of them really had time to think of anything but the wedding preparations. Bertie's list of names and addresses came the next morning while Kitty and Rosie were making the wedding cake. Jim and Mary went to the registry office to settle the date on Wednesday afternoon and came back feeling pleased with themselves because it was fixed for three o'clock on Saturday the thirteenth ofSeptember, which Mary reckoned would just about give them time to have a honeymoon. The next day, Rosie and Kitty walked to the Wells tenements to book the hall, and that night Kitty and Jim and Rosie sat round the kitchen table sending out the invitations. It was all happening so quickly it seemed a bit unreal.

The days rushed by. The acceptances came back quickly and turned up in batches in Rosie's postbag, to Kitty's amusement. Bertie's father wrote to say he would provide the beer. A car was booked to take the bride and her father to the town hall in style. Flowers and button-holes were ordered. Mary came home to pack a bag and stay overnight in her old room. And the great day arrived with a bright sun warming her even through the curtains, and the birds singing as clearly as a choir, and her wedding dress hanging on a hook from the picture rail, clean and pressed and ready for her.

It puzzled her to realise that she wasn't excited. The day swept her up in its own momentum, and she simply went with it, eating the breakfast her mother had cooked for her, bathing and dressing, greeting her neighbours, hugging Sam and Gracie, being driven to the registry office with her dad, standing in front of a huge desk in a large panelled room while her guests sat behind her and her dear Bertie stood beaming beside her, and finally emerging into the sunlight in front of the town hall when the ceremony was over, to be showered with confetti.

It wasn't until they'd been driven to the hall, and she and Bertie were standing by the entrance greeting their guests as they trooped in, smiling and laughing, that she began to realise that she was married and happy about it.

It was an excellent wedding breakfast; good food, happy company and three entertaining speeches. Sam started off by telling them what a good bloke Bertie was in a crisis. 'Always cool, calm and collected. Couldn't want a better oppo.' Her dad looked along the table and said, 'I just found out our Bertie's dad is a docker same as me, only he comes from Bermondsey, an' I was bred in the Borough. But I won't hold that against you, mate. I'll tell you what though, us dockers breed damn good kids,' which made Bertie's family cheer, and Edie called out, 'Us yokels ent so bad at it neither,' and got a cheer from her side of the family too. And Bertie thanked them all for coming, in the traditional way, and confessed that he wasn't much cop at speechifying, but he had to tell them 'Mary is the best girl alive,' which got the third and loudest cheer.

And then the afternoon was over, and their driver appeared to take them to Waterloo and their train to Salisbury, where he'd booked a room for them in a lovely hotel called The Red Lion, because Sam had told him how very good it was.

'OK?' Bertie asked as they settled into their seats.

'Very,' she said and meant it.

'So I can kiss you?'

'If you don't mind getting a mouthful of confetti.'

'I'm quite partial to a mouthful of confetti,' he said, pulling her towards him. And when the kiss was over, he smiled into her eyes and said, 'Roll on tonight,' in such an amorous voice it made her shiver at the thought of the pleasure that was coming.

'Tonight and the next six nights,' she said.

He grinned at that. 'If the War Office is agreeable,' he said, stroking her cheek.

The War Office allowed them five of their seven nights, but when they came happily down to breakfast on their sixth morning, there was a letter stamped OHMS waiting by Bertie's plate. Mary could feel her heart shrinking at the mere sight of it. She watched him as he read it.

'Is it…?' she asked

''Fraid so.'

'When?'

'Eleven hundred hours.'

She wanted to howl that they couldn't do it, that it wasn't fair, but she knew she had to stay calm, the way they'd taught her at the hospital. 'When will you have to leave?'

'Bus at ten thirty. They've sent a chitty.'

She found she could be sensible. 'Just time to have our breakfast,' she said, 'an' then I'll help you pack.'

He gave her a bleak smile. 'Yes,' he said.

So they ate as much breakfast as they could although neither of them had much of an appetite, and then she packed his clothes while he went to settle the bill and to explain that they would both be leaving, and she managed to keep smiling until his bus was out of sight.

Then she wept most bitterly and was still weeping as she stumbled back to the hotel to pack her own bag. And there was Gracie waiting at reception. And oh, it *was* so good to see her. She ran towards her with her arms outstretched for comfort. Now she could say all the things she wanted and needed to say. 'It's not fair. They could've let us finish our honeymoon. Oh why, why, why do we have to have these stupid wars? What am I going to do now, Gracie?'

Gracie cuddled her and kissed her and stroked her damp hair out of her eyes. 'You're going to come back to my bedsit with me,' she said, 'and stay with me till it's time for you to go back to Guy's. It's all fixed. I'd say stay with me till they get sent to Africa, but we don't know when that'll be, and your leave'll be up in a day or two, won't it? I've phoned in to say I won't be at work for a couple of days. Told them why. They were half expecting it anyway. Come on.'

So that's what they did, and they were very glad of one another's company, for Gracie was every bit as worried and upset as her sister, and for exactly the same reason.

*

The Eighth Army was sent to North Africa at the end of September, just as Bertie had predicted. By that time Mary was back at work in Guy's, and Gracie was working out her notice in Salisbury so that she could return to Guy's too.

'They could be out there for months,' she said to Mary when they were phoning each other, 'and I'm damned if I'm going to stay in this place if that's the case.'

Sam and Bertie wrote to them every other day to keep them informed, not that there was very much they could tell them, because they were only fighting in an occasional skirmish, and nothing major seemed to be happening.

'Skirmishes sound all right to me,' Mary said to her sister. 'At least there's less chance of them getting wounded in a skirmish, or…'

The two of them were in the hospital canteen, eating their supper before they went on duty, and they'd been passing each other the information they'd gleaned from their letters and saying what a wicked waste of time this campaign was turning out to be.

'We need a new general who knows what's what,' Gracie said, piling pie on her fork.

'That's what Dad says,' Mary told her. 'He reckons this lot are bone-heads.'

But a general who knew what was what was still proving very difficult to find, and the campaign dragged on.

*

Life was a drag for a lot of people in Great Britain in the last months of 1941. Tinned food was put on ration using a points system, in which everybody had a certain number of points to spend and could use them on whatever tinned goods they needed. Mrs Totteridge said she'd never be able to work it out in a million years, but with Rosie and Kitty and Sonia to help her she managed it after a week or two.

The news from Russia got worse with every bulletin. Food shortages got worse with every week. The weather seemed to get worse with every day, with fogs and drizzling rain that made everything damp and dark and depressing, but at least you could grumble about that without feeling you were letting the side down.

But on 2 December the papers were full of disquieting news about a new call up. Single women between the ages of twenty and thirty were going to be conscripted into the forces and the papers reckoned that 1,700,000 of them would be eligible. And as if that weren't ominous enough, men were now going to be conscripted from the age of eighteen to fifty.

'They'll be after you,' Rosie said to Jim, looking anxious.

'Oh Jim!' Kitty worried. 'They won't, will they? Not after all you done the last time.'

'No they won't,' Jim said, grinning at them. 'Don't worry. I done my bit. An' anyway, I wouldn't pass the medical, not with this leg. If they call me up, I shall take a stick with me an' limp like a good un. But I'll tell you what they *will* do. They'll take our Josh an' that'll be a real blow. I shall have a job to find someone as good as him.'

'We'll face that when we have to,' Rosie said.

'We could do with some *good* news,' Jim said.

Good news of a sort was reported four days later. The German high command had announced that the expected attack on Moscow wouldn't take place until after the winter.

'Well at least that's given the poor old Russkies a bit of a respite,' Kitty said, as she and Rosie enjoyed the picture of a group of German soldiers trying to struggle through a snowdrift, with their eyebrows frozen solid. The Russians, on the other hand, were making good use of the bad weather and had been bringing in supplies to Stalingrad across the frozen Lake Ladoga for several weeks. On the inside of the paper was a picture of horse-drawn sledges travelling over a solidly frozen lake.

'Good luck to 'em,' Rosie said, 'they know how to handle their winter.'

'Well, they're used to it,' Kitty said.

'The Germans should never've gone there in the first place,' Jim told them dourly. 'Serve the buggers right.'

'It makes you wonder what's gonna happen next,' Kitty said, sighing.

What happened next was reported the very next morning –and it was something that nobody expected.

CHAPTER SEVENTEEN

The velvety voice of the newsreader that Sunday morning was so smooth and soothing that, for a few seconds, Jim, Rosie and Kitty couldn't take in the horror and enormity of what he was saying. They sat on their saggy sofa and that well-worn armchair and stared at the wireless in disbelief.

'At just before eight o'clock this morning, local time,' the newsreader said, 'Japanese warplanes attacked and bombed the American fleet, which was lying at anchor in Pearl Harbour. There had been no declaration of war from the Japanese embassy and the attack was completely unprovoked. Many ships, including the USS *Arizona* were destroyed and sunk. It is estimated that over two thousand American personnel have been killed.'

Kitty was the first to find her tongue. 'Good God alive!' she said. 'They can't do that! Ain'tcher supposed ter declare war first, 'fore you start bombin' people?'

'It's barbaric,' Rosie said, still staring at the wireless. 'What chance did all those poor devil sailors have?'

Jim's response was more pragmatic. 'Well that's settled that,' he said. 'The Yanks'll have to come into the war after this.'

'Two thousand dead,' Rosie mourned. 'Poor things.'

But Kitty was thinking over what Jim had said. 'Will they?' she asked. 'I mean to say…'

'Yes,' Jim said, rather grimly. 'They will. They got no choice. Not now. An' high time too. They've sat on their backsides quite long enough.'

He was proved right the next day, when the headlines shouted, 'Pearl Harbour bombed: US at war,' and reported that President Roosevelt had addressed a specially-convened session of Congress as soon as the news came through. He had spoken passionately and from the heart. 'Yesterday,' he said, '7 December 1941 – a date which will live in infamy –the United States of America was suddenly and deliberately attacked by naval and air forces of the Empire of Japan.' And he urged Congress to take action

By the end of the day, Congress had declared war on Japan.

From then on, one declaration followed another.

In the small hours of Monday morning, following their now established principle of striking first and declaring war afterwards, the Japanese bombed Singapore. This time they declared war on Great Britain a few hours later. The retaliatory declaration from London came by mid afternoon. Three days later, Germany and Italy declared war on the USA, and Congress answered by declaring war on Germany and Italy on the same day.

By next morning, when Rosie and Sonia walked up to the Borough Market to get their shopping, the place was fizzing with shock, excitement and satisfaction.

'Quite right too,' people said to one another. 'High time they come in ter the war. They should ha' done it years ago. We been on our own a bleedin' sight too long.' One or two asked, 'What price them bleedin'

Japs?' and said they didn't think 'much a that fer a way ter go on', but most of the talk was about the Americans.

'My Jim'll be in his element this morning,' Rosie said, grinning at Sonia. 'This is just what he said when we heard the news.'

But although Jim was smiling at his customers the way he always did, he looked anxious when he turned away from them.

'What's up?' Rosie asked when he started to serve Sonia.

'Josh's got his call-up,' Jim said. 'Goin' Saturday.'

'Blimey!' Sonia said. 'That was quick. What'll you do now?'

'Try to find someone to replace 'im, I s'pose,' Jim said. 'I reckon I'll have me work cut out to find one though. He'll be a hard act to foller.'

Sonia grinned at him and made him an offer he didn't expect. 'I could come down an' give you a hand to tide you over, if you like?' she offered.

'Straight up?'

'Yeh,' she said. 'I'd love to. I'm pretty good at maths. I used to work in an office 'fore I got married.'

He thought about it as he tipped her potatoes into her basket. Then he asked, 'Could you start Saturday?'

'Yes. Course. What time?'

''Alf past seven.'

'I'll be here,' she promised.

'You're a dark horse,' Rosie said as she and Sonia struggled home with their laden baskets. 'I never knew you were job hunting.'

'Nor did I,' Sonia admitted. 'Not 'til your Jim told us about Josh. The thing is, I get lonely on me own. I miss the company down the tube. We had a lark down there most nights, singin' an' chattin' an' doin' our knittin', an' now I'm on me own. I wouldn't wish the Blitz back for all the tea in China – don't misunderstand me – but I miss the company.'

'You could always come in to us,' Rosie said.

Sonia grinned. 'Not at two in the mornin' I couldn't,' she said. 'No. This job'll suit me fine. Providin' I suit your Jim.'

It took him three days to make up his mind. On the fourth he told her he was taking her on 'permanent'.

'Good,' Rosie said, when he told her too. 'Now all we want is for the Yanks to start doing something about the Germans.'

'If you ask me, they got their work cut out for the moment, dealin' with the Japs,' Jim said, dourly.

It was hideously true, as the headlines shouted at them nearly every day. The Japanese were bombing and invading all sorts of places, most of which they'd never heard of, like Guam, Kotu Bharu, Thailand, Malaya, the Phillipines and Kowloon. And on Christmas Day, as a final blow to finish the year, they captured Hong Kong.

By that time, Gracie had served out her notice in Salisbury and had come back to work at Guy's, so she and Mary came home for Christmas dinner, such as it was. Jim had tried hard to get them a turkey or a chicken, but there were none to be had, so they had to make do with a leg of mutton. But it was lovely to have them home, sitting round the table, pulling crackers and wearing paper hats, cracking jokes with Kitty and singing the old songs with Sonia and Mrs T, feeding tit-bits to the cat, which sat between them and reminded them of her starving condition from time to time by piteous mewing, and complaining to their mother that they never got any real news from Sam and Bertie.

'They say they're well, and they've got a tan, and they don't think much of sandstorms, and the grub's not bad,' Mary said, 'but they can't tell us where they are or what's happening because the censor would put his blue pencil through it.'

'An' quite right too,' Jim said. ''Ave some more beer.' And when their

265

glasses were full, he raised his own in a toast. 'Here's to 1942,' he said. 'An' victory to us an' the Yanks.'

Personally Rosie thought that 1942 wouldn't be very different from 1941, but she didn't say so. They needed a bit of hope or the world would be a very dark place. I'll wait and see what happens when the Americans get here, she thought. I hope they buck their ideas up.

The Americans arrived in England and Northern Ireland at the end of January in long, cheerfully straggly columns, chewing gum and singing and tossing handfuls of sweets, which they called candy, at the kids who'd come to watch them arrive. They were escorted by funny little square jalopies, which carried three men and were called jeeps, and by shiploads of kit and provisions of all kinds, but mostly tinned: cans of Coca Cola, cigarettes, medical supplies. As Jim said rather enviously, 'You name it, they've got it.' But whatever you might think of their provisions, they'd obviously come prepared for a long stay.

Three weeks later, the US Eighth Air Force followed them over and began to look for suitable sites for their airfields.

'Now,' Rosie said, 'we shall see a difference.'

'Let's hope so,' Jim said morosely. 'I can't see much difference in the newspapers.'

It was true enough. The news seemed to be uniformly bad, whichever war zone was being featured. At the end of January, the Germans captured Benghazi and started to push the Eighth Army back towards Egypt. In February, the Japanese overran Singapore.

But spring arrived, despite the bad news, to spread sunshine in the parks and gardens with a boldness of daffodils and forsythia, tulips stood to attention like guardsmen, the cherry trees bloomed as if there were no such thing as war, their blackbird sang from the may tree as he always did, and when they weren't delivering letters, Rosie and Kitty gave the kitchen a good spring clean. Josh sent Jim a letter to say he'd finished his square bashing and was coming home on leave in a day or two, which he did, wearing his new RAF uniform and looking older than he'd done when he left them, which was a bit disconcerting. But he was given a hero's welcome in the market and patted on the back by his customers until he laughed at them and begged them to 'give over'.

'Now what will he do?' Rosie asked, when he'd gone lolloping off through the crowds to see his grandmother. 'I mean, where will he go?'

'Wherever they send 'im,' Jim told her. 'You don' get a choice once you're in the forces.'

That's true, Rosie thought, and wondered what Sam and Bertie were doing and where they were. The girls told her whenever they got a letter or a card, and it was always the same – they were well, they were brassed off with being in the desert, the grub was OK, they sent their love. And in the meantime, as far as she could see from what the papers were reporting, the Eighth Army was being steadily pushed back, closer and closer to Egypt. In May the papers reported that they'd reached a place called Mersa Matruh, which wasn't in Gracie's school atlas, but which, from the sketch maps in the paper, looked dangerously close to the frontier with Egypt.

Yet it was a superb summer, no matter what was happening in other parts of the world; the sunshine strong and warming, the sky as blue as a postcard, and a glut of plums in every greengrocers. They had plum pie and plum crumble to top off nearly every meal and ate them raw like sweets, letting the juice roll down their chins as if they were kids. If it hadn't been for the bomb sites they passed on their rounds, and the bad news on the wireless, Rosie and Kitty could have been entirely happy.

But the news pulled them back to reality in frequent and searing bulletins.

BERYL KINGSTON

On 10 June the newsreaders reported that there had been a massacre in Poland. One of Hitler's prized henchmen, a man called Heydrich, had been driving his sports car through Prague when it received a direct hit from a bomb and was blown to pieces. It was claimed that the bomb was thrown by someone in the Polish resistance, and Hitler and Himmler had decided to take revenge for it. They chose a small village called Lidice, which was just outside Prague, rounded up the 199 men and boys who lived there, and shot them all dead. Then they packed the women and children off to two separate concentration camps and set fire to their homes, using high explosives when the flames began to die down to ensure that there was nothing left of the place at all.

Rosie and Kitty heard the news when they came home from their afternoon round and both of them wept at the brutality of it.

'What sort of people can do things like this?' Rosie said, struggling to make sense of such cruelty.

'Monsters,' Kitty said. 'That's what they are, an' when this bleedin' war's over, I hope they take the whole bleedin' lot of 'em and put 'em up against the nearest wall an' shoot 'em dead.'

It was something she would say with increasing frequency over the next few weeks, because the news was full of horrors. In fact, one of the things they read at the end of the month was so absolutely dreadful that Rosie couldn't bear to believe it.

It was a report about a new concentration camp that the Nazis had built in Poland. There was nothing new about German concentration camps, of course. Most people knew that the Nazis had been herding the Jews into camps, where they'd be hidden away and out of sight, ever since they started moving them out of the cities where they lived. That was bad enough. But this was worse. For if this report was true, the

268

Nazis had now built a camp in a place called Treblinka, which would have what they called 'a facility' in which the Jews would be killed.

'It can't be true,' Rosie said. 'They couldn't possibly do a thing like that. It'd be murder.' But she was remembering Gerry de Silva and the things he'd told her when they were saying goodbye. 'They will kill us because we're Jews,' he'd said. 'Jews, gypsies, communists, anybody they don't like. They call us the *untermensch.*'

Kitty made a grimace. 'I wouldn't put it past 'em,' she said. 'They think they're the lords a the earth. They can do whatever they want.'

That was Jim's opinion of it too when he read the paper. 'It's got a name,' he pointed out, 'so if you ask me, it's real, an' someone's found out about it.'

'What sort of world are we living in?' Rosie said. It made her feel desperate to think about a camp built for murdering people.

'One what needs changing,' Jim said. 'An' we'll have to beat the beggars first before we can change 'em.'

'I wonder what our gels'll think about it,' Kitty said. 'They're bound to have seen the paper.'

They had, but they hadn't paid much attention to it because both of them were hard at work nursing their newest casualties, who had been flown back from the desert seriously wounded and needing a great deal of care. One in particular, a private called Jock, was in a very bad state, with a shattered right leg that had to be amputated below the knee and shrapnel wounds all over his back, which meant that he had to lie on his chest after his wounds had been dressed and was obviously extremely uncomfortable. At first he simply groaned with the pain of what they were doing to him, and they gave him morphine whenever he would accept it, but he resisted strongly, saying it made him feel worse than the pain did. Then Gracie checked his notes and discovered that he'd been a gunner in an artillery regiment in the Eighth Army and, in an effort to distract him from the pain, she asked him what it had been like in the desert.

Her question unleashed a torrent of such foul language that it shocked everybody in the ward, nurses and patients alike. 'Like?' he roared. 'You dare to ask me what it was fucking like! You wasn't there. It was a fucking hell hole. That's what it was. A fucking hell hole. Like being in a fucking oven. An' it stunk to high bleedin' heaven. We was covered in muck an' filth from morning to night, and the nights was so bleedin' cold they froze yer bollocks off, an' the days was so bleedin' hot the sweat poured off us in buckets. An' there was bleedin' great black flies crawling all over everything, in an out yer wounds, all over every fucking thing, piles a fucking shit, burnt out fucking tanks, stupid fucking guns blown inside out, bleedin' corpses. It was a fucking nightmare. That's what it was. A total fucking God-awful nightmare.' And then his face crumpled and he began to cry in great gulping painful sobs that made his chest shake. And two of the nearest nurses rushed to comfort him. And he shook them away and told them, 'Fuck off!'

'Leave him be,' Gracie said. 'He'll have to get over this by himself.' She was badly shaken because she knew that this was what Sam was enduring. It had to be. But she was determined to stay under control. 'Go and look after young Paul,' she told the younger of the two nurses. 'He's crying too and he could use some comfort. Hold his hand. And Frances,' turning to the other nurse. 'Go and find sister.'

When the incident had been reported, and Jock was quiet again, and the ward had been smoothed back into its usual running order, she felt too weary to stand and went to sit down at the nurses' station to try to get her thoughts back into running order as well. But they were spinning round and round in her head, and she couldn't push them away. Sam was out there in all that filth, with the flies and the heat and the corpses. Tanks could take a direct hit, and what happened to the crew then? She ached to talk to Mary. But that would have to wait until her supper time, when she'd be off duty. She wanted to weep and howl that these terrible things should never have to be endured, but nurses didn't behave like that. I hate war, she thought, looking down at her hard-working hands. It's ugly and brutal and destructive. There ought to be some other way to tackle fascists. But she couldn't think of an answer, and one of her patients was calling for attention. So she got on with her job.

That weekend, when Gracie and Mary went to tea at Coney Street, they both had news they wanted to pass on to their parents but, instead of being able to do so, they found themselves in the middle of a serious discussion. More bad news had come out of Poland that morning, with a horrible report from Warsaw. According to the journalist, the Jewish ghetto was '*now effectively a concentration camp*' with thousands of Jews penned in, living nineteen to a room, with no medicine and precious little food, and dying from disease and starvation every day. This time Rosie said it was horrible but she could believe it.

'I mean, they're not killing them, are they?' she said. 'Not deliberately killing them.'

'They're cramming 'em into ghettos an' not letting 'em out,' Kitty said hotly, 'an' they're starving 'em to death an' not lifting a finger to help 'em. To my way a lookin' at it, that's just as bad.'

Rosie clung on to her faint hope. 'But they're not shooting them,' she insisted, 'or gassing them or whatever it is they're going to do to them in that horrible concentration camp. They've got a chance if they can hang on.'

Her face was drawn and distressed and, watching her, Gracie felt so sorry for her she knew she couldn't tell her about Jock and the way he'd carried on. That would be cruel. Dad'll have to sort this out, she thought, looking at him hopefully.

But Jim didn't know what to say. He was almost as distressed as Rosie, because he wanted to comfort her and he knew how much she needed him to agree with her, but he simply couldn't do it. 'Trouble is,' he said, 'Hitler and his gang a prize thugs promised their voters they'd get rid a the Jews once an' for all, an' now they got to do it. One way or another. I think this is one of the ways.' And when Rosie winced, 'I'm sorry, kid. I know it's bleedin' awful, but that's how I see it. I ain't gonna tell you lies.'

Gracie and Mary passed rapid eye-messages to one another, and Gracie shook her head to show that she wasn't going to mention the swearing outburst and raised her eyebrows in a question and, to her considerable relief, Mary found something anodyne to say.

'Is there any more tea? she asked, lifting the lid and looking in the teapot.

'I'll make a fresh pot,' Rosie said. 'That'll be stewed by now.' And she went to fill the kettle.

'I had a nice letter from Bertie this morning,' Mary said as the kettle boiled. 'It made me laugh.'

'What did he say?' Gracie encouraged, pouring the dregs from their cups into the slop basin.

'He was telling me how brassed off they are with having one new general after another,' Mary said, looking round at them all, 'and he said they wouldn't mind if any of them were any good at the job, and then he said, "*Good ones are as rare as a cock's egg*". I've never heard that before. I thought it was rather good.'

Jim laughed at it. 'That's what comes a growing up in Bermondsey,' he said.

Mary laughed with him. 'Oh is *that* what it is?' she said and, having got their attention, went on with some more news from the letter. 'He says they're all chuffed about the Yanks declaring war. They've got new equipment coming, and he says it could make all the difference.'

'Let's hope so,' Rosie said, putting the refilled teapot back on its trivet. 'Now, who's for another cuppa?' and Gracie gave her sister a nod of approval, thinking how deftly she'd responded.

But the bad news went on, and no matter how cheerful they tried to be, the weeks passed slowly without the slightest sign of a victory anywhere. By the beginning of July, the Germans had pushed the British army back to a place called El Alamein, which was alarmingly close to the Egyptian frontier.

'Now what'll we do?' Kitty said.

'Send out another bleedin' useless general,' Jim told her. 'If I'm any judge.'

'Well let's hope they pick a good un, that's all,' Kitty said.

They picked a man called Lieutenant-General William Gott. But his reign as a general didn't even begin because the plane that was taking him to the war zone was shot down en route, and he was killed.

'Now what? Rosie wondered.

''Now they'll pick another one,' Jim said miserably, 'an' if he runs true to form he'll be as bad as all the others.'

But he was wrong. The replacement they chose was Lt Gen. Bernard Montgomery, and he was a general who meant business. Within a week he had taken over command of the Eighth Army, and by early September, three hundred Sherman tanks and one hundred self-propelled guns began to arrive from America. It wasn't long before Sam was writing to Gracie to report that their new general was '*the real McCoy. He knows what we need when we're stuck out here in the desert for one thing. We have showers ready for us when we come off duty, which is bliss after a day when you've been sweating torrents. It's only a bucket of water in a raised tarpaulin, but give us that and a bar of Wright's coal tar and we're like new men. You wouldn't believe how hot it is here.'*

Not to be outdone, Gracie wrote to tell him she'd heard a lot about life in the desert from one of her patients, so she knew what they were enduring. '*Just look after yourself,*' she wrote. '*I'd like you home in one piece. I worry about you every time we get a new patient.*'

'*You can stop worrying for a few weeks,*' he told her in his next letter, '*because we shall be on manoeuvres, learning how to handle our new machines.*'

Although he couldn't tell her much, he and Bertie were actually learning how to handle the new Mark 4 Sherman tanks that had arrived from America. They were very impressed by them because they were a marked improvement on the old ones, with greater manoeuvrability and much more powerful guns. It was obvious to all of them that their new general was preparing for a battle in a thorough way. The gunners now had the latest self-propelled guns, and there were Wellington bombers training in the desert too, and rumours that they were soon to have the new B-25's from America as well.

'I wish I could tell Mary what's going on,' Bertie said morosely, as he and Sam and the rest of the crew were taking time off for a fag.

'I reckon they know quite a bit without us telling them,' Sam told him. 'They nurse the wounded, don't forget. Gracie says *they've* been talking about it quite freely.' Poor old Bertie was looking a bit glum and, as Sam was newly promoted corporal, he felt responsible for him. Then he noticed men on their feet a few hundred yards away. 'Hey up!' he said. 'We're off again.'

*

They spent the rest of September getting used to manoeuvring their new tanks over different terrains, while Gracie and Mary wrote to them every day and listened to the wireless whenever they could –even though it never told them the news they wanted to hear. It was a long month, and very little seemed to be happening except in Russia, where the German troops were attacking again, and in the Far East where the Japanese seemed to be getting things their own way wherever they invaded. There were rumours that they treated their prisoners very badly, starving them and beating them and making them march hundreds of miles to get to their POW camps. Rosie said she hoped they *were* rumours but secretly felt that, after Pearl Harbour, the Japanese were capable of anything.

But it was news from North Africa they were all waiting for. Kitty grew more impatient for it by the day.

'What are they playin' at?' she said. 'They been faffin' about in that stupid desert for months. Why don't they get on with it?'

If Sam and Bertie had been there, they could have told her exactly why they were taking such a long time. Over the last few busy weeks, they learned that to fight a major battle you need to be fully prepared, down to the last little detail – and probably beyond that. It was something their new general had been dinning into them ever since he arrived, and they understood it very well. They knew he wouldn't start this battle until everything was good and ready. And they knew he expected to win it. They couldn't say they were looking forward to it – that would have been foolhardy – but they were facing it with more confidence than they'd felt in months. They knew they outnumbered the Germans in men and tanks and that they were better equipped with their new tanks and anti-tank guns, and they also knew that Wellington bombers were on hand to give them support and protection.

But they also had a sneaky feeling that old Monty was up to something. They were used to his clipped way of talking and had accepted that he was eccentric, but this seemed to be a step further than eccentricity. On two occasions he'd ordered the brigade to take up positions further south than they were expecting to, and when they camped, cardboard shapes were handed round to every tank with instructions that they were to put them over their vehicles and keep them there until they moved on again.

'Very odd,' Sam said.

'There'll be a reason for it, you mark my words,' Bertie said, drawing on his fag.

'Oh well, we shall see in time,' Sam said, lighting up. 'It won't be long now.'

It began with a roar of gunfire on 23 October at 9.40 pm . Nearly six hundred allied guns opened up simultaneously along the El Alamein front, from the Mediterranean to the Qattara Depression, and they fired non-stop for fifteen minutes. To the men of the Eighth Armoured, waiting just behind the forward positions, the noise was deafening, and the blaze from the explosions so bright it hurt their eyes.

They were all taut with fear and excitement, although none of them spoke about it. In fact none of them said very much at all. They were ready; orders would come through sooner or later. As they did, with an abrupt calm that was oddly reassuring. And then they were off, driving into battle.

There was a full moon that night, and the desert was burnished with bronze, but it was a long night too and sometimes a confusing one because things seemed to be happening so quickly that it was almost impossible to take them all in. They knew the gunners had taken out several enemy tanks in that first attack because they'd seen the fires, and they'd heard the Wellington bombers as they passed overhead and watched the distant explosions from their raid, but there were moments when it was all they could do to obey orders, keep their tanks steady and fire at their distant targets. By the time the sun rose they were drenched in sweat and extremely tired, but the sight that was revealed in that smoky dawn was worth all the effort. There were burnt-out panzers in every direction and no sign of any German advance.

'If you ask me,' Bertie said, 'they didn't know we was coming. Or at least, not from this direction. I reckon we caught 'em on the hop. Maybe that's what all that cardboard was about.'

It wasn't until twelve days later, when Rommel's army was obviously retreating, and the Eighth Army was in cheerful pursuit, that the full story of Monty's cunning was passed along the British lines. They heard how he'd left piles of rubbish under tarpaulin until the German reconnaissance planes had seen it and had then removed the rubbish in the dark of night and replaced it with full petrol cans, ready to refuel his tanks; how he'd sent troops south so that Rommel would think they were going to be attacked from the south and driven into the sea and would move his panzers accordingly. It reassured them to think that their general was so splendidly devious and had every detail of this campaign under such control.

Back home, the news of Montgomery's victory was published at the end of October, and from then on his advance was followed day by day. It was the best news they'd had since the war began, and it got better daily. Three hundred German tanks had been destroyed and over 25,000 Axis troops killed or wounded. Tobruk had been captured.

'I'm beginning to think we might win this war after all,' Rosie said to Jim and Kitty.

'There's never been the slightest doubt about it,' Jim said, stolidly. 'Not in my book, anyway.'

On 15 November the church bells were rung to celebrate the victory. It was the first time their joyous clamour had been heard since the outbreak of the war. And that evening Mr Churchill gave a speech in the House of Commons, which caught the mood in the country to perfection.

'Now this is not the end,' he said. 'It is not even the beginning of the end. But it is, perhaps, the end of the beginning.'

Yes, Rosie thought, that's exactly what it is. The end of the beginning. And the words were an enormous comfort to her.

CHAPTER EIGHTEEN

Kitty erupted into the kitchen laden with shopping and in a state of such excitement she looked quite wild, her hair tousled, face pink, glasses slipping down her nose, waving an official looking booklet in the air with her free hand.

'Look at this!' she yelled at Rosie.

Rosie was making a pie, but she paused and grinned at her sister-in-law. 'What is it?' she said, pushing back her own hair and smearing her face with flour.

'It's a bleedin' revolution,' Kitty said, triumphantly. 'That's what it is. A bleedin' revolution. After all that fuss with the vote an' the way they led us on an' played us around, I never thought I'd live to see the day one of *them* would talk about revolution. But he has an' this is it.'

She put the leaflet on the table next to the mixing bowl and beamed at it. 'Read it. Start at page four. Read that bit. *Three guiding principles of recommendations.*'

Rosie would have preferred to read it from page one so as to make sense of it, but under the pressure of Kitty's driving excitement, she did as she was told and read it.

'*6. In proceeding from this first comprehensive survey of social insurance to the next task – of making recommendations – three guiding principles may be laid down at the outset.*

7. The first principle is that any proposals for the future, while they should use to the full the experience gathered in the past, should not be restricted by consideration of sectional interests established in the obtaining of that experience. Now, when the war is abolishing landmarks of every kind, is the opportunity for using experience in a clear field. A revolutionary moment in the world's history is a time for revolutions, not for patching.'

She was so impressed by the final sentence that she read it aloud.

'Ain't it grand?' Kitty said happily. '"*A time for revolutions, not for patching."* Never thought I'd live to see the day. Read the next bit.'

But Rosie was looking at the title page. 'Ah,' she said. 'Now I know what this is. It's the report they were talking about on the wireless this morning. The Beveridge Report.'

'Ol' Mrs Totteridge told me about it in the market,' Kitty said. 'That's why I was late getting back. She reckoned it was the best thing she'd read in the whole of her life, so I thought I'd stop off an' get a copy fer myself to see what was what, sorta thing. Had to queue for ages, mind you, and it cost me two bob, but it's worth every penny. I read it outside the shop. Look at the next bit about the Giants.'

'What giants?' Rosie said, a bit bemused by the speed Kitty was going at.

'Read it an' see,' Kitty urged.

So Rosie read on. '*8. The second principle is that organisation of social insurance should be treated as one part only of a comprehensive policy of social progress. Social insurance fully developed may provide income security; it is an attack upon Want. But Want is only one of the five giants on the road of reconstruction and in some ways the easiest to attack. The others are Disease, Ignorance, Squalor and Idleness.'*

'Well he's got that right an' no mistake,' she said. 'We'll read the rest of it tonight when Jim's back, shall we? I *must* get on with this pie.'

'Good idea,' Kitty said. 'To tell you the truth I only got that far with it, but I had to show you.'

So that's what they did. It was a riotous meal because Jim was as excited about the report as Kitty. He began to read it slowly and carefully while they were setting the table and dishing up the pie and, when he set it to one side and took up his knife and fork, he was grinning like a Cheshire cat.

'I knew it'd be good,' he said, 'on account a the way they been talking about it in the market – on an' on an' on – but I never thought it'd be *this* good. Have you read it all?'

'Not yet,' Kitty admitted. 'We got as far as the Giants. We thought we could read it together this evening. We could take it in turns to pick things out an' read 'em. Whatcher think?'

'I'll say one thing fer the man,' Jim said, as he cut off his first slice of pie. 'He's put his finger on what's wrong with the country. Want, Disease, Ignorance, Squalor – we seen enough a that in the Borough, ain't we Kitty? And Idleness. We seen enough a that too. Men moochin' about the streets trying to earn a livin' selling matches an' bootlaces. An' think a the Jarrow March. All that way just to ask fer a job. Which they never got. They was desperate times.'

'I wish he'd called it unemployment, though,' Kitty said. 'That would've been more accurate than idleness. Ter me, idleness means not gettin' on with yer work when you know you oughter be. Herbert was allus callin' my poor kids idle – when they didn't clear the table quick enough to suit him or they was laughin' when he came in. He couldn't stand 'em laughin', poor little devils.'

'It don't matter what he calls it, kid,' Jim said easily. 'I mean, we know what he means an' that's what counts. It's what he reckons we could *do* about his Giants that's the main thing. Did yer get to that bit?'

'No,' Rosie said, teasing him. 'We left it for you to read. Didn' we Kitty? Out the kindness of our hearts.'

'Well ta very much,' he said, grinning at her. 'I'd better get on wiv it then.'

He read for half an hour, sitting very still in his old armchair, holding the booklet in both hands and concentrating hard, while Rosie and Kitty listened to the wireless and pretended not to watch him. It was the most difficult thing he'd ever read in his life, and he had to go back over it from time to time to be sure he understood what was being said, because he knew how important it was. And finally, just as they were announcing the nine o'clock news, he got his reward.

'Well damn me!' he said, looking up from his studies. 'Never thought I'd ever see one a the nobs writin' like this. I dunno how he's done it but I'll tell yer this. He knows what it's like ter be poor. I mean, really knows. Understands. He's listed all the times when you can't manage ter feed yer family an' you're worried sick – when you're out a work, or you're too ill to work, or you're injured, or you're too old. Got it bang ter rights. And he's got the answer to it an' all. It's brilliant. He don't think much a the dole and that bleedin' means test. He's seen right through that. No, he thinks we should 'ave '*a scheme of social insurance*'. Jest listen ter this.' And he picked up the booklet and found the page he wanted and read it to them.

'"*Under the scheme of social insurance, which forms the main feature of this plan, every citizen of working age will contribute in his appropriate class according to the security he needs, or as a married woman will have contributions paid by the husband. Each will be covered for all his needs by a single weekly contribution on one insurance document. All the principle cash payments – for unemployment, disability and retirement will continue so long as the need lasts, without means test, and will be paid from a Social Insurance Fund built up by contributions from the insured persons, from their employers, if any, and from the State. This is in accord with two views as to the lines on which the problem of income maintenance should be approached.*" And just listen to this. "*The first view is that benefit in return for contributions, rather than free allowances from the State, is what the people of Britain desire.*" Ain't that amazing! No one wants ter be beholden.'

Somewhere in the background to his excitement, the newsreader was talking about North Africa, and Rosie held her hand up to warn them to listen, which they did. It was good news. The British Eighth Army was still steadily driving the German army back towards Tripoli and were expected to reach the town in the next few days.

'Let's hope they do,' Kitty said. 'Then they can drive the buggers right out of Africa altogether and have done wiv 'em. They should never 'ave gone there in the first place.'

'They went fer the oil, kid,' Jim told her. 'Same as we done.'

'Well now they can scarper,' Kitty said, firmly. 'That's another bit a good news.'

Rosie was still thinking about the impact of the report. 'I wonder what the papers will make of our Sir William,' she said.

'We'll see in the morning,' Jim said. 'I could do with a pint. Let's go up the pub.'

It was a lively evening because so many of the regulars had heard about the report and wanted to know more, and some of them had read it and were spreading the news.

'Is it as good as they say, mate?' one of Jim's cronies asked him and beamed when he said it was 'Even better' and explained how the new services were going to be paid for. And old Mrs Totteridge was there with the best, extolling its virtues while she sipped her pint. It was, as Jim and his two 'gels' told one another on the way home, the best evening ever.

The next morning the papers gave their seal of approval. *The Times* called the report 'a momentous document which should and must exercise a profound and immediate influence on the direction of social change in Britain', the *Manchester Guardian* described it as 'a big and fine thing', while the *Daily Telegraph* said it was 'a consummation of the revolution begun by David Lloyd George in 1911.'

The Archbishop of Canterbury said it was 'the first time anyone had set out to embody the whole spirit of the Christian ethic in an Act of Parliament', and a fortnight later, the TUC announced that it was putting its considerable clout behind the report, too.

In fact, as far as Rosie could see, there was only one dissenting voice, and that came after a meeting of the British insurance companies who attacked it furiously and said it would never work. That made Jim and Rosie laugh.

'Poor little diddums!' Jim mocked. 'If we vote in a new health service, they're gonna lose their big fat profits an' they don't like that a bit. Our Kitty's gonna love this!'

'Our Kitty' had gone down to Binderton that day to see the twins, but Gracie and Mary came to tea and they were very excited about the new health service that the report was proposing.

'High time we had a proper health care system,' Gracie said. 'I saw how awful the present one was when I was in Salisbury. They had an infirmary there for the poor, where they had to sit on the benches and wait for hours, poor things, and when they were finally seen, the doctors were too exhausted to care for them properly, although they did the best they could. And in the rest of the hospital, the rich were being given really excellent service, constant attention, private rooms, good meals, the best doctors. I thought it was very unfair. I still do. If you're ill, you need to be looked after properly.'

'This new health service of his sounds a wonderful idea,' Mary said,' but will the government allow it? I mean, won't they vote against it?'

'They will if there are enough of them in favour of it,' Jim told her. 'We just got ter see there's plenty a the right kind elected.'

'And can we do that?'

'I've no idea, kid,' Jim admitted, 'but we can have a damn good try. We gotta get this war won first.'

'We're going in the right direction,' Rosie said. 'How are Sam and Bertie?'

'Laconic,' Gracie said, which made them laugh.

'I wish they'd let them home for Christmas,' Mary said wistfully, 'but Bertie said that'd be asking for the moon.'

'Next year maybe,' Rosie said, trying to comfort her.

'I wonder where we'll all be by then,' Gracie said. 'I'm beginning to feel we're all living in limbo.'

'We'll be here, with a bit a luck,' Jim said, grinning at her, which was his way of trying to encourage his daughters. 'Keep yer pecker up. Now the good news has started to come in, there'll be more of it.'

He was right. Just before Christmas the papers reported that the Beveridge report had sold 635,000 copies and outsold all the other books in the bestseller list. Better still, they also reported a poll that showed how very popular it was. Nineteen people out of twenty had heard of it, and no fewer than nine out of ten wanted it to be put into action when the war ended. They drank a toast to that particular bit of news at their Christmas dinner, and Kitty said it had made her day. And then Jim raised his glass in a second toast.

'Here's to 1943,' he said. 'An' may it bring a few more victories.'

*

January was a dismal month, cold and grey and far too often soaking them with rain, but it obliged them with a victory on its very first day when the papers reported that the Japanese were withdrawing from Guadacanal. Then, just over a fortnight later, on a very dull day when Jim and Rosie were huddled by the fire listening to the wireless, they heard that the Soviet army had broken their sixteen-month-long siege of Leningrad and finally driven the Germans out. It was estimated, the announcer said, that 100,000 German troops had either been killed or had died from starvation and extreme cold since the Russian army started their siege.

'Hitler bit off more than he could chew when he invaded the ol' Russkies,' Jim said, with great satisfaction, 'an' serve the bugger right. Now they'll start pushin' *him* around, an' he won't like that.'

And as if to prove him right, a few days later they heard the news that the Germans who had occupied Stalingrad had surrendered. Hitler had promoted General Von Paulus, who was in command there, to the rank of field marshal, saying that 'field marshals never surrender'. But field marshal or not, Von Paulus surrendered to a young Soviet lieutenant which, however you looked at it, was humiliating for him and his boss.

But the news that Gracie and Mary ached to hear, still didn't come. The Eighth Army were still slogging it out in Africa, but they hadn't captured Tripoli, which everyone knew was their next and probably final target. Bertie and Sam sent them letters at reassuringly regular intervals to report that they were 'OK,' and Bertie ventured to say that when they'd pushed Mussolini out of his African empire, they ought to be due some leave. But there was no news of victory or leave. And the wait went on.

Then, on 21 January, some local news was brought to them by the tram telegraph, and it was as bad as it could be. On the previous afternoon, a German bomber had managed to dodge under the radar and had bombed the Sandhurst Road School in Catford, where 150 children were gathered in the hall, waiting to watch a performance of *A Midsummer Night's Dream*. There'd been no air raid warning, and the barrage balloons weren't up, so the German plane had a clear run to dive-bomb the place and blow it to pieces. Forty-one children between the ages of five and fourteen were killed along with six of their teachers and many more were injured. It took all day and most of the night to dig the dead and injured out of the wreckage.

It took a long time for local people to digest such a horror, and there was a lot of painful and useless anger, especially in the pubs and the market.

Mary and Gracie were still waiting for the news they wanted to hear.

It came a few days later, as all news, good or bad, eventually must. And this time it was very good indeed. The Eighth Army had captured Tripoli, as the announcer told them in his calm and measured way. *'Armoured cars of the Eleventh Hussars entered the town before dawn. By midday the Union Jack was flying in the main square, the Piazza Italia. General Montgomery, in his familiar Tank Corps beret and battledress, received the formal surrender.'*

The next day they crossed the border into Tunisia. And a month later the two girls got the letters they'd been yearning for. *'We've got some leave coming at last. Be home soon. Probably in May.'*

CHAPTER NINETEEN

It was a rapturous homecoming on a magical afternoon in May, when the sky was the colour of milky opal and distant buildings were bleached to pale blue shadows. Everything about it was easy and lethargic. The passengers emerging from their newly arrived train at London Bridge ambled along the platform, as if it was too much effort to put one foot in front of the other. Nobody banged the doors. Even the steam from the engine hung suspended above the funnel, too exhausted to rise and disperse.

But Mary and Gracie took one look at the two khaki-clad figures easing out of the second coach and ran towards them, shrieking their names, 'Sam!' 'Bertie!' And the two soldiers dropped their kitbags on the platform and waved to them. And seconds later, with an impact that took their breath away, they were standing with their arms round their lovers, where they'd yearned to be for so long, being bombarded with kisses and more kisses and more kisses until their lips were sore, and held so close they could barely breathe, and nothing else mattered because everything was right with their world. At last, at last.

The platform had emptied before they came to their senses and began to breathe normally.

'Now then,' Bertie said. 'We got everything planned. Ain't we Sam? We're all gonna stay with my old dears up the Elephant. They've found two bedrooms for us, an' they're gonna feed us of a morning, an' we'll have the rest a the day to ourselves. We've got our ration cards an' everythin'. Come on.'

'I thought you lived in Bermondsey,' Mary said, as they ambled off toward Borough High Street. 'Wasn't that what you said?'

'I did as a kid,' he explained, 'but no-one can live there now. The old dears got bombed out. So now they're living up the Elephant.'

That sounded alarming. 'Were they hurt?'

'No,' he said easily. 'They was in the shelter in the next street. They always went there of a night. Jest as well really – 'cos when they come out that night, most a their street was gone. They was in a church hall for a week or two, an' the WVS fed 'em an' found 'em clothes an' that, an' then they got this place. Bit rough an' ready, but it's home. You've got the address. I gave it to you when we got married.'

Mary was full of sympathy for his poor parents but as he wasn't making a fuss, she didn't either. She'd forgotten the address he'd given her but then there'd been so much to attend to with that wedding, she'd just handed it across to her mother. There's a lot I don't know about my Bertie, she thought, and we've only got ten days together.

'I used to live in Newcomen Street,' she told him. 'Not far from here. We'll be passing it in a minute. That part of the Borough's taken a pasting too.'

'Was your place bombed an' all?' he asked.

'No,' she said. 'It's still standing. Me an' Gracie cycled down one evening to see. The south side of the street's been flattened but the shop where we used to live is still all right.'

'We turn off at Harper Road,' he said. 'That's in a bit of mess, too.'

And that's an understatement, Mary thought, when they finally reached the place. Even in the gentle light of that hazy afternoon, it looked grubby and battered. But the pub was still in one piece and so was a small terrace of sooty houses, and her mother and father-in-law were watching for them out of the window and came out into the street to kiss their son and welcome them all in.

'We got it all arranged,' Mrs O'Connor said. 'Ol' Mrs Grey's gonna put you up. She's got two rooms upstairs she don't use on account of her legs, and she says you can have one each. She's a nice old lady. You'll like her. We'll have a little cup a' tea, an' then I'll take you in an' introduce you an' you can get settled.'

It was a nice large mug of tea, hot and strong and accompanied by a plate full of scones 'to keep you goin' till supper.' And then they picked up their bags and walked down the street to Mrs Grey's.

Mary and Gracie took to Mrs Grey as soon as they saw her. She was old, gentle, amiable, rather timid and very well named, for everything about her was grey. Her hair, which she wore in a straggling bun, was almost white, her skin so pale it hardly had any colour at all, her few remaining teeth grey-brown, her eyes a faded slate-grey but smiling her welcome. Even her clothes were grey, for she wore an old grey skirt and her blouse was ecru. But she gave them a timid smile and said they'd be nice an' private upstairs. 'I don't get up there on account a me legs, so you'll have it all to yourselves. Go on up. They're both the same size more or less, so you can choose which one you want, can't yer?'

Bertie tried to tell her how kind she was, but she held up her hand to stop him. 'It's the least I can do,' she said. 'With you out in the desert an' all. Go on up. The beds are all made. Your mum done 'em.'

So they carried their bags upstairs and took to their beds and began their second honeymoons. And oh it *was* so good to be together again.

*

Rosie was disappointed that her two girls and their husbands only visited her once during their leave, but she kept her thoughts to herself and made some scones to welcome them. And she was glad she had when she saw how relaxed and happy they all looked.

'We went to Hampton Court yesterday,' Mary told her. 'It was lovely there down by the river. Wasn't it, Bertie?'

He agreed that it was, grinning at her. And watching them, Rosie remembered the day she and Jim had taken their little daughters up river to the self-same palace in an old steam boat, and what a rattling old tub it was and how much they'd enjoyed it. They were very young then, she thought, remembering, and now they're married women with separate lives.

'Did you go on the river trip too?' she asked Gracie.

'We went up West to see a show,' Gracie told her.

'Good?' Jim asked.

Gracie and Sam answered together, she saying 'Not bad', he saying 'Very funny.' And that made them laugh at one another.

'We're learning which eye to look out of,' Sam explained, looking rather shame-faced. 'We don't always see eye to eye.'

Eyes were sending unspoken messages to one another all around the room, Bertie's sending a question to Mary, Mary's sending sympathy to her sister, Rosie and Jim signalling sympathy for Sam to one another.

'I wouldn't worry about it if I was you,' Jim told him, laughing. 'Takes an age to see eye to eye. We don't. Not all the time. Do we Rosie? An' we been married fer donkey's years.'

'We agreed about the bomb damage though,' Gracie said, feeding him a new topic. 'Didn't we Sam?'

'Terrible the amount of it round here,' Sam said, earnestly. 'Whole streets, just gone. I couldn't believe it. It's going to be a huge job to build it all up again.'

'Ah!' Kitty said, getting up from her chair. 'That reminds me. Hang on a tick. I got summink ter show yer.'

'Where's she off to?' Gracie said, and noticed that her parents were grinning at her.

She soon found out because Kitty was back within seconds. She had a copy of their much-thumbed Beveridge Report in her hand and was waving it at Sam and Bertie.

''Ave you seen this?' she said.

It was Bertie who answered her, and his answer was rather a disappointment because she was looking forward to enlightening him. 'Yeh! Course,' he said. 'We seen it when it come out. One of the fellers had a copy sent out to him an' he handed it round.'

Kitty sat down, still clutching the leaflet, belligerently. 'Whatcher think of it?' she asked.

'Great stuff,' Bertie told her. 'Once we've won this war an' given Herr Hitler what-for, we'll get cracking an' make sure we elect the sorta government that'll deliver it. Anyway, that's what we reckon, don't we Sam? My local MP is all for it. I wrote to him, an' he wrote straight back an' said so.'

Kitty was impressed. 'Really?' she said. 'Did yer?'

'Course,' Bertie told her.

'I did too,' Sam said. 'An' mine was in favour of it too, or so he said.'

'What about yer mates?' Kitty asked. Did they write an' all?'

'Some of 'em,' Bertie said. 'Probably.'

'Didn't you tell 'em to?' Kitty said. 'I know I would've.'

'You don't tell tankies what ter do,' Bertie said. 'That ain't the way of it. They're the most independent men alive, tankies are. Don't take orders from no one. Only Monty.'

Sam grinned at that. 'And then only sometimes!' he said. Which made them both grin happily.

Kitty was looking surprised and cross so Rosie moved in to rescue her. 'Kitty was a Suffragette,' she explained. 'She likes action.'

Sam was impressed and showed it. 'No!' he said. 'Were you really?'

'Yes,' Kitty said briefly. She was flattered by his admiration but still annoyed by Bertie's complacency. If he made an effort he could have a whole tank corps writing to their MPs. What was the matter with the man?

Seeing how aggressive she was getting, Jim changed the subject. 'So now you got the Eyeties on the run,' he said to the two young men. 'What's gonna happen next?'

'That's what *we* want ter know,' Bertie said. ''Course they got to deal with all the prisoners first, an' there were thousands and thousands of *them*. The Eyeties surrendered in battalions an' they've all got to go *somewhere*. They're sorting all that out now. But there's been a lot a' talk about a second front. In Normandy.'

'Likely?' Jim asked.

'Very,' Bertie told him. 'But not without a lot a' preparation, an' that'll take months. We was months preparing for El Alamein.'

'Perhaps they'll send you home,' Rosie said.

'Fingers crossed,' Sam said, smiling at Gracie.

'Oh I do hope they will,' Rosie said, and got smiled at by all four of her children, daughters and son-in-laws alike.

They're such good kids, she thought. I do so want everything to work out for them. If I there was anything I could do to make it happen, I'd do it like a shot. But of course, you can't influence things in a war. You just have to sit tight and take what's coming.

*

The longed-for honeymoon continued, the weather held, there was no news from Africa or anywhere else much. And soon – oh, far too soon – Mary and Gracie were kissing their darlings goodbye, and they were all on their reluctant way back to reality.

'I know there's a censor and all that,' Gracie said, 'but if you're off on some new campaign and you can't tell me, write and ask how our cat is and then I'll know.'

He gave her a grin and promised he would, and then the train began to puff and tug in a totally unnecessary way and they were being pulled apart. She and Mary waved until the heartless thing was out of sight. Then she lifted her chin, squared her shoulders, gave her sister a hug and said, 'Ah well! Back to work.' And the real world reached out to grab them.

From then on Bertie and Sam sent regular letters home, but there was no news of what was to come and no coded messages about cats. May slid into June without any new events, June became July and still no cats were mentioned. But on the tenthof July the papers reported that the Allies had invaded Sicily, and Mary and Gracie got letters to say that they might not be able to write again for a few days, but that they were fit and well and thinking of them.

'So the Yanks are in it now,' Jim said with great satisfaction. 'That ought ter speed things up.'

It certainly seemed to. Thirteen days later there were jubilant headlines in all the newspapers saying that the Allies had captured Palermo, and they'd obviously done it at speed.

'*In a rapid thrust to the north from the Allied held southern part of the island,*' the paper said, '*US troops overwhelmed the city yesterday, trapping an estimated 45,000 Axis troops who must now either surrender or be annihilated.'* And the journalist went on to give details. *'General Eisenhower, the Allied C-in-C, described the success as "the first page in the history of the liberation of the European continent".'* And even better, from Mary and Gracie's point of view, the paper then went on to give details about the British Eighth Army, who, *'under the command of General Montgomery, were advancing on the port of Catania from the south while Canadian forces were advancing on from the east.'*

'Now that's been well planned,' Jim said, beaming his approval at the paper.

'Whatever next?' Rosie said. After the long-drawn-out campaign in Africa, this invasion seemed wonderfully speedy.

'They'll invade Italy,' Jim told her. 'That's where they're heading.'

Two days later, on 25 July, the Sunday papers reported that Mussolini had been deposed. King Victor Emmanuel had assumed command of the Italian armed forces and had appointed Marshal Badoglio, whom the papers described as 'anti fascist', to be prime minister. And the next day there were demonstrations in the streets of Rome celebrating Mussolini's downfall, and Marshal Badoglio asked the Allies for peace terms.

It was almost too good and too quick to be true.

*

That year, summer soothed them into a gentle ease. Rosie and Kitty took themselves off into the garden when they got back from their afternoon delivery and sat in the rickety deckchairs – rather gingerly at first because they weren't sure they would hold their weight – and did a spot of sunbathing, and took it in turns to nurse the cat. Sometimes old Winnie Totteridge came down to join them.

'It makes a nice change ter sit in the sun,' she said. 'Providin' the canvas'll 'old us up. I used ter sit out in my garden a lot afore the war. Can't now on account a the shelter. They don't 'alf take up a lot a' room, them things. Very useful in the raids, I ain't denyin' that, but they don' leave yer much garden.'

'No, they don't,' Rosie remembered, glaring at her own shelter. Despite its usefulness she'd never really forgiven it for being there. It was stupid of her because she knew what excellent protection they'd been. She'd seen people dug out of their shelters alive when their houses had been flattened. But she still missed her garden. 'I had a lovely garden here before the war,' she said. 'I used to spend my afternoons out here, weeding my vegetable patch, watering my beans, that sorta thing.'

'You miss it,' Mrs Totteridge understood.

'Yes,' Rosie admitted. 'I do. It was lovely having fresh fruit and vegetables.'

'She's a country gel,' Kitty teased. 'Born wiv a spade in her hand, wasn't yer, Rosie?'

'You'll get it back again when the war's over,' Mrs Totteridge commiserated, patting her hand.

'*When* the war's over,' Rosie said gloomily. 'We've got a long way to go yet. We'll be into our fourth year come September.'

'I shall be into my seventy-fifth come October,' Mrs Totteridge said. 'Think a that. Don't seem possible to me. When I was a nipper they said I'd never make old bones.'

'Well you've proved 'em wrong, ain'tcher,' Kitty said, grinning at her.

'I wonder how long it'll be before them stupid Eyeties give in,' Mrs Totteridge said.

'Not long, I shouldn't think,' Rosie said. 'They ent too keen on fighting.'

'Good,' Mrs Totteridge said. 'Then your boys can come home.'

296

Rosie sighed. 'They'll still have the Germans to contend with,' she said, 'an' they're a different kettle of fish altogether. They won't give up without a struggle.'

That was the general opinion among people who'd been on the receiving end of Hitler's bombs, and the general opinion was proved right.

*

On 3 September the papers reported the Allies had invaded the mainland of Italy. The next day the headlines said, *'Allies Capture Reggio di Calabria'*. On 8 September, Marshall Badoglio signed an armistice and the Italians were out of the war.

But the next day, when Allied troops landed at Salerno ready to capture Naples, they found the German troops waiting for them.

'Fucking Jerries!' Bertie said, as he and Sam and their crew sat in their tank waiting for orders. It was hot and they were all tense, knowing they had a battle ahead of them.

Sam shrugged his shoulders in resignation. 'You got a fag?' he said.

It was over a week before they managed to drive the German panzers back from Salerno, and that was because the troops who had crossed the Straights of Messina and captured Reggio di Calabria had fought their way north to join them, so that they formed a continuous line across Southern Italy. And by that time, German troops had occupied Rome. The attack on Naples started on 20 September, but it was ten hard-fought days before the Germans pulled back and the city finally surrendered.

It had been a long month.

CHAPTER TWENTY

'Is that a cake I can smell?' Kitty said, sniffing the air and looking at the icing bag lying on the kitchen table. 'Wiv icing?' She had just been down to the market to get the potatoes and greens, and an iced cake was just her idea of a treat. 'Are the gels coming?'

'It's a birthday cake,' Rosie explained. 'For old Mrs T. It's her seventy-fifth birthday tomorrow, and I thought it'd be nice to make a bit of a fuss of her. And yes, the girls are coming to tea too.'

'Ain't she got no family?' Kitty said, putting the vegetables into the cupboard. 'I've offen wondered. Never heard her mention any, and you don't like to ask, do yer?'

'Her husband was killed in the first war,' Rosie told her, opening the oven to inspect her cake, 'an' her little boy got took with the diphtheria when he was just a kiddy. She told me about it once. She said she'd been on her own ever since.'

'Poor soul,' Kitty said. 'Then we must make a proper fuss of her termorrer. She's earned it. I could make her a card an' we could all sign it. Whatcher think?'

The cake, the card and the fuss were duly made, and they all sang 'happy birthday' to their guest until her old face was pink with pleasure.

'An' here's me thinkin' I was jest poppin' in fer a cuppa,' she said. She was sitting in the place of honour in the middle of the sofa in the living room with everybody else grouped around her.

''Nother slice of cake?' Rosie asked her.

'Is there one?' the old lady hoped.

'There is, an' just for you,' Rosie told her. 'Top brick off the chimney for you today.'

'I'd rather 'ave the cake,' Mrs Totteridge said, grinning at them.

'Time fer the news,' Jim said, looking at the clock. And he got up and switched on the wireless, just in time to hear '...*and this is Alvar Liddell reading it.*' They settled to hear it whatever it was. It'll be another battle, Rosie thought, resignedly.

But it wasn't. It was a surprise, and it made them all wide eyed. The newly-appointed Italian government had declared war on Germany.

'Well there's a turn up fer the books,' Jim said. 'I thought they was buddy-buds.'

'I wonder what'll happen now,' Mary said.

'The Germans'll give the Eyeties hell,' Jim predicted. 'It's a public kick in the teeth an' their beloved Adolf won't stand for that.'

'I think it could actually turn out to be good news,' Gracie said. 'They'll have two armies to fight now. Maybe they won't have so much time and energy to shell our poor bloody men.' There'd been too many badly injured soldiers in their wards since the Italian campaign began, and the sight of every new arrival clawed her heart raw and made her aware of how easy it would be for Sam to be injured too, or even killed – although she tried not to think about *that*.

'Don't you believe it,' Jim said. 'They'll bring in more troops.'

'*Are* there more troops?' Mary wondered. 'I mean, they've got armies all over the place, all over Russia and occupied Europe, and they've had lots of casualties; the supply can't be endless.'

'There's millions a the beggars,' Mrs Totteridge said. 'Swarmin' all over the bleedin' place. I mean ter say, when you come ter think about it, they 'ad ten million unemployed when Adolf come ter power, an' they all went in the army, every man jack of 'em, 'cause they didn't 'ave nothink else ter do.'

'I offen wonder where 'e got his money from for all the uniforms an' the guns an' their pay an' everything,' Kitty said. 'That must ha' cost a packet an' 'e wasn't a rich man by any manner a means. War's expensive.'

'I don't know who financed *him*,' Jim said, 'but I can tell you who the Mr Moneybags was behind Oswald Moseley and his stinking blackshirts.'

They turned their heads to look at him, waiting for him to tell them.

'Lord Rothermere,' he said. 'That's who it was. Lord Rothermere what owns the *Daily Mail*. He gave them lots of money and praised them to high heaven on the front pages of his stinking rag. That's who it was.'

Mrs Totteridge was impressed. 'How d'yer know that?' she asked

'My old sergeant told me,' Jim said. 'Wasn't much he didn't know about the beggars. Used ter come out on the streets an' fight 'em. That's how I met up wiv 'im again. Out on the street in Worthing, standin' up to 'em and getting punched for it.'

'I remember that,' Gracie said. 'It was a horrible dark night and down by the pier. The Blackshirts had been having a meeting in the theatre, and they came strutting out in their jackboots, all red in the face and itching to hit someone. It was the first time I'd ever seen them and they scared me stiff. An' then Dad suddenly yelled out that they were thumping his sarge and he wasn't having that, and he went striding off and knocked one of them right down on the ground. It was amazing.'

'Well good fer you,' Mrs Totteridge said to Jim. 'I allus knew you was the right sort.'

'Mr Johnson,' Gracie remembered. 'That was his name. He used to come and have supper with us when we were little. Him and his wife. Where is he now, do you know?'

'Yorkshire somewhere,' Jim said. 'I've got his address in me book. His daughter married a farmer out there somewhere, an' when the war began, she wrote an' told him he an' Minnie was to come an' live with her out a' harm's way. Wouldn't take no for answer. Bit of a tartar, his daughter, by all accounts. Anyway, he done as he was told. He's a good bloke. Sends me a card every Christmas, reg'lar as clockwork.'

'You miss 'im,' Mrs Totteridge said, sympathetically.

'Yeh,' he admitted. I do. Now an' then.' And then he made a joke about it because her sympathy was making him realise that he missed his old sarge quite badly. 'When I ain't bein' run off me feet.'

'Listen,' Mary said, holding up her hand and moving in to rescue him. 'It's ITMA. We mustn't miss that.' Jim had turned the volume down when the news was over, but the sounds of the opening song were clear to be heard.

So they settled down to listen to their favourite programme and finished the birthday tea with laughter. And Rosie had to admit to herself that there were some good things in life, even in the fourth year of the war. Good things give you a breathing space, she thought. And God knows, we need it.

*

The war continued in its juggernaut way. At the end of October the Allied armies ran into trouble when they reached a mountain called Monte

Cassino. The Germans had taken over a decaying monastery on the top of the mountain and turned it into an almost impenetrable fortress.

'*It's a difficult terrain,*' Bertie wrote to Mary. '*The land is marshy, there are very few roads and what there are aren't very good, and we've had fog for the last three days. We shall get through eventually. It's just a slog at the moment.*'

He was right, but it wasn't just a difficult terrain, it was a very hard-fought struggle, and there were increasing numbers of casualties, as Mary and Gracie knew only too well. They had a new drug now called penicillin that was very effective in treating wound sepsis but even so, some of the injuries were very bad indeed.

'Somebody ought to do something to stop this,' Mary said, when the latest bunch of casualties were due to arrive, and she was making the beds ready for them.

'Short of blowing the whole bloody mountain up, I don't see what,' Gracie said, stripping the next bed of its soiled sheets. 'That's what I'd do if it was up to me. All this tosh about it being an historic building. Men are being killed.'

Eventually, when the fight had gone on for three and a half bloody months, General Eisenhower agreed with her and gave the order for the mountain to be bombed by a squadron of Flying Fortresses. In an official bulletin he said that historical monuments '*were bound to be respected, as far as war allows, but if we have to choose between destroying a famous building and sacrificing our men's lives, then the building must go.*'

According to Bertie, it was a magnificent sight. He wrote to Mary, sitting beside his tank at a safe distance from where the debris was falling. '*Huge flash of light,*' he told her. '*Hurt your eyes to look at it. I seen plenty of explosions one way and another but never nothing like that. Then there was a huge column a smoke, must've been 500 feet high if it was an inch, and that was the end of that. We've got rid of the buggers. Good riddance to bad rubbish.'* He didn't tell her what a hideous mess of churned earth, discarded helmets, soiled dressings, burnt out tanks and lorries and stinking filth lay between him and the wrecked monastery. That was the price they'd had to pay to get past the bloody thing, and there were some details it was better for her not to know.

When he'd finished writing his letter, he turned to Sam and gave him a V sign and a grin.

Sam was lighting a fag. 'Now what'll happen?' he said.

'We'll move on,' Bertie said, feeling happily confident now that he'd seen what the Yanks could do. 'We'll move on an' mop up the rest of Italy. With firepower like that it'll be a doddle.'

Sam grinned back and crossed his fingers. 'Just so long as we can get out of here when we've done it,' he said. 'I'd like to go home for a week or two.' And when Bertie grimaced at him and shook his head, he said, 'Yep. I know. Faint hope a that.'

Then the signal to advance was given, so that was the end of the conversation. But not of the thoughts and dreams.

*

'Take a look at that,' Jim said, passing the newspaper across the table to Rosie. He'd finished his bacon, tomatoes and fried bread and was on to his third mug of tea, and she'd only just sat down to begin hers –but no matter. This was important. The headlines were fairly yelling it at them. '*BRITAIN BECOMES AN ARMED CAMP.*'

Rosie couldn't make sense of it. 'What are they talking about?' she said.

'Read it,' he said. So she did.

'Britain has become one huge armed camp as General Dwight D Eisenhower completes his plans for the Allied invasion of Hitler's Fortress Europe. All coastal areas have been banned to visitors, and all overseas travel by foreign diplomats in London has been forbidden, as has the privilege of sending diplomatic dispatches without inspection.

Large scale military exercises are taking place in different parts of southern England. Railway timetables are being reorganised to enable hundreds of thousands of British, American and Commonwealth troops to be moved to the invasion assembly points. Airborne landings by parachutists and glider troops are being rehearsed. Amphibious operations are being practised, with special equipment for landing tanks, heavy guns and supplies. The enemy's rear areas are being softened up by day and night air attacks in railway marshalling yards, airfields and military positions in France and Germany.'

It made the hairs stand on Rosie's neck. There'd been a lot of talk in the last two or three months about this Second Front, but it had never amounted to anything. And now this. 'Ye gods,' she said. 'Then it's imminent.'

'Looks like it,' Jim said, putting down his empty mug.

Rosie looked round at her peaceful, comfortable kitchen, taking it all in as if she was seeing it for the first time; the battered kettle simmering on the hob; her cat purring on her lap; the ironing airing on the dryer above her head; plates and cups neatly arranged on her nice clean dresser; her garden green through the glass of the back door where the sun shone through in a palpable column, so solid she felt she could touch it; the lingering smell of bacon and fried bread, and she was overwhelmed with pity for the young men who would soon be risking their lives in France. 'Those poor boys!' she said.

Jim grinned at her. 'Which ones?' he said.

'All of them,' she told him. 'Sam and Bertie naturally, but all the others who are waiting for the invasion. All the hundreds of thousands. I hate war.'

'We all hate war,' he said sombrely, 'but there ain't a bleedin' thing we can do about it except fight the bleedin' thing, so there's no point in thinkin' about it. We jest 'ave to get on with it. Least this lot are bein' prepared for what's ahead of *them*. Which is more than we was. They give us a rifle and showed us how to fire it an' that was that. Most of us didn't know what 'ad hit us when we got ter the trenches.'

That's true, Rosie thought, but it didn't comfort her.

'Got ter be off or I'll be late,' Jim said, standing up. 'Drop in when you've done yer walk an' I'll put some titbits by for you.' And he walked into the hall and shouted up the stairs to his sister. 'Come on lazybones. Stir yer stumps or you'll be late fer work.'

He's so stolid, Rosie thought, admiring him. He never seems to be thrown by anything. I wonder what my girls will think of all this.

*

Her girls didn't see the paper until they were having their dinner, and then they merely glanced at it. Their minds were focussed on what was going on in Italy.

'I wonder when they'll send them home,' Mary said. 'It shouldn't be too long now. I mean, once they've taken Rome, they'll be due a bit of leave. Surely to goodness. They've earned it.'

'I shouldn't bank on it.' Gracie said, shaking a dollop of HP sauce onto her rissolle. She opened the paper idly to scan the middle pages, and what she found there *did* interest her.

'Take a look that,' she said to Mary.

'What is it?'

Gracie pointed to the paragraph with her fork: *'500,000 prefabricated houses promised'*. 'Read it,' she said.

Ever obedient, Mary read it, but without much interest until she reached a sentence where the journalist told her that these homes were for *'demobilised servicemen and bombed-out families.'* 'That could be us,' she said.

'Just what I thought,' Gracie said. 'Let's go and see them. It says they're on display in the Tate Gallery, and that's not far. What d'you think?'

By the end of the week, they'd bought two tickets, swapped shifts and were on their way to Millbank. Neither of them had much idea of what to expect of a house that had been designed and built by a car manufacturer and had been erected in five hours. But once they'd seen it, they were thrilled by it. From the outside it looked like a painted box with windows. It had a flat roof, and it looked clean and neat, and that was really all that could be said about it. But inside it was a totally different story.

They were escorted round by a lady with the sternest pince nez and the warmest smile, who said she was there to answer any questions they might have. They followed her from room to room, admiring everything they saw. The furniture had been built into the house and very good it was; a wall full of chests of drawers and wardrobes in both the bedrooms, and shelves and cupboards in the living room on either side of a gas fire.

'No more raking out ashes of a morning if you live here,' Gracie said, approvingly.

Mary agreed. 'No more black leading the grate either.'

There was even a table that you could fold back into the wall when you weren't using it, which they both thought was very sensible.

But it was the kitchen that really sold the place to them. It was like something from another world: clean and white and modern with every bit of equipment they could think of, a brand new gas cooker, spotlessly clean, a geyser for hot water whenever they wanted it, a modern gas-fired copper for washing the clothes, another entire wall of shelves and cupboards where they could keep their food and, standing in the corner of the room, a little white cupboard that turned out to be one of the new refrigerators that they'd heard about but never seen.

'We think it's the best thing that's ever been invented,' their guide said, opening it up to show them how it worked. 'No more runny butter or sour milk. No more flies. There's space here for everything you want to keep fresh. That's for the milk, butter there, eggs in their own little cups, plenty of room for meat and fish. What do you think of it?'

They thought it was wonderful and said so.

'All we need to know now is how we could apply to have one,' Gracie said. 'We've not been bombed out, but we're both married to servicemen so I think we'd be eligible.'

'You would indeed,' their guide said. 'Would you like to bring them to see it, too?'

Gracie laughed. 'We'd love to,' she said, 'but they're in Italy with the Eighth Army.'

Their guide smiled at them. 'Ah well,' she said. 'You'll have to write and tell them all about it. I'll give you a form so that you can register your names to be considered. Good luck.'

That night, when they finally came off duty, the sisters sat down and filled in the forms, which turned out to be surprisingly simple, and wrote long happy letters to their darlings, describing the new prefabs detail by detail, reminding one another of things they ought to put in and breaking off in mid paragraph to jog one another's memories and enjoy them all over again. It was a real labour of love, and by the time they'd finished they'd covered every single aspect of these new amazing dwellings and run to three sheets of paper.

'Won't they be surprised?' Mary said, when she finally put down her pen.

'They'll be gobsmacked,' Gracie said, grinning. 'I can't wait to hear what they'll say.'

It was four days before they got an answer, and that was longer than any exchange of letters had ever been. So long, in fact, that they were both getting seriously worried, although they kept their worries to themselves, both of them thinking the same thing – if we don't get a letter tomorrow we'll know something's up.

Something was. But it was something positive and something they didn't expect. The Eighth Army had been posted back to Britain.

'We should be home in a few days,' Sam wrote, 'and we should have a few passes then. The prefabs sound amazing. Have you sent in the forms?'

Bertie was more forthcoming. 'Prefabs sound just the ticket,' he wrote. 'I can just see us living there. We shall be home in a few days if everything goes according to plan. Don't think they'll give us leave to go house-hunting just yet awhile though. We're going to be busy on manoeuvres and such like. I'll tell you more when I see you what I can't wait to do.' He signed it ATLITW, which was their shorthand for 'all the love in the world', and squeezed a row of kisses into the margin with a note underneath them. 'Use your imagination.'

By the time they tumbled through their parents' front door the next weekend, Mary and Gracie were fizzing with excitement and both talking at once. 'They're coming home,' they said. 'We've got it in writing. Imagine that!' 'And they're building prefabs for us. Wait till we tell you about *them.*' 'D'you think they'll be demobbed?' 'Oh isn't it the best news ever?' 'As soon as we know where they're based we're going to get rooms there to be with them. Can't wait!'

Rosie laughed at them and kissed them and told them it was the best news ever, and Kitty said she never did, 'I mean ter say, what a surprise!' And Jim grinned and wondered whether they would ever get any tea.

They talked non-stop and sometimes all at once until it was time for the two girls to cycle back to the hospital.

'What an extraordinary thing,' Rosie said when they were out of sight, and she and the others were walking into the living room.

'Bit too good to be true if you ask me,' Jim said, settling into his armchair.

'Oh you old misery guts!' Rosie teased. 'If they say they're coming home, they'll be coming home. What could go wrong with that?'

'Depends what they're coming home *for*,' Jim said. 'They might want 'em here fer the Second Front.'

Rosie and Kitty stared at him in disbelief. It was like having a bucket of cold water thrown over them.

'They couldn't do that,' Rosie said. 'I mean, it wouldn't be fair. Not after all they've been through.'

'They're seasoned troops,' Jim told her. 'Very valuable, seasoned troops are. They know what's what.'

'I don't believe it. They couldn't,' Kitty insisted, glaring at him. 'You're bein' an old kill-joy.'

He held up his hands to ward off her anger. 'OK,' he said. 'I don't want it ter be true neither. I was only sayin.'

'Well don't,' Kitty said. 'And don't go sayin' stupid things ter the gels, neither.'

'Oh Kitty! Kitty!' her brother said, rebuking her as gently as he could. 'Don't yer know nothink about me kid?'

'He wouldn't, Kitty,' Rosie said, siding with him but trying to placate her too. 'None of us would. We just got to keep our fingers crossed.' And she switched the wireless on and was relieved to hear Vera Lynn's lovely voice. That should soothe them.

But the doubt was in all their minds now that it had been roused, and only the cat was unruffled.

*

Gracie and Mary made tentative plans whenever they weren't on the wards, lay awake most nights thinking of passionate reunions and waited for more news with a never-ending, itching impatience. And finally their impatience was rewarded by the arrival of two postcards in the same post, both saying the same thing. They were back, they were on Salisbury Plain, they would get a pass on Saturday night and ending 'See you soon'.

Now they'd got the green light, Gracie and Mary moved into action like the seasoned troopers *they* were. Gracie was needed on men's surgical and couldn't get time off during the week, so Mary took over and set off to Salisbury on her own, saying she wouldn't be back until she'd got a room for both of them. It wasn't easy, because so many rooms had already been taken. 'Soldiers' wives, you see,' one landlady explained. And when Mary said, 'Like us,' the landlady said, 'You and half the world,' which was rather discouraging. But she found two rooms in the end, although it took her until late evening to manage it, and when the job was done she caught the last train back, feeling pleased with herself.

Then it was just a matter of rearranging their shifts and waiting till Saturday, which was only three days away but felt like a lifetime. And then at long, long last, and in such a state of tremulous excitement, they were in Salisbury on a balmy April evening, waiting in the bus station for the lorries that were bringing their warriors back to them. And they looked so handsome and so brown and kissed them so lovingly that nothing else mattered.

They didn't talk about the war at all that Saturday, nor about when Sam and Bertie were going to be demobbed, and nothing was said on the following Saturday either. They were too fully occupied making love and enjoying one another's company. But on the third Saturday, which was the first one in May and had been wonderfully warm, they all went out to supper in the local British Restaurant because Bertie said they'd had a long hot day and needed sustenance, and when they reached the spotted dog and custard stage of the meal, Mary said something that turned their light hearted chatter in a different direction.

'Why don't you two come up to London next week? We can take you to see the prefab.'

'Can't be done,' Sam said. 'We're lucky to get passes for a Saturday evening. We shan't get any more than that until all this is over.'

Mary was disappointed because she'd hoped he would say yes, but his choice of words had alerted Gracie to a disturbing suspicion. 'All *what* is over?' she asked.

'The Second Front,' Sam told her. 'We've missed the April window but it could be May. We're working flat out.'

'What are you talking about?' Gracie said. She was needle sharp now and close to anger. 'They're surely not going to send you back into the war again? Not after all you've been through. It wouldn't be fair.'

'War ain't fair, Gracie,' Bertie said, taking over the conversation because he could see how upset Sam was to have told her when she wasn't ready for it. 'Never was, never will be. You just have ter get on with it.'

'You sound just like my dad,' Gracie said, scowling at him.

311

'Very likely,' Bertie said, smiling at her to try and placate her. 'He's an old soldier too. Good bloke.'

Gracie was in her stride and wouldn't be placated. 'And what's all this nonsense about windows?'

It was Sam who answered her, trying to make amends for his clumsiness. 'There are only a few days in each month when the moon's full and the tides are right for an invasion. They call them windows. They're at the start of the month. We've missed the April one and I can't see everything being ready for the May one, so it looks as though it will be...'

'June,' Mary said, her voice high with distress. 'Oh dear God, Sam. June.'

'Now look,' Bertie said, looking round at them all. 'This is hard for all of us an' we don't make it no easier going on about it. So let me tell you. We're well equipped – we've got the most up-to-date tanks going and the most powerful guns – *and* we're very well prepared, *and* we've got Monty on our side and let me tell you, he's a cunning old bird. He pulled the wool right over the Germans' eyes at El Alamein. They got quite the wrong idea about where we was going to attack 'em, an' we caught them on the hop, good an' proper. An' now he's doing it again.' He paused and looked at Sam before he went on, while Mary and Gracie waited, wondering what was coming.

'Let's settle up and go for a walk,' he said. 'Walls have ears.'

So they did. And when they were strolling along a virtually empty road towards the water meadows, he told them what he knew.

'This is all hush-hush,' he said, 'so fer Christ's sake don't spread it around. They've had it planned for months, and the advantage of it is that the Germans don't know what we're doing, so we've got to keep it that way. The plan is to make them think we're going to invade across the Pas de Calais in July, so that they'll base their crack troops an' their Panzers an' their heavy artillery up there. Monty's invented a new US

Army Group based in Kent and Sussex – all fiction of course – but he's got a bona fide general called Patton to command it, and he's made dummy trucks and tanks and landing craft and put them all along the coast. He keeps moving them about as if they're on manoeuvres. It's bloody clever. You got to hand it to the man. We don't know the half of it any more than we did at El Alamein. But believe me. Trust me. We're well prepared.'

'Oh Bertie,' Mary said. 'I do love you.' And she put her arms round his neck and kissed him passionately.

'Steady the buffs,' he said, 'or you'll have me off me feet.'

*

When the lorries had driven their two darlings away, and Mary and Gracie were on the last train heading to London, Mary wondered whether they ought to tell the aged Ps what they'd heard. 'They might be worrying too,' she said.

'Better not,' Gracie said. 'You heard what Bertie said. The fewer people that know what's going on, the better.'

'If it's going to be in June,' Mary said, 'we haven't got very long.'

'Then we'll make the most of it,' Gracie told her.

CHAPTER TWENTY-ONE

'Did they phone?' Jim asked as he walked into the kitchen. He was tired after a long day at work, but his poor Rosie looked so worried he had to ask.

'They both did,' Rosie said, filling the tea pot. 'One after the other, but they didn't say anything. Just what a lot of work they'd got to do and how they're going to Salisbury again on Saturday.'

'Still keeping it to themselves then,' Jim said. It was silly really, because everyone knew the Eighth Army was going to be part of the invasion now. It had been in all the papers. But there you are, it showed how upset they were.

He sighed and changed the subject, sitting in his chair rather heavily because his leg was aching. 'Kitty get off all right?' His sister had gone off on one of her regular trips to Binderton to see the boys.

'Yes,' Rosie said listlessly. 'She was fine.'

He decided to take another tack to see if *that* would interest her. 'You'll never guess who came into the market this morning,' he said.

Rosie was stirring the tea. 'No idea,' she said flatly, and her voice showed how little she cared about it. He told her anyway because he thought it might cheer her up.

'My ol' sarge,' Jim said. 'Old Jack Johnson. I was pickin' over the spuds, an' 'orrible manky lot they were, I'll be glad when the new ones come in. Anyway, I was picking over the spuds and there he was. Large as life an' twice as gruesome. And wait till I tell you this. He's livin' in the Borough. Whatcher thinka that?'

This time she looked up at him, plainly interested. 'I thought they'd gone for the duration,' she said.

'So did I,' Jim said, spooning sugar into his tea. 'But apparently not. He said they was homesick on the farm. Didn't suit him. So he reckoned they might as well come back, the Blitz bein' over an' all. An' that's what they done.'

'I bet they had a job finding somewhere to live,' Rosie said. 'Specially here.'

'They got a house by the John Bull Arch,' Jim said, grinning at her. 'Where they bombed the railway line that time. D'you remember that?'

She was remembering it as he spoke, and what an ugly, blood-soaked shambles it had been. 'I wouldn' ha' thought there was much there worth living in now,' she said.

'Four houses just about habitable, so he says,' Jim told her. 'He's rentin' one of them and doin' it up. He's quite proud of it. Anyway the long an' the short of it is, he'd like us to go and have supper with him an' Minnie. You an' me an' Kitty an' all.'

'When?'

'This Saturday. What d'yer think? He said he'd come in again termorrer so's I can tell him.'

'Well why not?' Rosie said. It would be better than sitting at home, worrying about the girls.

So they went. And it turned out to be a treat she hadn't expected. Although it began with a powerful feeling of being thrown bodily back into the past.

She'd passed the John Bull Arch on a tram on several occasions since the night of the bomb and hadn't given it much attention, but once she and Jim and Kitty stepped down from their tram that evening and had begun to walk towards the bridge, she found herself back in the nightmare, remembering the incident in vivid detail; waiting in the ambulance in the heat and noise of the raid, ready to collect the next batch of casualties as the rescue teams struggled to dig them out of the rubble; that heavy broken girder slanting above the wreckage and trembling with every explosion as if it was going to fall to the ground and crush everything beneath it; her nostrils full of the familiar stink of escaping gas, shit, shattered brick and plaster; billowing clouds of grey dust everywhere, bulging and swelling and growing with every second. It made her shiver to remember it, and it was several minutes before she realised that Jim was talking to her, and it took an effort of will to pull her mind away from her memories and listen to what he was saying.

He was looking at the railway line above their heads and talking to Kitty. 'You'd never believe what a state it was in to look at it now,' he said.

Kitty was staring at the bomb sites. 'What are all them flowers?' she said.

'Weeds,' Rosie told her. 'Dandelions, nettles, ground ivy. The tall one with the pretty pink flowers is called London Pride. We rather like that one.'

'You got a good name for it,' Kitty said. 'Very suitable. So come on Jim, where's this house?'

'Only place it could be,' Jim said. 'Over there. See? Terrace of four.'

They were standing all on their own in a wilderness of dusty earth and weeds: four small houses built of sooty brick, each with a front door and two windows, one above the other and with a patched side wall where a chimney-breast with a large crack running through it rose crookedly into the roof. And there was Mr Johnson bounding towards them out of the second house, beaming like a Cheshire cat, with his wife following behind him, wiping her hands on her apron.

'Come on in,' he called to them. 'Grub's all ready.'

From then on, the day and the place were swept into a new direction. Jack and Minnie were so happy in their refurbished house and so proud of the work they were doing on it and the plans they had for it, that they hardly stopped talking long enough to eat their supper. And when the meal was over and the dirty dishes had been cleared into the kitchen, they took their guests on a conducted tour of the place, showing them where they'd mended the stairs and re-plastered the walls and put up a new picture rail, and displaying all the things they'd bought.

'We've been pickin' up the furniture an' the curtains bit by bit,' Minnie told them. 'Flea markets usually. An' the china. You'd be surprised what you can get in the markets if you know what you're looking for.'

'We wouldn't,' Rosie said, laughing at her. 'That's where we got most of our stuff, didn't we Jim?'

'You've furnished it lovely,' Kitty said. 'Where'd yer get the nets? They're nice.'

'Petticoat Lane,' Minnie said, as they trooped down the stairs again. 'Ain't got no pictures yet, but we're workin' on it.'

'I'd ha' liked to paper this room really,' Jack said, as they walked back into the living room, 'only you can't get wallpaper fer love nor money. There ain't a lot a paint on offer neither, but we thought this white'd do to be goin' on with. Nice an' clean. We're gonna turn it into a little palace, ain't we Minnie?'

'It looks a treat,' Rosie told him because he was so obviously asking for approval.

'It's not bad, is it?' he said, happily. Then he thought of something else. 'You got time fer a quick one? We got a good boozer just round the corner.'

So they finished their evening with a couple of pints and emerged into an evening pearly with mist that swathed the bomb sites and made them look almost romantic.

'It's been a great night,' Jim said as they parted.

Jack was flushed with beer and success. 'We'll do it again,' he promised.

*

'I wouldn't like ter be him living there,' Kitty said, when they were on the tram going home. 'It ain't 'alf ramshackle. I'd be frightened it'd fall down.'

'Don't you believe it,' Jim told her cheerfully. 'Be good for a few years yet. He'll turn it into a little palace, like he said. You watch.'

'And at least it ent gonna be bombed,' Rosie said. 'That's the main thing.' Having the Blitz over and done with was such a comfort.

'I wonder how the gels are,' Jim said, gazing out of the window at the smoky darkness in the street. 'I miss 'em comin' round of a Sat'day.'

'They said they'd pop in tomorrow,' Rosie reminded him.

'Good,' he said and grinned at her.

*

The next day was cold and stormy and very unseasonable for the start of June. The sky had been overcast since mid-morning, and there was a strong wind blowing and a lot of rain, some of it quite heavy. The girls arrived just before tea time, shaking the rain from their capes.

They were both looking so downcast that Rosie was worried at once.

'What's up?' she said, as she filled the kettle.

'The invasion's coming,' Gracie told her. 'That's what's up. We should've told you this before. Sam and Bertie are going to be in it. That's why they brought them back from Italy.'

'It's OK kid,' Jim said, trying to soothe her. 'We guessed as much.'

She made a rueful face. 'We didn't like to say in case it upset you,' she said. 'Bit silly really. Only we've got to tell you now because it's any day. They've been water-proofing the vehicles and getting ready for days. There's no more leave. Not even a pass. And Sam reckons they'll be moving to the embarkation area today or tomorrow. He said he didn't know where it was, but they were all prepared.'

'So this is it,' Jim said, giving her a hug.

'Looks like it.'

'Bertie predicted it all along,' Mary told them. 'The weather's not good, but the tide and the moon are right for it, and that's what they've been waiting for. So yes, this is it. I wish it wasn't'

Jim reached out with his free arm and gave her a hug too because it was horrid to see her so woe-begone. My poor gels, he thought, cuddling them close.

Just like us, Rosie was thinking. Torn apart and nothing they can do about it. I hate war. But she made the tea and didn't say anything. What was to come would come, no matter what they said or did.

*

The Seventh Tank Brigade sailed to Normandy in late afternoon. The weather was still very bad, and they had a rough crossing. They'd been told to expect a rough ride, but it was worse than they'd imagined it

319

would be. There was a strong sou'wester blowing, for a start, and the sky was oppressive with low, blue-black clouds threatening rain and giving all of them a horrid sense of impending doom which none of them talked about – naturally. But the sea was the worst thing. It was an ominous slate-grey with huge rolling waves that threw them about and made them feel sea-sick within minutes of leaving port. But, seasick or not, to know that they were part of such a formidable, well planned armada was exalting. There was no other word for it.

There were ships everywhere they looked. The Channel was full of them, some sailing out of harbour, rolling heavily, others on their way back, their prows carving white parabolas of foam, and the further they went into the Channel, the more there were of them; sleek grey warships, bristling with guns, LCTs like the one they were sailing in, liberty ships, even rusty old colliers, bobbing over the waves like corks, landing craft like huge square mouthed barges, and so many troop-ships they couldn't count them, their decks packed with khaki vehicles and thousands of men in full kit, their helmets reflecting the limited sunlight. It could have been a film set, Bertie thought, if death wasn't waiting at the end of it. But that was a thought that made him give an involuntary shiver, so he decided it was better to turn his mind to something else. Like the last time he'd been with his darling, his lovely, cuddly Mary-Pary, breathing in the musky scent of her skin, his face in her hair, holding her close, close… and now she was in London and he was here. But at least it was safe in London now they'd stopped bombing the place, and that was something.

There was a sudden roar as the battleships opened fire behind them and, looking up, he saw the shells streaming inland, thousands and thousands of them, dark in that threatening sky. Jesus! he thought. Now that's some bombardment. I wouldn't want to be on the receiving end of that. And then the ship gave a sudden lurch and, when his guts had realigned themselves and he wasn't feeling quite so sick, he looked up again, this time staring straight ahead to steady himself, and saw that they were approaching the beach. He could see it clearly; long, sandy and full of vehicles and troops, all on the move, some wading ashore from the landing craft, others marching in shuffling columns, with beach masters waving their arms, giving directions. And there were the dunes they'd been told about and above them the expected row of houses, most of them roofless and pitted with shells.

'This is it,' their sergeant said. 'Let's be 'avin' yer.'

They obeyed him at once, climbing onto their tank the way they'd learnt to do and easing into the turrets, quick and nimble as monkeys.

'Least it's not Dunkirk,' Sam said, flicking his dog-end into the sea before he started his climb.

The day changed into another gear as they took up their allotted positions, Sam in the driving seat with young Roddy, his co-driver, to his left, Bertie beside his gun with his loader Taffy beside *him* and Sergeant Merryweather in the rear seat where he could see everything. The interphone was switched on. Orders were given. Sam turned on the ignition and drove. They arrived with a bump as the ramps were lowered, inched their formidable war horses onto the sand, were signalled forward by the beach masters. Everything going according to plan.

They're moving us on before we can see what a blood bath it was this morning, Sam thought, but if that *was* their intention it wasn't working, because they'd all got their heads out of the turrets and could see everything clearly.

The dead and injured had been carried away, but the beach was ribbed with tyre marks, and there was debris all over the place that gave the game away – empty shell-cases, blood-soaked rags, smashed helmets, discarded vehicles. And driving carefully through it, he could see the mine detectors still at work, stepping delicately, the long sticks of their detectors swinging backwards and forwards before them like pendulums.

He climbed across the sand dunes, drove cautiously through a gap between the wrecked houses and arrived in open country. The barrage was still going on, but they were accustomed to the noise of it by then and were concentrating on following instructions. There was a complicated signpost ahead of them and, following the Sergeant's orders, he slowed to examine it. And there was the familiar pink desert rat of the Seventh Armoured pointing them to the west. That'll be Caen, Sam thought, as he followed the sign. It was all going according to plan.

It was a surprisingly uneventful journey. The smoothness of it pleased him and was a secret relief as they trundled on. From time to time they passed little groups of rough earth mounds where the dead had been temporarily buried, each marked by a rifle with a helmet hanging from it, British and Germans side by side. And when they'd been going for about a mile they came upon one of the German's most powerful 88-millimetre guns, still in its emplacement but with its muzzle shattered like one of Groucho Marx's cigars. They gave it a cheer as they passed and waved their berets at it. You might treat their corpses with respect – that was only right and proper – but the way to treat German guns was to blow them to blazes. And then they were on the road to Caen.

*

Back in London, the news of the invasion was greeted with reserved satisfaction. Most people either had someone there or knew someone who was, and nobody was under any illusion about how difficult and costly it was going to be.

'They're not much more than boys, poor little devils,' Mrs Totteridge said, stirring her tea. 'An' now they're in the firing line. It don't seem right.'

Rosie was scrubbing the draining board. 'It *ent* right,' she said. 'Never was. There ought to be some other way to settle things without killing off our young men.'

'P'raps that ol' Beveridge feller could think a somethin',' Mrs Totteridge said. 'He's got the sense for it. You ain't got any more tea 'ave yer? I'm as dry as a bone this afternoon.'

'Help yourself,' Rosie said, scouring diligently.

'Tell yer one thing though,' Mrs Totteridge said as she poured herself another cup. 'At least they ain't bombin' *us* now. They give up on that lark.'

Six days later, she was proved wrong.

*

The air raid siren sounded just before dawn when it was still quite dark. It was such a rarity those days that Jim and Rosie were startled by it.

'Now what?' Rosie said, sitting up in bed and rubbing the sleep from her eyes.

''Nother plane lost its way,' Jim said, easily. They'd had one or two stray planes recently. 'I'll get up an' go down the post an' see.' Which he did.

Seconds after he closed the front door, Kitty wandered into the bedroom, yawning widely and carrying the cat, which was looking puzzled. 'We need ter go in the shelter?' she asked. 'Whatcher reckon?' The ack-ack guns had started firing, and for a few seconds they lifted their heads and listened to it, judging how far away it was.

323

'Quite a distance,' Rosie decided. 'If it's anything, Jim'll ring us, like he done last time. Get in under the covers or you'll catch your death.'

But Kitty had barely reached the edge of the bed before there was a very loud explosion. It was some way off, but it reverberated for a very long time.

'What the hell was that?' Kitty said.

'God knows,' Rosie said. 'It was something big, whatever it was. Stray bomber maybe. Brought down with a full load on board. Jim'll know.'

'So what'll we do now? Go in the shelter?'

Rosie didn't think so. 'If it *was* a stray, it's come down now. We might as well stay where we are and see what happens next.'

So they settled into bed and waited, and after a while the all clear sounded so they relaxed and dozed off again. But it didn't seem any time at all before the dawn was threading a narrow ribbon of bright light between the black-out curtains, and the birds began to chirrup and sing in the garden.

'No peace for the wicked,' Rosie sighed, easing out of bed and walking across to pull the curtains back. 'I'm getting up. Jim'll be home any minute now, and I want to know what that was.'

'We'll all get up,' Kitty said. 'Won't we, cat? An' then he can tell us all.'

But, to their disappointment, he had nothing to tell them apart from the fact that, whatever it was, it had fallen in Grove Road in Mile End and that there'd been a lot of casualties. 'We'll know a bit more when they've cleared the site,' he said. 'We got any bacon?'

How stolid he is, Rosie thought. Nothing ever seems to throw him. 'Oh well,' she said, forking their last three rashers into the frying pan, 'they'll tell us when they know, I suppose.'

But by the end of the day she knew as much as anybody, and maybe even more than most.

There were two more massive explosions that morning, every bit as loud and alarming as the one they'd heard in the night, and considerable speculation about them in the market. Kitty and Rosie were still talking about it when they set off to do their afternoon deliveries. They both agreed there couldn't possibly have been three fully-laden bombers shot down in a single day. Somebody would have seen at least one of them, and word would have got round. But if it wasn't a bomber, then what was it? They were no nearer finding an answer when they left the post office with their post bags and set off in their different directions.

And then, just as Rosie was removing the elastic band from her final packet of letters, she heard a sound like several clapped out motorcycles all roaring by at once and, since it was coming from somewhere above her, she looked up into the sky to see what it was. And there, hurtling through the wispy cloud, not far above her head, was the most peculiar plane she'd ever seen in her life; an evil, sinister-looking thing, black with square-ended wings and a long trail of flame pouring from its stern. It was travelling so fast it had disappeared behind the houses before she could take it all in.

She became aware that a young woman with a shopping basket was running down the road towards her, calling as she ran. 'Did we ought ter go in the shelter?'

Rosie pulled her mind back to earth with a palpable effort and tried to remember where the nearest shelter was. 'I shouldn't think so,' she called back. 'It's gone over now.' Then she realised that the engine must have stopped because she couldn't hear it, and seconds later there was another enormous explosion, and she looked up into the sky and could see smoke and debris pluming into the air and was relieved because it looked a good way away. But there'd been no sound of any other plane and no ack-ack, so it certainly hadn't been shot down.

'What was it?' the woman was saying.

'I've no idea,' Rosie admitted. 'But someone else is bound to know by now. That was the fourth.' And she was thinking, if there've been four, others'll follow. Jim'll know.

But it wasn't Jim who enlightened her. He didn't know much more than she did. It was Mr Kennedy, who rang her just after she'd had her supper to tell her that he'd been told to gather his teams together again. 'It'll be our usual rota,' he said. 'I'll send you a copy. Eight hours on, eight on call, eight resting. These things could come at any time so we've got to be ready round the clock.'

'I saw one of them this afternoon,' she told him. 'It didn't look like a plane.'

'We think it's some sort of rocket,' he said. 'Loaded with high explosives. We might know more tomorrow. You're on the night shift, if that's all right.'

We're getting ready for another blitz, Rosie thought, as she hung up the receiver. Only this is one with a difference. How the hell are we going to cope with rockets? The question was chilling. Nevertheless, she handed in her notice at the post office, put on her uniform the next evening and cycled to the depot, ready to face whatever had to be faced.

Mr Kennedy had made it his business to find out as much as he could about the new German weapon. 'I haven't been able to dig much out,' he said, as they sat round the table drinking their usual tea from their usual mugs. 'They're being a bit cagey at the Ministry of Defence at the moment, as you can imagine. But the bloke I spoke to confirmed that they *are* rockets, and they're being launched from the Pas de Calais region in northern France, so the sooner our lads get up there and send them packing, the better. He also told me they travel at three hundred miles an hour and carry a payload of a thousand kilograms of HE, which is pretty formidable.'

There was an intake of breath all around the table.

'So they're big,' Sister Maloney said, dourly.

'Very.'

'In that case,' Sister Maloney said, 'I shall take my cape, so I shall.'

That made them laugh and old Frank, who was the oldest driver in the team, teased her, 'It's goin' ter be very hot work, Sister. You'll need a fan, not a cape.' Which made them laugh again.

They got their first call out thirty minutes later and it *was* a major incident. They were all ready and waiting for it because they'd heard the explosion and knew what they were in for, and it didn't surprise them when three ambulances were called for, they simply set out in convoy.

But the scene they found when they arrived was worse than anything they could have imagined. The rocket had demolished four houses, and the dust cloud was so high they couldn't see the top of it. The warden on duty told them it had been so thick when he arrived that he couldn't see the pavement under his feet either. Rescue teams were already hard at work among the rubble, and there were several ominous shrouds laid out on the road.

'I'll take them,' old Frank said to his fellow drivers. 'You look after the casualties. You're quicker than me.'

They worked methodically, giving first aid and comfort where they could and driving carefully to hospital with their casualties. It took several hours before the site was cleared, and by then they'd heard three more explosions and knew they would be called out again. It was just like the Blitz, only worse. And it didn't let up.

As the days passed there were more and more explosions, and the rockets acquired two irreverent London nicknames, *buzzbombs* and *doodlebugs*, because of the odd noise they made. The Ministry of Defence passed on whatever information they had, advising people to take cover as soon as a rocket's engine cut out. 'You have thirteen seconds to get into a safe place,' their leaflet said. 'More street shelters are being constructed, and the underground stations will remain open at all times.'

There were also plans to evacuate women and children from London and from the areas in Kent and Sussex which was the flightpath for the new weapons on their way to the city. So many rockets had landed there that it was being called 'buzzbomb alley' and had become an official danger zone. There were also some heartening stories about how RAF pilots were flying so close to the rockets that they managed to clip their wings and turn them off course: and one amazing photograph to prove it.

'They needn't think they can lick *us,*' people said to one another with determined bravado.

But Rosie wasn't so sure. She didn't say anything, naturally, that would have been letting the side down, but she noticed things. She saw how shabby and weary people looked, how dirty London was, how very little food was on offer in the market and how unappetising it looked, and what a lot of new bomb sites there were; she saw the pressure the ambulance service was under and how valiantly they were trying to cope with it. She looked at her face in the mirror in the morning and thought how old and tired she was. This dreadful war's been going on for nearly five years, she thought, staring at her reflection, and five years is much too long when so many people are in danger, Sam and Bertie in Caen fighting those German Panzers and all those other young men fighting in France and Italy and all of us here with these foul buzzbombs. It's all very well telling us to take cover. You could take cover and the bomb could fall on you wherever you were. We can't stop them falling. She felt defeated. Trapped. She wanted to weep. But what good was that?

She had to be at the ambulance station in less than an hour, and there was breakfast to cook. So she lifted her chin in the air and squared her shoulders and told herself to get on with it.

*

During the next few weeks, more brick-built air raid shelters started to appear in the streets, and on 11 July , the second evacuation took place as planned. The papers reported that it had gone well and that more than 41,000 women and children had been taken to places of safety. Rosie was glad they'd gone because it was always horribly upsetting to watch a dead child being pulled out of the rubble, but she missed their voices when she went to market and felt that the place was emptier and sadder without them.

And the days passed, and the buzzbombs continued to arrive in greater and greater numbers.

CHAPTER TWENTY-TWO

It had all started so well, with everything going according to plan. They were fairly bowling along, making good time, and Sam was whistling as he drove. The Third Infantry were doing their best to keep up with them on the foldable bicycles they'd all been given, and they grinned and waved at them as they drove past. They could see that these men weren't the entire brigade, but they assumed the rest were following on. And they were cheered when the Lancasters and Halifaxes flew overhead, and watched as their bombs fell on the city.

And then it all went suddenly and catastrophically wrong.

They were only a few kilometres from the northern outskirts of Caen when Panzers appeared out of nowhere, firing as they came. There were German troops swarming round them, and within seconds men were falling like flies, and a tank had taken a direct hit and was brewing up. They watched as the crew struggled out of the hatches, two of them obviously wounded, and Sam manoeuvred into a better position, and Bertie fired and fired and fired again as Taffy reloaded. There were tanks firing all around them, the sergeant was hollering orders, and the infantry were being shot and falling. It was a scene out of hell.

It was a great relief to all of them when Sergeant Merryweather told them that HQ had sent the instruction to retreat. They were hopelessly outnumbered and had taken more than enough casualties already. It meant the capture of Caen would have to be postponed until later, but better postponed than dead.

That night they ate their grub ravenously. There were no field kitchens yet, so it was cold and out of tins, but they were very hungry and glad to have any food at all, and they ate while they were servicing their tank because that had to be done first and they were too hungry to wait. Then they dug makeshift latrines and piddled behind trees and slept on tarpaulins on the ground alongside their tanks, intermittently and uncomfortably, grumbling that bare earth was bloody uncomfortable and they preferred sand. And they woke at dawn, tense and filthy dirty, to hear what was ahead of them.

As they'd half expected, the new attack was to be led by the Seventh Armoured and the Fifty-First Highland Infantry Division.

'Well what do you know!' Sam said bitterly.

'Shows we're the best,' Bertie said, grinning at him.

'Quite right too,' the Sergeant said, but the rest of the crew growled and Taffy swore, 'Fuck that for a game a soldiers.' At which Bertie laughed and whacked him between the shoulder blades. And so they set off, all five of them taut and sweating, to face the second day of the campaign.

It was every bit as bad as the first had been and every bit as costly. The Germans were obviously putting all their troops and armour into defending this place. Nobody could count the buggers, but they could see that there were hundreds of tanks and several battalions of troops in action and dozens of those bloody eighty-eight millimetre guns all solidly emplaced and doing appalling damage. Even so, under the sergeant's instructions, they managed to circle the northern area of the town and to hold their positions for nearly four days. But they couldn't break into the town, and they were still taking far too many casualties, so it didn't surprise them when *this* attack was called off too, and they had orders to retreat.

This time the field kitchen was waiting for them and they were able to wash.

'I reckon it's going to be a bit longer before they send us back for a third time,' Bertie said.

'How do you work that out?' Taffy asked.

'I'd lay money on it,' Bertie told him. 'It's not old Monty's style to do things in a rush. He'll take his time now. Bring up reinforcements. Make sure of our supplies.'

'D'you reckon we'll get any mail?' Sam said. He and Bertie had sent cards whenever they could to say they were still in one piece and that sort of thing, and he'd been aching for a reply.

The letters came the next morning, when they were eating their breakfast. Sam and Bertie had two each, and Sam read his second with some alarm.

'The Germans are bombing London with some sort of rocket,' he told his mess-mates.

'Pilotless planes, my Mary says,' Bertie told them.

Others from London had got the news too and it was discussed at length.

'They must be firing 'em off from somewhere over here,' Bertie said. 'It's a fair old range to reach London.'

'Tell 'em we'll blow 'em to smithereens,' Taffy said.

But then the sergeant arrived to give them the latest information on their position – 'the current situation's under consideration so we could be here for a few days' – so speculation about rockets had to stop. But later that day they both wrote back urging their darlings to look after themselves and to send them letters whenever they could. '*I don't have time to breathe here, but I will worry about you,*' Sam wrote, and he was telling the painful truth.

They stayed where they were, ate hot meals, got a change of clothes and slept uncomfortably but more easily for the next twelve days. Then news came through that they were to be joined by the 1st, 8th and 30th Corps, which consisted of sixty thousand men, six hundred tanks and seven thousand guns, under the command of General Richard O'Connor, and that the new attack was scheduled to begin on 23 June. It didn't work out as planned, because a storm blew up in the Channel that day, and their food supplies and fuel and equipment were blocked aboard the ships, which were riding it out at anchor or worse, were still in England unable to get out of harbour. And in the meantime the Germans were taking advantage of the lull and bringing in more tanks from other areas.

'If we're not careful we're going to be outnumbered again,' Sam said, sitting with his back against a tree and smoking dolefully.

'Look on the bright side,' Bertie encouraged him. 'At least they won't be beating the hell out of our other armies.'

But Sam just smoked and scowled.

He was still scowling on Sunday, when the weather improved and they set off for Caen yet again. This time they attacked from the west of the town, and the Scots actually broke through the German front line and advanced for ten kilometres before the German troops managed to stop them. But apart from that, it was another costly stalemate, and it wasn't long before they were pulled back for a third time.

'I'm beginning to feel like a bleedin' yo-yo,' Sam complained, as he drove back to their temporary base. 'I can't see why they don't bomb this bloody town to blazes an' flatten the whole bloody thing, Jerries an' their bleedin' Panzers an' all.'

'It's because there are civilians there,' Sergeant Merryweather said. 'And you can't bomb civilians.'

'They're bombing civilians in London,' Tom said, sourly. 'With bleedin' rockets.'

'That's as maybe,' the sergeant said. 'It don't mean we have to do the same.'

But apparently HQ shared Sam's view. On 7 July, British bombers dropped two and a half thousand tonnes of bombs on the outskirts of Caen. And two days later, the Third Canadian Division and the Third British Division occupied the northern part of the town, and the German troops and panzers retreated until they were south of the river Orne. It took another terrible bombardment, from land, sea and air, and another long and very costly fight in which six thousand allied troops were killed and nearly four hundred tanks destroyed, before the Germans were finally driven out. But on 20 July Caen was liberated at last, and the Desert Rats drove their tanks down what was left of the main road into the town.

It was an eerie journey because there were hardly any shops or houses left standing and no sign at all of any people.

Sam and his crew had their heads out of the hatches and were peering about them. 'Where are they all?' Taffy said, and the words were barely out of his mouth before Sam saw a small skinny child standing in the rubble, gazing at them anxiously.

'N'ayez pas de peur,' he said, finding enough French to speak to her and hoping it was correct. It was a long time since he'd learnt what little he knew. 'Nous sommes Anglais.'

She didn't answer but continued to stare, which unnerved him. So he decided to try something easier. 'Comment t'appelle-tu?'

That provoked an answer. 'Mauricette, monsieur,' she said. 'J'ai faim, monsieur.'

He translated for the others. 'She's hungry. Have we got any food on board?' The tank was always full of things stashed away in case of need – fags, water – but he wasn't sure about food.

'Hang on a tick,' Taffy said and disappeared for a few seconds to return with a rather battered bar of chocolate which he tossed to the child, calling 'Catch hold!'

She didn't manage to catch it, but she retrieved it from the debris and tore off the wrapper and began to eat it at once, ravenously.

'She's starving, poor kid,' Taffy said. 'Tell her we'll get 'em to send in food as soon as they can.'

That was beyond Sam's limited French, so he told her in English and hoped she would understand. But she ran away.

The sergeant was already on the phone reporting that there were still some inhabitants left alive and that they needed food. 'They say it's under control,' he told the others when he'd finished the call and stuck his head out of the rear hatch again.

'Let's bloody hope so,' Bertie said, as Sam drove on through the wreckage of the town. 'That was bloody awful. Poor kid.'

Sam didn't say anything, because he was too near to tears to be able to speak without weeping. It was all he could do to keep his face under control and to concentrate on driving the bloody tank. His chest was crushed with such pity for the child, he could barely breathe and, worse, he was torn by a terrible, searing sense of guilt. He'd been wishing for that bombardment, demanding it, saying they should bomb the bloody town to blazes. He could hear the exact words. And now this. Oh dear God, he thought. Why does war have to be so cruel?

*

335

Much later that evening, when they'd returned to their camp outside the town and serviced the tank and eaten a good meal, although in Sam's case, rather guiltily, Bertie tried to compliment him on speaking French.

'You're a dark horse,' he said. 'Didn't know you could speak French.'

Sam didn't really want to talk about it. 'I learnt it at school,' he said shortly and fished in the pocket of his tunic for a cigarette.

'I was very impressed,' Bertie said.

'I don't care how fucking impressed you were,' Sam said, drawing on the fag. 'I did it for the kid, that's all, and a fat lot of fucking good *that* was.'

'You got her some food.'

'Big fucking deal!'

'OK! OK!' Bertie said, holding up his hands as if he was trying to ward Sam off. 'Don't mouth off at me, sunshine. I didn't start the war.'

Sam rose wearily to his feet. 'I don't fucking care who fucking started the fucking war,' he said. 'Just leave me be.' And he walked away into the field, kicking the long grass.

'What was all that about, boyo?' Taffy said, wandering across and offering Bertie a cigarette.

'God knows,' Bertie said, taking the cigarette. 'Ta.'

'Touch a the 'eebie-jeebies, I shouldn't wonder,' Taffy said, wisely. 'Leave him be, poor bugger. He'll get over it. It gets to us all in time.'

But now that he was out of earshot and where none of them could see him, Sam was weeping, and he wept until he had no more tears to shed. If only I could be back in London with my darling, he thought, as the sky darkened and the trees turned into black silhouettes, and the fields were as grey as those awful bombed streets. He yearned to be hugged and comforted, just for an hour, or half an hour even. That would make all the difference.

*

Gracie was in admissions that evening and hard at work, removing a messy temporary dressing from the badly injured leg of an old lady who'd just been brought in from an 'incident'. She was a valiant old thing and determined not to make a fuss, even though she was in a lot of pain. They were waiting for Dr Clements to arrive, and Gracie had already decided that this injury needed penicillin. It was a wonderful drug and worked on infected wounds better than anything else she'd ever seen. There aren't many good things to come of this hideous war, she thought, but that's certainly one of them.

The ward was crowded because they'd had two doodlebugs within twenty minutes of one another, and it was taking Dr Clements some time to visit all the casualties. But there she was at last, walking in through the curtains, smiling her nice, reassuring smile, looking at the notes at the end of the bed and saying 'Mrs Stefanovic?' in her gentle voice. We're a good team, Gracie thought, and she was glad they were working together.

That afternoon she'd written a long letter to Sam. She'd tried to make it as encouraging as she could because his last letter had been so short and he'd sounded down. So she'd told him that it looked as though the number of doodlebugs that were coming over might be diminishing and wondered whether the sites had been bombed or maybe even captured. She didn't say how weary they all were or mention how long the doodlebug raids had been going on, because she wanted to cheer him up, not cast him down even further. But it had been nearly seven weeks now, and the pressure of being continually on alert was wearing them all out. There were times when she wondered privately how much more of it they could stand. But then she decided that if Mum and Dad and Mary could take it, so could she. She couldn't let the side down.

Even so, it was a long hard summer. Every day of it brought more deaths and injuries, and although there were slightly fewer buzzbombs, the damned things kept coming. They checked the papers every day to see whether the sites had been captured, but it was September before they heard what they wanted to hear. And then the news didn't come through the papers but in a letter from Bertie.

The two girls shared their letters from France whenever they weren't too personal and had long accepted that the two men wrote in very different ways. Sam's were wonderful love letters telling his Gracie how much he missed her and how much he loved her but, if they wanted to know what was happening on the campaign, it was Bertie who told them. He wrote cautiously and often in hints so as not to alert the censor, saying they were '*motoring*' once they'd got out of Normandy, and that the locals were coming out in support of them. '*The partisans have landed in the south of France with an Allied army.*' '*Marseilles has been freed by the partisans.*' '*The Germans in Paris have surrendered.*' '*Belgium next stop.*' '*The German tanks are running away. We have to drive slowly or we'd run into the back of them.*'

'He's making a joke of it,' Gracie said, rather disapprovingly.

'That's his way,' Mary told her, feeling pleased to think that *her* husband was the one who was keeping them informed. 'He doesn't want us to worry.'

His next letter justified her understanding. '*Rumour has it,*' he wrote, '*that a certain launch pad, which has been causing you problems, has been bombed flat.*'

'Well thank God for that,' Rosie said, when his prediction proved true. 'Now we can have a bit of peace.'

It was short-lived. At a quarter to seven in the evening of 8 September, when Jim and Rosie and Kitty were eating their supper, there was a sudden massive explosion, louder than the buzz-bombs had been and without sight or sound of a buzzbomb or a plane.

'What the hell was *that*?' Rosie said, peering out of the window. There was the usual dust cloud rising somewhere to the west of them but no sign of a plane of any kind. Whatever it was had come out of the blue.

The next morning the papers explained that a gas main had blown up in Chiswick, and for a couple of hours Jim and Rosie and Kitty thought no more about it. But then there were two more explosions.

'And don't tell me, they're gas mains as well,' Rosie said. 'One I might believe, but not three in a row.'

And after two more days the authorities finally decided to tell them that the Germans were firing a new kind of rocket at them. It flew at speeds greater than the speed of sound and carried over a thousand pounds of high explosives. It was chilling news, but Jim and Rosie understood what it meant.

'That's why we don't hear the bloody things coming,' Jim said. 'The sound they make arrives after they've exploded.'

'That's gruesome,' Kitty said.

'And how the hell can we get out of their way?' Rosie said. It seemed dreadful to her that they'd got to sit and wait for these foul things to fall on them. At least they'd been able to duck out the way of the buzzbombs when they heard their engines cut out.

His answer was short and honest. 'We can't,' he said. 'We've just got to endure 'em.'

Which is what they did.

*

The explosions continued by day and night, and every single one did appalling damage and caused a lot of deaths and injuries, and Jim was proved right, there was nothing they could do about it, except turn up for duty when it was their shift and face whatever horrors every shift would bring. So the times when they were both off duty at the same time were rare and precious, and they made the most of them, silently keeping their fingers crossed that a rocket wouldn't fall on *their* house while they were in it. There was something very comforting about spending an evening together. As it was on Guy Fawkes evening.

It began like an ordinary evening and was an easy one. Kitty was in Binderton visiting her twins, Jim was off duty and Rosie was on standby, and they were in the kitchen enjoying a quiet cup of tea together before she started to cook their supper. And the phone rang.

She drifted off into the hall, cup in hand, wondering which of her daughters it would be. But it wasn't either of them.

'Ah!' Mr Kennedy's voice said. 'Sorry to do this to you Rosie, but we've got to use you tonight. Mr Colgate's off sick. He's fallen off a wall and broken his arm.'

Stupid man, Rosie thought. I know he's a good driver but what was he doing climbing up walls? A man his age. But she didn't pass any comment, she simply agreed to be at the station as soon as she could get there and took her cup back to the kitchen to tell Jim the news. 'And just as I was looking forward to my nice chump chop,' she said.

'Never mind,' he said, smiling at her. 'We can have 'em termorrer. They'll keep. Nip up an' get into yer uniform an' I'll rustle you up a sandwich.'

He's such a dear, Rosie thought, and she walked to the sink and put her cup in to soak, and she stopped to stroke his face on her way to the door.

He caught her fingers and kissed them, smiling at her. 'What would I do without you?' she said, smiling back.

'Starve I 'spect,' he said. 'Go on. Nip an' get changed. It'll be ready for you when you come down.'

As it was of course, all neatly wrapped in greaseproof paper. So she put it in her shoulder bag and cycled off to her unwanted work.

*

The ambulance station was fully manned and ready for anything. They'd had two very bad incidents in the afternoon and were hoping they wouldn't get another that evening.

'Fat chance a that!' Sister Maloney said, setting aside her knitting. 'They're sending them over by the dozen, so they are. I see we're working together again, Mrs Jackson. Could you fancy a cup of tea?'

Rosie accepted the tea and unwrapped her sandwiches and settled down to wait. An hour went by and there were two explosions, one to the north and the other to the south, but they weren't called to either. Another hour passed, and there was a nearer incident to which the first three ambulances were called, so Rosie moved her ambulance into position, and she and Sister Maloney gave it a thorough check. More time passed, and she was just beginning to think she was going to get through to twelve o'clock without being called out when there was a thunderous explosion, very close by, so close that they could feel the shock waves under their feet and so massive they could see the debris falling all around the building.

'Jesus, Mary and Joseph!' Sister Maloney said and crossed herself. 'It's next door.'

'When the debris stops falling I'll go outside and see,' Mr Kennedy said. But it was still falling when the call came through.

'It's the John Bull Arch,' Mr Kennedy said when he'd put the phone down. 'Three ambulances at least, they reckon. It's brought the bridge down.'

341

'We'll go first,' Rosie told him. 'I've got friends there.'

'You sure?'

'Yes, of course,' she said. 'If they're hurt they'll be glad to see someone they know.'

They drove the few hundred yards to the bridge in convoy, noticing as they drove that the wreckage was getting deeper by the yard and that it was still falling along with dark chunks that looked like shrapnel. When they'd finally inched their way through and got as close to the site as they could, they couldn't see the full extent of the damage because the dust cloud was still so thick, although they could see that the bridge was down. The steel girders had been flung in the air by the explosion and now lay spread-eagled across the wreckage and what was left of the road. There was no sign of the shelters that used to stand under the bridge. They were just piles of broken brick. And there was no sign of Mr Johnson's house, either.

A warden appeared out of the murk, coated in dust and grime with his notebook in his hand. 'There's four houses gone here,' he reported. 'Two empty, two occupied, one by an old feller called Jake something-or-other and the other one by a couple called…'

'Johnson,' Rosie told him, as he consulted his notes. 'I know them. They're friends of my husband's. Give me first shout when you get them out.'

It felt like a long wait. But the dust seemed to be settling, there was no more shrapnel falling and she and Sister Maloney could see the teams digging over the wreckage where the house had been and the heavy duty boys lifting a wall with their crane. A wall with a broken chimney still attached to it.

'They'll have them out in no time once that thing's out of the way,' Rosie said.

They were lifting someone out of the rubble as she spoke, and the warden was beckoning to them. So they took up their stretcher and picked their way through the debris in the road until they reached the site. The figure lying on the ground was ominously still.

'Is this your friend?' the warden said.

It was but, now that she was bending over him, she could see that his chest was caved in, and there was blood all over his face. He was dead. 'Yes,' she said. 'Poor man. That's Mr Johnson. He went all through the first war without being injured and now this.' She was full of pity for him. He'd been so happy in that house, decorating it and buying furniture. She could hear his voice. '*We're gonna turn it into a little palace.*' And now it was smashed to smithereens and he was dead.

'Hang on a tick,' the warden said. 'They've got another one out.'

'That'll be his wife,' Rosie said, hoping *she* was alive, and she watched as the two rescuers carried their next casualty gently across to them and laid it neatly alongside Mr Johnson's body.

But then the scene split in two as though someone had ripped it in half, and she fell to her knees in the rubble and howled. 'No! No! No! No! No! No! No!'

For this time, the man lying dead at her feet was Jim.

CHAPTER TWENTY-THREE

The world had disintegrated. There was nothing left now except dirt, darkness, the stink of the explosion and Jim's dead body lying on the ground. Rosie stayed on her knees among the debris on the pavement, holding his poor injured hand and groaning. What else could she do? She felt powerless, unable to think or speak or even move. From time to time, faces swam into her line of vision out of the darkness and she looked at them vacantly, because she couldn't recognise them. And anyway, what were they to *her* when Jim was dead?

At one point, two men with a stretcher came up to her and asked if they could take him to the ambulance, and she found the energy to scream at them to go away and leave him alone. Somewhere, a long way away, people were talking, but that was nothing to do with her. Oh he couldn't be dead. Not her Jim. He couldn't be.

*

Sister Maloney had been so upset to see her nice Mrs Jackson grieving so terribly that she'd gone straight back to the ambulance and phoned Mr Kennedy. He took his time to answer her – dratted man! – but, when he did, and had listened to everything she had to tell him, his advice was sound and practical.

'I was just going off duty,' he told her, 'but not to worry. This is important. We will deal with it together. I shall start by ringing Guy's to see if Sister Vernon's there. She should be at this time of the morning. Their daughters need to know what's happened, and she'll break the news gently. I'll get Mavis to send out another ambulance and a second driver. We've just changed shifts and she's in charge now. And then I'll drive over and see what else can be done.'

Sister Maloney thanked him with some relief. 'You're a good man, so you are,' she said.

'I'll be with you presently,' he said.

He arrived at the same time as one of his ambulances, which was on its way back to base and had brought Gracie and Mary to the site. He and Sister Maloney watched as the two girls ran through the rubble to their mother and knelt beside her. Then they watched and waited.

*

Mary and Gracie had been so terribly upset to hear that their father had been killed that for a few minutes they were too shocked to weep or speak. Not Dad, Gracie thought. Oh dear God, not Dad. He's always been there. Always. Then she realised that Sister Vernon was telling them something else and summoned up her reserves so that she could take it in.

'Your mother is with him,' the sister said, 'and from what Mr Kennedy told me, I would say she's in a state of shock. We have arranged for you to take time off so that you can go and help her. Mr Kennedy will drive you there. Take your capes. You will need them.'

So they got their capes and packed their night clothes and, still in full uniform, were driven to the site. Neither of them spoke during the drive, and although Mary wept she managed to do so without making too much sound, while Gracie held her hand and patted her back. But when they walked across the rubble to where their mother was crouched and saw their father on the ground, they howled with distress, and it was some time before they could pay attention to their mother, who was sitting on her heels and rocking backwards and forwards. Then they remembered their training and because that sort of rocking was a sign of extreme grief, they managed to get themselves under sufficient control to deal with it.

'We're just going to lift you up, Mum,' Mary said.

Her mother looked puzzled. 'What for?' she asked.

But before Mary could answer, there was a noisy explosion on the other side of the river and, while it was reverberating, the two girls counted to three, the way they'd been taught to do when lifting a patient, 'One, two, three, up!' and lifted her until she was standing. She was unsteady, but she was on her feet.

'Now let's see if you can walk,' Gracie said.

'I've got to stay here with your father,' Rosie told her, doggedly. 'I can't leave him.'

'He'll have to go to hospital,' Mary tried to explain.

Rosie couldn't understand that, although she'd ferried enough corpses to hospital to know it was true. But there was a gulf between knowing things and understanding them now. And this was Jim they were talking about, not somebody else. She stood shakily between her daughters, crushed to realise that her brain wasn't working properly. Then she saw Mr Kennedy walking towards her and wondered what he was doing there. Nothing made any sort of sense at all.

He was very calm and gentle. 'Are you able to walk to the car?' he said. And her daughters began to walk, holding her arms so that she had to walk with them. And then, somehow or other, they were in Mr Kennedy's car, all three of them squashed together on the back seat, and Sister Maloney was talking to her through the window, saying, 'I'll look after your Jim, so I will. You go home and have a nice warm drink and get into a nice warm bed.' And then they were driving, and she didn't have the strength to ask where they were going, but just shut her eyes and let things happen. What did it matter? What did anything matter now her Jim was dead? It was as if she wasn't really there anymore.

They arrived in Coney Street, and the girls unlocked the door and took her upstairs and undressed her and put her to bed, with a hot-water bottle at her feet and a cup of cocoa on the bedside table. They were being so kind to her, and she couldn't even find the energy to thank them, but she did her best to drink the cocoa and, when they'd tucked her in and told her they would be in Mary's room if she needed anything, she turned on her side and tried to settle to sleep. It was useless. Sleep wouldn't come, although tears came unbidden and in profusion, and after a while she resigned herself to the fact that she wasn't going to sleep that night and just lay there thinking. And the hours passed on very sorrowful feet.

*

When Kitty came striding back to Coney Street the next morning it was twenty to twelve, so she was rather surprised to find the curtains still drawn. She'd spent two gossip-filled days in Binderton with her twins, which had been nice in its way, but now she was more than ready to be back in her home town with Rosie and Jim. She knew Jim would be at work, but when she put her key in the lock she expected to see Rosie in the kitchen and was a bit disturbed to find that the room was empty and the house was quiet.

'Come on you ol' slug-a-bed,' she called as she climbed the stairs. 'Time you was up!'

Then she saw Mary and Gracie at the top of the stairs, still in their dressing gowns, and she knew there was something the matter. Gracie had her fingers to her lips and was walking down the stairs. So they all went quietly down to the kitchen.

'It's bad news ain't it?' Kitty said.

'Yes,' Gracie said. 'The worst.'

'Is it Jim or Rosie?'

'It's Dad,' Gracie said, but even saying the words made her cry.

'Dead or wounded?' Kitty said, surprising them all by how calm she was being.

But when they told her, her face crumpled with distress, and she cried like a child and that set them all off. They stood in the kitchen, holding one another, and wept together until the phone rang and made them all jump. Gracie was the first to recover, so she went to answer it.

It was Mr Kennedy, as unruffled as ever to say that he was back on duty and had heard from the undertaker who would like to visit them that afternoon, and was that in order?

She reported back to the others, and Kitty said she'd better go up and warn poor Rosie, which she did. It took her a long time because Rosie was still in such a state she had to be helped to dress, so by the time they came downstairs again, the undertaker was at the door.

He was a very old man, and a gentle one. He told them that the only space he could find for them within distance of their home was the Peckham cemetery and asked if it would do and, as Rosie was quite incapable of answering him, Kitty took over and agreed with the site and made all the arrangements. It felt unreal to all of them, and they were glad when he'd left them.

'We shall have to go back to the hospital now,' Gracie said to Kitty, 'if that's all right?'

'Yeh. Course,' Kitty said. 'I'll look after her. I'll hand in my notice at the post office otherwise I shan't have the time, It's all right. I can always find another job later.'

So they began to pick up the pieces of their lives and to learn how to live round the anguish. It was very, very difficult.

*

Over in Belgium, Bertie and Sam were cock-a-whoop. The campaign was going according to plan, the Germans were still in retreat and they were now only ten kilometres from the Dutch frontier. The weather seemed to be holding up too, although it was very cold, but no snow had fallen yet, and their progress was pretty steady.

'With a bit a luck this could be over by Christmas,' Bertie said, as they sat side by side on the canteen benches with their mess tins full of warm food.

'An' we can go back home.' Sam said, savouring the idea along with the bully beef.

They were slightly upset to hear that their father-in-law had been killed and wrote back to their girls at once to say how sorry they were and what a good man he'd been. But the truth was, it was one death among so many that they were almost inured to it. There was a war to be won before they could grieve.

*

The funeral turned out to be a very big affair, much bigger than Rosie had imagined it would be, with scores of his customers there and all the men and women from the wardens' post and everybody from Binderton, and lots of people she'd never seen before. It was a miserable day, dark and cold with a constant drizzle to dampen them all, but that seemed right and fitting to her. She was still in a state where words passed over her head, and she heard them but didn't understand them. She didn't hear the sermon, partly because it was drowned by coughing, but mostly because she wasn't listening, and although all sorts of people came up to her afterwards to tell her how sorry they were, she shook their hands without really hearing *them* either, and hung on to her daughters' arms knowing she would fall if they hadn't been there. She was quite glad when they were on the tram and heading home. It had been an occasion, but it was nothing to do with her or Jim.

She noticed that old Mrs Totteridge and Sonia had come back to the house with them and had brought a sandwich lunch for them all, which was very good of them, and they all crowded into the living room, the way her family always did, and sat wherever they could and ate and drank. She saw that her brother and sisters were on cushions on the floor and that the twins were jammed against the book shelf as close to Johnnie as they could get. But there was a dreamlike quality about it all, and she watched as though it was nothing to do with her. It wasn't until her daughters had gone back to the hospital and her visitors had left to catch their train, and she and Kitty and Sonia were washing the dirty dishes in the kitchen, that an element of reality crept through the cracks in her life and made her stop and notice.

'I hope you won't mind me sayin' this,' Sonia said to her, taking a dripping plate and drying it rapidly, 'but I'm having quite a hard time runnin' the stall on me own. I wouldn't say nothin', but there's so many things your Jim dealt with, an' to tell you the truth, I don't know where to begin with 'em.' She looked rather shame-faced, and the look jerked Rosie back into feeling responsible.

'You need some help,' she said. 'Course. I should've thought of it.'

Sonia smiled at her, apologetically, caught between need and delicacy. 'I wouldn't bother you, not with all this goin' on,' she said, 'only it's the weekend coming and we need stocks.'

'Me an' Kitty'll go to Covent Garden first thing tomorrow morning,' Rosie told her. 'Won't we Kitty?' And when Kitty nodded, she put her arms round her old friend, soapy-handed though she was, and kissed her. 'I'm sorry I didn't think of this before, Sonia. I should've done. He kept a notebook in the bookcase with all sorts of details in. I'll look it out an' bring it down with me, when we've finished at the Garden. I can't have you struggling along all on your own.'

Until that moment she hadn't been able to think straight about anything at all, but now she knew where she was going and what she had to do to prepare for it. That stall had been Jim's lifeline, and he'd worked all hours to run it well and profitably. Now she would take it over and run it for him. It wouldn't be easy, but it was necessary. When Sonia and Mrs T had gone home, she found Jim's tattered account books and took them up to bed with her. She would study them until she knew what sort of prices she ought to pay at the Garden, even if it took all night.

It took until after half past one before she was satisfied that she knew enough to be able to bargain, and then she slept as if she'd been pole-axed. And woke at five just as *he*'d always done. Then everything had to be done at speed. She called Kitty, who got up at once, made tea and toast, found the tin where he kept his cash, and then the two of them set off across London Bridge on their bikes.

Covent Garden was a confusing place, crowded, quick moving, busy and extremely noisy. But she found the dealers he'd noted and bought the goods she needed, feeling easier with each purchase she made. Kitty stood beside her with the note books and opened them at the appropriate pages to remind her, but for most of the time she remembered the prices she needed to know and managed to bargain, hesitantly at first but with increasing confidence. Some of the traders knew her Jim and asked how he was, so she had to tell them, even though she was afraid she might weep. But they were kind and full of sympathy, so she weathered it.

'Bleedin' war,' one of them said to her. 'It's allus the best what go.'

Eventually all the necessary supplies had been bought and stashed in baskets ready to be delivered, and Rosie and Kitty cycled back to the Borough, where the opening bell was just being rung.

'I feel as if we been workin' fer hours,' Kitty said.

Rosie laughed at her. 'We have,' she said, thinking what a wonderful thing it was to be laughing again.

And so they began their new lives as stall holders. They were still grieving most painfully, and Rosie had accepted that *that* would never stop, but it had shifted gear a little, and that was enough to give her hope.

*

'Well there you are fellers,' Sergeant Merryweather said, striding across to them over the rough ground. 'Bang goes our Christmas leave.'

It was a depressing morning. They'd woken to thick swathes of fog, a chorus of coughs, sentries shivering and complaining that they were frozen solid, and a December chill that ate into their bones. When the sergeant came cheerfully across to give them bad news, they were all annoyed and looked it.

'Now fucking what?' Sam growled.

'The Jerries have invaded,' the sergeant said.

'Bloody hell fire,' Taffy said. 'You'd ha' thought they'd've run out of places to invade be this time. Specially after what the ol' Russkies are doin' to 'em. Who're the lucky buggers they've invaded now?'

'Us,' the sergeant said, grimacing. 'They've come in by the same route they took at the beginning, through the Ardennes. History bloody repeating itself. Now we've got ter send 'em packin' again. Stir yer stumps.'

'Shall we tell the girls?' Sam asked, when the sergeant had gone.

But Bertie said 'no'. 'They'll hear in the papers soon enough,' he said. 'We'll send cards nice an' reg'lar an' tell 'em we're still in the land of the living. No point worryin' 'em for nothin'.'

But of course the news was all over the front page, and both girls were more worried than they let on to their mother. They talked about it to one another, naturally, but agreed that they would say as little as they could to her.

'She's got enough on her plate without this,' Mary said.

It was a tender and understandable concern but wasted because Rosie read the papers along with everyone else and knew what bad news it was. But, oddly, grief had made her more stoical.

'What's to come, will come,' she said to Kitty, as she cooked some baked beans and bacon for their breakfast. They were working hard and needed a good breakfast. 'It's no good worrying before the event.'

'No,' Kitty said, rather sadly. 'But you do, don'tcher.'

'There you are,' Rosie said, putting a full plate on the table in front of her. 'Get that down you. We'll hear if anything happens.' In one way she was quite glad they were so hard at work, because it *did* take your mind off the possibility of disasters.

Soon, the papers were calling this new battle the Battle of the Bulge and reporting it in as much detail as they were given by the War Office. Bertie and Sam sent regular postcards which the girls brought to show her, which was comforting. But the rockets kept coming and coming, so there were more and more casualties and more and more bombsites. There was a really bad incident in New Cross on the Saturday before Christmas, when a rocket was dropped on the local Woolworths. It was crowded with Christmas shoppers and, naturally, many of them were children. The tram-telegraph spread the news over the next three days, stage by stage, as more and more bodies or bits of bodies were found, some of them in pieces on the roofs and some in trees. At the final count, the official figures were 160 people killed and 108 seriously wounded. It was the worst bomb of the war.

Rosie's customers were hot with anger at the enormity of it. 'Bastards!' they said. 'Let's hope they catch the foul man who invented these bleedin' things an' put him up against a wall an' shoot him dead. He oughter've been drowned at birth.'

And Kitty and Rosie agreed with them.

Later that evening, when Rosie and Kitty were sitting by the fire, getting warm and listening to Vera Lynn, with the cat cuddled between them, Rosie suddenly remembered Jim's Christmas decorations. 'We ought to put 'em up,' she said. 'People'll miss them.'

Kitty was all for it, so the next day they left for work a quarter of an hour early and dragged out the step ladder and found the box where the decorations were kept and started work, and when Sonia arrived she joined in too. It wasn't long before they drew the usual crowd and discovered how difficult it was. It had been all well and good for Jim. He'd been a lot taller than they were. It was soon obvious to their audience that they couldn't reach the far corners and were in danger of falling. Volunteers were called for and offered their services, and it wasn't long before the occasion became a ribald comedy turn.

'What a lark,' their customers said, when the job was done. And Mrs Totteridge, who'd enjoyed it immensely, grinned at Rosie and said, 'He'd a been proud of yer, duck.' Which brought a cheer and a few tears.

So despite bad news, a shortage of food and horrible weather, the year ended on a high, rude note.

CHAPTER TWENTY-FOUR

Over in the war-ravaged fields and waterways of Belgium, the weather was against the Allied armies and they all knew it. If there wasn't a fog to obscure their vision and hide the German panzers from their sight, it was blowing a blizzard and snowing, which made things even worse. For far too many days it had been impossible to see where the panzers were, and the roads were icy which made driving the tank horribly difficult and, to make matters worse, the allied planes had been grounded for weeks, so they had no air support. They *had* managed to prevent the Germans from crossing the Meuse, but what they all wanted to do was to drive the buggers back into Germany and go home.

Ever since he'd found that kid in the wreckage of Caen, Sam had been acutely –but privately –aware of how cruel, foul and filthy this war was. He didn't say anything because his years with Bertie had taught him the need for tight self-control but, every time they went out on a sortie, he winced at the sight of all the damage they were doing; the morass of mud and slush, spent cartridge cases and debris that their treads were churning up, the litter they left behind wherever they went, the rows of shallow graves marked by the usual helmets stuck on sticks or rifles and now covered in snow, the hellish noise, the stink and the constant fear they were all living with. If I get out of this hell-hole alive, he thought, I'll settle down with my Gracie in a nice, warm, clean, peaceful house and never leave it. Ever.

Bertie had similar thoughts, but he kept them to himself too, hanging on until the weather broke, as it was bound to sooner or later, and they could get on with the job. But it was several more days before the wind dropped and the snow stopped and visibility improved. And then, to the relief of the men on the ground, the bombers flew overhead within an hour, scores and scores of them: Wellingtons, Halifaxes, Flying Fortresses, in formidable squadrons. 'Give 'em hell, boys!' they shouted, waving their arms.

Then they checked their tanks and vehicles as they listened to the massive explosions of the raid and cheered when they saw a petrol dump go up in flames – and waited.

*

Rosie and Kitty had done well that Christmas, rather to their surprise because there wasn't a great deal for them to sell and very few titbits; no dates or oranges or sugared almonds – ah those were the days! – and very few chestnuts, although they'd bought as many as they could. But by Christmas Eve they had cleared the stall.

'This is the sixth Christmas of the war,' Rosie said, as she and Kitty and her daughters sat down for their Christmas dinner in the kitchen with Moggie lurking hopefully at their feet and a good fire waiting for them in the living room for once.

'And let's hope it's the last,' Gracie said, holding out the wishbone to Mary. 'Come on sis, make a wish!'

Grief lurched at Rosie in its now familiar way, making her want to crawl away somewhere quiet and cry, so she took a strip of chicken skin from her plate and fed it to the cat. When she looked up, she saw that Kitty was smiling at her, her smile so sad and full of sympathy that it said more to her than any words could possibly have done. We find new ways to talk to one another when we're grieving, she thought, and smiled bleakly back.

'Here's to the new year', Gracie said, holding up her glass and rescuing them in her perceptive way. 'And let it be a good one. We've earned it.'

So they drank to the new year, and although Rosie had serious misgivings about it, she didn't say so. And to be fair, it started well, with the news that the German army had been pushed back into Germany and the Battle of the Bulge was over. Two days later, Gracie and Mary had letters from Sam and Bertie to say that the Germans had admitted defeat and were on the run and that they were well and motoring across the frontier.

'So this has got to be the beginning of the end,' Gracie said. And it certainly looked and felt like it.

The rockets kept coming, so they were still coping with serious casualties, and wounded men were still being flown in from various parts of Europe, among them a tankie who had lost a leg struggling to get out of his burning tank before it exploded, which upset them both, although they were careful not to let him know. He was impressively sanguine about it, saying, 'Better me leg than me life,' with a wry smile. So they made him a medal for bravery and pinned it to his pyjamas, remembering how they'd decorated Sam all those long years ago when *he* was their patient.

The year limped towards spring. Sam and Bertie wrote regular letters to say that the Germans were fighting like maniacs but they were OK and it would soon be over. And all sorts of nations like Peru and Paraquay and Egypt and Norway were declaring war on the Germans. There seemed to be a new one every day.

'Climbin' on the bandwagon,' Mrs Totteridge said, scornfully. 'It was a different thing when we was on our own. I never seen none of 'em rushin' to join us *then*.'

The news bulletins were held up while they played all their national anthems, and the more there were of them, the longer it took. Mrs Totteridge wasn't impressed by that either and called it 'bleedin' ridiculous.' But there was plenty of news when the newsreader finally got around to reading it, and the papers were full of what was happening. Most of their news came from the campaigns in Europe, as their readers expected, although they did report on events in the Far East from time to time, once telling their readers that American marines had captured an island called Iwo Jima after four day's heavy fighting. It didn't impress Kitty.

'They should try six years,' she said, peeling potatoes furiously.

Rosie laughed at her. 'Oh come on Kitty,' she said. 'We ent been fighting *all* the time.'

'Well however long it's been, it's a damn sight longer than four stupid days,' she said.

'I tell you what,' Rosie said wearily. 'I shall be glad when it's over. It's all so vicious.'

There was some very disquieting news among the accounts of battles, and she was finding it very upsetting. The Russians had liberated a concentration camp at a place called Auschwitz and revealed that it was a death camp where they took anybody they'd labelled as an 'undesirable' like Jews and gypsies and all sorts of others, and killed them in underground gas chambers. It was monstrous beyond belief, particularly as it soon turned out that it wasn't just one they'd found. There were scores of others, and the reports of their discovery turned up at regular intervals as the Russians powered towards Berlin.

And then, as if to prove that the Germans didn't have the monopoly on cruelty, there was a report about an air raid on the German town of Dresden that had been bombed by Allied planes for a night and a day. At first there was no report about how many casualties there'd been, but after a week terrifying totals began to emerge. Some papers said it was '*about sixty thousand*,' others put the figure as high as a hundred and thirty thousand, explaining that the bombing had caused a firestorm and that many bodies had been hard to find and difficult to identify.

'Dear God,' Rosie said. 'That's dreadful. What did the poor buggers do to deserve that?'

'Same as we done, when we was bombed,' Mrs Totteridge said, sourly. 'That's war for yer.'

'Then the sooner it's over, the better,' Rosie said. But the last stage of this dreadful war seemed to be taking a very long time.

At odd moments when they weren't serving their customers, Rosie and Kitty and Sonia read the papers to see what was going on and something always was. At the end of February they were full of triumphant maps showing the progress of the American and Russian armies which had crossed the Roer and Oder rivers and were storming towards Berlin. But there was little news about the Eighth Army, which was what they really wanted to hear. They seemed to be still stuck the wrong side of the Rhine.

Kitty couldn't understand it. 'What's the matter with 'em?' she said, putting the paper down on a pile of discarded potatoes. 'I mean ter say, it don't make sense ter be hanging about. They should be over that river and closin' in on Berlin along wiv all the others.'

Sonia tried to be understanding. 'There'll be a reason,' she said. 'There's bound to be.'

And she was right. As Bertie could have told her if the whole thing hadn't been under such careful and censored wraps. Monty was playing his usual skillful and careful game, pulling the wool over the German's eyes as to where they would cross the river and ensuring that supplies were in the right place, plentiful and ready. By this time, his men knew how necessary all this was and waited patiently, knowing that his method would mean fewer casualties. As it did, for when they finally crossed the river on 25 March it was a relatively easy crossing and not a costly one.

Sam and Bertie wrote home in triumph. 'Now we shall push the Jerries back to Berlin,' Bertie said, 'and when it's over, we'll be among the first to be demobbed, because they're doing it on the principle of first in, first out, and me and Sam have been in from the beginning. See you soon. ATLITW'

April brought one victory after another, which was cheering. The Russians and Americans met up at a place called Torgau, which meant that Berlin was now surrounded, Nuremburg was captured along with a place called Osnabruck and, despite Hitler ranting that the Germans would fight to the last man, his subjects had other ideas. There were stories of villages flying a white flag from their churches and reports that millions had surrendered.

'Won't be long now,' Kitty said happily.

But Rosie felt it hard to respond to the news as she knew she should be doing. There were other things being reported too, and they worried her. Now that the Allied armies were pouring into Germany from both directions, more and more of those terrible concentration camps were being discovered, places with unfamiliar names like Buchenwald and

Dachau, and there didn't seem to be much doubt that they really were places where the Jews were being deliberately murdered. The British army had found one at a place called Bergen, and the BBC had sent one of their top reporters, a man called Richard Dimbleby, to film and report on it. She tried not to think about it too much because there was nothing she could do about it, but the thoughts were there and so were the images they conjured up, and they troubled her dreams and cast her down into grief.

'What we need's a nice night at the flicks,' Kitty said, when Rosie had been far too near tears all day. 'Let's see what's on.'

They chose a nice cosy musical starring Fred Astaire and Ginger Rogers that was on at the Troc. 'Just the thing,' Kitty said. 'That'll cheer us up no end.'

And so it did because it was everything they needed; a light, candy-floss romance with lots of singing and dancing, wonderful dresses, a predictable plot and a lovely happy ending. Perfect.

It was followed by the familiar tune of Pathe News.

'Shall we stay on an' watch it?' Kitty asked. 'Whatcher think?'

'Might as well,' Rosie said, adding as she always did when the news came on, 'We might see our boys.'

But they didn't –not that she really expected it. What they saw were the gates to Belsen concentration camp, looking forbidding but standing open to allow you and the cameras to move inside.

Rosie just had time to think how glad the prisoners must have been to be liberated, when she found herself moving between crowds of the most pitiful men she'd ever seen in her life. They were shuffling about in a nightmare compound, hemmed in by barbed wire and wearing a uniform like filthy striped pyjamas worn down to bits of rag, and so thin and dirty they looked like skeletons. She could see every bone;

ribs, knees, spines, even their skulls because their heads had been shaven bare. Nothing about them seemed human; their eyes had an impossible weariness about them and their hands like claws, reaching out to the soldiers for food and help. They looked like walking skeletons; lost, deserted, at the limit of their endurance, waiting to die. She wanted to get up and run away or shout to the cameras to stop, but the scene was changing.

There was a child. It could have been a boy or a girl. There was no way of telling. It was squatting on the bare earth, with its back to the camera, naked and filthy, its head shaven, without an ounce of flesh on its body. And there was a huge bug crawling up its back. Rosie felt her gorge rise at the sight and watched in horror as the child put a stick-thin arm over its shoulder and tried to knock the bug away. But it hadn't got the strength to reach the horrid thing. All it managed was to pull up the loose skin on its back. Oh, God! Rosie thought. To be starved like that and have a bug that size crawling on you and be too weak to knock it off. She was aching with pity for the poor little thing. She wanted to leap into the picture and squash the bug and pick the kid up and give it something to eat and wrap it up warm. How could the Germans be so cruel?

The commentator was still talking but she couldn't hear what he was saying because there was another picture on the screen, and that one was so utterly dreadful she started to cry. It showed a heap of dead bodies all piled up on top of one another, hundreds and hundreds of them, all completely naked and covered in filth, with stick-thin legs and heads like skulls with terrible sunken eye sockets. And there was a man in uniform with a bulldozer pushing them into a pit as if they were rubbish. He had a mask over his mouth, and she could see that the tears were running out of his eyes and streaming down his cheeks.

Make it stop! she thought. Please make it stop. It's too dreadful. She wanted to hide her eyes but she couldn't. She *had* to see. It was making her ache from her throat to her stomach. These people have been starved to death, she thought. Deliberately starved to death. Men, women and children, deliberately starved to death. I've been complaining about the rations and sitting in the sun and living a normal life while these terrible obscene things have been going on. And then a combination of grief, revulsion and horror overwhelmed her, and she couldn't bear to watch any longer. She struggled to her feet, crying aloud like a baby and staggered from the auditorium with Kitty following behind her.

Once they were in the foyer, Kitty found a chair and made her sit in it.

'It should … never… 've been…allowed,' Rosie wept, trying to control herself. 'That poor… kid.

'No, it shouldn't've,' Kitty agreed, patting her back. 'An' it wouldn't ha' been neither, if we'd known what was goin' on. Only nobody did.'

'Gerry de Silva did,' Rosie remembered.

'Oh well! He was an artist, wasn't he?' Kitty said, as if that was all that needed to be said about him. 'Now then, if you're a bit better we'll get off home. I got an idea.'

Rosie followed her to the tram obediently, still weeping, but rather more quietly, and by the time they reached Coney Street she had more or less recovered.

At home Kitty made a pot of good strong tea and set Rosie's cup in front of her with a flourish. 'Now then,' she said. 'I'll tell you what we're gonna do.' Then she sat down with her own tea in front of her, took a long satisfying draught of it and explained.

'This war's gonna be over in a matter a months. That's obvious. An' high time too, cause we've had quite enough of it. So what we need now is somethin' to keep us goin' and give us somethin' ter work for, until it's the peace.'

Rosie felt suddenly tired. 'Do we?' she said. She'd have thought they had more than enough to do without taking on anything extra.

'Yes,' Kitty said, firmly, 'an' I'll tell you fer what.'

Rosie drank her tea and settled more comfortably in her chair and prepared to listen.

'When the war's over we shall have a general election.' Kitty said. 'I think that'll come quick an' all, because the Tories'll want ter cash in on Churchill bein' so popular, but whenever it comes, it'll be a chance to vote for someone who'll give us the revolution that ol' William Beveridge has been talking about. The Tories won't do it. The very idea of a revolution must be turnin' 'em pale. But the Labour Party will. They're pledged to it already. So I think we should join the party and help 'em get ready for it. The more of us there are, the more likely we'll make it.'

Rosie drank some more tea and considered. 'I don't join parties,' she said.

'I do,' Kitty said, and grinned at her. 'Well you know that, don'tcher. Come on in, the water's lovely.'

Rosie gave it thought but she wasn't convinced. 'I don't think I'd have the energy for it, Kitty,' she said. 'Not now.'

'You never know till you try,' Kitty told her. 'I wasn't keen on the suffragettes neither, till I joined 'em. Tell you what, the local group are having a meeting day after tomorrer – an' that's a bit a luck cause they don't have many – anyway, it's tomorrer at one of their houses. Sonia told me. Why don't we go along and see?'

So, rather against her better judgement, Rosie ironed her skirt, polished her shoes, put on a clean blouse and went along and saw. And got a few surprises.

For a start, the meeting wasn't in a house but in a flat over a shop, and it was already full of people and wreathed in cigarette smoke when they arrived. And then the man who walked across to greet them turned out to be one of the butchers from the market.

'Name of Morris,' he said, shaking their hands. 'I'm the chairman of this group, for my sins. And you run Jim Jackson's greengrocers, don't you. Rosie, isn't it? And Kitty? Is that right? And this young man,' pulling a white-haired man out of the crowd, 'is our secretary, and you couldn't get a better one. We did try, but we couldn't get a better one.' And the white-haired man turned round and laughed at him and walked towards them. And he was Mr Kennedy.

'Hello you two,' he said. 'Welcome aboard. You're just in time to help us plan a public meeting.'

'They're ahead of us,' Rosie said to Kitty, as the people in the room found seats so that the meeting could begin.

'We'll soon catch up, don't you worry,' Kitty told her, grinning. 'This is only the beginning.'

It was a lively meeting, and it began on a high note with their secretary reporting that twenty-seven new members had joined the party since their last meeting. 'It's beginning to look like a trend,' he said. Then they got down to the serious business of planning how they were going to support the public meeting that was coming in two weeks' time. The MP for Southwark Central, who was a man called John Hanbury Martin, was the speaker, and his theme was going to be how the party would put the Beveridge report into operation as soon as they were elected. 'So it's important to get as many people as we can to come and hear him.'

The meeting was going to be in the school hall in Lant Street, and now they needed people to be out on the High Street handing out leaflets to publicise it. There were plenty of immediate volunteers. By the time they all parted company at ten o'clock, Rosie and Kitty had decided to join the party and had offered to join the leafleteers, too.

The weeks that followed were full of cheerful activity, and Rosie made a lot of new friends and discovered that a lot of old ones were already committed to Beveridge's ideas, which gave her a wonderful sense of togetherness. And the meeting was excellent for Mr Martin was a powerful speaker, and his audience were with him from the moment he began to speak.

'If we could get in with a big enough majority,' Kitty said, as she and Rosie were walking home, 'we could 'ave our revolution.'

'It's a big if,' Rosie said. But there'd been such a strong feeling of optimism at the meeting that she couldn't help feeling hopeful just the same.

And the war was now definitely coming to an end, which was the best thing of all.

Hitler might still be bragging that the Germans would fight to the last man, but most of the Germans and Italians now seemed to have other ideas. On 28 April, news came through that the partisans in Italy had captured Mussolini while he was hiding under a pile of coats, put him on trial and found him guilty and shot him dead. They'd hung his battered dead body from the façade of a petrol station in the Piazza Loretto in Milan, tied by the heels and upside down There was a picture of it on the front page.

'Good riddance to bad rubbish,' Kitty said with great satisfaction.

The next day the Germans in Italy surrendered 'unconditionally' to Field Marshal Alexander, and the day after that the Americans and Russians met up in the virtually demolished centre of Berlin. Hitler was reported to be hiding in a bunker somewhere in the city. But later in the day another report came through to say that he had committed suicide.

'Best thing he ever did in his life,' Kitty said.

'Now what will happen?' Rosie said. It seemed almost too good to be true that this dreadful war was nearly over.

What happened next was the unconditional surrender of Germany, which took place in Montgomery's tent on Luneburg Heath at on 4 May, and a few days later in the little red school house which was General Eisenhower's HQ in Rheims. At long last, the war in Europe was officially over.

Gracie and Mary went up to Trafalgar Square that evening to join the riotous celebrations, but Rosie and Kitty stayed at home with the cat. Their loss was still too raw, and neither of them had much appetite for singing and dancing.

CHAPTER TWENTY-FIVE

The general election was called on 23 May, ten days after the end of the war, just as Kitty had predicted. Polling day would be on 5 July . But because there were still so many men on active service all over the world who couldn't get home to vote, the election was going to be taken to them. They would cast their votes at special polling stations wherever they were, and then there would be a three week interval between the vote and the count, while their papers were collected and flown home.

'It's a pity they couldn't have flown you home to vote here,' Mary wrote to Bertie. 'When are you going to be demobbed? Have they told you?'

'There's too many of us to fly us all home,' he wrote back reasonably. 'And anyway, we're all busy coping with prisoners and refugees and what they call displaced persons. There are millions of them. You never saw such a muddle. But I'll be back with you as soon as I can, I promise. It's just going to take a bit of time.'

'I know there's a lot of men out there,' Mary complained to Gracie during their next tea break. 'He didn't need to tell me that, but you'd think they'd make more of an effort than this. After all, they've been out there for six years.' She'd counted every day.

'They'll get them home as soon as they can,' Gracie tried to comfort. But Mary wasn't appeased. 'Well I don't think much of it,' she said.

So Gracie tried another tack. 'We ought to phone Mum and tell her when we'll be visiting,' she said. 'I promised I'd find out when I phoned her on Wednesday.'

But Mary was determined not to be pleased by anything. 'She'll only talk about that wretched Labour Party of hers,' she said and looked at her watch.

That wretched Labour Party was keeping Rosie extremely busy, for now that the election was only six weeks away it was important to tell as many people what was going on as she could. She was only too well aware that, if they were going to win enough seats to make the revolution a possibility, they would need every vote they could get. She and Kitty handed out leaflets in the streets whenever they had a free moment and delivered posters to their supporters so that they could put them up in their windows and attended every meeting they could. The best one was an enormous affair because the speaker was a man called Nye Bevan who was reputed to be a great speaker, and who'd worked down the pits in south Wales since he was thirteen, so she had a particular sympathy for him.

It was held in Central Hall which was absolutely packed, but he spoke so strongly and passionately in his lovely Welsh voice that, even though it was thickened by coal-dust, they could hear every word he said, even at the back of the hall. 'If the revolution is to come,' he told them, 'as I believe it must, then it will come because it is the will of the majority of the people in this country, a majority that has been ignored and downtrodden for far, far too long, denied help when you were sick, denied help when you were unemployed through no fault of your own, denied a living wage. Now is the time for all of you to make your wishes known, to say to the men in power: enough is enough.'

When he finally sat down, his audience rose to their feet and roared their approval. It had been a magical occasion.

From then on Kitty and Rosie worked even harder than they'd been doing before they heard him, sitting up into the small hours, addressing envelopes ready for their candidates' electoral statement, or folding leaflets to slip into the doors of their neighbours in the Borough.

Mary was not impressed. 'I hardly ever see her,' she complained to Bertie. 'She's always out on the streets somewhere or other.'

But Gracie was full of admiration. 'I don't know where she gets her energy from,' she told Sam. 'She's out all the hours that God sends.'

'She's a very good woman,' he wrote back, 'and on the right side. Give her my love.'

But by the time polling day arrived, even Rosie had to admit that she could do with a rest.

'We've got three weeks of enforced rest now,' Kitty said, 'and believe you me, that's going to take a long time.'

It did, although excitement and speculation mounted day by day. Would they get enough seats? Was it possible? And if they didn't, what would happen then?

But at last the day of the count arrived and everybody who could get time off from work was in the town hall to hear the results. The place was so crowded they could barely see across the room for cigarette smoke, and the noise was deafening. Three long trestle tables had been set up in the centre of the hall, one for each of the three candidates, with chairs for the sorters and tellers, and the mayor was standing on the platform looking rather splendid in his robes. After a while the candidates began to arrive, which was interesting, because the Labour candidates didn't seem at all concerned, and the Liberals were talking to one another rather earnestly, and the Tories were braying. It was the first time Rosie and Kitty had seen a large group of Tories together, and it was a revelation to both of them. They spoke in such loud, upper class voices and seemed so sure they were going to win, it was painful to hear them.

'They're so full of themselves,' Rosie said to Kitty. 'To hear them talk you'd think they owned the world.'

'They do,' Kitty said, grinning. 'For the moment.'

'It's no surprise really,' Rosie said. 'All the newspapers think they're going to win this election.'

'Not all of them,' Kitty said. 'Not the *Daily Mirror*.'

'I wish we could hear some results from one or two of the marginals,' Rosie said. 'That would show us the way the wind was blowing.' They seemed to be waiting a very long time.

There was a slight disturbance in the crowd all around them, and Mr Kennedy eased his way through until he reached them. 'No news yet, I gather?' he said. 'I had to come and check. There's nothing on the wireless yet.'

But there was a result in the hall. The candidates for Southwark North were being called to the platform, the mayor was adjusting his robes, tapping the microphone and giving a preliminary cough. It was a safe Labour seat, so they expected to win it, but not by such a huge majority. There were gasps all around the hall. And it was obvious from the excited expression on the mayor's face that he had other dramatic news for them, but they had to wait until George Isaacs had made his speech, which felt interminable to Rosie and Kitty because he thanked everybody. But at last he sat down, and the mayor stepped forward with a paper in his hand to tell them that he had news of other London results too. 'They've come through on the wireless,' he said. 'There's been a Labour gain in Dulwich, both the Lewisham seats have been won by Labour and at Peckham, the Labour majority has risen from one hundred last time, to seven thousand this.' The applause in the hall was deafening.

'There's no doubt about it now,' Rosie said.

And Mr Kennedy gave her a huge beam and said, 'no doubt at all.'

It wasn't long before the two other results were announced in the hall, and they were both comfortable wins, just as Rosie and Kitty expected. It was almost too good to be true. They sang all the way home to Coney Street.

That night the evening news gave them the final count. It was staggering. The Labour party had won 393 seats, the Tories 213, the Liberals twelve and the Independents twenty-two. It was a landslide.

The next day, Churchill resigned and the new Labour prime minister, Clement Attlee, was sworn in. For the first time in its history, the country had a Labour government with a huge majority.

'Now,' Kitty said triumphantly, 'we shall see the sparks fly.'

'Now,' Rosie said, 'you'll see me taking a bit of a rest, I'm knackered!'

'We'll rest together,' Kitty said, 'but not until after Saturday. Our stocks are getting low.'

Rosie groaned. 'They would be!' she said. 'All right then, we'll start resting on Monday. That's usually an easy day. We can take it in turns to have a day off.'

But their lives had speeded up now. And events were rushing them along.

Four days after the election, Mary and Gracie rang up to say that they'd had a letter telling them that the prefabs they'd asked for had been built and were ready for occupation. Mary was so excited she could barely breathe. But she did manage to ask her mother if she would like to come with them when they took possession. So naturally, Rosie did.

The houses they'd been offered were side by side on Clapham Common, and Rosie was very impressed by them. 'You're not going to need much in the way of furniture,' she said. 'Just a bed and a few chairs and bedlinen and china and such. We could go to Arding and Hobbs and get it all in and settled before your fellers come home.'

And tired though she was, it was a splendid day out, buying beds and bedlinen and treating them both to a full set of china. By the end of the week they were settled into their new home, impatiently waiting for Bertie and Sam to be demobbed.

It seemed to take for ever and ever, although they wrote to one another every day. Sam was full of the news that he'd decided what he wanted to do once he was out of the army, and that was to take up teaching. He'd discovered that the Ministry of Education were setting up Emergency Training Colleges for ex-service men and women to provide the teachers they knew they would need, and he'd already made an application for a place in one of them. He wrote to Gracie every day, telling her how impatient he was, and she wrote back every day to tell him it could only be a matter of time, and eventually he sent the letter that told her what they both wanted to hear. He was being demobbed at the end of August and had been awarded a place at the Emergency Training College at Wandsworth. 'It's on the common,' he wrote, 'and quite a place by all accounts.'

Gracie and Mary took time off to go and see it and were quite impressed with it, although Mary said it reminded her of something out of *Alice in Wonderland* with those funny towers. 'But at least he's found out what he wants to do,' she said. 'Bertie doesn't seem to have the least idea.'

He still didn't have the least idea when he arrived at the prefab on a hot August afternoon, dressed in a demob suit that didn't suit him and carrying his uniform in his kit bag. But he was home, that was the main and happy thing. And three days later, Sam followed him. His demob suit was a pinstripe and looked quite good on him, but he said he didn't care if it did or not, just so long as he was home.

That evening all four of them went to the Windmill and drank until they were ridiculous. Oh it was *so* wonderful not to be at war, to have the days spreading out before them, simply there to be enjoyed.

Sam started at the college at the end of September, after having worked out that if the course was only to last eighteen months, he would be ready to start work after Easter in 1947.

Once he'd gone, Bertie felt lost without him and realised that he'd been back in London for several weeks and hadn't visited his family or gone to see Rosie. He felt quite guilty about it, because he was the only one at home in the two prefabs now, what with Sam at college and Mary and Gracie at work in the hospital.

'I think I'll go an' visit your mum,' he said to Mary. 'It's high time.'

'Give her my love,' she said, kissing him briefly as she always did when she left for work. 'Tell her we'll come and see her this weekend.'

*

The Borough had hardly changed, except for all the gaps in the houses, and the market was exactly the same. But Rosie looked worn out, which worried him. She's working too hard, Bertie thought and kissed her affectionately. 'How's things?' he said.

But three new customers arrived before she could tell him, and she had to haul a new sack of potatoes into position to serve them and was rather obviously wearied by it.

'Let me do that for you,' he said, stepping forward and lifting the sack. 'Bli' ol' Riley. That weighs a ton. Where d'yer want it?' He didn't stop to think whether the offer was acceptable or proper. It was simply something he could do to help her, and he did it.

'Thank you,' she said, pushing her hair out of her eyes. 'That's very kind. Could you empty it here?'

He emptied it and smiled at her, and then waited until her customer had been served. 'Now is there anythin' else that's needs moving?' he said. He'd made it sound like a joke but they both knew he meant it.

'You're a dear,' she said. 'You're just like my Jim. Yes there is, if you wouldn't mind.'

'Pleasure,' he said.

He stayed with her and Kitty and made himself useful until the end of the afternoon and, when they'd packed up the stall, he went back to Coney Street with them because they'd invited him to tea, and Mary wouldn't be home yet awhile, and he'd got an idea he wanted to test out on them.

Kitty made the tea, and they sat in the kitchen and drank it like three old friends. I must choose my moment carefully, he thought, and waited. And eventually Kitty showed him the way.

'This bleedin' market's breaking my back,' she said, rubbing it wearily when she stood up to refill the kettle.

'It's all that lugging things about,' he said. 'You need a man about the place.'

'Too bleedin' right,' she said, 'only all the buggers are in uniform.'

'I ain't,' he said, grinning at her. 'Would I do? I'm a big, stronger feller fer me age!'

'We'd have to pay you,' Rosie told him seriously, 'to make it all proper and above board. I mean to say, would you want to make a proper job of it?'

'Try me,' he said. But he already knew that he would and that he could do it well.

*

That Christmas, which was special because it was the first one after the war, Bertie was the one who climbed the ladder to put up the decorations and got jeered for his pains. But he knew he was making a very good fist of this job, because Rosie looked so much better than she'd done when he first walked into the market.

'I'm so glad you're married to my Mary,' she said. 'You're just like my Jim,' and gave him a kiss when he climbed down off the ladder.

Yes, he thought, I've found what I want to do.

CHAPTER TWENTY-SIX

It was a lovely hot summer in 1946 and perfect for a Victory Parade, or at least Rosie thought it was perfect, until she got a phone call from Mr Kennedy asking her if she'd like to take part.

'Well,' she said, 'I'm not really sure, I'd have to ask my girls and see what they think.'

'Take your time,' Mr Kennedy said, 'as long as you can tell me yay or nay by the end of the week.'

She'd only put the phone down for twenty minutes when it rang again. This time it was Gracie bubbling with excitement because Bertie and Sam were going to be in the Victory Parade. 'Imagine that!' she said. 'Me and Mary are going to ask matron if we can be in it too. Then we can all go up together.'

'Heavens!' Rosie said. 'And I've just had a phone call from Mr Kennedy asking me if I'd like to be in it.'

'I hope you said yes,' Gracie said. 'Then the entire family will be there.'

'Except Jim,' Rosie said. 'I'd hate to be there without him.'

Gracie could understand that perfectly. But she had an answer for it. She wasn't going to say it was what he would have wanted her to do, because she thought that sort of talk was very silly. But she had a bribe to offer.

'Tell you what,' she said, 'if you take part in the parade me and Mary will be right behind you, and if you're a very good mother and behave yourself beautifully all the way, we'll tell you a little secret.'

Rosie was intrigued. 'What little secret?' she said.

'Join the march and we'll tell you!' Gracie teased. 'Go on, you'll have fun.'

So Rosie rang Mr Kennedy and said she would join them. She wasn't really at all sure she was doing the right thing, but she was intrigued enough to try.

*

Rosie and Kitty woke up when the birds were singing on the day of the Victory Parade, partly because they were both rather excited, despite missing their Jim, and partly because Rosie didn't want to be late arriving at the meeting point.

'It's bound to take longer this morning,' she said, 'because there are bound to be crowds of people going up to see us.' And despite her sadness at being there without Jim, she felt proud to be able to say such a thing. If only he could've been with them, and the people could've been cheering *him* as well.

'And quite right too,' Kitty said. 'Chin up, our Rosie! I think it's gonna be fun.'

And it was. There were crowds everywhere they looked, and all of them excited. The tube was full of people talking to one another about what they were going to see and what they were going to do, and when they changed to a different line at the Bank, they were carried along the tiled corridors by a stream of cheerful people all talking about the parade. Some of them had bags full of sandwiches

and drinks to sustain them during the day. Rosie was impressed by
how clean they all smelled and realised as she walked that the tube
smelled good too. It had gone back to the peace time smell of metal
polish and oil and dust that she remembered from before the war.
At the end of the first corridor Kitty headed off to catch her tube to
Charing Cross saying, 'See you at Lyons' Corner House.' And the
crowds swept Rosie on again.

She arrived at the Marble Arch with time to spare, which was just as
well because there were marchers gathering from all directions, some
on foot from tubes and buses, some in coaches, and all in uniform, and
she could see it would take her some time to find out where she was
supposed to go in a crowd that size. Fortunately, there were marshals
everywhere too, some of them holding up cards labelled '*NFS*,' '*Civil
Defence*,' '*NAAFI*,' so she knew she could follow their instructions until
she found her place. In front of her allotted meeting point, there were
men and women in all three service uniforms and, waiting with their
instruments ready to lead the whole thing off, a splendid military band
in full dress uniform, busbies and all. There was no possibility of finding
her girls and Bertie and Sam in all that crush, but they would meet by
the arch when it was over. And it was certainly going to be very grand.

Behind the card marked '*Civil Defence*' people were being sorted
into their relevant marching orders and greeting old friends. It seemed
extraordinary to see so many men and women in the old uniforms,
and surprisingly there were several of *her* old friends there, which she
didn't expect. And among them was Mr Kennedy, who told her he
was going to march alongside her and look after her, which was kindly
and comforting, because she was beginning to feel lonely in such a
huge crowd. And then at last, after standing about for what seemed an
unconscionable time, the first part of the procession set off; armoured

cars, tanks, jeeps and every kind of motorised vehicle you could think off. It seemed to take a very long time until they were all gone, but at last the long file came to an end, and the next band was standing ready to head the marching columns, followed by flag-bearers that seemed to come from everywhere. The first group to follow the band consisted of men and women from the British Empire who'd served in the navy, the air force and the army, and after them the Royal Navy stepped out behind their own band, swinging along in their tiddly suits looking very handsome. And then they were off themselves, and Rosie knew that Mary and Gracie would be among the doctors and nurses, and that Sam and Bertie would be behind them with the various army units, and she felt comforted to know they were there. And so they walked between the cheering crowds. She'd expected cheering, but not on this deafening scale. There were people packed on either side of Oxford Street, six and more deep, all waving to them and cheering themselves hoarse, and so it continued along every inch of the route.

'There must be thousands here,' she called to Mr Kennedy, shouting above the noise.

'And quite right too!' he called back.

They swung down Charing Cross Road, marching easily with the whole road to themselves and cheers to encourage them all the way, their own band echoing in front of them, and the following band playing a different tune behind. At Trafalgar Square, the crowds were packed around Nelson's Column and perched on the lions and standing on the steps of the National Gallery. And she knew that Kitty would be somewhere in the crowd, even though she couldn't see her.

There's so much history here, Rosie thought, and some of it's ours, and she had a sudden, clear memory of that suffragette meeting she'd attended by accident all those years ago, on the night she'd met Kitty

381

and Jim. And oh! how splendid he'd been, striding across the square, pushing his way through the crowds to sort out the bullies who were throwing paint about and shouting obscenities. He was so like a lion that afternoon. She could still see him, punching one of the bullies to the pavement and walking back to them flexing his knuckles, grinning at her. Oh dear God, she did miss him.

Big Ben boomed into her thoughts, sounding midday in its wonderful, triumphant way. And the crowds seemed to be cheering that, too.

They were turning into Northumberland Avenue, where there were more crowds packed from the edge of the pavement to the front of the buildings. Then they arrived at the Embankment and marched south with the Thames on their left hand side; clean and grey-blue for once and sparkling in the sunshine in honour of the occasion. And then they were in Bridge Street and marching into Parliament Square, past the Houses of Parliament and Westminster Abbey and Central Hall where she'd seen the great Keir Hardie speak all those years ago and where she'd listened to Nye Bevan. Even when it came on to rain, her excitement wasn't diminished.

'I wouldn't have missed this for the world,' she called to Mr Kennedy. 'Nor me!' he called back.

And then they were walking past St James' Park, where Jim had kissed her under the trees, and they'd had their first row, although for the life of her she couldn't remember what it had been about. And she missed him all over again. Dear, dear Jim.

The rain stopped as they were turning into The Mall and setting out on the last leg of their march. Ahead of them in the long, straight distance was Queen Victoria's plinth and the luxurious façade of Buckingham Palace. And there was the saluting base, with a huge royal coat of arms in the middle of the canopy, and the King and Queen and the two princesses on the plinth with Attlee and Churchill standing to attention beside it, and it was 'Eyes left,' and they were all saluting, and the King and Queen were saluting back, and the cheers of the crowds rolled over them like waves. They'd been on their feet for over four hours but it felt like four minutes.

'Just as well I told our girls exactly where to find me,' Rosie said to Mr Kennedy as they headed for Hyde Park. 'I've to stand on the left-hand side of the Marble Arch and not move.'

'They're good girls,' Mr Kennedy said. 'If you stand still, they'll find you.'

Which they did, appearing one after the other with their husbands beside them. The day had gone entirely according to plan. Now it was simply a matter of finding Kitty, and they would all be together again. That was a little more difficult because the crowds were so thick around Lyons' Corner House, which was jam-packed with customers, but at last they were all together, and a wait for a table didn't matter.

Despite loss and grief and doubt, it had been a superb day.

'Now then,' Rosie said to the girls when they were all settled at a long table together and had given their order. 'You owe me an explanation.'

Kitty looked very surprised. 'What explanation?' she said.

'I was told that if I came on the parade I would be told a secret,' Rosie said. 'Wasn't I girls?'

'You were,' Gracie said.

'So am I going to be told?' Rosie asked.

'Oh I think so,' Gracie said, 'don't you Mary?'

'Yes,' Mary said and grinned quite devilishly at her mother. 'How would you like to be grandma?'

'Seriously?!' Rosie said, examining them both for signs. 'Which of you is it?'

'Both of us,' Mary said, and they both went off into peels of giggles. 'Mine's due in November, round about Guy Fawkes day, and Gracie's is going to be a Christmas pudding.'

'It's the perfect end to a perfect day!' Rosie said and kissed them both.

*

The next morning, when the cat had been fed and Rosie and Kitty were having a leisurely breakfast, the newspaper arrived. It was full of pictures of the march, showing the long column filling The Mall and the King and Queen taking the salute and tanks rolling past the podium. But it was the headline in the paper that pleased them most. '*CITIZEN ARMIES ON THE MARCH*' it said, in bold block capitals.

'An' ain't that exactly what we was!' Kitty said, grinning at Rosie. 'Citizen armies. It wasn't jest the army an' the navy an' the air force what won the war, it was all of us.'

And it was, it was. 'Quite right!' Rosie said.

'Now all we got ter do,' Kitty said, 'is win the peace.'

'Which'll take a bit of effort.' Rosie said. 'But we've got a good government now and we'll do it.' She began to check off all the tasks ahead of them. 'First we'll have to repair all the damage the bombers have done, then we'll build new houses and set things to rights, then…'

'Then?' Kitty laughed. 'Ain't that enough?'

'Then,' Rosie said, gazing through the kitchen door, with Moggie purring on her lap, 'I'm going to cultivate my garden and play with my grandchildren.'

Lightning Source UK Ltd.
Milton Keynes UK
UKHW010918270620
365672UK00005B/1422